Chasing Shadows

Books by Louisa Dawkins

Natives and Strangers
Chasing Shadows

~ Louisa Dawkins ~

Chasing Shadows

Houghton Mifflin Company   Boston

1988

Library of Congress Cataloging-in-Publication Data

Dawkins, Louisa.
Chasing shadows/Louisa Dawkins
p. cm.
ISBN 0-395-44143-9
I. Title.
PS3554.A946C5 1988   87-26459
813'.54—dc19   CIP

Printed in the United States of America

S 10 9 8 7 6 5 4 3 2 1

This book is for Jane, Jo, and Sheila,
with love and gratitude.

April 1950

Chapter 1

Morehaven

JAMES DRAYTON was making his way along Platform Three at Paddington Station. He edged past trunks and suitcases, stepped round a traveling cage containing a black rabbit, pushed through a mob of squealing gray-uniformed schoolgirls. "Excuse me," he said to a sturdy young woman whom he had identified by her clipboard as being in charge. "I'm looking for the Morehaven train."

"That's us all right," the woman replied with a grin that revealed regular white teeth. "Sorry about the din. These kids always make a hideous racket when they meet up after the holidays. I can hardly hear myself think!"

"I believe you're expecting my sister, Joanna Drayton."

"I certainly am! I'm Miss Buchanan," she added, shaking James's hand emphatically. She wore a kilt, golf shoes, and a fair-isle sweater; a stopwatch hung on a cord round her neck. "I teach lacrosse and ballroom dancing and swimming when it's warm enough, which isn't terribly often. And where, I wonder, is Joanna?"

"Right here," said James. But the girl beside him wasn't Joanna and neither was the girl behind him. "A moment ago I had her," he said, frowning. "I'd better take a look."

He found her fifty yards up the platform, a slight, mournful figure on a bench, her raincoat and overnight bag beside her. "I was afraid you'd bolted and I'd have to call in the police! Come on." He took her hand and pulled her to her feet. "That woman's harmless."

"Joanna's trunk is in the luggage van and her ticket is in her pocket," James told Miss Buchanan as he reappeared with Joanna. "I'd better be off now. I've got a school train to catch myself."

"Joanna will be fine with us," Miss Buchanan assured him. "We'll have her settled in no time."

James leaned from his great height to kiss his sister.

"Don't go!" she whispered, burying her face in his white shirtfront.

"I've got to," he whispered back.

"Take me with you!"

"You know I can't do that." He kissed her again and quickly disengaged himself. "I'll think about you often and I'll try to write." She watched as he strode away up the platform, fair hair just brushing the collar of his black coat. At the barrier he turned and waved once before the crowd swallowed him up.

Miss Buchanan propelled Joanna over to the nearest carriage. Its worn maroon plush interior held seven excited occupants who embraced, whispered, giggled, shrieked with delight at seeing one another. Above their bobbing heads were faded color prints of celebrated locomotives — Empress of Portsmouth, Weston Whistler, Basingstoke Bullet, Taunton Belle — steaming regally along riverbanks, across bridges, over the Berkshire Downs. Leaning through the door Miss Buchanan announced, "This is Joanna Drayton. She's new. Introduce yourselves and treat her decently!" She gave Joanna a little push, ducked out, and made off.

In the sudden silence following her announcement seven pairs of eyes regarded Joanna. "The corners are all occupied," a girl with bright red hair announced. "So you'll have to sit in the middle."

As Joanna bent to push her bag under the seat, tears slid down her cheeks. She wiped them away surreptitiously before straightening up and taking the only remaining place. In the face of so much joy it wouldn't do to weep.

The redhead leaned forward, elbows on knees, chin in freckled hands. Her fingernails were bitten to the quick. She narrowed her eyes and scrutinized Joanna. "How old are you?"

"Almost eleven."

"Almost eleven means ten. A bloody infant! So you haven't had it, have you? I'm Lucy, by the way."

Joanna pulled on the tops of her knee socks. "Haven't had what?"

"Mummy didn't tell you about those tricky times?" said another girl with pink-rimmed eyes.

Joanna blushed furiously.

"So Mummy *did* tell her," Lucy observed, "only they haven't started yet. They will, ducky. One day you'll start to feel fruitful, like a ripe plum, ready for some marvelous male to eat!"

A gale of laughter swept through the carriage.

"When are we going to see *you* ripen?" said Pink-eyes.

"It depends on one's genes," Lucy replied, tossing her curly hair. "In my family we're late developers. Why waste energy producing eggs that no one's going to fertilize for years?"

A whistle blew. The train lurched back and then forward, throwing Joanna against Pink-eyes, whose long nose quivered. "Watch yourself!" she said sharply as the train pulled away down the platform.

They passed engine yards and blackened walls with "Vote Labor" in tall letters chalked across them and drab huddled houses and wind-swept playgrounds. Eventually they reached damp spring countryside, where sheep and cattle grazed. Joanna stared out the window while her new companions zestfully recalled and recounted events from the holidays just over. No one spoke to her.

"We're here!" Lucy shouted joyfully as, an hour later, the train pulled into Beldon Station. She jumped up and swung the carriage door open. In the station yard two green buses waited to take the children to the school.

At one time Morehaven Court had been a proper country-seat, but the town of Beldon had crept closer and closer until now, all along the road, right up to the great wrought-iron gates, suburban bungalows squatted in tidy gardens with crazy paving and birdbaths and here and there a plaster leprechaun. Morehaven's last noble owner, suffering from syphilis and paranoia, had had the stone wall round his park topped with eighteen-inch iron spikes. Successive headmistresses of the girls' school, which had established itself on the premises after his lordship's heirs had sold out and gone to live abroad, had never had the cash to get the spikes removed. From the gates a drive wound up the hillside to a whitewashed porticoed Regency mansion. To the left towered three cedars of Lebanon; a huge copper beech in newest purplish leaf stood to the right. Daffodils, past their finest, edged the broad lawn.

As the buses drew up to a side door, girls seized their belongings, plunged over one another and out.

Joanna wanted to curl up in a corner seat and ride back to wherever the bus had come from, but the driver was impatient to be off and had no intention of taking any of his passengers with him. He cleared his throat, coughed twice, and stared meaningfully at Joanna in the rearview mirror. She squashed her gray felt hat down on her head, picked up her bag and her raincoat, and got off the bus.

A handful of girls chattered in front of the open door. They were waiting for the late arrivals whose parents were bringing them back to school by car, and they paid no attention as Joanna slipped by them and started off down a wide corridor paved with green and white marble. Wherever this leads I might as well go, she thought, walking past framed photographs of victorious lacrosse teams on primrose-colored walls.

A door swung open and Miss Buchanan dashed out, running full tilt into her. "Christ in Heaven, I'd forgotten about you! You should be upstairs."

Joanna, who had dropped her coat and bag in the collision, replied wearily, "I don't know where upstairs is, or how to get there."

"You don't? Of course not, how could you. Well, follow me."

Miss Buchanan set off at great speed, turned at a notice board decorated with stringless tennis rackets, and sped along a second corridor, this one dingier and pine-floored. Then she leapt, two steps at a time, up a narrow staircase. Her well-muscled legs and rubber-soled shoes gave her a good grip on the carpetless stairs, but Joanna, whose soles were leather and new that morning, slipped, banged her knee, and scrambled up again. On the landing Miss Buchanan caught her breath and nodded through a doorway. "Miss Grant, our matron. She's the fount of knowledge, count on her to tell you all you need to know about this place."

Miss Grant stood in front of a gray metal medicine cupboard, staring out at the majestic copper beech on the side lawn and rhythmically massaging her long red neck. Her hair, dyed chestnut, was set in elaborate waves. She had thinly plucked eyebrows, heavily powdered skin, and a crimson mouth. Below her white medical coat extended solid legs, a surprising contrast to the aging film-star face above them. She yawned widely and rubbed her eyes before turning to Miss Buchanan. "Thanks for the introduction, I'll do my best to live up to it. I assume this is the Drayton child," she added. "They didn't tell me her Christian name."

"It's Joanna," said Joanna, in awe of her eyebrows that remained up, despite the change in her expression.

"They took you in at the last moment, some sort of family emergency, right?" Miss Grant remarked, and as Miss Buchanan hurried away. "Lord, child, take off your hat!" When Joanna, having done so, stood before her, eyes averted, she said with a sigh, "I see trouble looming with that hair. Come here a second." She produced a battered blue brush and a rubber band from the medicine cabinet and set to work sweeping Joanna's wiry dark hair behind her ears and into a clump at the back.

"Not so hard!" Joanna begged. "You're hurting me!"

"Either we tie it back or we cut it," said Miss Grant dryly. "First time away from home," she went on, "and used to being waited on hand and foot, right? You'll learn to look after yourself here, they all do. We put you in the Pigsty. There are only two beds in there as a rule, but we managed to squeeze in a third. It's very near the kitchen — the kids say they like it because they can tell what's for lunch ahead of time."

"Who would *want* to tell ahead of time!" redheaded Lucy remarked from the doorway.

"You're due for a bath on Mondays, Wednesdays, and Fridays," Miss Grant continued, ignoring her, "and Miss Norton — she's the assistant matron — will wash your hair every other Saturday. That brings us to your personal habits . . . Which is it, Joanna, morning or evening?"

"It depends," replied Joanna, blushing.

"She'll have to work on those habits then, won't she, Miss Grant," said Lucy with a grin. "Here at Morehaven we don't like it to depend."

"Don't interrupt, Lucy Wheelock," Miss Grant said quickly. "Now prayers. If you want someone to hear them at bedtime, Miss Norton will be glad to oblige." She frowned. "What else is there of pressing importance? Oh, beds, can you make one?"

"Yes, of course!"

"With hospital corners?" Joanna shook her head. "Well, somebody will show you by and by." Miss Grant threw the blue hairbrush onto the top shelf of the medicine cupboard. "That's enough info from me for now. Take her down to the Pigsty, Lucy, there's a good girl."

Joanna followed Lucy through a warren of staircases and landings. This part of the mansion had been the servants' quarters in the aristocratic period; now it housed the most junior students. Peeling cream wainscoting bore black scuff marks, beige curtains hung unevenly at narrow windows, brown linoleum buckled on the stairs. The only cheerful note was provided by scarlet fire extinguishers, bracketed at regular intervals along the corridors.

"Grant's quite unique and we're awfully lucky to have her," Lucy remarked eagerly. "She was the toast of the Royal Air Force in the war. She ran an airfield cafeteria and all the boys flew off to fight and die for her. If you get her in a good mood she'll tell you how they'd leave their teddy bears with her when they went to bomb Germany, and if they didn't come back, she'd keep them. She still has several lined up on her bed." Lucy stopped in a doorway. "This is it! I slept in here when I first came to Morehaven. It isn't bad, except in hot weather, when the stuff in the dust bins in the yard down below begins to stink."

Iron bedsteads lined three walls of a very small room. Along the fourth wall, under the window, stood three chests of drawers. Beside the head of each bed was a cane-seated chair. There was one flyspecked mirror next to the window and one light fixture in the middle of the ceiling. Its opaque glass shade was cracked. The splintery floorboards were partially covered by worn coconut matting.

Two girls sat together reading *Blighty,* twenty pages of cartoons showing full-breasted, scantily clad women being pursued and captured by men in spacesuits. "Here's Joanna," Lucy said. "These people are Jocelyn and Eliza and they're best friends. They do simply everything together. Now I'd better go and feed my guinea pig." If you were thirteen or over, Joanna discovered, you could bring a guinea pig, rabbit, or hamster to Morehaven and keep it in the shed behind the art studio. The idea was that having a pet encouraged an interest in the natural sciences. Lucy ran off down the stairs.

Jocelyn and Eliza stared silently at Joanna. After a moment Jocelyn, whose black hair hung in two plaits down her back, pointed at the bed farthest from the window. "That's yours. Did you come by train?" Joanna nodded. "Bad luck. They won't bring your trunk up from the station till tomorrow."

"The chest of drawers with one top handle missing is for you," Eliza added. She looped a strand of straight pale hair behind one ear and went back to reading *Blighty*.

Joanna opened her overnight bag and began to remove familiar objects. A photograph frame contained a picture of her father, hatless, on an early autumn day. A second frame held two snapshots: one of her mother in a deck chair on a Welsh beach, the other of James and Miss Cathcart, seated side by side on a log in the park at Widleigh. Miss Cathcart wore her cream linen summer suit from Buenos Aires, her navy blue blouse with polka dots, and tortoiseshell combs in her hair.

"Can we see?" Jocelyn asked. She took the frames from Joanna and gave one to Eliza while she studied the other herself. "Who's this old man?"

"My father."

"Good Lord, he's so *ancient,* I thought he was your grandfather."

"He's not so ancient," said Joanna quickly. "He's sixty-five."

"Who's this, then?" Eliza asked, pointing at James. "Whoever he is, he's looking pretty happy."

"That's my brother on his eighteenth birthday. I took the picture myself with his camera. He's in his last half at Eton."

"Really?" said Eliza with sudden interest. "My brother was at Eton, too, only last spring he was sacked. His tutor's wife caught him in the maze at Hampton Court, kissing the Austrian ambassador's daughter. He should have been in Greek Prose." She went on, "I suppose the lady with him is your mother."

"No, that's Miss Cathcart."

"Who's she?"

"My governess."

"She looks too elegant to be a governess. You should have seen the one *I* had! She wore brown lisle stockings, a brown coat and skirt, and a droopy brown hat. Every garment she owned was brown, even her knickers."

"Miss Cathcart used to live in Argentina and she brought back heaps of made-to-measure clothes from there. South Americans have a real sense of style, that's what she says."

Jocelyn peered over Eliza's shoulder. "Is the person in the deck chair your mother?"

"Yes."

"She's old, too."

"She just *looks* old, because her hair's white. She says it turned white the year after she married Daddy, because of the strain of having to adjust to him and to living in the country. In fact she's forty-six — that isn't old really."

Eliza grimaced. "How awful to have such antique parents! My father's thirty-four and my mother's thirty-three."

A gong boomed far away at the other end of the building and instantly the corridors and staircases came alive with voices and running feet. "Tea!" Jocelyn yelled, jumping up. "Let's go, I'm starving."

Everyone had her assigned place in the oak-paneled dining hall except Joanna, who found herself standing alone in the middle of the room. Behind her a door clanged shut, a sonorous female voice said grace, and with much scraping of chairs a hundred fifty girls sat down to mountains of bread, margarine, and pipless raspberry jam. Chatter, which had stilled briefly before the meal began, returned to fever pitch.

Suddenly a handbell tinkled and the chatter ceased.

"Why does that child not have a chair?" At the head of the

longest table a woman rose. "Let her come over here and sit next to me!" Eyes lowered in shame, Joanna did as ordered. A long, veined hand appeared at waist level. Confused, she stared at it until, realizing what it was there for, she shook it. "We haven't met before," the woman said. "I'm Mrs. Kirkland, your headmistress, and you, of course, must be Joanna. I'm sorry you were left standing for so long." She poured Joanna a cup of tea and offered her a plate of bread and margarine.

"No, thanks."

"We have a rule here," said Mrs. Kirkland carefully. "At least one slice, unless you're ill. When you left home this morning you were quite well, I assume?" In a more casual tone she added, "By the way, where *is* home? It's slipped my mind for a moment."

"Widleigh Park, Herefordshire," said Joanna.

"Then you're bound to know the Ryland-Greens! *Dear* friends of mine. They live at Kennelton, ten miles out of Hereford in the Shrewsbury direction. Heavenly house, been in the family forever. I often stay there."

"I've never heard of the Ryland-Greens."

"Well, you wouldn't necessarily know the older generation."

The Honorable Etheldreda Kirkland sipped her tea. A shade under six foot and strikingly handsome, she resembled her father, Lord Trenchard, the First War general. Her friends and enemies alike agreed that her former husband, a wispy thing who had long since left for southern Africa, was no match for her. Well-connected but impoverished, she found "running a school for the children of one's friends," as she always put it, far more satisfactory than catering business luncheons in the city or giving viola lessons, the dismal fates of all too many female acquaintances down on their luck. The fact was, she thoroughly enjoyed the role of arbiter in the lives of a hundred fifty girls, ages eleven to seventeen. She made a point of getting to know each child as soon as she arrived and from that moment on kept herself closely informed about the details of her social maturation. She welcomed wholeheartedly the responsibilities of being *in loco parentis*, for she was convinced she had something of great value to offer the young people committed to her care: *standards* which, if identified with and approximated, guaranteed one the capacity to cope with virtually any situation in which one found oneself. For "people like us" (herself, her friends, their daughters), the essential ingredient for success was self-confidence based on a conviction of unassailable superiority.

Mrs. Kirkland's first impulse had been to put the Drayton child off until the autumn. Unlike most applicants, she hadn't been put down for Morehaven at birth; for that matter, she hadn't been put down at all, and autumn was preferable to spring for starting one's boarding-school career. However, the mother was an Old Girl, and she'd sounded desperate when she'd telephoned on Easter Monday with an involved tale about a governess who couldn't be kept in the house a day longer. And so, rather against her better judgment, Mrs. Kirkland had agreed to take the child, who, with her hair dragged back, certainly did look dour. Of course it could be that she was petrified. Mrs. Kirkland remembered how even *she* had felt quite scared the first time she'd walked into the dining hall and been confronted by a sea of distrust and apathy. But she'd taken that unpromising response as a challenge and had instantly set about wooing and winning. She would woo and win this dour little creature, too.

"So what did your mother tell you about Morehaven, Joanna?" she asked with a smile.

"Nothing."

"But she attended the school herself, did she not?"

"It was her seventh school and she went to several others after this one. My grandmother could never make up her mind whether she wanted to live in England or on the Continent —

she was constantly moving back and forth. And so after going to so many schools, my mother doesn't remember much about any of them. All she said about this one was that the headmistress wore a cloak with a red silk lining. You don't, though."

"No, that's not quite my style."

"And she rode a tricycle, my mother said."

"I don't ride a tricycle, either . . . Well, let me tell you what we know about *you,* Joanna. For one thing, we've heard that you're immensely musical, which is welcome news. We have a very fine school orchestra. It's such great fun, and we happen to need another cellist."

"I'm a pianist," Joanna said.

"You could take up the cello, though . . . If you're as musical as your mother says you are, you'd learn quickly."

"But I'm about to take up the organ," said Joanna firmly. "Miss Cathcart promised."

"Miss Cathcart?"

"My governess. She plays brilliantly herself and she was going to start me, only my parents suddenly got rid of her. Before she left she swore I could start the organ here instead."

Mrs. Kirkland smiled wistfully. "I've often thought the carriage house would make a charming chapel, but I'm still waiting for that special bequest to finance the conversion. Meanwhile, I'm sorry to say that we have no chapel and no organ, either."

"I didn't want Miss Cathcart to leave!" Joanna burst out, pushing her plate away. "I didn't in the least want to come here!"

Although Mrs. Kirkland observed that Joanna had not finished her slice of bread and margarine, she decided not to press the issue. "Drink up your tea," she said briskly.

"Can't I have milk?"

"At teatime we drink *tea,* Joanna."

"But I don't *like* tea."

"Here at Morehaven we soon *learn* to like it."

*

Joanna was to join Jocelyn and Eliza in form one. Their teacher's name was Mrs. Overton; she wore lacy blouses, Jocelyn said, and galoshes even when it wasn't raining, and her pink slip showed below her skirt.

Immediately after tea they took Joanna to see their classroom. Intended originally as a larder, it had one tiny window high up near the ceiling, and the electric light had to be on all day. A picture of a combine harvester cutting wheat on the Canadian prairies graced one wall, opposite an old framed photograph of the king and queen, their daughters, the princesses Elizabeth and Margaret Rose, and three corgis. Next they went in search of two seventeen-year-olds called Gillian and Rowena, with whom they were madly in love. They soon spotted them sprawled on the front lawn, and for half an hour they had Joanna crouch with them behind a clump of lilacs in order to observe these goddesses.

"It's finally happened!" whispered Eliza ecstatically.

"What has?"

"Gillian has become a woman!"

"How can you tell?"

"By her hair — look, it's six inches shorter than it was before Easter! After she'd given herself to him, he begged for something precious to remember her by. 'Let me cut off your golden tresses,' he said, 'so that when you're gone I can gaze at them and make believe you're still here with me.'"

"Are you sure she didn't just go to the hairdresser?" Jocelyn whispered and, when Eliza didn't deign to reply, added, "Who is *he,* anyway? The groom?"

"Heavens, not that bowlegged fellow, smelling like a muck heap! She's never looked twice at him. *He* is the gamekeeper, of course. They're the best."

"Best at what?"

"Making love," said Eliza, matter-of-factly.

"How do you know?"

"It says so in English literature. Anyway, the gamekeeper —

his name's Bertie — had watched her budding year by year. Then last Tuesday he glimpsed her in the woods when she was out riding and he saw how big her breasts had got. He said to himself, She's ready! No words passed between them, words weren't necessary. After her ride she handed her pony to the groom — Alf, the one who's bowlegged — and went inside for lunch. Meanwhile Bertie went back to the woods with a blanket which he spread over a bed of bracken."

"Couldn't it be sweet-smelling bracken?" whispered Jocelyn.

"Oh, if you like, it can be. After lunch Gillian washed her hair and dried it in front of the radiator in her room. She'd eaten hardly any lunch. She ate no tea at all and only picked at dinner. Her mother did wonder where her appetite had gone, but she was too worried about the maid, who was pregnant and beginning to show, to say anything.

"After they'd had their coffee, Gillian said she was going up to bed. She kissed her parents, went upstairs, took off everything, including her underpants, and put back just her skirt and jersey."

"Then she climbed down the fire escape . . ." Jocelyn whispered.

"They haven't got a fire escape, silly."

"How do *you* know? You've never been within a hundred miles of Gillian's house!"

Eliza shrugged. "For that matter, neither have you. Gillian climbed down the lime tree that taps at her window."

"She's *my* Passion, not yours," Jocelyn whispered fiercely. "I've a right to put in some details."

"Your details wreck the story."

"You don't even *know* Gillian," Jocelyn growled.

"I know her better than you do. You collapse whenever you're anywhere near her. You can't even look at her straight!"

"Beast!" Jocelyn lunged at Eliza and they scuffled behind the lilacs, punching each other and pulling one another's hair.

When at last she had Eliza pinned to the ground, Jocelyn demanded, "Now tell me whose story it is!"

"Yours," groaned Eliza.

But meanwhile the goddesses had arisen from the lawn and were strolling round the corner of the house, out of sight.

"You clot!" hissed Eliza as she struggled to her feet and brushed twigs and leaf mold from her gray skirt. "We've lost them and it's all your fault!"

That night, after Miss Norton had turned out their light, Jocelyn and Eliza decided to enact the seduction scene. They asked Joanna to be Gillian's mother, searching for her daughter in the moonlight. Saying she was too tired, Joanna turned to the wall and pulled the blankets up to her ears, but she couldn't shut out the squeaks and giggles of the other two, who bumped repeatedly against her bed and once, as the gamekeeper drew his beloved onto the sweet-smelling bracken, collapsed on top of her. Eventually both girls climbed into Eliza's bed and fell fast asleep.

As she lay across from them and listened to their slow breathing, Joanna thought, They love being here and with each other; they haven't said a word about home. Home . . . This morning when she left Widleigh her mother hadn't kissed her. She'd turned straight up the steps to the house — she'd been so glad to see the last of Joanna, she hadn't even waved. How could Miss Cathcart have let this happen? After promising to stay for ever and ever, she'd left.

January 1950

~~~~~~

Chapter 2

Widleigh

JOANNA SAT on the schoolroom table, waiting for Miss Cathcart. They should have gone out for a walk at three o'clock and
it was already half past three. The afternoon's dank drizzle
wasn't to Miss Cathcart's taste at all, and the prospect of going out in it would keep her upstairs in her red-flocked wallpapered room, full of memorabilia of life on the far side of the
planet, until the last possible moment. Since the weather that
winter had been singularly wet, even by Herefordshire standards, Miss Cathcart had been consistently late for their walks.

Joanna slid off the table and went to the window overlooking
a short side lawn ringed by leafless elm trees that dripped in the
rain. In the middle of soft grass was a plinth on which lay a
lichened greyhound. She breathed hard on a window pane and
when it was all fogged over, made her wish: The clouds will roll
away and a crimson sunset will bring Miss Cathcart racing from
her room. But when the pane cleared, the clouds hung as low as
ever and the elm trees still dripped.

The schoolroom wore its unoccupied holidays look. The
blackboard was blank on its easel; the surface of Miss Cathcart's mahogany desk was bare; encyclopedias stood in even
rows on the bookshelves; the keyboard of the upright piano
was shut. Joanna was supposed to have been reading, but she'd
lost her book, and because she was quite uncurious about *The*

Old Curiosity Shop, she wasn't going to look for it until she had to. She retreated to the table again. If only James were in! But he'd gone to Hereford by bus to get his hair cut. Her father was out as well, and even if he hadn't been, he wouldn't have welcomed her company. Pickering, the gardener, had gone to the hog sales at Leominster in the farm Ford. Agnes, the cook, was off until six-thirty, and the dailies had both gone home.

Joanna felt like crashing out a *marche militaire* on the piano and making the whole house shake; but her mother was in her sitting room, writing poetry, and *must* not be disturbed. Any loud noise between the hours of two and four ruined her concentration and gave her a migraine headache as well.

Overhead purposeful footsteps were crossing the landing. They continued down the steep back stairs. "Did you finish your reading, Joanna?" Miss Cathcart demanded as she swept in. She had fine blue eyes and a wide red mouth that glistened ever so slightly. She wore her honey-colored hair in a great netted bun at the nape of her neck. Her shoulders were square, her bosom firm; this afternoon it was swathed in rich cream crêpe de Chine. She looked a good deal like the illustration of Boadicea, queen of the ancient Britons, in the schoolroom copy of *Our Island Story.* Direct questioning had failed to elicit her date of birth, and her passport, which bore it, was locked from prying eyes in a cabinet to which she alone had the key. "I'm as old as my ears and a little older than my teeth" was the extent of her self-revelation. Agnes put her at thirty-seven, give or take a year.

"You haven't even opened your book, have you?" she said in a sadly disappointed voice, and when Joanna shook her head, she added, "In that case, how exactly *have* you spent your afternoon?"

It was on the tip of Joanna's tongue to say, Waiting for you, as usual — you're half an hour late again, but she said nothing. She knew that pointing out the facts would get her nowhere:

Miss Cathcart could always find a way of putting her in a worse light yet. Joanna had long ago adapted to the role of miscreant, having discovered that if she accepted whatever blame was in the offing, things generally took a turn for the better. Provided Miss Cathcart felt justified, she was amenable to letting Joanna decide what, together, they would do next.

Joanna had decided that this afternoon they would go down to the riverbank so that she could climb along a particular branch of a particular tree which reached far out over the water. In wet weather, when the river was swollen and angry, it was thrilling to sit astride that branch and swish up and down above the racing torrent.

"I'm afraid I was daydreaming," she admitted with a sigh of contrition, adding, "Your rain hat's on a hook in the pantry. I'll fetch it, you wait here!"

"When are you going to learn to use time properly," Miss Cathcart murmured, shaking her head.

"We'll need our Wellingtons and waterproofs too," Joanna announced as she returned, rain hat in hand.

"Wellingtons?" Miss Cathcart frowned. "What precisely do you have in mind?"

"We're going to the river."

"Are we? But it's so wet there! Why not a quick turn round the village? They might have got some licorice in at the shop."

"None till tomorrow. Pickering told me, he went down to check." Joanna added, "You needn't come *all* the way to the river. You can keep an eye on me from the gate."

"All right," Miss Cathcart conceded grudgingly. She loved dramatic weather — the burning skies of drought in southern latitudes, tidal waves, Andean blizzards, hurricanes. But Herefordshire drizzle eroded the soul, she often said.

In the view of Joanna's father, Major Henry Drayton, childhood was a time of perilous disorder from which only strict adherence to routine offered deliverance. Having spent his own childhood and adolescence learning punctuality and precision, he had entered the Royal Military College, Sandhurst. From there he had gone into the Thirteenth Hussars, the cavalry regiment that the Draytons had been going into since the Peninsular War, and his need for order had been satisfied for decades. But in retirement, with no junior officers to instruct and organize, he attempted to exact military precision from his family and household instead. He always said — with absolute truth — that he asked no more of others than he asked of himself, since he did the same thing at the same time each day, without fail. Joanna rather wished he were still with his regiment. He must have got much more satisfaction from his junior officers than he ever did, for example, from her.

Miss Cathcart was not by nature orderly, either. She believed in "responding to the particular situation" and in "not having one's spontaneity squashed." It was a constant source of wonder to Joanna that Miss Cathcart's inconsistencies were borne by her father, since in anyone else he would have considered them indications of poor moral character. But then, he had to make exceptions for Miss Cathcart because she had been entirely his own doing. He had put an advertisement in the *Times: Governess/companion wanted; imagination and initiative essential.* He had selected her from the other applicants, sight unseen; an interview would have meant his going up to London, which he loathed.

In her letter of inquiry, Miss Cathcart wrote that she had just got off the boat from South America, where she had spent the war with a large Anglo-Argentine family called Acland. Before that, she had been with the Talbots at Billingham Place in Northamptonshire. In the Argentine she had often stayed on the family estancia, a hundred miles from anywhere, for six months at a stretch; apart from educating the Acland children, she had shorn sheep, branded cattle, organized polo matches, and even played in them, until she'd had a bad fall on the pampas. After that, she had been told that she must never ride a horse again, and hadn't. In terms of her academic background, she had taken her higher school certificate and had spent a year near Lyons, so she was a good French speaker, although after Argentina, Spanish was her better language. Last, she had attended the Royal Academy of Music but, owing to family difficulties, had been unable to complete her course. Nevertheless, she played the piano and the organ, also, with considerable facility. For a time she had been assistant organist at the Anglican Cathedral of St. John the Divine in Buenos Aires.

To Henry Drayton, Sybilla Cathcart sounded like a sensible sort of woman who ought to fit in well at Widleigh Park. Her musical expertise especially appealed to him because his father had installed an organ in Widleigh parish church in memory of his mother, but there had never been anyone in the village properly competent to play it.

He didn't bother about references. He'd been at private school with Allen Talbot fifty years before, had thoroughly disliked him, and had kept away from him ever since. As for Arturo Acland, he'd never heard of him. Besides, he didn't give tuppence for other people's opinions. And so he sent Miss Cathcart money for a one-way train ticket from London to Hereford.

On her arrival two days later, Henry outlined his ideas concerning the education of females. (Since he hadn't had sisters, these were very largely speculative.) For boys, he told Miss Cathcart, boarding school was a necessity. Those who stayed with their indulgent mothers would never be braced sufficiently to withstand life's rigors. Hence both he and his son, James, had been sent away to Winterfields, soon after their seventh birthdays. Girls, however, were different; generally much tougher in character to begin with, they could remain at home.

Having read her letter very carefully, he had every expectation that Miss Cathcart would provide Joanna with a thorough grounding. An appreciation of Britain's historical role and of the Victorian novel were, of course, essential. Diary keeping, natural history, a grasp of arithmetic principles, and regular exercise were very important, too. (Given Miss Cathcart's unfortunate pampas accident, he, himself, would take charge of Joanna's equestrian training; this included fox hunting on winter Saturdays, whenever the meet was within hacking distance . . . There was a quite decent Raleigh bike in the garage; it had belonged to his mother, who used to pedal all over the Welsh Marches in search of Norman fonts. Miss Cathcart might possibly enjoy following the hounds on it?) He hastened to assure her that he was merely establishing guidelines designed to produce the sort of woman whom he, personally, would find agreeable to live with. But how she set about fleshing out his guidelines would be left entirely to her.

After almost four years at Widleigh, Miss Cathcart was unquestionably a success as a teacher. Every subject she made her own: osmosis — she had identified the process; the Magna Carta — she had been both a draftee and a signatory; the *Lays of Ancient Rome* — she had written them. Joanna, at eight, had been stunned to discover that Sir Francis Drake, not Miss Cathcart, had defeated the Spanish Armada! Her account of the proceedings had been so vivid; how could she remember the action in such detail without having been the architect of victory? Dramatic gesticulation always accompanied poetic recitations, descriptions of historical events, accounts of scientific discovery — for she had learned to use her hands, kept soft with a precious, secret, clove-scented skin oil, in a thoroughly Latin manner. But the best use to which she put her hands was playing the piano. She played with a ferocious joy and was doing her best to transmit the same sense and spirit to Joanna.

Her talents and enthusiasm had proved even more wide-ranging than her letter of inquiry had indicated. She had turned out to be an avid fly fisherman, a pretty fair shot, a passionate armchair cricketer. When the MCC toured Australia in the winter, she would bound from her bed at two in the morning to listen to the Test Match broadcasts on the smoking room radio. She knew a lot about steeplechasing, dogs, herbaceous borders. Furthermore, in character she complemented her employer perfectly. He was shy, she was extroverted. She stood firmly, encouragingly, between him and a recalcitrant world.

In a word, Henry Drayton's original presentiment that she was the right choice — both for Joanna and him — had been borne out completely.

Henry Drayton was a great lover of the English countryside, and he believed that the best way to see it was on foot. After lunch he took a short nap, but by two-fifteen at the latest he was up and out, whatever the weather, walking over his own and other people's property at a steady three and a half miles an hour. With ten minutes to spare until tea at four, he would be back in the park, expecting to see Joanna and Miss Cathcart hurrying home after their afternoon's exercise.

As they came out the front door, Miss Cathcart's customary eagerness vanished, and a general air of discontent took its place. She had agreed to this expedition but it was not of her own choosing. The clock in the stable yard said twenty-five minutes to four. Twenty-five minutes of chilling discomfort — water seeping through the seams of one's rubber boots, dripping off the brim of one's hat between the back of one's neck and one's collar, curling tendrils of hair round one's face into corkscrews. How she longed for the high, dry skies of Argentina! In silence they set off riverward.

Joanna glimpsed Dulcie, her pony of uncertain age and unreliable disposition, in the lee of a grove of walnut trees in the park. Like Miss Cathcart, Dulcie had been entirely Henry Drayton's doing, the child concerned never having been consulted. In Joanna's opinion, her father's choice of pony had been much less satisfactory than his choice of governess. She deeply disliked and distrusted Dulcie and made no attempt to attract her attention now. Miss Cathcart's poor frame of mind was problem enough. The task of the moment was to coax her into a better one.

Turning a bright face to her governess, Joanna said, "Tell me about the time you saved the lives of Ana María and María Antonia!" These were the two youngest Acland children. Señor Acland was of British descent and an Anglican, but his wife was an Argentine and what Miss Cathcart called an R.C., hence their three sons and four daughters. Miss Cathcart never spoke about her own childhood — that's too long ago, too far away, she'd say when Joanna pressed her — but she was *raconteuse par excellence* about her former charges, whose photographs she displayed on her chest of drawers: Luke Talbot in cricket whites in the first eleven at Winterfields, Alison on a pony, the Acland children lined up in front of their country house, and, in an especially large photo, the oldest Acland son, Felipe, a wonderfully handsome boy about James's age, smiling on a beach in Uruguay. Miss Cathcart had dozens of stories to tell about the Aclands and a great many about the Talbots, too. (Luke Talbot was now a first lieutenant in the Coldstream Guards; his sister was married and a mother and living in Washington. At Christmas Miss Cathcart received cards from both of them — beribboned, crested regimental ones from Luke, lavish American ones from Alison — with letters telling all their news. Strangely enough, no cards or letters ever arrived from Buenos Aires.)

"You've heard that rescue tale too often," said Miss Cathcart irritably.

"But you were such a heroine, tell it just once more!"

Beneath the brim of her rain hat Miss Cathcart's austere expression softened a little. "Oh, all right then, where shall I begin?"

"First say what they were wearing." Joanna knew that most of the time on the estancia Ana María and María Antonia wore corduroy trousers like she did at Widleigh, but their city wardrobe was exquisite.

"We were going to have lunch with their father in a very smart restaurant indeed," said Miss Cathcart with a glimmer of a smile at the memory. "So we chose broderie anglaise with pink sashes and pink hair ribbons to match."

"Starched petticoats?" Joanna asked, and when Miss Cathcart nodded, "Did they wear their lockets with Grandmother's baby hair?"

"They always wore their lockets on special occasions."

"White shoes, white gloves, lace-edged pocket handkerchiefs? Did you let them use your lilies of the valley toilet water?"

"Of course."

"Which car did you go in?"

"The Daimler. Their mother was using the Packard. They were so terribly excited that they couldn't wait for the chauffeur to bring it round — they rushed to the garage and jumped in. They'd both been so good and hard working, they truly deserved their treat."

But their treat never materialized. They arrived at the restaurant a little early, and while they were freshening up for Señor Acland in the ladies' cloakroom on the second floor, fire broke out in the kitchen; by the time they emerged with clean hands and smooth hair, flames were leaping up the carpeted staircase. In an instant Miss Cathcart had the two little girls back in the cloakroom, where she seized a jug of drinking water, poured its contents over all three of them, and, as flames licked under the door, hoisted the children to the window sill. Quickly she clambered up herself and then leapt, with Ana María under one arm and María Antonia under the other, into a bed of canna lilies twenty feet below. She suffered three broken ribs and a shattered ankle, but protected from the full impact of their fall by her body, neither child was hurt. By the time Señor Acland arrived, the restaurant had become a raging furnace. Many of the people in it, including the ladies' room attendant, suffered horrible deaths.

"You're always so good in a crisis," said Joanna when Miss Cathcart had finished her story.

"Some people seem to be born knowing what to do and when to do it," Miss Cathcart replied, smiling modestly. "It's a sixth sense, I suppose." At last the drizzle had ceased, the sky was clearing; and as she walked over the cattle grid at the bottom of the drive and across the road to the water meadow, Miss Cathcart exuded a sense of fresh purpose. When she spoke next it was in the voice she reserved for important communications.

"I want you to know, Joanna, that when I listened to your partita yesterday I was very moved." She paused significantly before going on. "An awareness that your talents are out of the ordinary has long been precious to me. I shall never forget the way you played the Beethoven G Major, years ago. Of course it's not technically difficult, but you had the phrasing and the mood — exactly the right spirit — and you were only seven! Alison Talbot was precocious also, and at one time I had high hopes for her. Like you, she seemed to *understand* music. What she lacked, though, was the right temperament."

Joanna experienced a small thrill of triumph. Until now Miss Cathcart had represented Alison Talbot as having had everything: the pink and white complexion of a quattrocento angel, beautiful penmanship, excellent spelling, an unusual sensitivity to horses. But there *had* been something missing after all!

Miss Cathcart came to a halt in the middle of the water meadow. "True musicality involves more than talent. It involves an invincible confidence in your own art, and that you seem to have, dear." Again she paused briefly. "In my opinion, a competition is what's needed next. It's time you were measured by standards other than my own. I mean," she added with a little chuckle, "before we're invited to play the Mozart two-piano concerto with the Hallé Orchestra, we have to win our spurs."

"We? Are you entering the competition, too, Miss Cathcart?"

"Of course not! It's only for children. You'll be playing for us both, dear."

After a moment's reflection Joanna said, "I never do that well in riding competitions."

"That's not entirely your fault — we know that Dulcie isn't always cooperative. But in a piano competition everything is up to *you* — your head, heart, hands, memory — your *soul*, Joanna. Now off you go," she concluded, pressing Joanna's hand with warm fingers. "And do be careful! Remember, if you fall in the water I shan't go diving in to fish you out!"

On their way back up the hill to the house in the dusk they spotted Henry Drayton and his labradors, Dolly and Grizelda, waiting for them by the railings that divided the lawn from the park.

"Rain's stopped, thank goodness, though it looks like we'll have frost tonight," he observed when Miss Cathcart and Joanna came within earshot. He was only a shade over five foot five, but because he carried himself so straight, he looked taller. His brownish-yellow plus fours had belonged to his father. The pocket watch he now glanced at had belonged to his grandfather. His stick he had cut from the hedge an hour before. "How did you enjoy your walk?"

"An outing on an afternoon like this makes one very ready for tea," Miss Cathcart replied with a broad smile.

"There's something I simply have to talk to you about," said Henry urgently as he fell into step beside her. "As usual, it's Butrick. He's behaving badly over his farmyard wall. It's falling down and he does nothing. Of all the tenants he's the most obtuse."

"He needs to be approached tactfully," said Miss Cathcart.

"I approached him — half an hour ago — and he didn't listen to a word. Turned his back on me."

"I tell you what," said Miss Cathcart as she laid a hand on her employer's arm. "Let's leave him for a day or two, then I'll pay his wife a visit."

"I'd be so grateful! Mrs. Butrick's awfully fond of you," said Henry, looking a shade happier. As he opened the gate in the railings for Miss Cathcart and Joanna to pass through, he added almost cheerfully, "I remember Father used to have trouble getting Butrick to listen to him, too."

In the bootroom he changed his heavy shoes for a lighter pair and tied the laces with double bows; he washed his hands, dried them, and straightened his regimental tie. Then he brushed his hair, which, like his small mustache, was flinty gray. He expressed directly little of what he felt, but when he was agitated his nose twitched, and his nose twitched often. In the regiment he had been known as Bunny, a nickname he'd detested but had borne with resignation. After his father died in January 1930 he had resigned from the army and come home to Widleigh, and except for his honeymoon, he had rarely been away since. Nor, as he told Joanna over dominoes on winter evenings, did he intend to leave in the future. For richer, for poorer, here he would stay.

The Draytons had lived at Widleigh since the reign of James I, but the original house — which, judging from a painting in the hall, had been charmingly unpretentious if a trifle squat — had been torn down in 1858 by Henry's grandfather, who, after marrying a Manchester textile heiress, decided he required an establishment that reflected his amplified resources. Soon a new crenelated mansion of a local pinkish stone rose on a ridge above the river Wye. It included every sort of room a Victorian family could reasonably wish for: besides ten bedrooms, day and night nurseries, a drawing room large enough to give a ball in, a smoking room, a gunroom, and a dining room that seated twenty-four, there was a conservatory lined with plaster busts of Roman emperors and a library with seven thousand books. (Thirty-five hundred of them — scarlet, forest-green, and midnight-blue tooled leather — had been ordered by the yard, indiscriminate of title, to fill gleaming mahogany shelves.) Bathrooms and central heating were added much later. The estate itself consisted of the park, five farms, three of which were now let, one thousand acres of moorland, four hundred yards of fishing on both banks of the Wye, and eighteen well-constructed laborers' cottages in Widleigh village.

Disdaining the acquisition of wealth and unwilling to pay much attention to its conservation, Henry had put his stocks and government bonds in the hands of a cautious Hereford solicitor named Chadwick. Now and then Mr. Chadwick might sell a few shares of English Electric and buy a few of British Petroleum with the proceeds, but basically he left well enough alone. In this way, while no unmitigated disasters had occurred, his client's income had remained the same, give or take a thousand pounds, for twenty years, and what with inflation and increased taxation, it didn't go nearly as far in 1950 as it had in 1930. Sometimes Henry complained about being hard up, but his financial situation didn't worry him enough for him to change the way he managed his money. He had enough for leading a quiet life at Widleigh, which was all he asked.

Joanna came upon her mother with the tea trolley at the dining room door. "Are those hands clean, Joanna?" Mrs. Drayton said quickly. "Let's see."

"I washed them in the bootroom sink."

"Not well enough though, darling. They need a proper scrubbing with the nailbrush."

As she watched her daughter run back to the bootroom, Mrs. Drayton fingered the scarlet and green silk scarf that she had draped round her shoulders over her canary yellow twin set.

The drabber the day, the brighter the clothes she selected. "Why don't you wear what other women wear in the winter?" her husband used to ask her, but she ignored him. In fact, with her height — she was five inches taller than Henry — tweed suits and hand-knitted jumpers, the uniform of all the county ladies, would have suited Barbara Drayton much better, but, considering herself a thoroughly city person, she passionately rejected them.

"Where's James?" Joanna demanded on her return.

"He said he would come straight home from the barber, but I suppose he missed the bus. The next one leaves Hereford at six."

James had promised Joanna that after tea he would read her the story he'd just finished, up in his room with the door locked. (James wrote tales of mystery and imagination in the style of Edgar Allan Poe. Joanna, who sometimes found them hard to follow, had suggested he try writing historical stories instead — for instance, about Richard II, who was her favorite English king. But James said he hated history; there was too much of it at Widleigh.) Apart from Mrs. Burgess and Mrs. Crompton — the dailies — who had to get in to clean, the only person for whom James unlocked his door was his sister. But if he caught the six o'clock bus he wouldn't be home before seven, and by then Joanna would be getting ready for bed; there wouldn't be time for reading.

"Here, take the crumpets," said Mrs. Drayton, handing her a white paper bag. "The baker just delivered them, so we know they're fresh. Why don't you start toasting them."

On weekdays Joanna and Miss Cathcart had breakfast and lunch in the schoolroom, which lacked the least hint of elegance. Miss Cathcart hurried through her schoolroom meals. But at tea, which they ate in the dining room, with its chandelier and portraits of Drayton ancestors in taffeta and velvet, she took her time. Crested silver, Dresden china, candles, even if unlit on the sideboard, made the spirits soar.

Today, as usual, she dominated the conversation while others negotiated the eating of their crumpets without getting too much butter on their chins. Having dealt with the upcoming general election, prospects for an end to petrol rationing, and the latest news from the Argentine of Eva Perón, Miss Cathcart cleared her throat. "I have a proposal."

"Do tell us," said Mrs. Drayton lightly. "Is this another public venture?" On her arrival at Widleigh, Miss Cathcart had installed herself as organist and revitalized the choir, whose repertoire she had extended far beyond *Hymns Ancient and Modern* to madrigals, cantatas, and early Spanish chants. With the proceeds from half a dozen whist drives that she had organized herself, she had bought her people, as she called them, lavish royal blue gowns and mortarboards, and off they'd gone in a chartered bus to sing at sacred and civic celebrations up and down the Welsh border from Chester to Pontypool. Next, needing a further outlet for her energies, Miss Cathcart had started a dramatic society. "Are the women of Widleigh to embroider new hassocks for the church?" Mrs. Drayton drawled. "I must say, I'd noticed how shabby the old ones are getting, but there's no point asking me to pitch in, my dear. I've never mastered backstitch, let alone bargello."

"This has nothing to do with Widleigh," replied Miss Cathcart. "This concerns Joanna. I believe the time has come for her to get a wider exposure, musically speaking, I mean."

"What do you have in mind? Village hall recitals, Chopin waltzes for the Mothers' Union?"

"I'd like to see her compete for the Elgar Prize."

"You'll excuse my ignorance, but what is that?" said Mrs. Drayton, one eyebrow raised.

"It's a national piano competition."

"*National* competition! Good heavens, aren't we getting carried away! My daughter has never entered anything more glamorous than a Pony Club gymkhana!"

Undeterred, Miss Cathcart continued. "For the purposes of

the Elgar Prize the British Isles are divided into twelve regions. Joanna would be in the West of England junior division. The first round takes place in Bristol on January twenty-third."

Henry Drayton wiped each buttery finger with his napkin before observing, "January twenty-third is nine days away, so I assume your proposal to enter Joanna in this event is already an accomplished fact."

"The application had to be in by the first of December, actually."

"So this is a conspiracy!" Mrs. Drayton turned to Joanna. "Why didn't *you* tell me?"

"I didn't know about it."

"I only broached the subject while we were out this afternoon," Miss Cathcart admitted. "It seemed unnecessary to get her worked up too far ahead of time."

Elbows on the table, Mrs. Drayton leaned toward Miss Cathcart. "So in nine days' time, Joanna, who until an hour ago was quite unaware of this event, will walk out onto a concert stage and play — what?"

"She's got the Bach partita ready and the minuet and rondo from Opus ten, Number three. And in reserve she has her Mozart variations."

"It's abject *cruelty* to spring this on her!" Mrs. Drayton exclaimed. She turned to Joanna. "Aren't you terrified?"

"It couldn't be worse than a gymkhana," Joanna said with a shrug. "In the egg and spoon race my egg always falls off my spoon before anyone else's."

Unheeding, Mrs. Drayton swung back to Miss Cathcart. "Building confidence is so important in the early years, and this experience could *destroy* Joanna's!"

"Confidence is built by expanding horizons."

"But she could make a complete fool of herself!"

After a moment's silence, Miss Cathcart went on. "Two competitors will be selected from each division to go on from Bristol to London for the concluding rounds in the Guildhall

School of Music on the ninth and tenth of February."

"Bristol! London! What is this? Leopold Mozart dragging little Wolfgang around Europe! In the first place, how do you expect to get to Bristol?"

"We'll go down by train the night before, and I've booked a room at the Severn Bore."

"The Severn Bore's frightfully expensive, and since you didn't consult us before making your arrangements, you can't be counting on me or my husband to pay your way."

"I wasn't, Mrs. Drayton." Miss Cathcart's voice rang. "I expect to cover our expenses out of my savings." She sat back in her chair, put two lumps of sugar in her tea, stirred it, and drank it down.

But Mrs. Drayton was still giving chase. "Why exactly are you doing this?"

"I've already told you why," Miss Cathcart replied, color rising.

"For Joanna's sake, you said, only that's nonsense! You're doing it for *you*. You're making my daughter into a vehicle for your own ambition!"

"Enough of that!" said Henry Drayton sharply. "Another crumpet for me, please, Joanna, and I dare say Miss Cathcart would like another, too. What train will you two be catching on Friday?"

"The three o'clock to Evesham," said Miss Cathcart quickly. "We change there."

"Personally I doubt the Severn Bore could broaden anyone's horizons, but if you say so, I'll take your word for it, and I'll be glad to foot the bill."

Miss Cathcart beamed. "Oh, Major, thank you! I was hoping you'd understand the importance of this!"

Someone was ringing the front doorbell with great insistence. "Who *is* that impatient person?" Mrs. Drayton said, exasperated. "Joanna, run and see."

"If it's Saunders, tell him to wait in the smoking room," said

Henry. Saunders was the farm bailiff. "He's early. I told him five o'clock and it's only twenty minutes to."

Joanna raced from the room and across the hall to struggle with the great oak door, which had swollen in the winter damp. It sprang open to reveal Thomas Edgerton, vicar of Widleigh, a massive figure in black suit, pond-green woolen gloves, and black felt hat. "Is she here?" he asked anxiously.

"If you mean Miss Cathcart, she's having her tea."

Mr. Edgerton's face fell. "I'd forgotten it was teatime. In that case I'm interrupting."

"She won't mind. Come in," Joanna told him. "Do you want to talk to her about your manuscript?" Mr. Edgerton, whose great interest was fourteenth-century ecclesiastical history, periodically brought drafts of sections of his monograph on the bishoprics of Hereford and Gloucester to read aloud to Miss Cathcart, from whom he could always count on receiving frank criticism.

"This time it's parish business."

"D'you want to leave your hat?"

"No, thanks. I'm only stopping in for a minute."

"You'll stay much longer than that, you always do. Give it to me. Don't forget when you go out, it's here on the hall table."

Mr. Edgerton stood in the dining room doorway. "Is it all right, my popping in?"

Miss Cathcart looked up with a welcoming smile. "Thomas, how nice!"

"Of course it's all right," said Mrs. Drayton briskly. "We'd just finished one order of business and we hadn't got on to the next. Sit next to Miss Cathcart and have a cup of tea and some shortbread. Agnes made it this morning."

The friendship between Mr. Edgerton and Miss Cathcart was a source of great amusement to Mrs. Drayton, who generally referred to Mr. Edgerton as "the young man." However, it seemed to arouse a rather complicated response in Major Drayton. At one time he had been proud of Mr. Edgerton's scholarly endeavors, but nowadays, behind his back, he called him "our episcopal pansy." (This puzzled Joanna, because Agnes said a pansy was a man who shared a bed with another man, whereas Mr. Edgerton lived with his sister, Miss Hilary, and they practically never had anyone, male or female, to stay.) In any event, it was obvious that Miss Cathcart had a great deal in common with Mr. Edgerton and that this compatibility rather clouded Major Drayton's sky.

"What's the burning issue of the day, Edgerton?" he said dryly as the vicar sat down next to Miss Cathcart.

"An unfortunate mix-up in the schedule. Bridbury has picked the same date we have for their jumble sale, and since they have a better bus service than we do, they'll nab our crowd."

"We'll soon sort out this muddle," said Miss Cathcart soothingly. "Joanna" — she glanced round — "if you've had all you want to eat, you may be excused now. Don't forget, your trills need attention. I'll be along to hear them directly."

The drawing room grand piano loomed above skins of tigers that Henry Drayton had shot in India, Burma, and the Malay Peninsula. They had stuffed heads, full sets of teeth, red tongues, and glass eyes that glared as one stumbled over one's arpeggios.

Joanna was playing Beethoven when her brother dashed in, his overcoat flapping to his ankles. His hair was clipped high above the ears and up the back of his head. "The barber scalped you!" Joanna said, laughing.

"Forget that. I've got something amazing to show you!" James's eyes changed with his mood and with the weather. Mostly they were gray, like the English Channel in November, his mother had once said. In summer, though, on rare July days when the wheat was high and beginning to lighten, they were just that color, green on the verge of gold, and sometimes, when he was especially happy, they were a remarkable deep dark blue.

They were that color now.

"Let's go!"

"Where are we going?"

"Out!" He grabbed her hands off the keys and pulled her away from the piano, and together they raced over the tiger skins and across the hall.

"I left the lamps on," Joanna said.

James slammed the front door shut behind them. "There!" In a pool of light at the bottom of the steps stood a small green car.

"Whose is it?"

"Mine!"

"Since when?"

"This afternoon at four-thirty."

Last September, after practicing on the farm Ford over the summer holidays, James had got his driver's license and then he'd started looking for a car of his own. The week before, in the *Hereford Chronicle,* he'd seen an advertisement that sounded promising: 1935 Morris, single owner, thirty thousand miles. On Saturday he'd gone to take a look, liked what he'd seen, left a deposit, and arranged to come back with the rest of the money today.

"Was it a lot?" asked Joanna.

"All my Christmas and birthday money for the last four years! My savings account is down to nine and sixpence."

"Do Daddy and Mummy know?"

"Nobody knows except you. Now hop in and I'll take you anywhere you want to go."

"How about London? Let's go and see Granny."

"I haven't got quite enough petrol for that, but I'll take you to the back door of the Rose and Crown and buy you a ginger beer and a packet of potato crisps." He opened the passenger door and bowed low. "Your Rolls awaits you, madam." Then he took out a starting handle and ran to the front of the car to crank it.

"There isn't a key?"

"You can't expect everything, Joanna!" James laughed as the engine spluttered to life. He jumped in and off they bumped down the drive, over the cattle grid, left, and away from Widleigh village.

"Aren't we going to the pub?" said Joanna.

"First we're going for a spin over the moor."

"What about Miss C.?"

"What about her?"

"She was coming to the drawing room to hear my trills."

"Too bad," said James, "but she'll forgive you. She adores you — you're the apple of her eye!"

"She likes Daddy just as much as me and Mr. Edgerton more than either of us. She's having a tête-à-tête with him this minute, in fact."

But James didn't respond; he was concentrating on driving. "She handles beautifully. I couldn't ask for anything better!"

Since the afternoon the temperature had fallen precipitously, and the puddles in the road showed black and icy in the headlights. Joanna shivered. "Is there a heater?"

"Afraid not, this is the common man's car."

"I forgot my coat. I'm freezing."

"Hold on!" James slammed his foot on the brake and the car skidded to a stop. He threw the door open, jumped out, and fought his way out of his overcoat. "Here — you wear it!"

"Now *you'll* freeze."

"I shan't, I'm having too good a time!"

"What will Daddy and Mummy say when they discover? They hate one doing things behind their backs."

"Who *cares* what they say! This isn't their car. It's mine, I paid for it. I bought it for you and me to go on trips together. Tell you what," he added, "let's go to Spain!" James had been there once already with his school friend Gordon Burns, whose aunt was a marquesa. He'd loved the light, the food, the kindness of the people. He intended to live in Spain one of these days and, meanwhile, to visit as often as possible.

"When shall we go? At Easter?"

James shook his head. "Not quite that soon. I'm flat broke and it'll take a while to replenish the coffers."

"I've got fifteen pounds, twelve and thruppence in my savings account."

"That's certainly a start."

"We could borrow the money from Daddy and pay him back when we're grown up."

"I doubt he'd go along with that idea. You know he doesn't approve of Abroad, unless it's India."

As she snuggled into James's coat, Joanna considered credit possibilities. "There's Granny. She's rich and she likes us."

"Then next time you see her, you should feel her out for a loan. Meanwhile, we'll scrimp and save our every penny." After a moment he continued reflectively, "When I went to Spain with Burns his aunt translated for us, but we won't have her, will we, so we'd better learn some Spanish. With Miss C. as resident tutor, that shouldn't be too difficult."

"Will she be coming with us?" said Joanna in alarm.

"She's not invited this time."

They had turned off the valley road and were climbing steadily to the moors. "That's good," Joanna said, tingling with relief and happiness. "If she came, she'd take up the whole back seat and we wouldn't have room for our luggage."

Chapter 3

The Arlington Hotel

"I PACKED your Viyella dress for tomorrow, and long white socks." Mrs. Drayton stood beside her daughter in the front hall, fiddling with the buttons of her cardigan. She did them up, then undid them, and one popped off and rolled away under the hall table. "Damn!" She knelt to recover it and as she rose to her feet again, went on. "Your green velvet with the lace collar is in your bag as well, just in case. At Christmas, when you last wore it, it was already a bit short but I wasn't about to get Mrs. Burgess to let the hem down. I hate to count chickens before they hatch — I mean, they might eliminate you tomorrow afternoon, mightn't they. Anyway, if Mrs. Burgess had let down the hem, there'd have been an ugly line. I must say, Joanna," she added, "you're astonishingly calm. I'm the one who's on edge! I suppose it's just as well I'm staying here."

Having returned from Bristol with an illuminated scroll signed by four judges and the Lord Mayor, Joanna was off to London with Miss Cathcart for the concluding rounds of the Elgar Competition. In her coat pocket she had the letter James had written from Eton: "I'll be up for the finals on Saturday, ready to cheer my head off when they announce you're the winner. Then we'll go to Benticks to celebrate with hot chocolate and black cherry cake. P.S. How does my car look? Hope you're polishing it regularly."

James, like Miss Cathcart, was supremely confident of Joanna's chances.

Mrs. Drayton twisted her wedding ring round and round on her finger. "Your grandmother leads a very active social life," she said. "She makes no bones about house guests getting in the way — as soon as one arrives she asks what time in the morning one will be leaving. Her offer to have you and Miss C. from Thursday to Sunday is practically *unheard* of. It's only because you're musical like she is. She hoped I would be, but I wasn't, which added one more bitter disappointment to her list.

"You'll be good, won't you, darling," she went on. "And please do what you can about Miss C. Granny likes to tell her own stories — she's not interested in other people's and you know how Miss C. is, once she's off and running about gauchos."

"I like her stories," said Joanna.

"I'm glad you do, darling, since you're a captive audience so much of the time, but I doubt your grandmother would feel the same way." Mrs. Drayton glanced at the clock on the mantelpiece. "Speaking of Miss C., where is she?"

"With Daddy. Last night they were working on the quarterly accounts together, and they're just finishing up."

At that moment the smoking room door opened and out came Miss Cathcart in a narrow-waisted dove-gray pavement suit and hat to match. On her right lapel she wore her lapis lazuli brooch, which matched her eyes. The Talbot children had given it to her when she left for South America. "Ready to sweep those judges off their feet, Joanna?" she said with a smile.

"You've got her music, haven't you?" said Mrs. Drayton before Joanna could reply.

"She won't need her music; she knows it all by heart."

"What if she gets in a panic? Shouldn't she have it to refer to?" But Miss Cathcart didn't care to respond.

Henry Drayton, who had followed her out of the smoking

room, said, "You two wait for me in front. I'll bring the car round."

"Don't ring until it's all over," said Mrs. Drayton, bending to kiss her daughter on the forehead. "I'll assume no news means good news."

At half past six that evening Joanna and Miss Cathcart arrived at the Arlington Hotel in Knightsbridge, where Mrs. Gilbert Beresford had her flat. The doorman, in top hat and brass-buttoned blue frock coat, saw them from the cab into the lobby. "Madam is expecting you, Miss Joanna?"

"Of course she is, Standish!"

Nóting the suitcases, Standish observed, "You'll be spending the night."

"Possibly *three* nights. Since her spare room's only got one bed, my grandmother's taken a room on the fourth floor for us."

"So this is going to be a proper visit. I'll get a boy to take your things to the room while you go up and say 'ow-are-you and very-well-thank-you."

Joanna and Miss Cathcart took the lift to the third floor, and Joanna raced down the plum-colored carpeted corridor with its shell-shaped lighting fixtures to knock at her grandmother's door. "Just coming," a voice called gaily, and there in the open doorway was Leonora Beresford, diminutive in beige cashmere, diamond earrings, and crocodile shoes. "What a treat to see you, darling! What a great excitement this is!" She offered a smooth pink-tinted cheek to her granddaughter and shook Miss Cathcart's hand. "Take off that ugly coat," she added to Joanna, "and let's have a look at you." She cocked her head to one side. "It doesn't seem she's taking after my daughter, does it, Miss Cathcart? If she were going to be a giantess like Barbara, surely she'd be taller by now. No, Joanna's more on my scale, thank heaven!"

Leonora Beresford had been one of the most celebrated

beauties of her generation, and was still, at seventy, very pleasing to the eye. This was partly due to nature and partly to an establishment in Hans Crescent, where every inch of her was ministered to each Thursday.

Her banker husband, whom she had married when she was twenty-two and he fifty-three, had died a few years later, leaving her with Barbara and an excellent trust. Although she had had many opportunities to do so, she hadn't married again because being someone's wife would have involved a great many accommodations on her part; by remaining a widow, she had been able to suit herself. By now she hardly remembered what Gilbert Beresford had looked like. A portrait of him in evening clothes hung in the flat, but it had been painted when he was a young man, before Leonora Petrie had even been born, and she saw little resemblance between the husband to whom she had been briefly married and the man over the dining room mantelpiece. Anyway, she much preferred Augustus John's portrait of herself, in gypsy costume, which hung in her sitting room.

She found living in the Arlington, to which she had moved shortly after her daughter's marriage, suited her well. The hotel had a superb staff, so the usual trying intimacies between mistress and servants were largely avoided, and the food was at least as good and much more varied than what one's own cook might have produced in one's own home. Furthermore, there was always so much going on in a hotel. Swearing that she'd rather be blown to bits in London than endure a lingering death from boredom in County Kildare or, heaven help us, Herefordshire — she found the country intolerable after four days — she had refused offers from a dozen friends and relations with garden cottages aired and waiting, and remained in Knightsbridge all through the war. When the building next door received a direct hit and the Arlington plumbing went berserk, she was forced to move out, but only to another hotel across Hyde Park, and she was back the instant her lavatory could be flushed again.

"At what hour does the great event begin?" she asked as she hung up Joanna's coat in the closet.

"Nine o'clock tomorrow morning," said Miss Cathcart.

Mrs. Beresford wrinkled her nose. "That early!"

"You're coming, Granny?" Joanna exclaimed.

"Most certainly I am! I wouldn't miss this splendid occasion for anything. I've canceled all commitments until the competition's over. I told Cousin Humphrey I absolutely couldn't go to Paris with him for the weekend. He said 'Leonora, you promised, I've been looking forward to it so much, you can't back out!' I told him, 'Ah, but when I promised, I didn't know Joanna was going to win this competition.' "

"I haven't won it yet," Joanna pointed out.

Mrs. Beresford sank onto a gold brocade sofa. "There's lemonade in the fridge, darling. Run and help yourself. Do sit down," she added to Miss Cathcart, indicating a deep armchair near the fireplace. "I have to say, how you've managed to foster this young talent in such a Philistine atmosphere is beyond me!"

Miss Cathcart smiled. "It's not so extraordinary, really. Major and Mrs. Drayton leave Joanna's education up to me. They rarely interfere."

"Even so, you have to contend with unremitting blood sports and the tedium of the agricultural cycle, neither of which contribute to artistic endeavors. That Widleigh ambiance . . . " She shivered. "Death to the spirit!"

"The truth is, Widleigh suits me, Mrs. Beresford," said Miss Cathcart quickly. "I enjoy country life — I don't find it tedious or constricting. On the contrary, it provides me with a great deal of scope."

"One wouldn't have taken you for a rural type," observed Mrs. Beresford. "For one thing, you're far too well turned out.

That hat, for instance — it's pure Bond Street. You're a Londoner by birth of course . . . "

"Oh no, I was born in Yorkshire, and I spent most of my childhood in Rutland."

"Really? Do tell me where."

"Crowthorpe Hall."

"What a coincidence! I often stayed there in the thirties. I remember a lovely rose-red Georgian house with a pediment over the door and a temple or two in the garden. My great friend was Leslie Beaumont, a sweet but ultimately silly man, though I'm still fond of him . . . He lives in Madeira now. He must have bought Crowthorpe from your parents."

"From my guardian, Cousin Ronald. I went to live with him after Father and Mother died. I was nine."

Mrs. Beresford leaned forward in alarm. "You were orphaned? Appalling! How?"

"My parents were drowned in a boating accident and my little brother, Walter, drowned as well. I was the only member of the family who survived."

"My dear, Barbara never said a word to me about this!"

"I doubt she knows," said Miss Cathcart dryly. "My life before coming to Widleigh doesn't interest Mrs. Drayton. Or at any rate, not enough for her to ask me about it," she added as she unbuttoned her suit jacket and sat back.

"You were in that boat too?"

"No, I was at home in bed. I had mumps. Walter got them first and just as he recovered and could go out again, I came down with them."

"So at least you didn't see the tragedy!"

"I often wish I had, though," said Miss Cathcart quietly. "As it is, I've never quite been able to believe what happened."

Joanna came back from the kitchen with her glass of lemonade and Mrs. Beresford gave a little shriek. "How rude of me! I forgot to offer *you* a drink, Miss Cathcart. I'm having whiskey.

Will you join me? Do help yourself so you can get the ice and water right. Or don't you care for ice? I know a lot of people don't in the winter." But Miss Cathcart did want ice, and when she had her tumbler and was back in her chair, Mrs. Beresford said, "I hope you don't mind my asking so many questions. It's just that you're so very important to Joanna — she talks about nothing but you on her visits here. You've been her mainstay for years, and yet you and I haven't met more than two or three times, have we. I suppose you're too busy to come to London. At least from what I've heard, everyone at Widleigh depends on you entirely!" She sipped her drink. "Tell me, did your cousin have a large family?"

"He never married. He manufactured boots and shoes in Leicester and made rather a fortune shodding British soldiers in the First World War. His factory was his only interest. He'd go off at seven in the morning and rarely came back before eight at night."

"Not much of a home life for you then . . . So tell me, how did a person of such manifold gifts find herself teaching other people's children how to read and write?"

"I could read and write before I met Miss Cathcart," said Joanna indignantly from a stool at her grandmother's feet.

"I'm sure you could, darling. That was only in a manner of speaking. Well?" She looked expectantly at Miss Cathcart.

"Cousin Ronald was ruined in the Depression. To be precise, he went bankrupt in 1933. As my trustee as well as my guardian he had invested my inheritance in his business, and when it failed, that was the end for me. At the time I was in my second year at the Royal Academy of Music. Of course I had to withdraw and go looking for a job. Apart from being a governess, there wasn't much that I was qualified to do. But I've been lucky with my children," Miss Cathcart added quickly.

"They've all been smarties like Joanna?"

Miss Cathcart smiled faintly. "Each has been rewarding in

his or her own way, and since their parents have tended to be careless or occupied elsewhere, I've generally had them to myself. And that's what I like best about my work, you see."

Mrs. Beresford shook her glass and the ice tinkled. "Tell me," she said lightly, "supposing Cousin Ronald's prosperity had continued, what might you have done then? Married some squire and run his village for him?"

"I doubt that. As a girl I was never very interested in getting married. Actually" — her voice softened — "I used to daydream about becoming a concert pianist."

"Think of the glamorous life you'd have had!" Mrs. Beresford laughed gaily. "Fame, pots of money, adoration! Yes," she went on, "I remember dreams of that sort . . . You see, I'd hoped to sing professionally once. I studied for years in France and Italy, but then the Archduke Ferdinand was shot at Sarajevo, and I had to rush back here. By the time the war was over" — she shrugged — "I felt I'd missed the boat." As she got up from the sofa she added, "Unfortunately, for most of us things don't turn out as we'd imagined they would, so life is a matter of making the best of it." She reached down and touched Joanna's cheek. "Now we could either go to the restaurant or order up. On second thought, ordering up might be better. Tomorrow's a very big day, and I got a bossy letter from your mother, darling, saying that for no reason whatsoever was I to keep you up after half past eight."

"A little lower . . . ahhh . . . that's marvelous, dear." Miss Cathcart lay face down, hair streaming over bare shoulders, arms limp at her sides. Her back was broad and smooth and very white. A small black mole peeped up above the top of her mushroom-colored silk slip, which gleamed over her bottom and along her thighs. "I didn't realize how tense I was until the very last moment," she murmured. "Then it suddenly felt as if my spine had snapped." She was silent for some minutes. "I feel so much better. You certainly have the healing touch! Do keep on just a little longer, dear."

Miss Cathcart's back, which had never recovered entirely from that bad fall on the pampas, had required a lot of attention over the past four years. After lunch at Widleigh, Joanna would be summoned to the red-flocked sanctuary at the top of the front stairs. There, having liberally applied lilies of the valley toilet water to her neck and arms, Miss Cathcart would lie down in her underclothes on the four-poster bed and bid Joanna to go to work. Following a long series of deep sighs signifying growing and, ultimately, total relief from discomfort, Miss Cathcart would fall asleep and Joanna would tiptoe out, although sometimes so much sensual activity would have its effect on her and she would lie down beside her governess and sleep, too.

The telephone began to ring. "Answer it, will you dear? It must be your grandmother asking what we want from the restaurant for supper," Miss Cathcart said. But it was James ringing from Eton.

"What's up, Joanna?"

"I'm giving Miss Cathcart a massage. Her back's bad again. She's been under a lot of strain."

"Are *you* all right, though?"

"Why shouldn't I be?"

At the other end of the line James exploded. "You're impossible! What happened in the competition?"

"Oh, that! Well, I got into the finals of the junior division. Seven other people and me."

"That's marvelous! Was it terrifying?"

"Being on the stage was to begin with. After a bit you stop noticing, though. They gave us eclairs for tea and one of the judges wore spats. I'd never seen spats before, except in Babar books. And when Philip Emmanuel Davis wasn't selected, both he and his mother burst into tears!"

"Who's Philip Emmanuel Davis?"

"The other West of England semifinalist. He'd won nine out of the eleven competitions he'd entered, so being put out of this one was naturally a shock. He lives in Shrewsbury and his mother's invited me to lunch. I said yes, only I shan't go. Philip Emmanuel is only eight."

"Far too young for you," said James gravely.

"You're coming tomorrow, aren't you?" Joanna asked anxiously.

"Of course!"

"Will you be here for breakfast? They have brioche and papaya and lots of delicious things."

"I can't make it up to London that early, I'm afraid. I'll see you at the Guildhall, about eleven. Now can I have a word with Miss C.?"

Miss Cathcart eased herself up to a sitting position and took the receiver. One strap slipped from her shoulder and for an instant her right breast was almost totally revealed. But she felt for the strap and deftly hitched it up again. "How good of you to ring, James," she said languidly.

"Congratulations! As Joanna's teacher, half the credit goes to you. Is it okay if I join you tomorrow?"

"We'll be delighted, you know that."

"How does one get to the place?"

"Take the Tube to the Embankment. Mrs. Beresford and I will save a seat for you between us. We'll each hold one of your hands."

Nervous competitors, relatives, and teachers were milling about outside the Guildhall School of Music when Joanna arrived with her governess and grandmother the next morning. The competitors included an Indian girl in a tunic and tight white trousers, a lanky African boy whose mother was talking to him forcefully in a tribal language, a tiny Chinese girl with hair cut in a stern fringe across her forehead. Joanna nodded to Alexander Moore, aged eleven. Alexander was from Edinburgh; he'd played Chopin and Rachmaninoff in the semifinals. At tea the day before he had confided that of all contemporary pianists, he admired Arthur Rubinstein most, and when he grew up he was going to be at least twice as famous.

Doors swung open and the crowd pressed through. Once inside Miss Cathcart whipped a comb out of her handbag and ran it over Joanna's hair. "Remember to count in the fourth variation," she whispered. Mrs. Beresford, head to ankle in Canadian squirrel, gave Joanna a squeeze. They left her in a seat in the center of the concert hall and found themselves places at the side just as the judges, three men and an elderly woman, filed in and sat down in the front row. The woman had on a long evening dress; the men wore tailcoats and white ties. Each carried a clipboard and many sheets of paper.

An elegant young woman with coppery hair walked onto the stage. She welcomed the distinguished judges and the finalists who came, she said, from all over Great Britain and a number of Commonwealth countries and colonies as well. The junior division finals would be judged before lunch, the senior division after; tea was at four o'clock, and the awards would be announced at five.

Joanna was scheduled to play immediately following the midmorning break. James had promised to be there by eleven, but after tea and ginger biscuits had been served in the entrance hall, it was eleven-twenty, and still he hadn't arrived. He must have forgotten Miss Cathcart's directions, Joanna thought drearily; he was lost in the East End of London, he was far away in Essex, at the end of the Tube line.

"Get up," whispered Alexander Moore in her right ear. "They're nodding at you, it's your turn now." With despair in her heart Joanna slipped out of her seat, climbed the steps, crossed the stage, and sat at the great black piano. Her hands were icy, her head swam, every note of Bach, Beethoven, and Mozart had vanished from her memory. But suddenly out of the corner of her eye she spotted a rolled up newspaper waving frantically. James wasn't off in Essex — he was sitting between Miss Cathcart and her grandmother, waiting to hear her play the best she'd ever played. Blood flowed back into her fingers, her head cleared. With a smile she smoothed her velvet skirt over her knees.

"What's that you've got there, Miss Joanna," exclaimed Standish. "A beautiful silver cup! Let me 'ave a look at it then. You must be so pleased madam," he added as he helped Mrs. Beresford out of the cab.

"I am! We all are. We're absolutely thrilled! The Duchess of Gloucester presented the prizes, and there were lots of official-looking people taking photographs, so I think we'll see Joanna in the papers in the morning. She did a charming curtsy, without any practice, mind you. I was so proud of her, I almost burst! And they made a recording of her Mozart variations. They're going to play it tomorrow afternoon at two, on the Third Programme. You'll have to get Mrs. Standish to listen. Don't forget! We've just come back to bathe and change and then we're off to the Savoy to celebrate. I'm so excited, I feel like wearing all my diamonds, only they're mostly in the bank, which is shut on a Saturday night."

But Mrs. Beresford did wear her black lace from Hardy Amies and her best pearls. Joanna had on her green velvet, creased at the back from so much sitting. James, too, wore the clothes he'd been in all day, but he'd bought himself a scarlet carnation from a flower lady in the Strand and stuck it in his buttonhole. He looked very elegant, sipping his champagne. Miss Cathcart had changed from her dove-gray suit into purple crêpe de Chine with padded shoulders. With her honey-colored hair piled up on her head and held in place with her tortoise-shell combs, she looked more regal than ever. She wore bluish eye shadow, black mascara. No lipstick, though. Her lips were naturally so red, she never needed lipstick. The pain at the base of her spine had vanished and her face glowed.

Every table was taken by men and women in glamorous evening clothes; they had come to the Savoy to see Yves Guillaume in his first London appearance in three years. He was going to sing on the dot of midnight.

After smoked salmon and lobster thermidor, Mrs. Beresford suggested a short rest before the sweet. "Besides," she said, "I've got an announcement to make." She smiled as she ran a finger round the rim of her champagne glass. "I've never believed in letting the young have money because, generally speaking, I think it's bad for them. But I'm so excited by my grandchildren's promise — James's as an author, Joanna's as a musician — that I've decided to bend the rule a little. When I die of course your mother will get all the Beresford money, so in case I get run over by a bus and Barbara spends her inheritance like water and there's nothing left for the two of you, I'm going to provide you with a hedge against disaster. Not a high one, mind you, as I don't intend to break my rule entirely, but I shall give you each enough so that if need be James will be able to buy himself a typewriter, a desk to put it on, and a year or two of freedom, and Joanna, a decent piano. On Monday morning I shall go to see my solicitor." This was Petrie money, she said, from her own family, and hers to do what she liked with. "Mind you, you won't get anything on Monday," she continued. "In fact you're going to have to wait until you're twenty-four, by which time I have faith that you'll know how to spend it wisely. And now" — she raised her glass — "I propose a toast to your futures. I very much hope that I *don't* get run over because I want to live to a ripe old age and read all James's books and go to all Joanna's concerts, and I'm sure Miss Cathcart wants to, too! To James and Joanna — the first artistic Draytons in three hundred years!"

The band was playing a tune from the twenties, and James

asked his grandmother to dance. "That's sweet of you, darling, but what about the other two ladies?"

"You first, Granny."

"Oh all right, if it's age before talent and beauty, why not one little turn around the floor!" Mrs. Beresford had been dancing at the Savoy for as long as she'd been a widow. She'd once had a walk-out with a Savoy saxophone player called Ralph, long dead now. But *she* wasn't dead, far from it, and she still adored dancing. "You do move nicely," she told her grandson. And when the tune from the twenties was finished and one from 1948 began, she said, "Just one more trot round, darling."

Then it was Miss Cathcart's turn, and as James led her out to the dance floor, Mrs. Beresford remarked, "Quite splendid to look at, isn't she?" James pulled Miss Cathcart close and away they went, heads together. Their hair was exactly the same color. "Despite what she said the other evening," Mrs. Beresford continued, "about loving life at Widleigh and so on, I'm sorry for her. Such a handsome woman to be stuck down there! An odd existence, if you ask me, even if the child who's the focus of it does happen to be you, darling."

"What's odd about life at Widleigh?" Joanna said heatedly.

Her grandmother chuckled. "The whole setup strikes one as bizarre!"

"When was the last time you came to see it?"

"Before the war."

"Before I was born, then."

"Not at all! The purpose of the visit was to view you. You were just a few days old, and even then — eleven years ago, almost — your parents' rooms were fifty yards apart. It was a wonder you got here, Joanna!"

"Daddy snores. You should hear him! He sounds like the cannons at Trafalgar. He'd keep Mummy awake if they shared a room, and Mummy has to get a lot of good deep sleep or her migraines would come more often even than they do."

"A sorry situation if ever I saw one," said Mrs. Beresford with a shrug, and she turned to watch the dancers.

James's and Miss Cathcart's faces shone with happiness as they quick-stepped round the floor.

"I suppose you'll be off to school before too long," Mrs. Beresford remarked after a moment, "and she'll be free to go."

"Oh, no," said Joanna quickly. "Daddy wants me to stay at home with Miss Cathcart, though the day will come, Miss Cathcart says, when I've gone beyond her, musically, that is, and I'll need to study with someone else. So our plan is to move to London together and get a flat and a piano teacher for me. We'll go to concerts too. It isn't enough to listen to the BBC or records on the gramophone. Of course I'll go on learning history and geography and everything else with her."

"So that's the plan then, is it — yet another Drayton anachronism! But what about your having children to play with, darling? That's important too, so they used to tell me. Even though your mother seemed perfectly content to live abroad with me while I studied singing, people were constantly trying to convince me to send her back to boarding school in England so that she'd have friends. 'She's got friends,' I'd tell them. 'She plays house with the concierge's daughter and football with the cook's son.' 'Leonora,' they said, 'Barbara needs a circle that she'll keep up with all her life. After you leave Florence or Geneva or whatever, she's not going to see the cook's son or the concierge's daughter ever again.' In the end, I gave in and sent your mother back to Morehaven, and in fact she did make one or two friends there who've stood her in good stead."

"I've got friends," said Joanna.

Gabriella Cooper was one of them. The Coopers lived at Spurlock, which was only five miles from Widleigh, and in the deepest depths of war and petrol rationing, they had been pushed in their prams along gravelly back roads to dig in sandpits and slide on frozen ponds and throw blocks at each other, while their nurses marveled at how well their charges got along together. That they frequently did each other grievous bodily harm and broke each other's toys with malice aforethought was ignored, because Gabriella was such a suitable friend for Joanna, and vice versa.

Another friend was Mary Williams, daughter of the village postmistress. Mary talked a blue streak with a broad Herefordshire accent, and she indulged in what Mrs. Drayton termed guttersnipe language. Joanna first got to know her in July the year before when she and Miss Cathcart had gone to watch the haymaking; they came upon her building a house in the hedge with a gang of Widleigh children. "Fetch me some hay for the floor, there's a duck," Mary had called to Joanna, and Joanna had instantly obeyed. So long as the haymaking lasted, she had played with the village children every afternoon, while Miss Cathcart made a pillow out of her cardigan and snoozed in the shade. One afternoon when they had thrown themselves down to rest after a game of tag round the new hayricks, Mary announced to her companions, "I know how women have babies and if you'll just shut up and listen, I'll tell you."

Was Mary's astonishing account the truth? At first Joanna considered asking Miss Cathcart, but Miss Cathcart had never had a baby, she wasn't even married, she mightn't know. On the other hand, all the servants were married, all had children. They had to know. And so the very next morning while she was having her elevenses in the kitchen, she decided she had to get their opinion that instant; she mightn't have the courage to ask later on. "You know Mary Williams who lives at the post office?" she said loudly. "Well, she told me that to get a baby, a man puts his thing into a lady and squirts." (In a nutshell, this is what Mary had said.) "Is it true or isn't it?"

Mrs. Burgess and Mrs. Crompton blushed and looked at the backs of their hands. Pickering laughed and turned his laugh into a cough.

"I got my Jimmy in the hospital myself," Agnes said. (Jimmy

was her son, now grown up and married and living in Cardiff.) She spoke with finality; there was no more to add.

"That's right," Pickering agreed. The dailies sighed with relief and they all went back to discussing the rise in the price of coal.

Whether what she had said was truth or falsehood, Mary continued to be of absorbing interest to Joanna. The interest didn't seem to be mutual, however. The last few times Joanna had run into Mary in the village, Mary had pointedly ignored her.

Joanna's other friends were the twins, Persepolis and Cynthia Knightley. They were four months younger than she was, and they came each summer with their grandmother (who was Henry Drayton's first cousin on his mother's side) to spend a week at Widleigh; when they went home, they took Joanna with them. (Meanwhile Miss Cathcart took her annual break from routine in the Scilly Islands, where she bird watched and sat in the sun, whenever there was any.) Cynthia was exceedingly serious and clever. Sep was clever, too, but much more fun. At Widleigh he organized war games that continued from summer to summer. The summer before they had invaded Russia under Sep (as Napoleon), with Dulcie doubling as charger and pack animal. Next summer they were going to fight the Battle of Waterloo, with Joanna as the Duke of Wellington. In a huge glass case at home in Warwickshire — where they lived with their grandmother because their mother had nervous problems and often had to go to sanatoria, and their father couldn't cope alone — there was a stuffed elephant called Gangin that an ancestor had ridden into battle in India a century ago. Perhaps Sep's addiction to war games was inherited.

But Joanna saw the twins for only a fortnight every August.

Anyway, she said to herself, even if I haven't got a whole *circle* of friends, I've got James. I love him best, I'll love him best forever. And here he is with Miss Cathcart, threading his way back between the tables.

"It's your turn to dance now, Joanna," said Mrs. Beresford.
"I don't want to, thanks."
"As the star of the evening, you must!"
"I don't know how. I've never been taught."
"Who taught your brother?"
"He learned at Winterfields."
"You see, that's another very good reason for going to boarding school! If you don't learn to dance, you'll miss all the excitement."

James was standing above her, smiling. "Just hold onto me," he told her, "and you'll be fine."

But Joanna couldn't be persuaded. "I prefer to watch," she insisted.

James danced turn and turn about with Miss Cathcart and his grandmother, until Mrs. Beresford announced that she'd been up very early two mornings running and now she was ready for bed.

"Then let's go back to the Arlington," said James. He would spend the night in his grandmother's spare room and return to Eton after lunch on Sunday.

"Definitely not! You young people should stay on as long as you want to. I'm perfectly capable of going home alone in a cab." But Joanna was struggling vainly to keep her eyes open, and Mrs. Beresford added, "On second thought, I'll take this little girl with me and put her to bed. They haven't had the cabaret yet. It's that Frenchman, what's his name. The *Evening Standard* said he shouldn't be missed. James, you and Miss Cathcart will tell Joanna and me all about it at breakfast."

The sun was streaming through the gap between the heavy curtains when Joanna awoke. Miss Cathcart was fast asleep three feet away. Joanna jumped up and drew the curtains so that the sun fell across Miss Cathcart's face. She stirred and turned over, away from the sunlight. On the carpet beside her bed lay her purple dress. She always hung up her clothes straight away after getting out of them. "That's how you keep nice things nice," she would tell Joanna. Even so, there her best dress lay. She must have been in a dreadful hurry going to bed, or very tired or terribly distracted, Joanna thought.

The traveling clock on the bedside table said ten minutes past ten, and their train left Paddington Station at eleven.

"Wake up!" Joanna shook a pale shoulder. Miss Cathcart twitched, as if the hand were a fly she could brush off. "Wake up! Wake up!"

Miss Cathcart sighed, snorted, and opened her eyes at last. "Good heavens, we'd better get going!" she exclaimed when she saw the time.

"When did you get in?" said Joanna.

"Not late. We only stayed for half the cabaret. Your brother didn't care for the singer, so we left."

"What did you do then?"

"We came back here, of course."

"You weren't back when I got up to go to the loo at half past four. Your bed was empty."

"If I wasn't in my bed, where else could I have been?" said Miss Cathcart crossly, throwing back the covers. "Of course I was here! Quick now. I'll pack while you wash your face and do your teeth. We've no time to waste."

They said good-bye to Mrs. Beresford on the telephone. "I only just awoke myself," she told Joanna, "and James is still dead to the world. Too much excitement and champagne, that's why we all overslept. I had a marvelous time. Thank you for providing the excuse, darling! I hope you give us cause to celebrate again before too long. I do enjoy going out with my grandchildren — we get on so well! Oh, Lord!" she exclaimed, "do you know what, darling? I never telephoned your mother. I totally forgot, and so she still doesn't know you won the competition! . . . But I shan't ring her now, either. You'll simply get off the train with your beautiful cup. If that doesn't cheer her up, I can't imagine what will!"

~~~~~~~~~~~~~~~~~~~~~~~~~~~~~~~~~~~~~

Chapter 4

Spurlock

JAMES WAS COMING home for the Easter holidays and Joanna was planning a feast. "Did you order the suet?" she ran to ask Agnes in her five-minute break between French and English History.

"The butcher said he'd bring it when he calls. And there's plenty of strawberry jam."

"And cream?"

"Of course there's cream. What d'you think a whole herd of cows is for?"

"We've got tomatoes for the sauce, and cheese?"

"There's tinned tomatoes. Fresh is hard to come by at this time of year."

"So we'll have spaghetti first and then the roly-poly pudding."

"That brother of yours is a lucky young man," Agnes remarked.

"Why?"

"He's lucky to have such a devoted sister."

"Oh, no, *I'm* lucky to have *him,* don't you see!" James wasn't a stickler for routine like her father was; he didn't get headaches and shut the door against her like her mother did; he liked her company any old time.

Agnes was rolling out pastry for two apple tarts, one for lunch in the dining room, the other for lunch in the schoolroom. The dining room tart would have a top on it; the school-room tart, at Joanna's request, would be open and sprinkled with brown sugar and grated lemon rind. Agnes had come as kitchen maid when Henry Drayton was a Sandhurst cadet. She had left to marry Bartlet, the stud groom, and, after he died, had returned as cook, a good plain one, nothing elaborate. Now that her son, Jimmy, and daughter, Marge, were grown up, she lived in the cottage in the stable yard with a Siamese cat called Charlie and a mongrel called Chip, both of whom came to work with her each morning. Charlie slept on a shelf over the Aga stove, one eye open for scraps; Chippie lay under the kitchen table, waiting to bark at tradesmen come to deliver. "If I was you, young lady," Agnes said, glancing at the clock, "I'd go where I belonged, or I'd have that governess after me. Come back when Miss C. goes for her afternoon nap and we'll get everything ready."

Joanna stood on the front steps waiting for James. It had been drizzling earlier and it was chilly, but she didn't notice the weather. Tea in the dining room wouldn't take long. They'd eat one crumpet each and half a slice of cake. It wouldn't do to spoil their appetites. When James saw the feast she had prepared he'd say, You mean you made all this for me? And she would say, This is nothing compared with what I'd *like* to have made — leg of lamb and roast potatoes, floating islands, devils on horseback. And he'd say, I'm so glad you didn't, because I like spaghetti best! After the feast they'd go off in the car, up hill, down dale, never mind the darkness. They'd come back at last to James's room, to the two armchairs in front of the fire, and James would bring out the stories he'd written since January, stories he'd saved to read to her before anyone else, even before his school friend Gordon Burns, who wrote stories too. And this was just their *first* evening. They would have twenty-nine more holiday evenings — and mornings and afternoons — together, talking and walking and reading aloud.

She would make his bed and retrieve his dirty socks from under it and iron his shirts as well, if only Mrs. Crompton would let her.

She saw the dark-blue Bentley turning in slowly at the gate and her father's cap and, next to it, the pale oval of James's face. With much spattering of gravel the old car (inherited, like almost all Henry Drayton's possessions) drew up to the house and James sprang out. He dashed past Joanna, overcoat unbuttoned. His eyes were narrow, his mouth grim. Henry remained at the wheel. His eyes were narrow too, and his nose twitched.

"You didn't say hello to me," Joanna cried, running after her brother. "Whatever happened *this* time?"

"Nothing that hasn't happened three dozen times before!" James flung back.

"If you want your bags," Henry shouted up the steps, "you'd better come and get them from the garage," and he scraped into gear and drove off.

" 'Your hair's a disgrace,' " James mimicked. " 'One wonders how you dared come home, looking like that! First thing in the morning, you're going to get it cut!' On and on he went, would not, could not stop. Can you imagine a more trivial mentality! My hair grows quietly, it does no harm. Until this afternoon at four-fifteen it had offended no one. 'A nascent literary phenomenon, is that how you see yourself,' Dad said, 'waiting for the world to discover you? Meanwhile you think you have the right to attract the unfavorable attention of those of us condemned to live with you!' In the end I told him, 'Shove it!' "

"Parents have to have something to carry on about," Joanna observed. "Hair's one favorite topic. Fingernails are another."

"Time stopped for Dad the day that Queen Victoria kicked the bucket," James said in disgust. "Now, could you kindly tell me where they've hidden my mail?"

"They haven't hidden it. It's on the hall table, where it always is."

James threw off his overcoat, which Joanna caught. She ran with it to the bootroom, and having stood on tiptoe to hang it on a hook between an old mackintosh and a cricket blazer, she quickly felt in both pockets for the grape-flavored chewing gum that James always got for her from a half-American boy in his house at school. She found a ten-shilling note, two sixpences, a Tube ticket, a pencil stub, but no gum.

She rejoined her brother, who was sorting through his letters in the hall. "Grizelda's pregnant," she informed him, "and we don't know who the father is. If it's Agnes's Chippie the puppies will certainly look strange, though I'm sure they'll have nice characters. Will you want to keep one?"

"Don't be silly — I can't take a dog into the regiment." When he left Eton in July, James would be off to do his national service in the Thirteenth Hussars.

"The army's not forever. Your puppy could live here with me until you've finished." But then he would be going up to Oxford to become an intellectual.

"Christ Church doesn't encourage pets, either," he said grimly.

Joanna picked up a Manila envelope. It bore one and sixpence worth of stamps and had come registered post. "Is this your passport? I'll have to get a passport, too, for going to Spain." James grabbed the envelope away from her and stuffed it in the inner pocket of his tweed jacket.

"It's my car documents, not my passport, and we shan't be going to Spain in the foreseeable future because I'm broke."

"Golly, you *are* cross! Whatever is the matter?"

"I'm *here,*" James replied, gathering up the rest of his letters. "That's what's the matter!"

"Don't you like us anymore, then?" What she really meant was, Don't you like *me?*

"Like, dislike!" he mocked. "We've gone far beyond that! Ladies and gentlemen, may I present to you the tin-pot tyrant, the hapless prisoner, the crumbling castle, the cowed retainers. It's like some simply dreadful novelette!" He strode off to the stairs.

"Widleigh isn't crumbling," Joanna shouted after him. "The roof was mended just the other day. The repairs cost hundreds of pounds. And anyway, this is a house, not a castle, so don't exaggerate!"

Mrs. Drayton was pushing the tea trolley up the kitchen corridor. "There you are, James!" she exclaimed. "When I heard the car drive up and then off again immediately, I thought you'd decided not to stay." She gave a small sharp laugh.

On the bottom stair James stopped and turned back to greet his mother. "Hullo," he said, pecking her cheek. "Here, let me push that thing." As he took hold of the trolley his right hand touched her left. "Sorry!" they cried in unison and jumped apart as if they had been burned.

Mrs. Drayton said quickly, "I've come this far, I'll take it the rest of the way. Joanna, if you'll run and call the others, we can have tea."

In the dining room James pulled out a chair and sat down while his mother laid out the tea things. "One of the hinges on the teapot lid broke weeks ago," she told him. "I should have taken it into Hereford to be mended, but it keeps slipping my mind. I've become so forgetful lately. I'll forget my own name next." She sighed deeply. "How was your term? Did you play much squash?" She knew nothing at all about squash, but James was captain of his house team.

"Not as much as I'd have liked," he replied in a bored voice. As she watched him help himself to milk and sugar, Mrs. Drayton felt a familiar anguish. While he was off at school she would forget how far he'd grown from her; on his return this reality always came as a fresh shock.

"They're both coming," Joanna announced as she ran in. Miss Cathcart, in a deep-blue jersey that matched her eyes, was a few steps behind her.

James rose to his feet instantly. "It's marvelous to see you!" he exclaimed as he shook her hand. "You're looking wonderful! How's everything?" Suddenly he was at ease, animated, happy. "Sit here, next to me!"

He didn't smile at *me*, Joanna thought sadly. He didn't shake my hand; in fact he didn't even say hello.

Miss Cathcart beamed at James. "The music's going very well. We're doing Rosemary Spencer's wedding over at Sullerton on Easter Saturday. I'm playing the Bach Fantasy in G, with a Buxtehude toccata for the recessional. The Buxtehude is *especially* fun."

The prospect of James going off to the army and thence with the regiment to Germany, the Far East, Africa, filled Joanna with dread, alleviated only by the assurance that after two years he'd be back. But what if, like Rosemary Spencer, he fell in love and even got married and went away to live with someone else forever? What would become of her then?

"I think the Buxtehude would appeal to you," Miss Cathcart was saying.

"I'm sure it would!" said James.

"In fact I was planning to get in a little practicing this evening. Perhaps you'd like to come along and listen, provided, of course, your parents can spare you."

After a brief silence James said distinctly, "They can spare me."

"That's settled then," said Miss Cathcart gaily. "And Joanna has her composition on the Earl of Essex to keep her busy, haven't you, dear."

Earl of Essex? But he isn't due till Monday, Joanna opened her mouth to say. And what about our car ride, James? Why should you be made to listen to *her* in that freezing church when you could be dashing through the countryside with *me*? If you really want to listen to music, my Schubert impromptu is coming along pretty well. Miss C. told me so this morning.

But James was saying, "I'd been hoping for a recital." Clearly he wasn't being *made* to go anywhere. Joanna shut her mouth again. "By the way, we had quite a few concerts and plays at school this half," James went on. "I saved the programs for you."

"How sweet of you!" As Henry Drayton came in, Miss Cathcart flashed a brilliant smile. "What a superb education James is getting, Major!" she exclaimed.

"I should hope so, given what it costs me."

"I mean specifically his *artistic* education. How I do envy him! As a girl I never saw a single play that I can remember, and a concert was a great event."

"Music and drama were a very important part of my life when I was young," Mrs. Drayton said loudly. "We always went to Covent Garden when we were in London, and we went to the theater very often as well — we saw simply everything. What I enjoyed most, though, were the Promenade Concerts. They were splendid occasions! One year, old Lady Cornway had seats next to ours. Her jewels were simply incredible! There was one necklace in particular — diamonds and black pearls. Even Mummy stared! I suppose the Proms attract a different sort these days. At least," she added, "Mummy doesn't go."

"So that was the appeal, was it," said James sarcastically. "A chance to hobnob with the vulgar rich. Never mind the music."

Joanna decided it was time to warm up the feast she had prepared. She slipped out of her chair, ran off to the kitchen, and popped the dishes into the oven.

When she returned a few minutes later, her mother was leaning across the table. "If I ask my son a question, it's because I want an answer from *him*, not *you!*" she shouted at Miss Cathcart. "I'm not the least bit interested in your opinions! They bore me utterly!"

Scarlet in the face, Miss Cathcart stared back. Her scalp was moving in an odd way. One moment her forehead was smooth like marble and the next it collapsed into pleats, like an accordion. She looked like a puppet whose strings had got tangled. Beside her sat James, head bowed, hands clenched.

"For heaven's sake, control yourself, Barbara!" Henry Drayton pushed his plate away abruptly and his knife clattered onto the table. Miss Cathcart settled back into her chair and the wash of color slowly receded from her face and down her neck. Mrs. Drayton poured herself another cup of tea but did not drink it. She bit her bottom lip and played with the cake crumbs on her plate.

Suddenly she was on her feet. "If I were a lodger in this house, if I paid rent each week, I'd have the right to say whatever I wanted, but I don't pay rent, so I have no rights! This house is supposed to be my home, but it's not — it never has been — I just happen to be living in one end of it!" Tears streaming, she rushed from the room, and they heard her run across the hall and up the stairs.

For some moments they sat in stunned silence until Henry Drayton cleared his throat and said, "James, I want a word with you before dinner. I'm considering some improvements in the cowsheds and I'd like to go over them with you."

"You want to discuss the cowsheds with *me?*" said James in surprise.

"As a matter of fact, I do. Why shouldn't I? You'll be nineteen in August. It's time you took a responsible interest in this place and stopped treating it like a hotel," said Henry dryly as he fitted his napkin into his silver napkin ring and got up. "I'll expect to see you in the smoking room at seven."

"I'm afraid we've all been a bit anxious lately," Miss Cathcart remarked. "The Herefordshire winter gets even the best of us down. But your mother's the one who concerns me, James. She's been terribly on edge . . . You might suggest she take a little holiday. She has that cousin in County Kildare. A fortnight over there might do her a world of good . . . Now let's get these things to the pantry, then I'll run and change my shoes and we'll be off." She quickly piled plates and cups and saucers onto the trolley and rolled it away, leaving Joanna and James alone in the dining room.

"Delightful scene that was," James said.

"It's just that Mummy's jealous of Miss Cathcart being queen of Widleigh."

"She ought to be *grateful*, not jealous!" James exclaimed as he strode to the door. "She should be overjoyed that Miss Cathcart's here to take an interest in the village, given that *she* never has."

"You can't go off yet!" Joanna cried, leaping up and running after him. "Stay here just a minute and come to the schoolroom when I call. Please!" She stood squarely in the doorway, arm outstretched to stop him.

"Whatever it is you've got in mind, do be quick about it. I don't want to keep Miss Cathcart waiting."

Joanna raced to the kitchen, yanked open the oven, and removed the dishes to a tray. She needed salt and, oh yes, knives and forks. And spoons for the pudding. And the cream! Hurriedly she assembled her feast. She was just setting off when she spotted a candle on the mantelpiece. It was an ordinary tallow candle for when the electricity went off, which happened frequently. The schoolroom would look different, more glamorous, by candlelight.

In the schoolroom she set the table. She wished it were round, like a table in a French café, instead of rectangular, and in her haste she had forgotten a cloth, but it was too late to go back for one. She lit the candle, snapped off the overhead light, and called to her brother. "You can come now!"

"Good Lord!" James exclaimed from the doorway. "What have we here?"

"Come all the way in and you'll see!"

"Not another meal!"

"This one I cooked myself — with Agnes's help. You sit

here." Joanna pulled out a chair. The room looked quite romantic, really. On the top of the piano her silver cup shone in
the candlelight. She pulled the sleeve of her cardigan over her
hand and removed the cover of the casserole. The spaghetti lay,
a solid mass, in its sea of tomato sauce.

"Oh, *no*," James groaned.

"Last holidays you said spaghetti was your favorite thing to
eat."

"Yes, but since then I've eaten it three times a week for
eleven weeks. To save my life I couldn't face it again."

Crushed, Joanna replaced the lid and uncovered the other
dish. "Hell and damnation!" she gasped with pain. In her anxiety she had forgotten to protect her hand, and now she blew on
burning fingertips. "Would you like some roly-poly pudding,"
she said miserably. "There's cream as well."

James nodded. "This looks better!"

She gave him a serving from the jammiest part, and he ate
four spoonfuls before pushing his plate away. "It's good, but
that's all I can manage at the moment. I trust your meal doesn't
run to three courses."

"Only two." She added desperately, "I've polished your car
every Friday. Pickering promised to help, but mostly he forgot.
I was thinking we'd go for a ride now."

"But it'll soon be dark. Who wants to go for a ride in the
dark?"

"In January we did!"

"Did we?" said James, disbelieving. "Yes, so we did." He
shook his head. "I'm sorry, Joanna, I should have known you'd
want a ride. It's just that tea was so frightful, I jumped at an
excuse to get out of the house."

"But you'd just that moment walked in!"

He sighed. "Look. I promise we'll go out tomorrow, directly
after lunch. Is that okay? When Miss Cathcart is resting. And
thanks for polishing my car."

*

When Joanna awoke the following Saturday, the rain had gone and the few small clouds scudding across the sky were soft and fluffy. On dark days Widleigh, like a thousand other Victorian mansions, was just another monument to unbridled pretension, but the spring sunshine lent it warmth and charm. Below the crenelated parapet, banks of Neo-Gothic windows reflected the green of the park and the surrounding hills, and the first daffodils were out in the flower beds on either side of the front steps.

Saturday was Miss Cathcart's day off, and the routine that yoked her and Joanna together on the other six days of the week was set aside. When they met by chance on a Saturday, Miss Cathcart would assume a preoccupied look, indicating that she had serious business of her own to think about.

As Joanna came out of her room, she saw her mother's door was ajar, and so she poked her head inside. Mrs. Drayton was sitting up in bed with her reading glasses on; she was using her breakfast tray as a writing desk. The shawl that she had draped over her shoulders had slipped down to show her low-cut nightdress and part of her breasts. Joanna quickly looked away. She didn't want to see her mother's nakedness.

"What are you doing?" Joanna said after a moment.

"The usual," her mother replied. "I thought of a couplet during the night. Dreamed it, I should say, and I'm jotting it down before I forget. I'll see you later, darling. Just you run along."

After Joanna had gone, Mrs. Drayton sat staring at her notebook; her breakfast was untouched when Mrs. Burgess appeared to remove it. Occasionally she would write a few words, cross them out, and rewrite them in a slightly different order. Although she used a number of poetic forms, the sonnet was her favorite. She had written many more of them than Shakespeare. Once James had found four on a single sheet of paper tucked under the cushion of a chair in the library. Having glanced over them, he had handed them to his mother without comment. Apart from him, no one in her family had read Mrs. Drayton's poetry. When Joanna was older and might understand the feelings that her mother struggled to express, she would be shown some. Meanwhile, Mrs. Drayton entered competitions in *Time and Tide* and *The Listener*. She had received three honorable mentions, and the year before *Time and Tide* had actually printed her "Ode to Solitude." Miss Hilary Edgerton had rung up to congratulate her. "The Major must be thrilled that you're in print!"

"Thrilled? I wouldn't say so," Mrs. Drayton had replied. "He asked me to use my maiden name the next time."

When Joanna got down to the dining room, she found her father alone with the dogs, who were eating leftover porridge on the hearth.

"Good morning," he said cheerfully. "What have you got planned for such a beautiful day?"

"I'm going to the matinee in Hereford with James," she said. The truth was, though, that when she had suggested the matinee James had said he'd have to see. He was always putting her off these days. He'd only taken her out twice in the car, and she hadn't heard one of his new stories. Whenever she asked him to read them to her he said he was busy. "Where is he?"

"Sleeping in, I imagine," her father said. "Incidentally," he went on, "you haven't touched that animal of yours since Monday. Poor Dulcie! In the holidays things get frightfully out of hand."

Joanna claimed that Dulcie, who often bit and sometimes kicked, had an evil nature, but Henry Drayton said no, she had a perfectly reasonable nature. It was just that Joanna didn't handle her correctly — she was careless and perfunctory — and Dulcie's ill temper was justified. Miss Cathcart, who concurred with Joanna, would try to intervene on her behalf. "Isn't Joanna getting rather big for that pony?" she often observed. "Mightn't it be time to look for another?" But in this one instance Henry was deaf to her suggestions. He insisted that Joanna still had a lot to learn from Dulcie: patience, for one thing — and only when she'd learned it would she be ready to move on. A few holidays before, James had announced to his father, "I despise this horse busyness, and if you don't let me drop it, I shan't do my national service in the regiment, I'll join the catering corps." And so he'd got his way. But Joanna, who didn't care for horses any more than her brother did, had no such threat; she was condemned to the busyness for a long while yet.

"When I saw Dulcie yesterday," said Henry, "she was covered in mud. She's going to take a lot of cleaning, and you and your mother are lunching with the Coopers at Spurlock at half past twelve, so there'll be time for only a short ride."

"No one told *me* about going to Spurlock!" Joanna exclaimed. This meant that every moment of her free Saturday was filled. "Is James invited too?"

"Not this time. Giles and Steven are skiing in the Alps, and James would be bored to death with you and Gabriella."

So Joanna would be spending the afternoon with the Princess at the Palace, while James got off! She would rather sit in the dining room all day than do those things her parents had decided she should do, without even asking her. Ever so slowly she spread her toast with marmalade.

Meanwhile her father got to his feet and went to the window. "On a clear morning after a good night's rain you can't beat this view," he said happily. "I remember people telling me that, at sunrise, from a particular Nepalese village one would get a splendid view of Everest, the most splendid view on earth, they said. So once I slogged up there, and the next morning there indeed was Everest, and very pretty, too, only I soon got tired of looking at that snow. I've been looking at this valley all my life, though, and I'm not tired of it! Every time it's a bit different. River's higher, new colors on the hills." Then he glimpsed

Dulcie grazing among the Friesians and remembered the task at hand.

"Finished your breakfast, Joanna?" Summoning Dolly and Grizelda, he led the way from the room. Outside he produced an apple from his pocket and gave it to his daughter. "Let's see what you can do."

They climbed the railings into the park and Joanna trudged off.

As Joanna approached her, Dulcie raised her head and eyed the apple; then with a lightning thrust of her muzzle she knocked it from her hand into a cow pat. Joanna made a grab for her headcollar but too late. Dulcie shied away and broke into a trot and then a canter.

"You have to be a lot quicker off the mark than that!" Henry yelled. He brought out a second apple and polished it quickly on his sleeve. "Let *me* try!"

Joanna was deployed on the flank while her father took up a central position. This time as Dulcie circled round, she slowed, approached cautiously, and was tempted; she reached for the apple, whereupon Henry grabbed her. She sprang back and tried to shake off his hand, but he hung on to her. "Simple, you see," he told his daughter. "Now you lead her in."

Henry had two horses of his own and, to take care of them, a groom called Rhys, who joined Pickering in the garden in April once the fox-hunting season was finished. Since Joanna's ninth birthday Rhys had been forbidden to touch Dulcie; Henry wanted Joanna to be fully responsible for the pony. And so during termtime she got up at six o'clock three days a week to catch and groom and exercise her pony, under the exacting supervision of her father, who told her, if she complained, "I get up at six as well, young lady, yet you never hear *me* grumble!"

Now as Joanna led Dulcie toward the stables Henry hummed to himself. He was extraordinarily fond of animals. He knew all his neighbors' horses and dogs by name, but few of their children. "My poor girl," he exclaimed, giving Dulcie an affectionate slap on the neck, "from the way you look this morning, one might think no one cared about you at all!" Once in the stable he handed Joanna a currycomb. She hissed through her teeth the way Rhys did, in the hope of seeming more proficient, but her father wasn't satisfied with the performance.

"Here, give that to me!" He took off his coat and hung it on a hook by the door, rolled up his sleeves, grasped the currycomb firmly, and went to work, hissing for all he was worth. Surprised by the sudden change of pace, Dulcie lunged at him with bared, discolored teeth. Joanna watched with a mixture of alarm and fascination as the pony snapped within half an inch of her father's back. But she didn't bite him; she never did. Joanna was the only one who ever got bitten.

At midday Joanna let Dulcie loose in the park. On the whole the morning had been a success. Her father had been pleased by the way she had brought Dulcie over a row of hurdles. He said he could see some improvement at last.

Joanna changed out of her riding clothes and joined her parents in the hall. Her mother was wearing a blue suit — electric blue, Henry Drayton called it — and a blue and yellow scarf. The suit — broad-lapelled jacket, narrow skirt barely covering the knee — bought off-the-peg just after the war, wasn't Dior's new look exactly, but Joanna liked it and was hopeful that her mother would look smarter than Gabriella's mother. To Joanna this mattered enormously. As she climbed into the Bentley, she noticed grain on the red carpet; her father had been transporting cattle feed in the car again. They set off, and alone in the back seat, Joanna pretended she was Queen Mary acknowledging the cheers of the people, standing ten deep on either side of the drive.

From time to time Mrs. Drayton said to her husband,

"*Couldn't* you go a bit faster, Henry?" but he ignored her. He had the distance between Widleigh and Spurlock measured exactly. The clock on the dashboard, which still, after twenty-three years, kept time correctly, showed half past twelve when they turned in at the Coopers' gates.

Gabriella Cooper's grandfather had bought Spurlock at the turn of the century and by now the family had lived there long enough for most of their neighbors to have forgotten that their money came from manufacturing socks and underpants. The house was approached through a gateway surmounted by a pair of stone unicorns and flanked by two pretty lodges, where the head gardener and the head groom lived. The park boasted a thriving herd of fallow deer. (Widleigh's herd had fallen prey to brucellosis and had had to be destroyed. Henry Drayton, who thought fallow deer were silly creatures, did not replace them. He'd put Friesians in his park instead.) The gravel in the drive at Spurlock was at least five inches deep and every pebble looked as if it had been newly washed. It crunched opulently as Henry drove slowly to the front door, but the moment his wife and daughter were out of the car, he was off again. The Cooper affluence appalled him.

"Barbara, my dear!" Lady Harriet Cooper kissed the air close to Mrs. Drayton's cheek. "And how are *you,* Joanna? Gabriella's still out riding, but she'll be back very soon." Lady Harriet's voice trailed off at the end of a sentence and she couldn't look you in the eye for very long. It was as if she wanted to make contact but wasn't able to maintain the effort, quite. Her pale red hair had a lot of gray in it, and there were little lines all round her eyes. She had spent a lifetime on the verge of being lovely and now it was too late to bloom. She had a bad back and carried a cane everywhere. The truth was, her back gave her trouble only in wet weather and today was dry, but she felt quite lost without her cane, which gave her a sense of resolve in the face of a willful family. Now she leaned on it as she murmured, "I'm sorry Henry couldn't stay, but you two, do come in."

While Mrs. Drayton sat waiting for her sherry in the drawing room, the flower arrangement on the mantelpiece caught her eye. "Anemones, how beautiful!" she exclaimed. "Of course they're from your own greenhouse?"

Lady Harriet smiled shyly. "I'm awfully pleased with them, as last year none came up at all." Suddenly she was quite animated and had so much to say about garden plans, accomplished and proposed, that she barely touched her drink. "After lunch perhaps you'd like a tour?" she was saying eagerly when the door flung open and Gabriella came striding in.

As she shook Mrs. Drayton's hand, Gabriella curtsied — a little awkwardly — because she was standing and Mrs. Drayton was sitting, but Joanna only noticed the curtsy; the awkwardness escaped her. Joanna never curtsied when she shook hands, she hadn't been brought up to do so; she did wish terribly that she had. Although she would never in a hundred years have admitted it to anyone, she admired and envied Gabriella no end. While other girls their age were bony and inelegant, flailing their arms and legs, Gabriella was smooth and narrow and her limbs were properly coordinated. She gave the impression that she knew very well what she was doing, that whatever she did was right, and that she would be looked at and admired while doing it.

"Did you have a nice ride?" Mrs. Drayton asked, smiling up at Gabriella, searching her face. Gabriella looked down impassively at the woman in the loud blue suit. Grown-ups were always wanting her to like and approve of them. She turned away to the fireplace, where she stood staring into the fire, one foot on the brass rail, hands in jodhpur pockets. She was her father's favorite, and already her mother knew that before long Gabriella would evolve into just the kind of girl who had terrified and humiliated her, years before, when she was an unfashionable Irish bride in most fashionable London.

"Gabriella, darling, would you ring the bell? I forgot to tell you, Barbara," she added, "Nigel's going to be late and we should start lunch without him."

As Gabriella pressed the bell in the wall to one side of the fireplace, she caught her mother's eye, challenging her to tell her, That's enough; but Lady Harriet looked away and the shrill ring went on and on in the back of the house until Stillwell, the butler, in black morning coat and gray-and-black-striped trousers, appeared to announce lunch.

Despite mutual good will, Lady Harriet and Barbara Drayton had rather little to say to each other, and there were long pauses in the conversation. On Lady Harriet's left sat Gabriella's French governess, Mlle. du Lac. She smelled of mothballs and her hair, dyed with henna, was thinning at the crown. Although it had been doubtful whether Gabriella would learn anything from her, or if, indeed, she was capable of teaching anything, Mlle. du Lac had remained at Spurlock after Gabriella's older sister, Victoria, had gone away to school, because she was a known commodity and did no harm. She was not, however, talkative, and Gabriella, as usual, chose not to talk at all, since she was permitted to speak only French at meals when her governess was present. Joanna, then, was silent also.

They had finished roast beef and Yorkshire pudding and had started on plum tart when they heard the front door open and bang shut and firm steps advance across the hall. Colonel Nigel Cooper swept into the room in palest mole-colored riding breeches, gleaming boots, a bright checked jacket, which he got away with because, like his daughter, he had the gift of making everything about him look right. Not only was he an exceptionally handsome fellow, he was a clever one, too. Olympic Underwear had done remarkably well lately and was likely to do even better; but he was resolutely the country gentleman, and although he readily discussed blood sports, steeplechasing, Guernsey cows, and the Herefordshire Yeomanry, with which he had served during the war (hence his military title), he never men-

tioned his commercial activities — at least not in the country.

Now as he sat at the table waiting to be served, he stretched
out his long legs and explained to Mrs. Drayton that he had
driven down at crack of dawn to Wiltshire to see his racehorse
trainer. "Because Bingham's doing awfully well for me," he remarked, "it's worth having the horses so far off. This has been
my most successful winter since 1934." Stillwell appeared with
a plate heaped with roast beef and vegetables, and as he helped
himself to mustard, Nigel remarked, "You're looking very fit,
I must say, Barbara. What's *your* winter been like?" and he
gave her a most charming smile.

"Won't you tell me about your successes," said Mrs. Drayton
quickly, to avoid talking about herself; she knew little about
horse racing and cared less. Lady Harriet also gave Nigel her
complete attention. Disappointment though she might be to
him, he could count on her to listen to everything he said,
however many times he said it. But Mlle. du Lac didn't listen —
after almost two decades in the British Isles her grasp of English was still rudimentary. Gabriella didn't listen, either; she
followed stories at first telling only, and often not even then.

But Joanna listened to every word. Her father had once told
her, "That man's a smoothie, a social climber, an opportunist.
The only pleasant thing about him is his wife, whom he married
because she's the daughter of an earl. I give him as wide a berth
as possible, always have." But despite — or because of — her
father's opinion, Colonel Cooper intrigued Joanna. Like Gabriella, he fully expected admiration and throve on it, but unlike his beautiful daughter he had a spurious warmth and
generosity about him that made Joanna want to stay near him in
the hope that some of it might be directed at her. Listening
closely to such a glamorous man made her feel glamorous, too.

"We've finished, so we're going," Gabriella said in a loud,
bored voice, startling Joanna out of her absorption with Colo-

nel Cooper. "À bientôt, Mademoiselle," she added, slipping out of her chair.

"Wait a second." Nigel Cooper reached into his jacket pocket. "Andrew Bingham gave me something for you." But Gabriella walked away as if she hadn't heard. "Don't you want to know what it is?" her father pleaded. Gabriella's approval was something he specifically needed, and when she withheld it he became nervous, which he didn't like at all.

Gabriella paused. "I can't imagine what that old fool would want to send me," she said with a shrug.

"This!" Nigel Cooper exclaimed, pulling out a replica of a silver trophy. (Had one of the other children called Bingham an old fool he would have demanded an apology immediately.) "King's Man won this at Leicester in January. Remember? The odds were six to one against. Since King's Man has always been one of your favorites, Andrew thought you'd like to keep this."

Gabriella took the replica from him and examined it cursorily before handing it back. "Tell Mr. Bingham I only keep cups I've won myself. Come on," she said to Joanna, "let's go."

Joanna followed her out of the dining room and shut the door carefully behind them. Poor Colonel Cooper; he'd looked so put out!

Gabriella led the way through the baize door and down the long, dark kitchen corridor. She stopped at the pantry, where Stillwell was reading the newspaper, waiting to take the coffee to the drawing room. "Did you get what I asked for?" she said.

"Get what, Miss Gabriella?" said Stillwell.

"Come off it, Stillwell! Don't worry about Joanna. She likes fags as much as I do."

"I don't know what the world's coming to," Stillwell said with a smirk as he reached into the drawer where the fruit knives were kept. "Promise that if her ladyship catches you, you'll say you pinched them yourself," he added, taking out four Benson & Hedges cigarettes.

"I prefer Sobranies," Gabriella said. "They're stronger."

"The Colonel hasn't opened the new box yet, miss. You shouldn't complain, though, miss. The Colonel has these made up special in London. I tell you, I wish I could afford to smoke them myself!"

"Why *should* I get caught?" Gabriella said as she pocketed the cigarettes. "I never have been, have I?" and she gave Stillwell a radiant smile.

"There you go then," he said, and winked at her. He'll go on stealing cigarettes for her forever, Joanna thought.

Outside in the stable yard Gabriella giggled. "He's pathetic! Ever since I caught him drinking the brandy he's done whatever I want because he's terrified I'll tell Daddy."

Joanna found Stillwell more sinister than pathetic. She hadn't liked the way he'd winked at all.

"Is that your best skirt?" said Gabriella. Joanna nodded. "Too bad because we're about to climb a tree. You'd better be careful because if you tear your clothes your mother will make a stink and then *my* mother will guess what we've been up to and there'll be hell to pay." She led the way through old rhododendrons to a row of Douglas firs. "We're going up this one," she said, stopping at the tallest. "And for God's sake, watch it. If you get us into trouble, I'll never invite you here again!" She swung herself into the tree and in a few seconds was out of sight. "Aren't you coming?" she called down.

Joanna took a deep breath and started up in pursuit. When she had climbed what seemed a very long way without looking down for fear of getting dizzy, she heard Gabriella's voice just above her. "Lord, you're filthy — clothes, hands, face, everything!" Joanna scrambled onto the branch beside her and noticed that Gabriella had somehow managed to remain clean. "Well, it's twenty to three already, so we haven't got much time. Here!" She handed Joanna a cigarette.

Joanna was not an experienced smoker, but she put the cigarette between her lips and bent her head in what she imagined was a sophisticated manner so that Gabriella, who had lifted a mother of pearl lighter from Lady Harriet's sitting room, could light it for her.

"Do you come up here often?" Joanna asked, leaning back against the trunk of the tree.

Gabriella was blowing smoke rings. "Several times a week," she replied after a moment in a mock grown-up voice. "I find it restful and I awfully like the view, don't you?" They puffed in silence until Gabriella said, "So what shall we pretend to be today?" Pretending-to-be was the only game she ever wanted to play.

"You decide," said Joanna. Gabriella always overrode her suggestions anyway.

"How about Mrs. Welden and my father? I'll be Daddy and you be Mrs. Welden having dinner at Prunier's. It's her thirty-second birthday."

"Who's Mrs. Welden?"

"Daddy's girlfriend. She's got a hat shop in Beauchamp Place, which Daddy paid for, and red nails an inch long, and she wears flashy dresses with necklines down to here." Gabriella pointed to her navel. "You know, like *your* father and Miss Cathcart, only Mrs. Welden doesn't live with us — Mummy wouldn't stand for that — she lives in London and never comes down here. I told you about her before, remember? Daddy's had her for ages, ever since he got fed up with Gloria Hisbeach."

"Who was she?"

"His private secretary."

"Miss Cathcart isn't flashy," Joanna said quickly. "She's always well turned out."

"I suppose you're right," Gabriella agreed. "Well, anyway, let's start. We're in the restaurant." She picked up Joanna's hand and examined her fingers one by one. "Oh, Deidre, your nails, one simply never sees nails like yours in the country! Such hands have never weeded a herbaceous border in their life!" She burst into gales of laughter and had to clutch the branch above to keep herself from falling out of the tree.

Henry Drayton drove out of Hereford, where he'd done some errands and had a peaceful lunch in a pub, on his way back to Spurlock to pick up his wife and daughter. He wondered what Joanna did when she was with Gabriella, whom he trusted no more than her father. At Widleigh recently he had come upon the girls in the summer house just as Gabriella, dressed in a tablecloth and a gold paper crown, was being served her break-fast by Joanna, dressed in a dustsheet. "This egg is revolting, it's practically raw!" Gabriella had shouted. "Take it away! How many times must I tell you that I detest soft-boiled eggs? If you don't watch it, I'll send you back to Ireland and get a new lady in waiting!" At that point Henry had marched in, grabbed her by the arm, and yanked her out of her seat. "If I were your lady in waiting," he told her, "I'd go back to Ireland of my own accord! Your *manners* are revolting, never mind the egg!" Gabriella had looked up at him in utter disdain and said, "My dear Major Drayton, don't be so silly! *Where* is your sense of humor? This is only a game!"

He knew he hadn't taught the Princess a lesson because she was incorrigible; all the same, he hoped that Joanna had learned to stand up to her a bit better.

As he rounded a bend in the road a set of stone farm build-ings came into view. In the wall of the barnyard was a gate, and parked in front of the gate was James's green Morris. Why would James come here of all places? What was the attraction? Could he really have driven seven miles from Widleigh, using up precious petrol coupons, to go for a walk? But these days James's behavior was increasingly difficult to fathom.

Henry pulled the Bentley over to the verge and let the engine die. He got out quietly, went up to the Morris, peered through the cloudy windscreen, and saw James's tweed cap on the front seat. He wouldn't have gone for a walk, then, not without his cap. Perhaps he was in the sunny barnyard, chewing the end of a pencil, trying to draw inspiration from sunlight falling on old walls. At least it was healthier for him to write his nonsense out of doors instead of in his room, with all the windows shut. Henry decided to surprise his son.

He crossed the lane, unlatched the five-barred gate, and slipped through. The barnyard was deserted. No cattle, no sheep, no sign of James. On the far side a great wooden door sagged open. Heart pounding, Henry made his way toward it over cobblestones between which new grass grew. Once inside the barn he waited for his eyes to grow accustomed to the dark. For one long minute he heard nothing. Then straw rustled and a moment later the rustling came again, more loudly. A calf might have made that much noise as it heaved itself to its feet.

"Heavens, Jamie, d'you know it's almost four!" Henry heard Miss Cathcart exclaim from a corner to his left. "Our time has flown! It always does, though, doesn't it. Let's fold up the blanket, darling."

"I'll carry it," James said, and he added, "One of these days, I'm going to take you far away to somewhere with no routine, no interruptions, nothing, nobody but us."

For an instant Henry stood transfixed. Then he turned and tiptoed out to the lane, got into his car, started up the engine, and drove on.

Chapter 5

Sullerton

MISS CATHCART, seated at the organ in royal blue robe and mortarboard, broke into Buxtehude, and the congregation rose and craned their necks for a view of the bridal party receding through the chancel and the nave. Rosemary Spencer, wearing her family tiara and a dress of slipper satin with a neckline cut rather low for the chill of early April, trotted along on the arm of her new husband. She looked very pleased indeed. The bridegroom, though, seemed overwhelmed. His face was an alarming raspberry-red and his eyes were riveted to the cold stone floor. Behind them trooped seven grown-up bridesmaids in primrose taffeta with stephanotis in their hair.

Standing between her husband and her son, Mrs. Drayton noted that this was a standard union. Such couples were to be found all over the countryside. Their conventionality ensured them a long life together: early on, they would bring into the world several others in their own image, and later, though they might like to go their separate ways, neither, for lack of imagination, would go very far. Even so Mrs. Drayton, tears pricking, admitted to herself that she envied them — for not wanting anything different. Their complacency would shield them from expectations unfulfilled.

James sighed with satisfaction as Buxtehude soared.

The choir filed out of the choir stalls and down the aisle

behind the dean of Hereford Cathedral, who, assisted by the vicar of Sullerton, had performed the ceremony. Then guests poured from the pews and followed the parents of the bride and bridegroom out into pale sunshine.

With her husband, top hat in hand, scuttling behind her, Mrs. Spencer dashed through the graveyard and the wrought-iron gate leading to Sullerton Priory next door. "Marjorie, do please wait!" her husband called after her in vain.

This was her party and she was going to see to it that everything went according to plan. Alligator handbag clasped to her stomach, she sped towards the house, overtaking the bridal party on the lawn. Then she sprang up the front steps, across the hall, and into the library, where photographers waited. At one end of the room bronze urns of flaming lilies flanked a massive portrait of an ancestor in coronation robes.

"We'll have the pictures here," Mrs. Spencer announced, "and do make sure you get the Lord Chancellor in, too!" As she wasn't about to let her guests into the priory until she was ready to receive them properly, they would have to stand about outside until the photography session was concluded.

Major and Mrs. Drayton and James left the church together, but in the bottleneck at the gate between the graveyard and the priory garden, they were separated. Mrs. Drayton wandered among guests clustered in little knots all over the lawn. She nodded at some, greeted others, but did not stop to talk to anyone. She liked one or two, including Harriet Cooper, who had put on her glasses in order to examine the tags on the naked rose bushes in the circular bed in the middle of the lawn; but she couldn't think of a thing to say to her. All the rest she found snobbish, cold, contemptible. The self-pity that had brought her to the verge of tears in the church had receded, leaving her aloof.

With half an ear she listened to three women discussing the wedding dress. The material was pretty, they conceded, although almost any other design would have been more flattering to poor Rosemary's full figure. The tiara, of course, they knew well. It was undeniably impressive on Marjorie, who wore it at hunt balls, but it was too ornate and heavy for such a young girl; a coronet of flowers would have been more suitable. As for the bridegroom, although he did seem terribly shy, he had a huge place in Yorkshire and a baking powder fortune, so all in all Rosemary had done well. The next order of business was the wedding presents, laid out for public viewing and evaluation in the breakfast room. The three ladies planned to have a look at them the minute they'd had a glass of champagne.

When the photographers had finished and the guests were at last admitted to the house, Mrs. Drayton rejoined her husband and her son so they could go through the receiving line together. A butler with rheumy eyes and translucent skin announced each guest in turn.

"Jeremy and I were *thrilled* with your present and I *promise* to write, only I've been *so* busy!" the bride exclaimed to every woman. To every man she gasped, "Thank you, how very sweet of you," if he complimented her on her appearance — if he didn't, she murmured, "So glad you could come!" — and she smiled what she believed to be a radiant nuptial smile.

Meanwhile the bridegroom nodded indiscriminately to everyone; to every fourth or fifth person he thought to say, "Wonderful to meet you!" Earlier, in his anxiety, his appetite had deserted him but now that the afternoon's important business had been satisfactorily concluded he was longing for his tea. His new mother-in-law, too, was impatient for this phase in the ritual to be over so that she could dash off to check on the caterers, who had come highly recommended, but one never really knew. To her left her husband and other members of the wedding party shook hands with anyone and everyone who made motion to shake hands with them.

The library was divided from the drawing room and the

drawing room from the dining room by doors that were folded back on great occasions to make the length of Sullerton Priory into one huge room. "A wedding's so much more fun in the country than in London if one has a house like this to do it in!" guests exclaimed to one another as they demolished sausage rolls and sipped champagne. "And *where* did Marjorie find those lilies so early in the year?"

Mrs. Drayton stood by a window overlooking the spring garden. She smiled to herself as she remembered her first visit to Sullerton just after she was married. Over cocktails before dinner Marjorie Spencer had observed, "One gathers you don't hunt or shoot, Barbara, so what, one wonders, will you find to do in Herefordshire?" and having pursed her lips in what was intended to be a sympathetic smile, she had turned to talk to someone else.

Henry Drayton, who had never been known to do anything in a hurry, had met, proposed to, and married Barbara Beresford in one month flat, and Marjorie Spencer, among others, was naturally curious about what had possessed him. Such short engagements were unheard of, except if the girl was very pregnant or a war was on and the young man was due back with his regiment. Barbara, however, didn't look a bit pregnant and there was no war on, either, so she concluded that Henry had married out of desperate loneliness. His mother, Catharine Hannington, a wonderful woman — any committee you could think of, she'd been on it — to whom he'd been devoted, had died the previous summer and his father shortly thereafter, and Henry had come home from India to an empty house. Saddest of all, Betsy, his beloved labrador, had died in quarantine. People had to wonder, though, whether Barbara Beresford, towering over him in her smart London frock, would be much solace. She didn't seem a bit like Catharine Hannington, or a labrador, either, come to think of it.

"There you are, Barbara!" Mrs. Spencer, finished with hand-shaking and for the moment with the caterers, had Henry Drayton in tow. "I just have to tell you how delighted we were with Miss Cathcart! She was quite magnificent. That old organ hasn't been pushed so hard in decades. It must be so exciting to have such talent in the house! Such fun for you, Barbara, especially, since you were a musician, too, before you married, isn't that right?"

"No. I used to paint."

"I could have sworn you played the harp, or something equally exotic."

"You must be confusing me with someone else," said Mrs. Drayton testily.

Just then Miss Cathcart appeared at the far side of the room with James beside her. She had removed her mortarboard and gown to reveal purple silk and upswept dark gold hair. Her face bore an expression of diffuse good will. "How lovely," Mrs. Spencer exclaimed. "There she is! We're over here," she called, waving one gray kid-gloved hand. Across the room Miss Cathcart broke into a wide smile and, champagne glass held high to avoid spillage, edged her way forward through the crowd.

"We did so enjoy the music!" Mrs. Spencer told her. "I can't tell you how many people asked after you as they came through the receiving line. You're going to be in greater demand than ever. No one will *dare* get married or buried without you! You have been warned," she told the Draytons, "she's going to be away from home a lot! And what a lovely dress!" she added, turning back to Miss Cathcart. "It sets off your coloring so perfectly!" Mrs. Drayton stared over Mrs. Spencer's shoulder at a Gilpin painting of a broodmare; Henry Drayton's gaze focused on Mrs. Spencer's collarbone.

"I'm glad everything seemed to go well," said Miss Cathcart.

"By the way," Mrs. Spencer went on quickly, "last week I ran into your clever Mr. Edgerton. He was saying how enormously attached he is to you. What he said, actually, was that

you'd changed *his* life as well as the life of the village! The way
you've got people going — singing and dancing and everything
— was in and of itself a source of amazement, but your genius,
he said, lay in keeping them at it. That's a far more challenging
task."

"Widleigh's rather isolated," said Miss Cathcart. "People need
something to do. It's that more than anything which accounts
for their persistence."

"But you know you're not doing yourself justice! Beating
culture's drum isn't your cup of tea quite, is it Barbara?" Mrs.
Spencer continued. "I can imagine that after a childhood on the
Continent and a youth in London, a little place like Widleigh
wouldn't have looked too promising. How fortunate for all of
us that Miss Cathcart came along to fill the gap!" Mrs. Spencer
was beginning to enjoy herself. "Last year's Midsummer pageant was such fun! Tell me, Sybilla — I *can* call you Sybilla,
can't I? I do so hate formality! — what have you got up your
sleeve for this year? No doubt Barbara and Henry have heard
your plans but I'm sure they won't mind hearing them again."

Mrs. Drayton said loudly, "You're quite wrong, Marjorie. So
far as *I'm* concerned, Miss Cathcart doesn't make a habit of
sharing her plans."

"Mother!" James said urgently, "your glass is empty and
mine is, too. Let's go and get some more champagne."

"I don't want more champagne, James. I want to hear about
these plans."

Miss Cathcart's color had risen and she was breathing rapidly. "Our theme is the role the Welsh Marches have played in
British history from the Romans to the present."

"From the Romans to the present! Haven't you bitten off
more than you can chew?" Mrs. Drayton said. "And what do
you know about the Welsh Marches? You've only lived here
four years!"

"I admit that I'm no expert," said Miss Cathcart quietly,

"but Mr. Edgerton is a respected authority and he and I are working on the script together. If you have concerns about accuracy, Mrs. Drayton, when we've completed it, perhaps you'd like to check it over." She added, "I have to say, though, until this moment I have never heard you express any special feeling for Marcher history."

"Why would I express my special feelings to *you,* of all people? And suppose I did, you wouldn't listen! You never listen to a thing I say!"

People were beginning to nudge and stare.

Gaze averted, hands deep in the pockets of his striped trousers, James whispered, "Let it go, Mother, for Christ's sake!"

But Mrs. Drayton ignored her son. "All this adulation seems to have convinced you that you're the fount of wisdom, an oracle, in fact," she shouted at Miss Cathcart. "Well, I don't give a damn for your pronouncements! I find you utterly pedestrian, I always have!"

Although Marjorie Spencer was delighted to see Barbara Drayton make a fool of herself in public, she didn't like it happening in her house, at her daughter's wedding reception, in front of three hundred guests. "Henry, Barbara's not feeling well *at all* and you and I must remove her," she said firmly, grasping Mrs. Drayton's elbow. "Barbara, come along with us."

The crowd parted to let Mrs. Spencer and the Draytons through, and guests who hadn't had a ringside view of the proceedings demanded an explanation from those who had. "Such a *peculiar* woman!" Mrs. Drayton heard a man she'd known for twenty years say to his wife. "I've always said so, haven't I?"

Why was she letting herself be manhandled? On the threshold of the drawing room she pulled away from Mrs. Spencer. "Let me go!" she cried, but her husband had her firmly by the other elbow. At the front door Mrs. Spencer told her, "You're going to feel better in a minute or two. It's so hot inside! So many people in a quite small space." She remained with the

Draytons and sent the undergardener to bring round their car.

"Get in, Barbara," Henry Drayton ordered when the Bentley appeared.

"Why should I?"

"It's time to go home," said Mrs. Spencer quickly.

"What about *her*, though? How will *she* get home?"

"James has a car, hasn't he," said Henry. "Miss Cathcart will come home with him. He'll leap at the chance to show her just how well he drives."

Mrs. Spencer said through the car window, "Sorry this had to happen, Barbara. I'm sure we'll run into each other soon. Happy Easter! Good-bye!"

Henry Drayton drove in silence through Sullerton village. His nose for once revealed nothing. Mrs. Drayton watched his profile while she counted to a hundred. "What are you thinking? Tell me!" she shouted. Henry glanced at her for an instant before turning his eyes back to the road. "No, you don't have to tell me, I already know! You're thinking I should be locked up in a sanatorium, like your cousin Caroline Knightley — in that Swiss place, preferably — that would get me right out of the way so I'd never humiliate you and your son again! Well, if our little scene convinced you that you can't keep me and that woman under one roof anymore, I'm delighted it occurred! And even if it didn't convince you, it most certainly convinced me. She can queen it over you forever, I don't care, but she's not going to queen it over me one day longer! I'm off, Henry! It won't matter if you never give me another penny — I'll manage somehow for Joanna and me. James is entirely yours. He won't miss me. He despises me. You made sure of that!" Mrs. Drayton burst into hysterical laughter. "Alone with her at last! What a frenzied fleshly feast you have in store! Once Joanna's out of the house, there'll be no holding back!"

Henry Drayton jammed on the brakes, the car swerved, and the engine stalled.

"I'm going to give her notice as soon as she gets back from the reception."

Mrs. Drayton's mouth dropped open. "Have you gone mad?" she said, wiping away tears of laughter.

"Miss Cathcart isn't the woman I thought she was," said Henry quietly.

"She isn't?" Mrs. Drayton was momentarily confused; then again she was engulfed by laughter. "Can it be," she gasped, "that Marjorie Spencer is responsible for this? 'Mr Edgerton is so enormously attached to you,' she mimicked. 'He says you've changed his life!'" She took a deep breath. "So my lady is perfidious, is she? Now I understand! You haven't gone mad. It's the episcopal pansy. You're overwhelmed by jealousy!"

"I gather you haven't noticed our son's behavior," said Henry softly.

"Is it any more objectionable than usual?"

Henry emitted a long deep sigh. "James and Miss Cathcart are . . ." He stopped.

"James and Miss Cathcart are what?"

"They're having a love affair." In a sad, dry voice he added, "I don't know when it started but the wise thing would be to try to stop it, wouldn't you agree?"

"I'll be home about six," Mrs. Drayton had told Joanna when she left for Sullerton, but at four o'clock doors slammed and there she was in the front hall, home two hours early.

"You're back so soon! It wasn't fun?" Joanna cried, running down the stairs to meet her.

"Fun?" Her mother shrugged. "It might have been for some people."

"How many tiers did the cake have?" Joanna asked. "Did you bring a piece back for me?"

"We left before they cut it."

"Where's James?"

"Still there."

"Did *he* enjoy himself?"

"When he gets back, you'll have to ask him," Mrs. Drayton said, and as she started for her room she added, "I have a headache, I've got to lie down."

Meanwhile Major Drayton was walking through the kitchen and up the pantry passage to the smoking room. Joanna heard him shut the door and knew it meant that under no circumstances did he want to be disturbed.

Upstairs, Joanna knocked on Miss Cathcart's door. When there was no answer she knocked again more loudly. Still no response. Perhaps Miss C. was in the schoolroom, she thought, so she ran down there; but the excursion proved futile.

The house was perfectly still. Joanna went along the passage to the dining room and stared into the huge painting over the sideboard. She asked the turbaned blackamoor, who held a plunging horse, Why didn't she come home? The blackamoor was small and lithe and looked about Joanna's age. He had accompanied an eighteenth-century Drayton across the Great Arabian Desert and returned with him to Widleigh, where they'd had their portrait painted by George Stubbs. Sometimes he smiled in a very friendly fashion; sometimes he grinned insolently. This was one of his insolent days. You're no help at all, Joanna told him.

Next Joanna tried to play Schubert in the drawing room but she couldn't concentrate. She came away from the piano, opened a bureau drawer, and lifted out a stack of mounted photographs. Cross-legged on a tiger skin, she flipped through them. Most were of horses and hounds and servants, house parties and shooting parties, lined up in front of a new Widleigh, over which Virginia creeper had yet to grow; but one was of a boy on the seashore, in a striped bathing suit with sleeves. On the back was written "H. D., Abersoch, North Wales, 1894."

A car pulled up at the front and Joanna dashed into the entrance hall in time to see Miss Cathcart sweep through to the stairs.

"Why did you come home with James?" she demanded. James had promised her that she alone could ride in his car. She ran up behind her and tugged at a purple sleeve. "Why didn't you come home with my parents?"

"Let me go please, Joanna," Miss Cathcart said sharply, pulling away, and then she, too, disappeared behind a closed door.

For a moment Joanna stood on the landing, panic rising from her stomach to her throat. Then she dashed downstairs again and out into the stables.

James was coming from the garage in a gray tailcoat that had once belonged to Humphrey Beresford. He'd loosened the knot of his silk tie and it hung halfway down his chest. Was he drunk? But he was walking straight enough.

"You said the car was just for you and me," Joanna cried. "Not for *her*." As he came up to her she saw his face looked strange, greenish. "Are you going to be sick?" she asked in alarm.

"I *am* sick!" he burst out. "Sick of *them*! He bullies her and they both bully everyone who's foolish enough to go near them. If you don't see that yet, Joanna, one day soon you will, and then, God help you!"

"Where are you going?" She grabbed his hand. "Can I come too?"

"I want to be alone now."

"*I've* been alone for hours and hours. I want to be with you!"

"Can't you go and be with Agnes?"

"She's off, and anyway, she went to Hereford."

"Look" — there was a sudden hard edge to his voice — "you're too old to be needing so much attention. You can't expect other people to entertain you all the time!"

"I've been entertaining myself since lunchtime," Joanna

cried. "*I* haven't been to any wedding!" But James had pulled away. He walked quickly through the kitchen and off along the pantry passage. "You *promised* you wouldn't take Miss Cathcart in your car!" she shouted after him. "You shouldn't make promises you don't intend to keep!"

She ran up the back stairs to her mother's room and tried the door. It wasn't locked and she went in. Mrs. Drayton was sitting at her dressing table. She still wore her wedding hat; she hadn't even taken off her gloves.

"When you and Daddy came in you wouldn't talk to me. Miss Cathcart and James just came in and they wouldn't talk to me, either. What happened at that wedding?"

Mrs. Drayton shook her head as if to clear it. "Did you have tea?" she said vaguely. "I had no idea how late it was!" she exclaimed, looking at her watch. "It's your suppertime. Shall we see what Agnes left for you?"

"Why did Miss Cathcart come home with James?" Joanna demanded.

"Your father and I decided we'd had enough, so we left early. One always sees the same people at these things. I find them dreadfully dull but since Miss Cathcart *loves* even the most boring party, it would have been a shame to drag her away."

"Did she play well?"

"Mrs. Spencer seemed delighted and that's what counts, I suppose. Let's go and get your supper."

"Why d'you still have your hat on?"

"At times your father's claimed I'm mad," said Mrs. Drayton with a laugh. "He could be right!"

Joanna wasn't satisfied at all but she wanted to feel reassured and so she laughed, too.

When she came down to breakfast on Easter morning she found her father alone in the dining room, shut away behind the *Sunday Times*. She ate her porridge and her bacon and eggs, and as she got up to make herself a slice of toast she remarked, "Shouldn't I call Miss Cathcart? She must have overslept. She'll be late for church if she doesn't hurry."

"I'm not sure she'll be going to church today," said Henry Drayton from behind the newspaper.

"She *always* goes, unless she's ill. Is she ill now?"

"Not at all, she's perfectly well." Henry put down his paper and wiped his mouth carefully with his napkin. "I have something to tell you, Joanna. Please sit down." He waited until she was back in her chair and then he said, "Miss Cathcart will be leaving for London in the morning by the early train."

"When will she be back?"

"There's been a change of plan. She won't be back."

Joanna was thunderstruck. "Who will I have lessons with?"

"Your mother and I think it's time you went to boarding school."

"Boarding school!"

"You shouldn't be at home alone like this. It isn't good for you. You need companions your own age."

"But you don't *approve* of boarding schools for girls! They're dreadful, disorganized, sloppy places! You've said so yourself dozens of times!"

"There are some that aren't so dreadful."

"How do you know? Have you ever seen one?" Her father said nothing. "Why is Miss Cathcart leaving, when she's the most remarkable person we know?"

"Things aren't what they used to be," said Henry Drayton, looking miserable.

"In what way aren't they?"

"Take my word for it," her father said bitterly.

After a moment's thought Joanna said, "Can't I get another governess?"

"Miss Cathcart's irreplaceable. There's no one else like her anywhere." He went on, "You know, James went to Winter-fields at seven, so did I, as a matter of fact, and neither of us turned a hair."

"But you'd been warned. You always knew you'd be going. *I've* always known I'd be staying at home with her!"

"She thinks boarding school is best for you, too," said Henry Drayton deliberately. "We all came to the conclusion that this would be the best thing to do."

"Why did you change your minds so quickly?" said Joanna. Tears spilled down her cheeks. She dug up her sleeve for a handkerchief but found none. Her father handed her his. After a moment she said, "Where are you going to put me? Not that frightful place the Coopers sent Victoria — the bread had wee-vils in it. And I can't go to Cynthia Knightley's convent because I'm not a Roman Catholic."

But her father had had enough. He folded his napkin and stood up. "Your mother's going to look into things tomorrow. I myself *liked* boarding school and so did James. Even your mother did. Being on one's own is good for one. Come on, it's time for church."

"You haven't explained anything!" Joanna sprang up from the table and threw herself against the dining room door. For an instant her father stared at her, confused, but he quickly got control of himself. "Let me out," he ordered, and when she didn't budge, he pulled her away from the door, jerked it open, and marched through.

Joanna stumbled back to her chair, slumped into it, laid her head on her hands, and wept.

When Mrs. Drayton appeared a few moments later, dressed for church, she saw her daughter's tear-streaked face. "So you've been told," she said. Joanna got up and left the room.

"Where's James?" she asked her father, whom she found waiting at the front door.

"Taken off."

"Off? Where for?"

"Somerset. He's gone to stay with the Burns boy."

"He didn't tell *me* he was going," Joanna cried. "Did he leave me a note?"

"I don't believe so. He decided to go late last night and left before daylight. I suppose he didn't want to wake you to say good-bye."

Joanna shook her head in disbelief. "He's woken me up lots of times before. Does *he* know Miss Cathcart's leaving?"

"He does."

"Did he say good-bye to *her?*"

"To my mind, he's said quite enough to her already."

After church Joanna followed her mother into the library. "Are you going to send me to that Morehaven dump?" she demanded.

Mrs. Drayton picked up a book of verse and leafed through it. "Possibly," she said.

"What's it like?"

"These days? I couldn't tell you! I saw it last in 1915. It was nice then, though. I liked it."

"You did not! You left after a year."

"That was Granny's decision, not mine. When I went to Morehaven we were still living in Switzerland, but over the winter Granny moved back to London, where there were lots of good day schools. She said, 'Why go to boarding school when there's Queensgate round the corner?' That July she took me out of Morehaven — much against my wishes, mind you — and in September I went to Queensgate instead."

"Why can't *I* go to a day school?"

"Because there aren't any round here."

"Of course there are! Mary Williams goes to the Girls Grammer School in Hereford every morning on the bus. She loves it, the boys' school's right next door."

"You can't go there, though. For one thing, you'd have to pass an exam to get in."

"If Mary passed it, I could, too!"

"We don't know when they give it."

"We could easily find out."

Mrs. Drayton shook her head. "It's no good, Joanna, you can't go to that sort of school. No Drayton has ever gone to Hereford Grammar. Your father would never hear of it." She added, "If you went, you'd end up speaking with a Herefordshire accent."

"What's wrong with that?"

"It's dreadfully unattractive. Look," she said hurriedly, "there are some lines I must write before lunch. It's so nice outside. You should go out and enjoy the good weather while it lasts."

Joanna turned on her heels and left the room, slamming the door behind her. She ran across the hall and up the stairs. She hadn't laid eyes on Miss Cathcart since she'd come in after the wedding. The door to her governess's room, which was next to her own, had been shut whenever Joanna walked by. Her supper had been brought up on a tray; she hadn't come to breakfast. But now her door stood open. From the threshold Joanna saw that the photographs of the Talbot and Acland children were gone from the bureau and that the red walls had been stripped of South American memorabilia. Flutes from the Brazilian rain forest, a sequined costume from Carnival in Rio, a brown sarape from the Peruvian highlands, spurs from the Chaco, a carved wooden crocodile from Ecuador, together with the made-to-measure wardrobe from Buenos Aires, lay on the four-poster bed. Joanna knew the history of every garment, every artifact; she had handled and admired each one innumerable times and now they were about to be packed into trunks and cardboard boxes and shipped away.

Miss Cathcart was sorting her books into piles by category:

history, natural history, fiction, drama, travel, miscellaneous. She wore her paisley dressing gown, and her hair hung down her back in one thick plait. She seemed unaware of Joanna in the doorway.

"My parents say it's better for me to be at boarding school than here with you," Joanna said at last, "and that's why you're leaving, but I don't believe it."

Miss Cathcart glanced round, a book in either hand. "It's a good enough reason."

"Not good enough for me! I don't want you to go!" Joanna said desperately. Miss Cathcart was silent. She went on, "You've been promising for years you'd start me on the organ as soon as I could reach the pedals. Well, now that I can, you're off!"

"Organ teachers aren't too difficult to come by," said Miss Cathcart in a neutral voice. "There's bound to be one at the school you go to."

For four years she had watched Joanna, guided her. Now she was cutting her off.

"Where will you go?" said Joanna.

"This morning I telephoned a friend from my Royal Academy days. She'll be delighted to put me up while I look for another position." She could have been talking to the teller in the bank or the clerk behind the counter in the post office; but, Joanna realized, she would have smiled at those people.

"Will you be someone else's governess?" Joanna persisted.

"Perhaps. Then again I might decide to do something completely different."

"Are you fed up with children? Are you fed up with me? Is that why you're leaving?"

Miss Cathcart flushed. "Oh *no!*" She put down the books she was holding and came to Joanna. "That's not it at all!"

"Who will I play four-hands with?"

"You'll find someone."

"But it will never be as much fun as it was with you." She thought about pounding out Mozart with Miss Cathcart in the drawing room. Sometimes — even better — she had jumped off the bench and raced down the passage to the schoolroom, and then they'd crashed away on both pianos at once; the house had rocked on its foundations. "Have you been unhappy here? Is that why you're leaving?"

"On the contrary, I've been *very* happy, dear!" She touched Joanna's cheek. "In my entire life I've never been happier."

Joanna sighed enormously. "I don't understand."

"It *is* very confusing," Miss Cathcart said. They looked at each other in sad silence until Miss Cathcart added quietly, "Perhaps one day, when you're older, you'll understand. Now I'd better get on with my packing."

On Monday morning Joanna heard her governess moving about before daybreak in her room next door. Soon she heard Rhys and Pickering come to carry down the trunks and boxes and then Miss Cathcart's voice on the landing. She expected a knock, but none came. Miss Cathcart walked off down the stairs.

Joanna slipped out of bed, took a brown envelope out of the drawer in her bedside table, and ran after her.

There, at the front door, she stood in her dove-gray pavement suit, with Henry Drayton at her side. Joanna stopped abruptly; she hadn't thought out what to say.

"We're off now," said her father. "We've got that train to catch." Miss Cathcart, her back to Joanna, was putting on her gloves.

"Thank you for everything," Joanna said. Miss Cathcart started, froze, and then turned to her, and Joanna saw there were tears in her eyes. "This is for you," she added, thrusting the brown envelope into her governess's hand. "It's that photograph of me and the Duchess of Gloucester, from the *Daily*

Telegraph. The next place you go, will you put it up with Luke and Felipe?" She flung her arms around Miss Cathcart's neck and was engulfed by the scents of cloves and lilies of the valley. For an instant they clung together and then, ashamed of such a display of feeling in front of her father, Joanna pulled away.

"I'll write as soon as I'm settled. I promise we won't lose touch," Miss Cathcart said, and then Henry Drayton was ushering her out the front door.

Mrs. Burgess, crossing the hall on her way to clean out the grate in the smoking room, saw Joanna barefoot on the icy stone floor. "I'm sorry, love," she said. "Miss C. was quite a one, wasn't she. We shan't be seeing the likes of her again."

Chapter 6

The Arlington Hotel

THE TRAIN HAD LEFT Oxford and was running south through the Thames Valley. Mrs. Drayton was reading a volume of poetry by Edith Sitwell, whom she very much admired. Joanna, too, had a book. She turned the pages at regular intervals without absorbing a word.

There's been a change of plan, a change of plan, a change of plan, clacked the wheels of the train.

She was condemned to the stucco prison she had seen in her mother's photograph album. A form had arrived in the post the day before and her father had signed on the dotted line. The next essential step was buying the necessary clothes.

At the end of a long afternoon in Debenham and Freebody, which stocked, so the sales assistant asserted, the uniforms of thirty-seven girls' private schools throughout the length and breadth of England, Joanna and her mother took the Underground to Knightsbridge and the Arlington Hotel.

Standish hovered over a party of Americans who had just poured out of a charabanc. Regardless of sex they wore tan raincoats and mystified expressions. The men had very little hair between them and every one of the women clutched a Fortnum and Mason carrier bag. "Evening, Miss Joanna!" Standish called, but he had no time to chat.

An elderly gentleman trundling through the lobby, bowler

hat in hand, spotted Mrs. Drayton. "Up from the country to see your mama?" he boomed. "We lunched together yesterday. She's in amazing form! Going to Sicily next week with Humphrey and then on to Tangiers. You going too?"

Mrs. Drayton shook her head. "I have to get my daughter organized for school. She's off for the first time." She pushed Joanna forward. "This is General Mainwaring, darling. He's one of Granny's oldest friends."

"Met her on the beach at Dinard when she was four and I was six. Emptied my bucket of crabs and starfish over her and she hit me with her spade," he said. "How d'you do, and what school are you off to, Joanna?"

"Morehaven."

"Never heard of it, but I only had boys myself. Anyway, if you're anything at all like your grandmother, you'll take over the place in no time! Give her my love, won't you," he said, putting on his hat. "I'd better be going. Got to meet my boy Julian at the Cavalry Club."

As Joanna knocked at the door of her grandmother's flat, Mrs. Drayton straightened her hat and plucked lint off her jacket. "Do I look all right, darling?" she said anxiously.

"There's something wrong with the lock," Mrs. Beresford called through the door. "I reported it this morning but they've done nothing about it so far. It's you, isn't it, Barbara? You'll have to push."

Mrs. Drayton put her shoulder to the door, which burst open.

"I didn't ask you to push me *over!*" Mrs. Beresford exclaimed.

"I'm so sorry, Mummy! I didn't realize you were right *at* the door." Mrs. Drayton was visibly upset.

"I'll have a great black bruise on my arm where you hit me and it'll take weeks to go away! Oh, well . . . I hope you've had tea already because what's left here is stone-cold. I was expecting you a good deal earlier and I had mine ages ago." Mrs. Beresford seated herself on the sofa and patted the cushion beside her. "Give me a kiss and sit next to me, Joanna, darling. No more cups to show me yet? Never mind, there will be shortly." She went on, "I understand you've been buying the uniform. I hate uniforms! In my opinion, they desecrate the adolescent female body. I hope that when you come up from school to see me, you'll change en route." She offered maca-roons in a yellow Chinese bowl. "You've got to try one, darling. Strictly contraband from Paris."

"I thought that because of Joanna's competition you didn't go, Mummy."

"Humphrey went without me and brought these back . . . So that fine young woman left you! I must say, I liked her aw-fully. She had all sorts of nooks and crannies in her. Then of course there was her appearance, which was truly *formidable* — that high, wide, *noble* forehead and marvelous hair! And she did so wonderfully well with Joanna. Why did you get rid of her? You didn't explain on the telephone — I suppose Henry's such a miser he won't let you talk more than three minutes, even to your mama. My understanding was that she was a great suc-cess, but then, puff, that's the end of her!"

"She was Henry's idea from start to finish." Mrs. Drayton hadn't come to London to talk about Miss Cathcart, who had been over and done with for three whole days, and she certainly didn't want to talk about her in front of Joanna. "You know how he is when he gets the bit between his teeth. Last weekend he suddenly decided Joanna would do better away."

"Is that so?" Mrs. Beresford took a cigarette from an ivory box and lit it with a silver-fluted lighter. "I heard a rather curious story recently," she said, head cocked to one side. "You remember George Streatfield, don't you, Barbara? From Cannes in 1938."

"I didn't go to Cannes in 1938, Mummy."

"No? Well, *I* did, and I met George there and last week he came to dinner. He'd just been in the Argentine, staying with relations, and was full of tales of derring-do on the pampas and decadence in Buenos Aires. One tale I found rather intriguing was about the family's English nanny — this had happened some years ago, mind you — anyway, she ran off with the oldest son. By the time the parents tracked them down in Rio they were married. The woman dug in her heels — in effect, held the boy for ransom. She wouldn't agree to an annulment until they produced a hefty sum — in dollars, mind you. A quite unpleasant situation. Finally, though, cash in hand, she left on a boat to Southampton.

"After George had gone I remembered that your Miss Cathcart had come from that part of the world, so naturally, although she didn't really *look* like an adventuress to me, I had to wonder. In February when she was up with Joanna, and James joined us, he appeared to be quite smitten. So did *she,* as a matter of fact. To tell you the truth, I found them rather charming."

"Miss Cathcart's a governess, not a nanny," Joanna said quickly. "She doesn't like babies at all."

"That's a good point," said Mrs. Beresford, laughing gaily. "One mustn't let one's imagination get out of hand!" She tapped ash off her cigarette, uncrossed and recrossed pale legs, and said, "Tell me about Morehaven, Barbara. Was it one of the schools I liked, or not?"

"You never saw it."

"No? Of course we were living in Lausanne at the beginning of the war, weren't we, and it seemed wise to send you home, but you traveled back with Humphrey and I stayed on to pack. In those days it was considered rather an advanced school — Greek dancing, cold baths, fencing. What's it like now?"

"I know very little about it, Mummy," Mrs. Drayton said.

"Well, aren't you going down to have a look?"

"Henry's already paid the fees, so Joanna's going is an accomplished fact. There isn't much point in my looking at it. Besides, what would there be to look at in the holidays?"

"No students, I admit that, but one might learn something from the state of the furniture. I think it's *l'heure du whisky*," Mrs. Beresford added, getting to her feet. "I've booked a table at the Connaught for eight. Does that sound good to you two ladies? What about a drink now, Barbara? There's pretty much everything."

"Nothing, thank you. Perhaps later."

"What about you, Joanna, darling?"

"Don't give her anything, Mummy, please! She's simply too young."

But Mrs. Beresford ignored her daughter. "Have a little something, darling, do!"

"Have you got cider?"

"Afraid not. Cider does awful things to the alimentary tract. Is sherry any good to you?" She picked up a bottle of Amontillado.

"Please, Mummy, no!" Mrs. Drayton exclaimed. "I'd really rather you didn't give her any."

"Why ever not?" Mrs. Beresford poured half a glass. "It couldn't possibly do her any harm and it might actually cheer her up." She brought the glass to Joanna on the sofa. "You're looking so gloomy, poor pet! I don't understand why, really. I'd have thought you'd be quite pleased to get away from Widleigh. On the rare occasions I've been rash enough to go there it's seemed unremittingly grim. By the way, Barbara," she went on lightly, "did you ever do anything about the drawing room chairs — they were dark brown threadbare velvet, with antimacassars over the backs. When one sat down, clouds of dust wafted out of the cushions."

"You *know* I had them re-covered, Mummy! In green. You saw them yourself. You even said you liked the color."

"How long did it take to dig the money out of Henry?" said Mrs. Beresford with a little laugh. "Five years? Seven?"

Although she personally preferred not to be married, Mrs. Beresford wasn't opposed to marriage per se. To be amusing, single life required a certain sparkle and economic means, both of which she herself had in abundance. But despite a great deal of foreign exposure, quite nice hair, and pretty clothes, poor Barbara had little sparkle and no money; by the terms of the will of her late father she wouldn't receive any, either, until her mother was dead.

Gilbert Beresford died of a heart attack when his wife was twenty-seven and his daughter not quite four. Since a daughter is usually easier (if less fun) to bring up than a son, Mrs. Beresford always considered herself lucky. Furthermore, Barbara turned out to be a good traveler. By the age of six she had learned to chat up maids and bellboys in five languages. She hardly protested when one took her out of the lycée in Alexandria before Christmas, put her in a convent in Madrid for the winter term, and had her finish up the year in Geneva. She didn't make much fuss, either, about being left behind in Ireland with cousins or, failing that, with the housekeeper in Deauville, when one found another source of companionship, as one frequently did. In fact Barbara managed to grow up without aggravating her mother to speak of. She had a willing ear for melodrama; she was admiring, sympathetic, and loyal.

In April 1930, having spent the winter in Cannes, mother and daughter came to London for the Season and moved into Number Six Cardigan Square. Leaving Barbara to her own devices — after all, she was twenty-six — Mrs. Beresford plunged into an intense round of social activity, made all the more feverish by the arrival of her friend Maurice de Boulac, who had followed her over from Cannes. He had taken a suite round the corner in the Arlington Hotel, which he thought would be ideal for keeping an eye on her. As she told him on the day of his arrival, this was very silly of him. No one had the right to stop her from doing whatever she wanted to do! But Maurice de Boulac kept on trying, even so, which she increasingly resented, to the point where she found herself doing things almost deliberately, just to annoy him. Her affair with Adrian Fortescue being a case in point. Charming though he was, she mightn't have given Adrian a second glance if she hadn't been so furious with Maurice and his possessiveness.

Mrs. Beresford met Adrian through her daughter.

For the past few years Barbara had been painting seriously. She'd had a wonderful teacher in Florence, a good one in Paris, an indifferent one in Cannes. When she arrived in London she began looking about and several friends suggested Adrian Fortescue. He taught at the Central School of Art and took private students, too, if he found their work sufficiently interesting. With fear and trembling, Barbara, who painted seascapes out of her head — she had always found the sea soothing — took some of her canvases to show him. To her amazement he said he thought them promising and told her that although at the moment he had no other private students, if she liked she could come in the afternoons to his studio in Pimlico.

He was a little older and several inches taller than Barbara, who generally loomed over men. He had reddish hair and a luxuriant beard — she found beards, virtually unknown in her social circle, very attractive — and curling reddish hair on the backs of his broad hands as well.

After a week he told her, "Your cheekbones are remarkable. Why don't you stop what you're doing for a bit and let me make some sketches of you." He made two sketches before making love to her.

Barbara was quite used to lovers. Ever since she could remember she had observed her mother's comings and goings in rented flats and houses across Europe. However, Adrian was only *her* second lover, and much more accomplished than the first, an Italian, who'd fizzled, to her relief, since she hadn't really been in love with him. But she fell head over heels in love with Adrian.

They made love each weekday between two and half past five, and then Adrian would walk her home. The new leaves on the plane trees in the garden in the middle of Cardigan Square rustled with her happiness whenever she passed through.

One Friday evening as they turned into the square they ran into Mrs. Beresford and Maurice de Boulac on their way to cocktails in Cornelia Gardens. "This is Adrian Fortescue, my painting teacher, Mummy."

"So you're the one I make the check out to each week! Barbara never told me you were young and handsome. I'd been imagining a fat old bore like the teacher she had in Cannes last winter, who droned on interminably about pigment and tone. Perhaps, as a conscientious mother, I should come to Pimlico myself to see exactly what you're up to," Mrs. Beresford said gaily as she walked away.

The following Monday Barbara spent the morning having her hair done in a new style. She had her nails done, too, and chose a varnish called gloxinia which was the most exciting shade of pink she'd ever seen. She lunched lightly in a restaurant in Ebury Street, arrived at the studio at two sharp, and rang the bell. No one answered it.

It wasn't like Adrian not to be there, but perhaps he'd gone out to lunch with a patron. She went up to Victoria, bought a newspaper, came back, and rang again. Still no one answered.

For an hour she paced in front of the building before returning to Cardigan Square. The house was empty; her mother hadn't returned from luncheon with Maurice and it was the maid's day off. Barbara telephoned Adrian. The line was busy, which meant that he'd come in. But ten minutes later it was still busy, and ten minutes after that as well. She ran outside, hailed a cab, and went to Pimlico.

No one answered the doorbell.

Then it dawned on her that Adrian didn't answer the door, that he'd left the telephone off the hook, because he had another woman up there with him. With a heart of white-hot lead she dragged herself home.

The telephone was ringing when she got in. "Where's your mama?" Maurice de Boulac demanded. "I was expecting her for lunch."

"I haven't the faintest idea where my mother is. You can't expect me to keep track of her," Barbara replied, her voice rising. "She does what she pleases, don't you know that by now!" and she slammed down the receiver.

The telephone shrilled again immediately.

"When she comes back," said Maurice, "will you ask her to give me a ring?"

"What if she doesn't come back, what if she's in bed with a landscape painter half her age?" Barbara shouted. "If I were you, I wouldn't trust my mother further than I could throw her!"

At ten the next morning Barbara saw Adrian bound from a cab in the street below her bedroom window. He helped Mrs. Beresford out and stood beside her while she found her door key. After she entered the house he jumped back into the taxi, which drove off.

"Madam's very tired," the maid came to tell Barbara a few moments later. "She said to say she won't be having luncheon." So Barbara lunched alone. Afterward she went to Pimlico.

"I've come to collect my paints and brushes," she told Adrian, who answered the door this time.

"Aren't I a good enough teacher?" he said with a wry smile.

"On the contrary, I've learned a lot."

"Time to move on, is that it?"

"Yes, since you're so busy."

"It's my nature to be busy," he said softly.

Five nights later Barbara sat next to Henry Drayton at a dull dinner party. She noticed the careful way he peeled his peach. He seemed gentle. He was so much older than she was; perhaps he would be kind. He told her that he'd been back from India since January and was living alone on the Welsh border. He must be looking for a wife, Barbara thought. Why else would he have come to London and squashed his feet into patent leather evening shoes? My mother would hate Herefordshire, she'd leave me alone there, I'd be safe.

When Henry asked her to go dancing after the dinner party she accepted, and when he brought her home at three in the morning she invited him in and led him upstairs to her bed. He was touchingly surprised and pleased and grateful. He told her she was the first real girl he'd ever been to bed with, unless one counted Anglo-Indians.

"Doesn't one?"

"I don't think so," he said sadly.

They had dinner together six nights running and always ended up in her bed in the empty house. (Adrian, Mrs. Beresford had quickly discovered, was very demanding of her time.) At dawn after the seventh night together, as he was tying the laces of his patent leather shoes, Henry asked Barbara to marry him and she said yes. He came that afternoon to take her to Garrards to have his mother's engagement ring altered to fit her, and before dinner that evening he cornered Mrs. Beresford long enough to tell her their news.

What with Maurice on the one hand and Adrian on the other, she'd been having such a hectic spring that she'd hardly noticed Henry Drayton's comings and goings at Cardigan Square. But one June evening, as she dashed through the hall on her way out to Covent Garden to see *Così fan tutte* with Adrian, Henry intercepted her. "Got a minute?" he said grimly.

"I suppose just one," Mrs. Beresford said, doing her best to smile playfully. Adrian loathed being kept waiting. In her mind's eye she could see him marching up and down outside the opera house, getting crosser and crosser. Well, she'd put herself out for him a good deal lately — she'd lent him money she knew he'd never pay back, and yesterday, by not letting her get out of bed in time, he'd made her miss her massage appointment in Hans Crescent.

Henry looked so old-fashioned in possibly the very first dinner jacket ever created. Oh God, she thought in sudden horror, he's after *me*! and for an instant she considered escaping through the kitchen into the mews. But he went on, "I'd like a word with you about Barbara and myself. As she's legally of age, we don't require your consent, but it would be nice if you could be there."

"Be where?" Mrs. Beresford asked politely.

"St. George's. We're getting married at three o'clock on the twenty-seventh. That's a Monday."

Mrs. Beresford gazed at him, dumbfounded, but the next moment she had collected herself enough to say, "Today's the tenth, so that means in seventeen days' time."

Henry nodded. "Exactly."

"Let's see what else I have on that day." She felt in her evening bag for her glasses, which she found, and her diary. The diary, she realized, must be in her bedroom. "Excuse me," she said, turning up the stairs. "I'll be back in a second." She spotted the book on her dressing table and descended with it to the hall. "I've got nothing down for the twenty-seventh until eight in the evening, when I'm giving a dinner party for the Red Cross Ball." In a reasonable tone she went on, "Isn't this rushing things rather? I mean, how well do you know my daughter, and *she* knows nothing about India. In fact she's never been in the tropics at all. As a child she was rather anemic, and I imagine in the wrong climate she could become so again."

"Did I say anything about India? I've left the regiment. I've come into a place in the country and we'll live there."

"Barbara's never been in the country to speak of, either," Mrs. Beresford murmured. Henry Drayton was staring at her. He didn't appear to approve of her in the least. "What sort of place is it?" she asked.

"You can come and see for yourself if you want to."

"I've hardly got time if the wedding's two weeks from Monday. Why Monday, incidentally?"

"Because that's the soonest the banns can be read, and St. George's happens to be free that day."

"Is there any reason why you can't wait a week or two longer?" Mrs. Beresford said.

"I've got to be back at Widleigh for the haymaking."

"Why not get married *after* the haymaking's over?"

"Then comes the harvest."

"I see."

At that moment Barbara appeared, wearing a chiffon dress from Fouré. She positioned herself beside Henry, and her mother noted that she was half a head taller than he was. "Congratulations, darling! Henry tells me you two are engaged!"

Barbara frowned as if she had one of her bad headaches. "Yes, Mummy, we are."

That Fouré dress looked all wrong, Mrs. Beresford saw. Instead of fitting over the bosom like a second skin, it hung dispiritedly, like a garment one saw for sale on a dummy in the window of a thrift shop. Under her mother's scrutiny Barbara blushed.

"I imagine there's a lot to be done," observed Mrs. Beresford.

"There is," Henry agreed. He continued to look unsympathetic. "I've made lists."

"That sounds sensible. Are there some for me?"

"Yes, several. I'll come round in the morning and we'll go over them. I wouldn't want to hold you up any longer now. I'm aware from Barbara of the busy life you lead," and he nodded, dismissing her.

Extraordinary man! Mrs. Beresford thought. "I hope you'll both be very happy," she said as she put her diary into her evening bag and snapped it shut. "I have to say, though, this comes as rather a surprise!"

Despite a strong intimation that she wasn't going to get Henry to warm to her, through force of habit Mrs. Beresford did her best to win him over. (She told Maurice and Adrian that for the next fortnight she was *fully* occupied; she must concentrate *solely* on Barbara.) On the grounds that they needed time to go over lists together, she had several meals alone with Henry at a terrifically expensive restaurant, for which she paid. And while he took Barbara off to the country to show her her future home, she rushed from florist to church to caterer in a chauffeured car, hired for the duration. But for all her time, trouble, and money, Henry remained just as cold and disapproving. Finally, out of wounded pride, she switched to mockery, firing her opening volley at the prenuptial dinner, where she toasted "Henry Howard Hannington Drayton, my future son-in-law, slayer of tiger, wild boar, and panther, conscript of the empire on which the sun never sets."

The week that Henry and Barbara were off on their Dorset honeymoon (a week was all they could squeeze in before the haymaking was expected to begin) turned out to be beastly. First Mrs. Beresford found herself missing Barbara dreadfully. (She hadn't anticipated this.) Next Maurice went storming back to France in a jealous fury, and then she had a flaming row over money with Adrian. The morning afterwards, on her third cup of coffee, she decided that since she was feeling so down it might be wise to leave London for a few days — and Widleigh was the obvious choice. After all, as a conscientious mother, she ought to see what Barbara had got herself into, and while she was away, Adrian would have a chance to miss her and regret all the horrid things he'd said. So she telephoned Widleigh and spoke to the butler, who told her that yes, Major and Mrs. Drayton were expected back for lunch. Then she had her maid pack a bag and she was off in a taxi to Paddington.

But as she sat in the Hereford train she discovered that being away from London made her feel even worse. She toyed with the idea of jumping out at Oxford and heading back in order to attempt some sort of truce with Adrian. Then she thought better of it. Having embarked on a strategy, she would be foolish to abandon it before giving it a decent chance to pay off.

She arrived at Widleigh to find that the honeymooners had been back only an hour and that the suitcases containing Barbara's trousseau still stood in the hall. She shook hands briskly with her son-in-law and kissed her daughter, whose confusion on seeing her mother at such short notice was so tremendous she could barely speak.

"I lunched on the train," Mrs. Beresford told them, "so in terms of food, I'm fine. What I would like, though, is a bed to lie down on."

Barbara recovered enough to lead her upstairs, along a corridor, and into a grand but rather shabby guest room. "They call this the Prince's room," she said, proud that at last she had something to show off to her mother. Her father, of whom she had little memory, hadn't had an ancestral home. As the younger son of a younger son, he had grown up in a square brick house in Chiswick, which had since become a pub. There had been no ancestral home in Mrs. Beresford's immediate past, either. And after so much traipsing about Europe, three centuries in one place appealed to Barbara. "The Prince of Wales accepted an invitation to a shooting weekend," she explained, "and Henry's grandmother did this room up for him, only after all that effort, he never came."

"Disgusting old man!" exclaimed Mrs. Beresford with a shudder. "Once, at the Cottesmore Hunt Ball, he pinched my bottom. I wouldn't want to sleep in a bed *he'd* slept in!" She went to the dressing table, removed her hat, grimaced at her reflection in the mirror, put on some rouge though none was needed. Then she collapsed into an armchair by a window that gave onto a view of deer grazing in a deep summer park. But she didn't notice the view. "I've had a horrid week, darling. It's awful how I've missed having you to talk to! Why did you have to go and marry someone who lives so far away!" and she launched into an account of her trials with Maurice and Adrian.

Barbara listened to her mother's chronicle of woe; and when it was finished Mrs. Beresford turned wide blue eyes on the daughter who for so long had offered sympathy whenever she'd needed it. None was forthcoming. Barbara sat gaunt, ungiving, silent on the Prince's bed. Mrs. Beresford sighed. She ought to have followed her intuition and got off the train at Oxford. There was no earthly point in her being here!

Thereafter mother and daughter saw each other infrequently. Barbara would come up to London a few times a year and once, when Mrs. Beresford lacked a traveling companion, she invited Barbara to go to Paris with her for a week. However, she soon found lots of Parisian friends dying to entertain her; she really hadn't needed Barbara after all!

Whenever they met, Mrs. Beresford made it clear that in her view the tiger slayer and the mausoleum (Henry and his ancestral home) were absurdities from which anyone in her right mind would extricate herself.

Barbara, who had married in order to escape her mother's casual malice, had known very well whom she was leaving; she had had little idea, however, about whom she was going to. But she had sensed Henry's loneliness and rigidity and hoped that marriage would ease these, allowing trust and kindness to grow between them. (Since she had never felt loved, she didn't dare aspire to deserve love.) She hoped for children, thinking they would nurture this trust and kindness. But rather than forging a bond, James's arrival, fourteen months after the wedding, seemed to drive a wedge between his parents. *Whose was he?* That was the question. Henry wanted him for Widleigh, Barbara for herself. And Joanna, the product of a rare encounter the night after seven-year-old James had left for Winterfields, drove them still further apart.

Shame kept Barbara with her husband, whom she had deliberately seduced in order to achieve a desperately desired end; shame and, more important, an enduring dread of the damage her mother might yet do her if given the chance.

War provided a distraction: Barbara discovered that in the face of national peril, personal misery became more manageable.

In the spring of 1940 a small private school called St. Bartolph's was evacuated from the south coast, facing France and the Germans, to Widleigh, facing Wales. The house easily absorbed thirty little boys and four masters. Mrs. Marshall, the headmaster's wife, spotted an idle Barbara — Nanny Hastings had taken charge of Joanna the moment she came from the hospital; James was at boarding school; Henry was busy night and day with the Home Guard, growing beets and turnips and keeping the Herefordshire Hunt foxhounds alive. She put her to work darning socks, drying nettles, turning sheets sides to middle, and performing dozens of other essential tasks of which, hitherto, Barbara had had no notion. For the first time in her life she felt useful, and as Mrs. Marshall kept up a continuous flow of rumination, speculation, and humorous commentary, Barbara, whose principal childhood companions had been concierges, felt at ease if not at home.

But in the early months of 1945, as Allied armies flooded across Europe, Mrs. Marshall went back to Sussex with her school and Barbara was bereft. Two days after V-E Day, she wrote a letter to her husband saying that after fifteen years their marriage had ground to a halt and she was leaving. She packed a suitcase for herself and one for Joanna, slipped the letter under the smoking room door, and, before the morning mist had risen from the river, took her six-year-old daughter and set off. In the early afternoon they reached London, to find streets still thronged with crowds celebrating peace and victory, and took a taxi to the Arlington. Barbara hadn't telephoned ahead to say that she was coming. She wanted the second momentous decision of her life to be as much of a surprise to her mother as the first had been.

She found her with three male luncheon guests: Cousin Humphrey and two admirers. One Barbara remembered from Paris in 1935. The other, a much younger man, was a new involvement whom Barbara had not met before.

"You should have let me know you were coming," said Mrs. Beresford with undisguised displeasure. Barbara unannounced was bad enough, but accompanied by the little girl was worse yet. Sometimes, provided they were tidy, children could conceivably be an asset to a party, but after many hours on the train Joanna wasn't *at all* tidy. "Come in if you must. We're having coffee in the sitting room."

Humphrey, who was invariably kind to children, abandoned his coffee and took his brandy and Joanna to the window seat to play Counties of England. He was an elaborately handsome, immaculately groomed man of fifty, but Barbara remembered him as a scruffy schoolboy playing Counties of England with *her* in Switzerland, before the First World War.

But finally, at half past four, after expressing extravagant praise for her food and gratitude for her attentions, the guests left and Mrs. Beresford turned to her daughter to ask what she was doing in London.

"I've left Henry," Barbara replied.

Her mother stared incredulously. "Don't say you've got a boyfriend I haven't heard about!"

"Nothing like that, Mummy."

"Then why this mad dash all of a sudden?"

"It *wasn't* all of a sudden. I've been thinking about doing it for years, only I just didn't have the courage until now."

"I see." Mrs. Beresford frowned. "Of course I don't at all, really. What do you expect to live on?" She added loudly, "You can't live on *air*!"

"Please, Mummy," Barbara begged, "I don't want Joanna to hear." Joanna was still on the window seat and now that her partner at cards had deserted her she was looking through a pile of scrapbooks that highlighted her grandmother's social career.

"She's going to start asking questions very soon . . . Is James included in the party?"

"He's at Eton until the term ends."

"And then? Where do you expect to live? You can't stay here. I've only got one spare bed, as you well know, and you can't stay upstairs, either, if you haven't got the wherewithal to pay the bill."

"I know it's a lot to ask," said Barbara, "but would you be willing to lend me some money? I shan't need much. I'll find us a place in the country. Henry will have to make some sort of financial arrangement for the children and once we're settled I'll get a job and pay you back."

"*You* get a job! What kind of a job?"

"I'm not illiterate, Mummy."

"Even if you found a job, you could never support yourself on what you earned, let alone save enough to pay me back," said Mrs. Beresford as she poured herself some more brandy. "I shouldn't be doing this — I'll get a splitting headache later — but you're upsetting me so, I have to. Your lack of forethought simply amazes me! You say you've been thinking of leaving Henry for years, and yet, when you finally do, it's without having made any prior provision whatsoever! Or is it that at age forty-two you're expecting your mother to take care of you? During all the time you spent waiting for courage to come, you might have come up with a better plan than that!"

Barbara took a tiny room for her and Joanna on the fifth

floor of the hotel and they spent their days going from one jeweler to another until Barbara sold her engagement ring for four hundred and fifty pounds to Haddons in the Burlington Arcade. Then she telephoned her old Morehaven friend, Phyllis Buxton, who lived in Inverness-shire. Barbara had never been to Inverness-shire, nor did she know Phyllis Buxton well anymore, but Phyllis was the only person she could think of who might help and Inverness-shire was a long way from both Widleigh and the Arlington. "Husbands can be dreadful," Phyllis had said. "Mine was. Do by all means come! I've got a cottage standing empty in the village. It's wedged between the post office and the Nonconformist chapel and it's primitive, but we're into May now, so it shouldn't be too bad. I'll meet the overnight train."

On their last afternoon when Barbara and Joanna were going down to the lobby to pay the bill, Mrs. Beresford stepped into the crowded lift. Her white hair curled softly round her raw-silk turban, her make-up, applied with brush and magnifying glass, was perfect, and her eyes, in the midst of such artistry, were a most brilliant blue.

"Good afternoon, madam," the lift boy called out to her.

"Good afternoon, Patrick!" Mrs. Beresford replied. "How's your dear mother today? Better, I hope?" and she smiled her lovely smile, making Patrick feel that even though his mother wasn't at all better, her illness was somehow justified because it was of interest to this exquisite creature.

Joanna struggled through a forest of legs to seize her grandmother's hand. "Granny, you didn't ask us down to see you yesterday, or the day before either!"

"That's because you were so terribly busy, I knew you wouldn't have time for poor old me," Mrs. Beresford replied, quick as a whip. She laughed and the other people in the lift laughed too at the absurdity of such a charming lady being either poor or old.

When they reached the lobby everyone held back so that Mrs. Beresford, leading Joanna by the hand, could get out first. "I was wondering what you were up to," she said when Barbara joined them. "As I told Henry, you came here, explained yourself most inadequately, and rushed off again."

"*Henry* rang *you?*"

"Why, yes, indeed! The night before last. A major event! He was more forthcoming than I've ever known him, too. As a matter of fact he was quite chatty! Said that since the winter you'd been increasingly strange. You'd been taking long walks — in the past you'd never been much of a walker — and crying at lunch. Given that we were defeating the Germans at last, after almost six years, and most people were simply euphoric, naturally Henry thought this was odd behavior. So when the two of you vanished last Thursday he thought at first you might have pushed Joanna into the Wye and jumped in after her. But someone reported having seen you get on a train at Hereford Station, so then he rang me.

"He wanted to know, had you seemed rational?" Mrs. Beresford said.

"What did you tell him?" Barbara demanded in a high, funny voice.

"That I doubted you'd throw yourself into any river as you lacked the spunk, but that you seemed to have no idea where your next meal was coming from — certainly not from me, I assured him!" Mrs. Beresford put on her gloves and nodded at a bellboy who darted up to her. "Ask Standish to get me a taxi, please. Well, what *are* you up to?" she added, turning back to Barbara.

"I'm about to pay our hotel bill."

"Really? With what?"

"I sold my engagement ring."

"Henry's not going to like that a bit! It was a Drayton treasure."

Barbara nodded. "I'm afraid so."

"And now I trust you've come to your senses and you're on your way back to Herefordshire."

"I'm not going back, I told you that! I'm going up to Phyllis Buxton's in Scotland."

"So you intend to divorce Henry? Don't tell me he's been adulterous!"

"Not that I know of, and without grounds, as they say, I realize I shan't be able to divorce him, as I'd very much like to do. But even if, legally, we have to remain married, I don't have to live with him."

"True, I suppose, but what about Joanna?"

"She's coming with me."

"In that case," said Mrs. Beresford with a shrug, "there's something you should be prepared for. Henry mightn't mind about *your* leaving, but he minds very much about your taking Joanna and he intends to get her back."

"But I'm her mother, she has to be with me!" Barbara's eyes widened in alarm.

"Has to? Who says so? He's a very determined man, is Henry," said Mrs. Beresford dryly. "I don't envy you a bit! My advice is, go straight back to Widleigh, because if you don't go of your own accord he'll make things very difficult for you later. Lawyers cost a lot of money and Henry will *hate* paying their bills, but he'll do so if he has to, and *you'll* suffer the consequences." She smiled pityingly. "I really *have* to go. They must have found a cab for me by now. May *I* give *you* a kiss this time, Joanna, darling?" She stooped to kiss the little girl. "Make sure Mummy feeds you properly in savage Scotland! Good-bye!"

For a moment Barbara stared after her mother, disbelieving, then she ran out of the hotel in pursuit. Mrs. Beresford was already seated in a taxi. "Wait a minute," Barbara cried, wrenching open the door.

"I thought we'd said our good-byes."

"Don't you want to know where I'm going? The address, I mean? If you've got a bit of paper I'll write it down."

"Why don't you send me a postcard once you're settled. You're making this poor cab driver hold up the traffic."

Barbara stumbled back onto the pavement as if she had been slapped and Standish reached round her to shut the door. As the taxi moved off Mrs. Beresford raised one gloved hand. She might have been the Queen Empress, bidding farewell to the blurred masses of India.

Now, five years later, Mrs. Beresford tinkled the ice in her glass and examined the freshly varnished nails of her left hand. "It amazes me that Henry's willing to pay Joanna's school fees," she drawled. "Morehaven didn't come cheap even in your day, Barbara. I hate to think what it costs now."

"Less than a governess's salary," Mrs. Drayton said quickly.

"That I understand, but Henry got some personal benefit from Miss Cathcart's presence, wouldn't you say?" With a smile Mrs. Beresford got up to pour herself another drink. "Still nothing for you, Barbara? . . . You know it's still a mystery to me why you went back to Henry. I suppose you simply weren't determined enough — faced with the prospect of supporting yourself, you simply caved in. Given that someone had always doled it out to you, you thought that money grew on trees. The discovery that it didn't must have come as a dreadful shock."

In a very low voice Mrs. Drayton said, "The judge ordered me to return Joanna. You heard. You were there."

"Yes, but *you* needn't have gone back, too. You should have grown mushrooms in someone's garage or learned to file documents or type. You should have got used to paying your own way. *Then* you would have developed some self-respect."

Mrs. Drayton stared at the carpet. "The whole year I was in

Scotland," she said, "Henry prevented me from seeing James. If I'd sent Joanna back to Widleigh, he wouldn't have let me see her, either. They'd both have turned out as eccentric as he is."

"Come now, Barbara, it wouldn't have been that bad! Henry did bring in Miss Cathcart, don't forget. *She'd* have been the mitigating influence and meanwhile *you'd* have had a life of your own." Mrs. Beresford sipped her whiskey. "Do you want your frock ironed for tonight? If so, I'll get the chambermaid to do it right away." Mrs. Drayton didn't answer. She was staring into the fire. "Do you or don't you want your frock ironed?" her mother repeated.

"I didn't bring one," said Mrs. Drayton looking up at her mother at last. "Henry gives me two hundred pounds a year to cover all my personal expenses, which is just enough for one to avoid being a public embarrassment. I didn't bring a frock to change into because I haven't had a new one for two years, and *that* was a summer frock I'd freeze to death in now. Is that what you call money growing on trees?"

"I'm not familiar with the details of Henry's financial situation," Mrs. Beresford pointed out. "Two hundred pounds may well be all he can afford. What I'm saying is, there's all the difference in the world between being handed money and earning it oneself." She took a cigarette from the ivory box and lit it.

Mrs. Drayton jumped up from her chair, dislodging her handbag, which fell upside down, spilling its contents across the carpet.

"Why the terrible hurry?"

"Joanna and I are going to have supper at Lyons Corner House and we'd better get there before they close."

"What *are* you talking about? I thought we'd agreed to go to the Connaught. My treat. Joanna was looking forward to it, weren't you, darling?"

Having recovered some of the coins from under the chairs

and the sofa, Joanna took them to the window seat and lined them up according to their dates. Invariably her mother got upset when she came to visit at the Arlington. On one most terrible occasion, owing to something Granny had said about James, she had thrown herself weeping to the floor and had beaten her fists on the carpet. The thing was, she always wanted Granny to pay attention to her worries; but Granny didn't *like* worries, especially not other people's, so Mummy ought to try to keep hers to herself.

"Remember what you just said," Mrs. Drayton was shouting. "That I should get used to paying my own way. I *can* afford Lyons, I *can't* afford the Connaught!"

"You always get so *excited*," said Mrs. Beresford with a sigh. "You should go and lie down now, then you'll feel calmer. Joanna and I can entertain each other very well." She turned to her granddaughter with a smile. "We always do, because we're so much alike, aren't we, darling? We'll play some Schubert duets."

Mrs. Drayton's face was white and she was trembling. "Do you *want* to stay here with your grandmother, Joanna?"

Joanna didn't answer. She bit her bottom lip and concentrated on setting her coins in order.

"Off you go, Barbara!" Mrs. Beresford ordered. "We'll see you downstairs at a quarter to eight." She threw her cigarette into the fire, went over to the piano, and began striking chords.

~~~~~~~~~~~~~~~~~~~~~~~~~~~~~~~~~~~~~~~

Chapter 7

Widleigh

AT MISS CATHCART'S DEPARTURE a fortnight still remained of
the Easter holidays. Joanna's commitment to maintaining the
routine alone wavered and collapsed. She threw *A Tale of Two
Cities* (her holiday reading) into the back of the schoolroom
cupboard and left the pages for the last half of April blank in
her leatherbound diary; Beethoven and Mozart got short shrift.
Neither of her parents, who were more preoccupied even than
usual, seemed to notice.

In the morning she would go to the garden to help Pickering
bed out wallflower and cabbage seedlings, or to the kitchen
where Agnes generally found a job for her to do. In the afternoon she went up on the moor to make believe that she was
Richard II, poor sorrowing king, come from Ireland and passing, captive, through the Marches on his way south. She en-
treated her nobles, exhorted her soldiers, pleaded with her
captors, but in vain. In the end, inevitably, came her abdication.
The speech she gave before her heinous death at Pontefract
moved the sheep, foraging around her on the hillside, to flap
their tails in sympathy.

Once she went into the silent room with the red-flocked
walls. She saw bare hangers on the rail in the wardrobe and
empty bureau drawers, half open on their grooves, and a dustsheet over the bed. Apart from a faint scent of cloves mingled

with lilies of the valley, no trace of her governess remained. She imagined her in dove-gray suit and hat to match, hurrying along London pavements to be interviewed for new positions. Would the next child learn to give massages? Every morning Joanna expected a letter, but none came.

After a week with the Burns boy in Somerset, James reappeared, but he'd only stopped in to drop off his car, having run out of petrol coupons, and to get clean clothes. He would be off by train to Lincolnshire in the morning, to stay with George Lifton, another Etonian friend.

"It was she who gave life at Widleigh meaning. With her gone, we're mere shadows, phantoms," he said without a hint of irony as he sat in his room with Joanna, in front of the empty grate. It wasn't cold enough for a fire, yet it wasn't warm enough to do comfortably without one.

Shadows, is that all we are? If she's not here to peg us down, will we waft away? Joanna wondered. And she saw herself drifting over the Brecon Beacons, across the breadth of Wales, and out to the Irish Sea.

"It's so sad here. Please don't go away again," she begged, "or if you have to, take me with you!"

"You don't know the Liftons. They invited *me,* not me and my little sister. But I'll be back in three days."

"James?"

"Yes, Joanna."

"Why did you go off to Gordon's so early in the morning? Had you and Daddy had a row?"

"I can't remember," James mumbled.

"You were in such a hurry, you didn't even wait till I was up. You'd never left without telling me before."

"Once I'd decided to go, there wasn't any point in hanging around."

"Had Gordon invited you?"

"Not exactly, but the Burnses aren't like the Draytons. They always welcome one, with or without an invitation."

After a moment's silence Joanna said, "What happened at that wedding, James?"

"Rosemary got married. Toasts were made. A good many people had too much to drink."

"Why did everyone come home so cross?"

"Why this interrogation?" James said testily.

"Because for almost as long as I can remember I've had Miss Cathcart, and the day after the wedding Daddy said she had to go, and the day after that she went."

"Your problem," James burst out, "is that you're used to having attention whenever you want it. You're *spoiled!* Before I went to Winterfields *I* didn't have a resident entertainer, believe me! I had lessons with Miss Hilary for three hours every morning and after lunch I was on my own. No one took *me* bird watching or played the piano with me, or even noughts-and-crosses! I considered myself lucky if someone read to me for ten minutes at bedtime. You've had everything your own way, admit it, and now that you're a bit bored and lonely, you come whining to me. Only I happen to have a great many things to do before tomorrow, so you'd better get out of here and stop wasting my time!" He jumped up and wrenched the door open. "Since you require so much attention, go and play your bloody piano, pretend you're Wanda Landowska, electrify the multitudes, make them roar for encores. Or if you lack that much imagination, how about helping Rhys muck out the stables? Rhys simply loves to chat." As she ran out he yelled after her, "I don't give a good goddamn how you entertain yourself — pick your nose, suck your thumb, for all I care — just stop buggering *me!*"

In her own room she threw herself down on the bed and buried her tear-streaked face in the pillow. James had never shouted at her like that before.

Three days later, when the telephone rang during tea, Joanna was sent to the smoking room to answer it. "My plans have changed," James told her. "I shan't be coming home — I'm going on to London. I've got enough clothes, Mrs. Lifton very kindly had my laundry done."

"Are you going to Granny's? I'll meet you there, then," Joanna said, hopes rising. "She'll fit me in, too. I'll sleep on the floor, I don't care."

But James wasn't going to the Arlington, he was going to yet another friend's and *she* wasn't invited.

"Aren't you ever coming back here?"

"Only when I feel like it."

She asked drearily, "Do you want to speak to Mummy or Daddy?"

"Can't *you* give them the message?"

"We should have the telephone number," she said, "so that if there's a disaster here we can let you know."

"I'd rather *not* know," James said, and hung up.

Joanna returned to the dining room and delivered the message. "What's the friend's name?" said Mrs. Drayton.

"I forgot to ask."

"Since you didn't get the telephone number, either, his whereabouts are unknown."

"That's exactly his intention, I imagine," Henry Drayton remarked.

On the last afternoon of the holidays, as Joanna lay in the bracken and looked towards Wales, she saw horses, out to grass for the summer, galloping across distant fields, a double-decker bus buffeting along a country road a half-mile away, and her father striding up the cart track leading across the moor. He had Dolly and Grizelda with him.

She felt like a bird wheeling very high above the ground, seeing everything and yet not being seen. But then her father glanced up and saw her. Watching carefully for rabbit holes, he came through the bracken to join her.

"Quite a climb," he panted, "though it's nothing to you, I don't suppose, with your young lungs and legs." He seated himself beside her and was joined immediately by the dogs. He took a small chocolate bar out of his pocket, broke it in two, and gave half to his daughter. "The Welsh hills are much grander than the English," he observed.

Joanna remembered him making conversation with Miss Cathcart, but never, hitherto, with her.

"Do you often come up here?" he added, rather formally, as if they were in a Hereford teashop or at a church fête.

"Only since Miss Cathcart left. She didn't care for the climb."

"Made her pant, too, did it?"

For a long while they sat in silence. As the clouds came and went across the sun, the hillside was sometimes in shadow, sometimes in brilliant light.

"Odd without her," Henry said softly at last. Narrowing his eyes he added, "I wonder how I'll get used to not having her here . . ."

Joanna was getting pins and needles in her legs so she shifted a little and disturbed Dolly, who got to her feet and shook herself, ready to resume the pursuit of field mice and rabbits. Henry glanced at his watch.

"It's ten past four and we're late for tea," he said, sighing. "It's so delightful up here that I forgot the time."

They set off down the hill and far below them the river ran now black, now silver, as the sun dodged in and out of clouds.

"If and when James *is* at home," Henry burst out all of a sudden, "he locks himself in his room and scribbles spy stories!"

"You mean, tales of mystery and imagination," Joanna corrected him.

"The point is, he's *in,* not *out.* At his age, I made the most of every moment I had here. Everything about Widleigh interested me — even frozen pipes in January. But James notices nothing, *he doesn't care!* Although I've asked him, pleaded with him, *ordered* him to come round the farm with me, he hasn't, not once, since last August, and here we are — it's almost May! Of course his attitude reflects his mother's entirely ... I remember the first time I ever brought her here ... It was June and the place was looking the way it had in my mind's eye in India — with two more years to sweat out before I got home leave — lush and green and cared for. Inside I showed her all the treasures, turned on all the lights, so she could see the pictures properly. She stopped in front of each in turn and eventually, with a long look on her face, she said, 'There isn't a single twentieth-century painting in this whole collection!' "

Joanna began counting her steps. She had reached twenty when her father continued. "That was only the beginning, mind you, when we were engaged. After we were married things got much worse. Everything was so old-fashioned, she said, or in poor taste. Frankly, I'd never thought about what sort of taste things were in. They'd always been there, that was what mattered, and compared with the rattan chairs in Indian army messes, which stuck bamboo splinters into one's bottom each time one sat down, the chairs in the drawing room were positively luxurious! Problem was, though, they were *brown* and she couldn't live with brown. They had to be recovered instantly! What she wanted was to turn Widleigh into one of those pastel flats she was used to. If I hadn't watched her like a hawk, she'd have installed a fake fireplace — a gas jet between plaster logs — in the drawing room. She even wanted two palm trees in the hall! I soon stopped that one. I told her, 'This isn't Monte Carlo. We've got three gardeners working ten hours a day, six days a week, to grow flowers native to the climate. Why don't you start cutting and arranging some of them?' " He sighed deeply. "I'm afraid your mother was dead set against Widleigh from the start."

They had reached the stile that led over the high wall into the park. Joanna scrambled up the steps and down the other side, but her father paused at the top of the wall. Below, in the middle of the park, stood the great house, mullioned windows shining. Pear blossom billowed white in the kitchen garden, bluebells carpeted the conifer plantation beyond the stables, celandines gleamed gold in bright spring grass. "I couldn't ask for anything better than this," said Henry, "so why should James?"

That night Joanna dreamed she was fleeing through Paddington Station. She raced past Lost Property, Refreshments, News, ducked into Ladies' Cloaks, and locked herself in a stall; there she waited, pressed against the wall, staring with dread at the dirty cement floor.

She heard a woman's voice shriek, "You can't hide from me, you're in here somewhere, I know it! If you won't come out of your own accord, I'll make you!" The door to the stall she was in swung open; her mother loomed immensely in the dim light. She seized Joanna and dragged her out to the middle of the station. "Coward!" she screamed, and shook her violently. People hurrying past stopped and, forgetting the trains they were supposed to be catching, joined in. "Coward! Coward!" they screamed, too.

Joanna fought to escape, but her mother held her back firmly. She fought harder, and this time she sprang awake.

She sat up and switched on the bedside light. Twenty to four, the clock said. The gray uniform hung on a hanger on the front of the wardrobe door. The trunk stood packed at the foot of the bed.

She switched off the light but sleep refused to come again, and so, as the blackbirds began their song of joy and heartbreak, she got out of bed and went to the window to watch the dawn seep across the park.

Later when she went down to breakfast, she found her mother sitting alone at the dining room table.

"Mummy, what are *you* doing here?"

"You don't sound very pleased to see me . . ."

"It's just that you always have breakfast in your room," Joanna mumbled.

"Well, your father just sits behind the paper and James, who got in very late, isn't likely to be chatty, so I thought, since it's your last morning, you might appreciate some company."

Joanna helped herself to porridge. She poured milk over it; then she sprinkled sugar over the milk and watched it sink out of sight.

"That's an odd way to go about things," remarked her mother. "Sugar goes on first and *then* milk. I suppose Miss Cathcart was always so busy talking that she never noticed your table manners. It's a good thing you're going to be with people who *do* take notice! I'm afraid that compared with other girls your age, you're quite uncivilized. If I were you, I'd look for a reliable sort of girl at Morehaven, one I could watch and model myself after."

Joanna stirred her porridge round and round.

"Eat some, darling, don't just play!"

"I'm not hungry."

"Have some Weetabix instead."

"I don't want Weetabix. I said I'm not hungry. I don't want anything at all." She stood up.

"Sit down! You have to eat *something*," said her mother, and she brought Joanna a poached egg from the hot plate, just as the door opened and Henry Drayton walked in.

"Good morning," he said gruffly, helping himself to porridge. He sat down and within seconds was immersed in the *Times* racing page. A few moments later James appeared.

"Bearing up okay?" he said to his sister with a nod. The night before Joanna had waited up for him and when, at ten o'clock, he still hadn't come home, her mother had made her turn off her light. Eventually she heard him coming up the stairs as the grandfather clock in the library struck twelve. She waited for him to come in but he didn't even pause at her door; he walked straight on down the passage to his room. Only two rides in the green car, no walks, no stories, not a single matinee. What talks they'd had had almost all been quarrels.

Now he took two eggs, bacon, and fried bread from the hot plate and sat down. He looked tired. "Today's the great day, isn't it, Joanna," he said. "You're plunging into the world of competition and I hope you're primed for the ordeal. Don't believe them when they tell you it's how you play the game that matters. *Winning* is what matters — forget the bloody game!" He picked up his knife and fork and began to eat rapidly.

"How was London?" said Joanna.

"Fine."

"You only just arrived and you have to go back there. Why didn't you come earlier?"

"My dear Miss Twenty Questions," James drawled, "won't you tell me about all the tremendous excitements that occurred while I was away?"

"There weren't any."

James shrugged. "In that case, how clever of me not to be here!"

Henry Drayton poured himself more coffee, put down the *Times*, picked up the *Telegraph*, and opened it to the racing page.

"Henry," Mrs. Drayton said, "I'd like to go to Hereford Station with all of you. I'd like to see Joanna off."

"You should have told me so earlier, then we might have made arrangements," Henry replied. "As it is, there won't be room. We're picking up the Cooper boys on the way, remember, and all their stuff."

"I know, but if Joanna sits on my knee, we'll all squash in somehow."

"I tell you, there won't be room," Henry said with relish, it seemed.

Mrs. Drayton appealed to Joanna. "You want me to come, don't you, darling?" But Joanna examined the flower pattern on her plate, as she had a thousand times before, through a thousand altercations, and said nothing.

"All right, if that's all the response I get," said her mother bitterly, "I'd better go and see to things upstairs. When you've finished your breakfast, send Rhys and Pickering for the trunks, would you please, Henry?" As she passed her husband's chair she grasped the carved back and gave it a shake, but Henry, who was reading about heavy-going at Chester, paid no attention.

When Joanna went up to her room she found her mother standing next to her trunk, holding a key ring with one new, shiny key attached to it.

"I'm about to lock now. Is everything in?"

"I didn't pack it, you did, so you must know."

Mrs. Drayton knelt to smooth a sheet of tissue paper over a folded blouse. "I'd been hoping that your last few days at home would be fun," she said, "but they weren't, were they?" Their expedition to the amusement park in Shrewsbury had been disastrous. Despite a strong protest from Joanna, Mrs. Drayton had invited Princess Gabriella, who'd been sick on the Dodg.'ems, so they'd had to come straight home. Their cinema outing hadn't been much better. The film Mrs. Drayton had chosen had sent Joanna to sleep in twenty minutes. "I don't know why, but you've been in a dreadful mood for a week at least. It's one thing if you're grumpy at home — *we* have to put up with you — but school's another matter. I hope you'll be more agreeable there."

As Joanna turned away to the window her mother got to her feet and followed her. "I was rather sharp with you," she said. "I'm sorry. This is difficult for me, too, you know."

A stretch of flattened grass showed where the cattle had slept the night before, but the cows themselves were nowhere to be seen.

"It may seem strange to you," Mrs. Drayton went on, "but I envy you. You'll meet so many people, you'll have so many new companions, and some of them have got to be nice."

"I'm going to say good-bye to Agnes and the others now," Joanna said quickly, and ran from the room. Behind her, Mrs. Drayton knelt to lock the trunk. As she got to her feet again, she looked about at the paraphernalia of childhood — stuffed animals, a French doll dressed in pink that had once been hers, a painted wooden farmyard made by Pickering — and picked up a teddy bear. Its rump was hairless, its nose squashed in, one eye was missing. With a sigh she let it drop and hurried out.

In the kitchen Joanna was showing her uniform to Agnes and the dailies.

"You look ever so grown up," Agnes said.

"It's a dismal color," said Joanna.

"Could've been a lot worse. Maroon, for instance, or black," Agnes said cheerfully.

"I think it's lovely," Mrs. Crompton said. "Sets off your dark hair."

"You'll look the best there," said Agnes. She opened a drawer and took out a little parcel. "This is from all of us."

"I know it's fudge," said Joanna, taking the package. "Thanks very much!" She hugged each one of them.

"When you come back home for the holidays we'll make some more together," Agnes said. "Mind you write to us. We'll want to know what sort of place you're at, and whether they're decent to you. If they aren't, we'll send Mr. Pickering after them!"

James poked his head into the kitchen. "Didn't you hear me calling? Dad's rearing to go." After a second round of hugs, Joanna followed him.

Mrs. Drayton stood at the hall door, twisting and untwisting her pearls. "You shouldn't have kept your father waiting, Joanna," she exclaimed. "I warn you, he's terribly cross." She picked up a gray school hat from the table. "Here, put this on!"

"No, I'll wait till I get to Paddington."

"If you don't put it on, you're bound to leave it in the car."

"I don't want to wear it now!" Joanna cried, but as she tried to slip by, her mother rammed the hat on her head.

"Leave it there, d'you hear me!" Mrs. Drayton ran down the steps and bent to speak to James, who was already in the car beside his father. "Don't let Joanna take her hat off, please, James." She attempted to kiss him but failed because the car window was open only a few inches and James didn't lower it. "Have a good last term, darling," she said to one side of his face.

"I'm sure I shall."

Mrs. Drayton stepped back and stumbled over Dolly and Grizelda, crowding round her feet. "You should have shut them in the smoking room, Henry!" she exclaimed, annoyed.

Joanna climbed into the back seat and as her father put the car into gear she saw her mother turn and go quickly into the house. Because of the argument over the hat, they hadn't said good-bye.

Chapter 8

Morehaven

MRS. OVERTON, the form-one teacher, soon perceived that she had been assigned one of a species rarely found at Morehaven: a child who gobbled up and digested information and then demanded more. This perception depressed her. She liked her students to be in good spirits and whenever one started exerting pressure inevitably one met with sulks and tears. The other students in form one, Jocelyn and Eliza, Jemima and Juliet (whose room, known as the Rabbit Hutch, adjoined the Pigsty), were accustomed to meandering. Although Juliet persisted in writing from right to left and Jemima still couldn't grasp why twelve and twelve made twenty-four, Mrs. Overton was unconcerned. Difficulties sometimes resolved themselves of their own accord, and if they didn't, summer would soon be here, the children would be gone; and when September came, they would be with Miss Hodgeson in form two.

But this little Drayton girl was eager to learn, she would insist on doing so, she would upset the others. As she bicycled home at the end of the third day of term, Mrs. Overton was anxiously aware that a well-established rhythm was being irrevocably disturbed. She calmed herself with the fantasy of finding a note in her box the next morning, telling her that a mistake had been discovered: the Drayton child belonged with Miss Hodgeson.

Joanna had arrived at Morehaven so late in the year that only the most junior music mistress, a shortsighted, acned, youngish person in a baggy coat and skirt, had time available. Miss Phipps had not until now been assigned children of discernible talent — indeed, her specific task was to endure the hopeless cases — and so when, at their first meeting, Joanna played *"Ah, vous dirai-je, maman,"* with which she had won the Elgar Prize, Miss Phipps was rendered speechless with apprehension. Was she up to this? She thought not, and her heart sank like a stone.

Joanna, used to Miss Cathcart deluging observations, suggestions, and (almost always) praise, found her reception by the grown-ups at Morehaven to be less than enthusiastic; her contemporaries — those companions of her own age so much touted by her parents — were less enthusiastic still.

They objected to her strongly on several counts: first, she hated riding; second, she scored ten out of ten on every test; third, and the most important charge against her, she threatened the emotional order. Jocelyn, Eliza, Juliet, and Jemima had been at Morehaven since the previous September, which was long enough for parents, brothers, sisters, servants — even pets — to be reduced to nebulous, insubstantial figures on the sidelines of their lives. The one who bore the burden of attachment now was the best friend. True, during termtime they sighed for the holidays, but when the holidays arrived, best friends parted tearfully. They wrote to each other daily, stayed at one another's houses for as long as possible, and counted the days until the new term began so they could be reunited. Four was divisible by two — two sets of best friends — but five wasn't, and so Jocelyn, Eliza, Juliet, and Jemima asked themselves, Will I be the one to get edged out? and resolved, whatever happened, not to be.

Of the four, Jocelyn was especially determined. Despite an eight-month hold on Eliza, she wasn't at all sure that she trusted her. Eliza Lancaster had a slippery streak, possibly the result of having been given in to by all the nannies and nursery governesses to whom her parents had entrusted her while they went, as they did several times a year, to America. (Lady Lancaster, born a Philadelphia Harrison, found post-war Britain drab.) Despite Eliza's daily protests of devotion, Jocelyn knew she had a roving eye, and even though Jocelyn herself couldn't see anything to recommend Joanna, she was deathly afraid that, in her perversity, Eliza might suddenly be smitten.

And so Jocelyn made it her business to make Joanna look as silly as she possibly could. She was always ready with a derisive comment on Joanna's looks, speech, attitude, facial expression. In class she made her comments sotto voce but loud enough for all to catch — except Mrs. Overton, who had suffered some hearing loss as the result of an air raid during the war. In the Pigsty she whispered them to Eliza and the two would giggle ostentatiously. On good days, when she felt confident of Eliza's attachment, she eased up on her attack, but the moment she sensed her friend's attention straying — perhaps to the enemy — she renewed it.

Eliza, who made a practice of doing what came easiest, found that by letting Jocelyn make most minor decisions her path was smoothed: her buttons were sewn on, her drawers straightened, her laundry sorted; Jocelyn often made her bed for her as well. If Joanna were to offer to perform an even wider range of services, Eliza would most probably accept, but short of receiving such an offer, she saw no immediate advantage to shifting her allegiance. Meanwhile, she enjoyed Jocelyn's derisive comments; she found some of them killingly funny, in fact.

To escape her constant companions Joanna would sit in one of the lavatories, which were legion — Morehaven had a much higher ratio of lavatories than staff to students — for as long as she could between lessons, after meals, before bed. There, in her mind's eye, she would repeatedly retrace the route back to Widleigh, and when, finally, she reached the front door, she would run in and search the house — rooms, closets, attic, cellar, even the crawlspaces under the roof — for her family. But although she searched a hundred times, she never found anyone.

A Sunday letter home was mandatory.

The first Sunday Joanna wrote, "Darling Daddy and Mummy, I arrived safely and my trunk came the next morning. I share a room without a view with Eliza and Jocelyn. Eliza's brother used to be at Eton. Jocelyn has a snow-white pony called Fantasia. She's won lots of prizes on her. The weather has been horrid. There isn't any organ here. Write soon. Love, Joanna."

To James she wrote, "I'm so lonely, my chest hurts, I can't sleep at night. Please help, please write, *please* ring me. If you say you're ringing for my birthday, a bit early, they'll let me speak to you. I miss you so much, I could die. All my love, Joanna. P.S. Did you know Rodney Lancaster? His sister's beastly."

Every evening she sat next to the telephone in the common room. Jocelyn's mother rang. Fantasia was lame; it could be navicular, the vet had said. A dread disease, no known cure for it. It was still too soon to tell. Jocelyn fled to the Pigsty and wept in Eliza's arms.

Eliza got a call as well, from her aunt Didi, already making plans for the half-term holiday. (Eliza's parents had gone to spend the spring on the Main Line; as her guardian, Aunt Didi was coping while they were away.) "We're going to Paris," Eliza told her roommates gleefully. "We'll be staying at the Ritz."

But the telephone didn't ring for Joanna. A week went by, and then almost another, and still no letter from James. He had squash and the Berwick Essay Prize to work for. Even so, if he truly loved her, he would find time to write. Her parents didn't write, either.

At meals Miss Norton constantly admonished her to eat.
Nibble she might but eat she could not.

After breakfast on the thirteenth morning of the term, Miss
Norton told Miss Grant that Joanna Drayton had lost her appetite. "She plays with everything, even roast potatoes. Just
pushes them about on her plate."

Miss Grant sent for Joanna and, when the last candidate for
cough syrup had departed, lit herself a cigarette. "I hear you're
off your food. Don't you like it? As school food goes, ours isn't
bad, believe me. I've been poisoned in lots of other schools but
never here."

Joanna bit her lip and said nothing.

Miss Grant tried again. "Look, if you're already feeling bad,
you'll feel ever so much worse if you get ill, too. And you're
bound to, if you keep this up," she added, smoothing the hair
off Joanna's forehead.

A dense dull pain had been sitting in the middle of her chest
since the moment she left Widleigh and now, as she felt Miss
Grant's cool touch, the pain rose and closed round her throat.
She shut her eyes fast and tried to swallow; suddenly she was
weeping — the brown linoleum at her feet was growing spotty
with her tears. Miss Grant took a quick puff on her cigarette,
pulled Joanna into the room, and slammed the door. Joanna
stood there, gasping like a fish.

The door flew open again and in came Miss Norton with her
clipboard. She had just finished checking the fingernails of students in forms three and four. "My goodness!" she exclaimed.
"Whatever's the matter?"

"When I asked her why she hadn't been eating, the flood-
gates opened and now she just won't stop." Miss Grant
frowned into Joanna's sodden face. "I can't even get her to
open her eyes. Any suggestions?"

"How about a cup of tea?" Miss Norton said. "*Whatever* is
the matter, tea might help . . ." She set her clipboard on the

table. "You'll do yourself mischief if you keep on." She pulled out a handkerchief and dabbed at Joanna's cheeks. "Come now, big girls don't cry so!"

At that moment Jocelyn burst in. "Oh my God, did someone die?" she exclaimed, eyes riveted on Joanna.

"Who asked *you* in here, young lady? Off you go!" Miss Grant seized Jocelyn by both shoulders, pushed her out, and slammed the door. She leaned against it, arms akimbo, watching Joanna helplessly. "This is beyond me," she said, and reached for the cigarette she had left burning in the ashtray on the top of the medicine cabinet. "Can you hear me?" she said loudly, and when there was no response, she took Joanna's face in her hands and said more loudly still, "If you don't stop this crying, we'll have to send for Dr. Reilly. You wouldn't want that, would you? Seems like she's about to drown in tears," she added to Miss Norton. "You'd better run and get Mrs. K. Perhaps *she'll* know what to do. One thing's sure — I don't." Miss Norton scurried off.

"I never would have thought it," Miss Grant mused, cigarette dangling from her lips. "Grim, I might have described you as, but certainly not hysterical . . . Is it Jocelyn?" she said after a moment. "Is she getting to you? Her bark's worse than her bite, I promise you. She's not a bad kid, really. Only a bit sharp to start with . . . Or is it Eliza? I wouldn't bother about her, either, if I were you." She belched loudly. "*Excuse* me!" Gingerly she felt her stomach through her white coat. "Lord, you and your misery, you're affecting my insides!"

Joanna imagined she was in a fortress surrounded by a moat. If she stayed where she was, obdurate, motionless, eventually Miss Grant would give up and go away. But after a while she heard another voice out there, beyond the water. She would not listen to that one, either. Instead she would retreat into the depths of her fortress, closing great doors behind her. One door, two doors. After the third she would be safe. She pushed with her whole will and strength but couldn't close it.

The new voice, she realized, was holding the door open. Get away from me! she tried to scream, but no sound came. Get away, leave me alone! and she opened her eyes to see Mrs. Kirkland peering at her in perplexity.

She shut her eyes again and pressed back into her fortress, but to her horror she discovered the portcullis had slammed shut and she was locked outside.

Mrs. Kirkland was holding her hands and saying softly, "If only you could tell me what's worrying you, I promise you'd feel better. Poor little thing! They'll have to have Prayers without me this morning while you and I go to my study for a chat."

Finding herself shut out of her fortress, Joanna opened her eyes and let herself be propelled to the door and through it, down staircases, along corridors. She wondered whether Mrs. Kirkland's talcum powder was supposed to smell of lavender or lilac. Lilac, she decided finally.

When they entered her study, Mrs. Kirkland shut the door behind them and led Joanna to the sofa. "Lie down," she told her. Although she had no intention of doing so, Joanna complied. The cushions were immensely soft. "Are you cold? Would you like a shawl to cover you?" Mrs. Kirkland asked.

Joanna sat up abruptly and swung her feet to the carpet. Bending to untie her shoelaces, she found that her eyes ached so much she couldn't see properly.

"What's wrong?" Mrs. Kirkland's voice seemed to come to her from some pinnacle high above her head.

"The laces, I can't undo them."

"So you haven't lost the power of speech! Miss Norton rushed in here, quite distraught. 'Joanna can't talk,' she told me. 'The linoleum's all awash!'" Mrs. Kirkland knelt to help Joanna take off her shoes. "There! Now you needn't worry about the furniture."

When people expressed admiration, as they often did, for the way Mrs. Kirkland surmounted life's great hurdles (a case in point being her husband's departure after dissipating her inheritance) she accepted it graciously; she knew she deserved it. She had, indeed, done admirably. However, she, personally, valued even more highly her talent for dealing with other people's crises. As Joanna lay back against the cushions, Mrs. Kirkland stood up and with a conspiratorial smile and an assumption of intimacy that did not exist — but undoubtedly would presently — said, "Now you've found your voice maybe you'll recover an appetite, too. Crying makes one awfully hungry."

Her biscuit box, which stood on her Chippendale desk, was made of laburnum wood. Her father had taken it to France in 1914 and had kept it with him, filled with Huntley & Palmer's chocolate biscuits, until Armistice Day. At his death Mrs. Kirkland had inherited it, and she had kept it filled with the same kind of biscuit ever since. To her, box and biscuits represented normality; they calmed her frayed nerves, and she assumed they had the same effect on her students', too. Opening it, she said expansively, "Do help yourself, my dear!" and when Joanna failed to do so, she took out the smallest size biscuit, shut the box, returned it to the desk, and sank to her knees beside the sofa. "Just *one*," she insisted, opening Joanna's hand and placing the biscuit in her palm. The scent of lilac was so strong that Joanna sniffed involuntarily. Mrs. Kirkland leaned forward and her double string of pearls swung an inch from Joanna's face. "You're exhausted, poor darling, absolutely worn out!"

Joanna's skin prickled. How she loathed that voice! But she was cornered; she couldn't escape.

The chocolate on the biscuit was melting fast. To avoid smearing the cushions, she thought she'd better eat it, so she did.

"That's better!" Mrs. Kirkland exclaimed. "Miss Norton says you've been starving yourself ever since you got here. Have we really made you so unhappy?" She rose from the carpet to sit on the sofa by Joanna's feet. She smiled reflectively and with one long finger traced roses on the cushion cover.

"I'm going to tell you a story," she said after a moment. "You like story-telling, don't you, Joanna? It's about a girl I knew a long, long time ago. She lived in the country and in the summer she always went with her family to the seaside. But one terrible summer, when she was about your age, she didn't go to the sea — her mother took her to Switzerland and left her in a hospital high up in the mountains. She had a lung disease. It was still in the early stages when, if you're lucky and take great care, it can be arrested and cured. This young friend of mine didn't feel ill, though. True, she'd had a cough since the early spring and hadn't been able to get rid of it, but she didn't see why she had to be in the hospital for *that!* She had never been away from home before. She was miserably homesick and frightened. The other patients were all older than she was, they spoke languages she didn't understand, and they were mostly much more ill than she was. All they talked about was their illness and whether they were getting worse or better. Mostly they got worse, too, and once in a while one of them would die in a room nearby.

"She begged her mother to come and take her home, but her mother always firmly replied that she had to stay in the hospital until she was completely well. So stay there she did, and often she thought she would die of unhappiness much sooner than she would die of her disease."

Mrs. Kirkland took Joanna's hand, the clean one that hadn't been holding the biscuit. "But do you know, by the following spring my friend had recovered and she came home to England. Then she was surprised to find she missed the hospital! Although she hadn't noticed at the time because she'd been so busy complaining, there had been plenty of people there who'd been very nice to her." After a moment she went on, "Perhaps you've guessed — that girl wasn't a friend at all, that girl was *me!* Once I got home and had had a chance to think, I was awfully ashamed of how rude and ungrateful I'd been to the doctors and nurses, of how I'd often snubbed the patients who had been friendly to me, and especially of those pleading, tear-splashed letters I'd written to my mother. Fortunately she knew that hospital was the only place where I'd get the help I needed, and her replies were always sympathetic but firm. For that, Joanna, I've been grateful all my life!" Mrs. Kirkland had told this tale with great effects innumerable times to innumerable homesick girls.

"*I* haven't had *any* letters," said Joanna.

"What was that?" For a moment Mrs. Kirkland was lost. She had been distracted by a smear of chocolate across a sofa cushion.

"*Your* mother wrote to you. *Mine* hasn't, not once! Nor has my brother. My father hasn't, either, neither has Miss Cathcart and she *promised* to keep in touch."

Father? Mrs. Kirkland frowned. But fathers rarely wrote letters. Hers never had, that she could remember. Miss Cathcart? Ah, yes, the governess who'd had to be removed. Mrs. Kirkland decided against dealing with that issue. Brothers and mothers were safer. "So there's a brother, too, is there? Older or younger?"

"He's eighteen."

Mrs. Kirkland sighed. "Big brothers tend to be very busy with their own lives — they rarely have much time for little sisters. But your mother's bound to write. Or is she very busy, too?"

"So far as I know, she doesn't do anything!" All of a sudden Joanna was crying again, eyes shut, mouth a little open. She looked just the way she had in Miss Grant's room twenty precious minutes before.

Mrs. Kirkland went to sit at her desk. She began to draw octagons on the blotting paper. Getting all the sides in evenly was the problem. She thought, If the mother *really* does nothing, then at ten in the morning she'll still be in bed, or at least at home. Joanna should speak to her on the telephone. That's sure to cheer her up! Simple solution! "I'll tell you what!" Mrs. Kirkland was all smiles now. "We'll ring your mama. You'll feel much better once you've talked to her."

Joanna remembered number four on the list of school regulations that had arrived at Widleigh: Girls may receive telephone calls on special occasions, but they are not permitted to ring home except in the case of great emergency. No, she definitely didn't want to ring her mother, who knew the regulations by heart. A telephone call could mean only one thing — trouble! Her mother hated trouble; she had enough of her own.

"She may be staying with my grandmother," Joanna said hastily. "She may have gone to London — she mightn't even be at home." But Mrs. Kirkland, wearying of the situation, took the list of parents' telephone numbers and found Drayton in the first column. Her back to Joanna, she gave the operator the number and Joanna heard all the buzzings and whirrings as connections were made between Berkshire and Herefordshire. At last the Widleigh telephone began to ring. Her father was out, Agnes had the kitchen door shut, nobody would hear it; but at the fourth ring someone answered. Mrs. Kirkland asked to speak to Mrs. Drayton.

"I'm so glad to catch you at home!" she exclaimed a moment or two later. "Etheldreda Kirkland here. We spoke a month or so ago . . . No, nothing drastic's happened. Joanna's *fine*. However, she's a little upset because she hasn't heard from you, so we thought it best to let her speak to you herself . . ." Mrs. Kirkland listened for several minutes while Mrs. Drayton talked and Joanna's heart thumped in her chest. Surely her mother was telling Mrs. Kirkland that Joanna had always been a shameful coward, afraid of ice cracking, the dentist's drill, the dark, being alone. Finally Mrs. Kirkland turned to her. "She wants to talk to you, she really does."

Despairing, Joanna took the receiver.

"Hello, it's me." She was shivering.

"You *know* I only write letters on Mondays," her mother said. She sounded very far away and very much on edge.

"You didn't write *last* Monday, you can't have, or I'd have got the letter by now."

"I didn't because you'd been gone for only six days and there was nothing to write about. But I wrote yesterday. You might even get the letter this afternoon." She went on, "I'm so sorry you've been such a problem to Mrs. Kirkland, who sounds charming, incidentally. How's the swimming?"

"It's been too cold for swimming."

"What about tennis? Do take advantage of those lessons. I remember how much I enjoyed tennis at Morehaven."

"You *did?* I didn't even know you knew how to play!"

"One doesn't have the opportunity here. Your father would never dream of sacrificing any part of the garden to make a court."

"How *is* Daddy?"

"As intransigent as ever! He's out today, which is lucky for you, given his views on making a fuss."

Joanna's shoulders drooped. Mrs. Kirkland hadn't noticed before how round-shouldered she was and made a mental note to ask Miss Grant about remedial exercises. She glanced at her watch; she had an appointment with the housekeeper at ten-fifteen and it was already ten past ten.

"How's the music going?" Mrs. Drayton asked, adding before Joanna could respond, "but I shouldn't keep you any longer. Tell me everything when you write on Sunday. You know how dull life is here, so I'll look forward to your news. And darling, don't give poor Mrs. Kirkland any more trouble, please!" Joanna plopped down the receiver.

"Feeling better?" said Mrs. Kirkland. Joanna nodded. It wasn't an emphatic full-scale nod but Mrs. Kirkland felt that it would have to do. "In that case, I'll write Mrs. Overton a note excusing your tardiness." She scribbled on a pad, tore off the page, folded it, and handed it to Joanna. "I've said you had a splitting headache and had to lie down. The *truth* need never be known. It's *our* secret, and if you ever feel 'that' way again, remember, you can always come and chat with me."

Joanna went to her classroom and gave the note to Mrs. Overton, who was just going off to the staff room for a cup of tea. "Glad to see you're better," she said. "The girls are doing their reading. *The Wind in the Willows,* page twenty-eight."

As soon as she had gone, Jocelyn whipped out a single sheet of paper. "Look what I've got!" she cried, jumping onto a desk.

"What?" the others demanded in chorus. Jemima tried to snatch the paper from her.

"Hold on! If you keep your grubby little hands off it, I'll read it. Shut the door!"

Jemima pointed at Joanna, who had her desk lid up. She was looking for her copy of *The Wind in the Willows.* "What about *her?* Does she belong here?"

"Never mind," said Jocelyn with a shrug. "She'll hear about it sooner or later, anyway. Might as well let her stay." She shook back her long plaits and began to read. " 'My Darling Rowena, It's only five and a half days since I saw you but it seems like five and a half *years!* These bloody boarding schools! Of course the Socialists are right, such bastions of class privilege should be abolished! And eventually, perhaps, they will be, only too late to do you or me any good.

" 'My considerate papa has just announced that *all of us,* the whole family, including cats and dogs, are to go up to Scotland as soon as the term ends. So I shan't see you until Xmas, unless you're prepared to come up, too. *If you are,* let's meet on the Isle of Skye on the twenty-ninth of July (I shan't be able to wait a day longer than that!) behind the fourth rock on the left after you get off the ferry. Bring pots of money, boots, a Windbreaker, a Thermos, and a Swiss Army knife. Skye's freezing, even in July. For you, though, I'll suffer all manner of deprivation, even — ' I only found page one," said Jocelyn. "It was on the floor of the loo at the top of the main stairs." She went on, "I like this part best: 'Of course the Socialists are right, such bastions of class privilege should be abolished!' That's exactly what my uncle Philip says. He's a Communist, he fought in the Spanish Civil War — well, he didn't actually *fight*, because before he had a chance to he got dysentery. He was heavenly to look at in those days, I've seen photographs. He still is, even though he's old. I wonder if this boyfriend's heavenly as well. Does Rowena swoon at the sight of his biceps? Or is he pale and spotty? If so she must be *thankful* not to have to see him till Xmas."

Eliza, who had been staring at Jocelyn, her color rising, burst out, "Give me that letter!"

Jocelyn said calmly, "*I* found it so why should I give it to *you?*"

"Because Rowena's *my* Passion, not yours. *I'm* the one who loves her!" Eliza grabbed the sheet of paper and pulled. It ripped jaggedly.

"Now you've gone and done it, haven't you," said Jocelyn in disgust. She let drop the torn scrap that remained in her hand just as Eliza flew at her, pushing her off the desk to the classroom floor, where she slapped and punched her until Juliet and Jemima managed to pull her away.

Jocelyn got to her feet slowly. One cheek, where her best friend had slapped her, flamed. Her plaits were coming undone. She'd lost both hair ribbons. As she watched Eliza run weeping from the room, she remarked, "I can't imagine why she's so upset . . ."

After lunch Mrs. Kirkland sorted through the second post and laid it out on the front hall table. She was still hovering when Joanna emerged with her classmates from the dining hall. (Form one's job was to wipe the tabletops and sweep the floor after each meal.) "I believe there's something waiting for you on the table," said Mrs. Kirkland in a low voice, "so everything's going to be fine!"

Joanna grabbed her mother's letter and ran upstairs to read it in the lavatory. "It's like winter here again," her mother wrote, "so I haven't been out. The dailies have been busy moving you into Miss Cathcart's old room. It's lighter and bigger than yours. (Daddy saw to it that she had the best room, naturally. It has the only new mattress — by new, I mean post–World War I — in the house. And the bedside light is rather decent, too.) I sorted through your things and the toys you're too old for I sent to the Waifs and Strays.

"Agnes has been ill; she says it's her insides and she might need an operation. I do hope not! Mrs. Burgess has been doing her best in the kitchen, but her best, alas, is far from satisfactory.

"Daddy's talking about getting rid of Dulcie. I thought you might be pleased to know."

Joanna put the letter in its envelope and went to her room, where she slipped it under the blouses in her drawer. It was the first letter she had ever received from her mother.

After their fight Eliza stopped speaking to Jocelyn. In the classroom she stared round and over her former best friend; in the Pigsty she turned her back on her and applied herself to three tattered copies of *Blighty*. When Jocelyn failed to clean her shoes, a self-appointed task she had been performing zealously for two terms, Eliza left them dirty, and Miss Norton put a cross against her name and warned her, "If this happens next week, you'll be writing 'I must keep my shoes clean and polished' a hundred times."

If Eliza could go it alone, Jocelyn was less independent. For two days she moped, but on the morning of the third she began making overtures to Joanna. Her hope was that when Eliza saw her taking up with someone else the worm of jealousy would wriggle into her heart.

Flopping down on Joanna's bed, she said loudly enough so that Eliza, who was tidying her bureau drawers, had to hear, "Will you spend break with me?"

"Get up a minute," Joanna said. "I'm trying to make my bed." She tugged at her eiderdown. "So long as you keep sitting on it, I can't get it straight." In spite of herself, she felt a fluttering in her throat.

"God, you're prissy!" Jocelyn exclaimed.

As she went to fold her laundry Joanna muttered, "If you like, I will."

Jocelyn glanced up to see whether Eliza had noted this communication, but by then Eliza was leaning out the window, purposefully regarding the dustbins down below.

When the break bell rang at midmorning, Jocelyn appeared beside Joanna. One eye on Eliza, she said, "We've only got fifteen minutes, so let's hurry!" They collected cartons of milk and currant buns from a trestle table presided over by Miss Norton and went outside. The stables of the aristocratic period had been converted into classrooms and the yard in the center was where, whatever the weather, a hundred fifty students consumed their milk and buns.

"There she is!" hissed Jocelyn. Across the yard Gillian stood talking with her best friend, Rowena. "Isn't she a dream!"

Joanna noted Gillian's strong shoulders, large red hands, and size-nine feet. The goddess sneezed twice, pulled out a grubby handkerchief, and blew her nose. A trumpet voluntary of a blow. Somehow, while stuffing her hanky back into her pocket, she dropped it, and as she bent to pick it up, she saw Jocelyn and Joanna staring at her. She blushed to the roots of her hair.

"Did you see that!" Jocelyn whispered ecstatically. "Did you see that blush! She *knows* I love her!"

Gillian and Rowena hurried away to sit on a wall, broad backs to the yard.

"Don't go too close to Rowena," said Jocelyn. "She's got B.O. — and a gap like a barn door between her two front teeth. Eliza's got terrible taste." She took a great chunk out of her currant bun and with her mouth full asked, "Have you picked yours yet, Joanna?"

"Picked my what?"

"Your Passion. One can't survive Morehaven without one — it's impossible."

"Why?"

"Because only if one has a Passion does one's life have any point at all. If I were you," she went on, "I'd choose someone who'll be staying on for a long time. I didn't think of that last October, when I chose Gillian, and at the end of this term she'll be leaving Morehaven. She's going to London to do a secretarial course and then she's coming out and then she's getting married."

"She is? Who to?"

"Does it matter? She's bound to marry *someone* pretty soon."

"Why should she?"

"What else is there to do?"

"I can think of things," Joanna said, but Jocelyn wasn't listening.

"I don't know how I'll bear it here without her. I might have to commit suicide! The gym would be an easy place to do it. I'd use one of the ropes to hang myself."

Are boys the same? Joanna wondered. At Eton does someone lie in wait for James and contemplate suicide, rather than face life without him? Being passionate about James was understandable but she couldn't conceive of Gillian making her heart leap or die.

When they came out of the dining hall after supper that evening, Jocelyn remarked to Joanna, "I've never tasted anything so disgusting in my life as that fish. It was rotten."

"Even so, you cleaned your plate."

"I had to. I was ravenous and rotten fish was all there was, apart from bread." She went on, "Do you know, Mrs. Kirkland's a thief."

"She is?"

"She steals our food money! That's why we get so little to eat and most of what we get is putrid. She buys stuff the butcher and the fishmonger throw out, or else it's been lying in some warehouse for a century. Do you know something else? She's got jam jars stuffed with pound notes under every bush in the shrubbery. One day she's going to dig them up and run off to Jamaica and laugh and grow fat on the proceeds of her wickedness." After a moment's reflection Jocelyn went on. "It's tragic, not just criminal . . . People our age have to get good food and plenty of it, or we'll be stunted, we'll never get the curse, we'll grow up hunchbacked, we'll go blind before we're twenty!"

"Mrs. Kirkland has her meals in the dining hall, too," said Joanna. "She eats what we eat — she's been doing so for years presumably — and *she's* not blind or hunchbacked."

"Of course not, she was fully grown before she set foot in this place. Besides, don't think putrid fish is all *she'll* get to eat tonight! She has her own supplies. Chocolates, potted shrimps, black cherry jam, tinned salmon . . ."

"How do you know?" The two girls were on their way to the music building, where Jocelyn would struggle with the recorder, Joanna with the cello, which Mrs. Kirkland had insisted she take up.

Jocelyn shrugged. "I also happen to know where she keeps the key to her special store cupboard. What about a spoonful of black cherry jam, Joanna, or a few Swiss chocolates? If we took a little of this and a little of that, old Etheldreda would never notice."

"You're making all this up."

"I bet I'm not!"

"Where's the key then?"

"Why should I tell *you?*"

"Okay, don't," Joanna retorted, and she walked into the music building and down the passage to Practice Room C, where string instruments were kept. She took the cello that had been assigned to her into Practice Room D and shut the door. She was putting rosin on her bow when Jocelyn slipped in.

"What if we went down tonight?" she whispered.

"Went down where?"

"To that store cupboard I was telling you about. I promise I know where the key is. If we wait till eleven when everyone's asleep, Etheldreda included, we shan't have any trouble. We'll need a torch, though, and my batteries are dead. Are yours good still? Well, what about it? Are you for going or not?"

"It would be stealing," Joanna said.

"Etheldreda steals from us all the time. Rightfully the food in that cupboard belongs to us!"

"Take it if you like, but I shan't."

"God! Never in my life have I met anyone as utterly dreary as you are!" Jocelyn exclaimed, and slammed out of the room.

The next night after lights Eliza suddenly appeared beside Joanna's bed. "Move over," she whispered. She hadn't spoken to Joanna for days. "There's room for both of us if you squash up." She hopped in and propped herself up on one elbow. "You know that letter," she whispered earnestly, "*the* letter, the one Jocelyn read aloud? Well, I've been thinking about it, and it's obvious that the stupid boyfriend can't love Rowena nearly as much as I do. *It stands to reason* that he can't. He hardly ever sees her, does he, whereas I see her many times a day. The thing is, though, I want Rowena to *know* I love her more than he does — I want to *convince* her." She went on, "You've seen those tattoos that sailors have on their backs and chests and arms, haven't you? Parrots and ships and naked ladies? Well, I've decided we should tattoo ourselves with her name."

In the darkness Joanna stared at her, wide eyed. "*We should?*"

"Yes. It'll be easy. We just dip a compass point in red ink and make lots of tiny pricks in our skin."

"Why should *I* do it? She's your Passion, not mine!"

"That's the point. It would be much more effective if two people tattooed themselves for her instead of one. You haven't got a Passion of your own yet, so if you do this with me, you won't be unfaithful to someone else. She's got to be impressed — we'll be writing on *ourselves*, our own *bodies*, not on some silly piece of paper that can be torn up or flushed down the loo . . . If we do it on our stomachs Grant and Norton won't ever see. And if we keep our backs to her while we're changing into our bathing suits, Buchanan won't see, either."

"How's *Rowena* going to see?"

"Simple! We'll follow her when she goes for a walk on the grounds and when she's far away from the house — in the water garden, for instance — we'll lift up our blouses so she'll see." Eliza put her hand under Joanna's pajama top. "Tell me you'll do it," she whispered. "Otherwise I'll tickle you and I'll go on and on till you go mad."

"Stop it!"

Eliza clamped one hand over her roommate's mouth and nostrils and with the other she started to tickle. Joanna tossed and squirmed and tried to roll away, but Eliza had her pinned.

Jocelyn sat up, slipped out of bed, and threw herself across Joanna's legs. "Give up!" she whispered. "It's two against one now." With Eliza's palm pressed against her teeth, Joanna lay still.

"She won't agree to my new plan," Eliza said, and as she described it to Jocelyn the dissension of the past few days was healed.

"Because of Gillian, I myself can't be tattooed," Jocelyn said, "so I'll be the tattooer. We'll have a proper ceremony," she added, caught up by the idea. "With costumes and everything. I'll be the high priestess and you two the sacrificial lambs."

"We can't do it tonight — we haven't got a compass," Eliza pointed out.

"Or red ink," Jocelyn added, "and without it the letters won't show up. So let's do it tomorrow night and get Juliet and Jemima to come as well. They'll be my assistants. They'll hold you two down while I do the artistic work."

Joanna struggled to a sitting position. "I hardly know who Rowena is. Why should I be tattooed for her?"

Eliza sighed. "My dear child, I've already explained why. Two sacrifices are twice as impressive as one." She went on, "Jocelyn, you should do Joanna first. After you've experimented and made mistakes on her, you'll do me perfectly."

"Good idea," said Jocelyn. "What time shall we hold the ceremony?"

"Sacrifices have to be at midnight and in the open air," Eliza said authoritatively. "We'll have it on the flat roof over the kitchen. We can climb out onto it through the bathroom window."

"For a proper sacrifice, there has to be a moon. What if there isn't one tomorrow?"

"We'll put the whole thing off till the next night."

"And afterwards," Jocelyn said, "we'll raid Etheldreda's store cupboard and have a celebration feast. The key's kept in the third drawer of the kitchen dresser. I saw cook putting it back there yesterday."

"So everything's decided." Eliza yawned and slipped out of Joanna's bed and into her own.

As she got off Joanna's legs, Jocelyn whispered, "If you go telling tales, little girl, we'll make life hell on earth for you."

Chapter 9

The Arlington Hotel

AFTER JOCELYN AND ELIZA WERE ASLEEP Joanna lay with her hands under her head and watched the shadows on the ceiling.

Maniacs! Barbarians! Savages! They could sacrifice each other but they weren't going to sacrifice her!

In her shoulder bag, which hung over the back of her cane chair, was a ten-shilling note that, in case she might have need of it, she hadn't given to Miss Grant for safekeeping, as school rules required. In the lavatory between classes, after meals, before bed, she had been considering the idea. Now, after this disgusting development, she embraced it. She wouldn't stay in this place where she'd been stowed for her parents' convenience. Tomorrow, hours before the kitchen roof ceremony, she would run away!

But where would she run to? Not to Widleigh. She wasn't welcome there. Her mother, in particular, wouldn't welcome her. Her sulkiness, untidiness, ingratitude, had exhausted her mother's patience.

As for her father, he would say, If someone bullies you, stand up to them! To him there could be no stronger indication of poor moral character than running away from school.

Would James take her? Surely he still loved her, surely he couldn't have stopped? But where would he put her? In her mind's eye she saw his narrow room at school littered with holey socks, squash rackets, scratched gramophone records, battered Greek texts. Last November when she'd gone down to Eton with her father to watch James play the Wall Game on St. Andrew's Day, the remains of a fried egg had been sitting in the middle of his bed. Obviously he wasn't set up to receive his sister. Besides, he hadn't telephoned, despite her letter baring her heart; he hadn't even written, although he'd sworn he'd try. Presumably he hadn't tried quite hard enough.

What about Miss Cathcart? She, too, had promised, and she hadn't written, either. For all Joanna knew, she'd gone right back to the Argentine.

So that left her grandmother. True, she had her temperamental side; she liked things her own way. But she'd often said how much she and Joanna had in common, so their two ways couldn't be as different as all that.

The Arlington Hotel was her solution. She would go to the same day school her mother had gone to after *she* had left Morehaven, and in the evenings she and her grandmother would play duets.

It was settled. Tomorrow she would run away to London!

After tea the following afternoon, Joanna, Jocelyn, and Eliza went upstairs to change out of their uniforms, as they were permitted to wear home clothes in the evenings. "I just heard the weather forecast on Grant's radio," Jocelyn announced. "South of England, clear, rain tomorrow. South of England means us, more or less, so it looks like we're set for the ceremony. I've been practicing writing *Rowena* in capitals all day."

"Aren't we posh," exclaimed Eliza to Joanna, who was tying the sash of her best cotton dress. "Most of your dresses look like potato sacks, but that one's not at all bad. Where did you buy it?"

"I didn't. One of our dailies made it."

"I wouldn't have guessed it was *homemade*." (Eliza's dresses were bought exclusively at Harrods.) "Coming to prep?" But Joanna had extra piano practice; she was playing with the orchestra on Friday.

"We'll see you at supper then," Jocelyn said.

As soon as she was alone, Joanna opened her shoulder bag and checked to make sure that her ten-shilling note was still there, in her little red purse. Then she popped in her toothbrush, which she had cleaned and dried that morning, and a comb. What else did she need? A handkerchief, the picture of James and Miss Cathcart. There wasn't room for underclothes. Her grandmother would buy her some in the morning. She took her cardigan from her bureau drawer and draped it carefully over her shoulders so that it hid her bag. She smiled at her reflection in the flyspecked mirror. No, she certainly didn't look like a runaway! After one last look at the narrow beds, the chipped furniture, the worn brown matting, she walked out.

As she passed her classroom she glanced inside and saw her classmates hunched over their desks. Maniacs! Barbarians! Savages!

She crossed the stable yard into the music building, but instead of turning into a practice room she walked straight down the corridor and out the back door into the shrubbery. There she broke into a run. The path was slippery from a recent rain and the bushes smelled dank. Round every bend she expected to meet Mrs. Kirkland out for her evening constitutional (or burying stolen cash in jam jars?), but there was no sign of her; she must have chosen a different route. After the path petered out, Joanna made her way through tangled undergrowth, stopping frequently to unhook her dress from blackberry brambles. On her left, topped by iron spikes, loomed the impenetrable park wall.

But just as she was convinced she would go stumbling on forever, she saw a gate, which, though padlocked, might be climbed. She made a bundle out of her bag and cardigan and threw them over onto the grassy verge on the far side. The first foothold was almost shoulder level, but she managed to pull herself up. As she reached the top she saw a blue bus plowing steadily towards her. She scrambled over the gate, spiked herself painfully in the groin, and, with tears in her eyes, lowered herself to the ground. Snatching up her bundle, she raced for the bus stop, pulling twigs and leaves from her hair and clothes as she ran.

Above her own breathlessness and the banging of her heart she heard the bus change gears behind her. The deserted bus stop was still a couple hundred yards away — she'd never get there in time! She'd have to wait for the next one, she'd miss the London train, she'd be apprehended by Mrs. Kirkland at the station and yanked back to school. But to her relief the bus slowed as it drew even with her, and she leapt for the platform, grabbed the pole, and scrambled on.

"Someone's in a heck of a hurry," observed the conductor. "Where might you be going so fast?"

He's guessed, Joanna thought. He knows because he saw me jump down from the gate. But no, he stood in the aisle waiting to sell her a ticket, quite friendly and unsuspicious.

"Beldon Station, please," Joanna told him as she took a seat.

"Going on a trip, then?"

"No. Well, yes, I suppose I am."

"That'll be fourpence."

For a panic-stricken moment she thought her purse had vanished, but there it was, red, in the bottom of her bag. She fished out her ten-shilling note.

"Got nothing smaller?" said the bus conductor. "Can't let you have all my change, you know."

They were drawing up to the next bus stop and she thought he was about to tell her, Seeing as I've got no change, you'd better get off and walk.

"Wait a mo', I can do it," he said, and sure enough, he counted out nine shillings and eightpence — four two-shilling pieces, two sixpences, five pennies, and a threepenny bit. "Here you are, plus the ticket."

Joanna's legs felt so much like rubber that she wondered if they would carry her when she tried to stand on them again. She took out her hanky, spat on it, and rubbed at the bramble scratches on her legs. They grew fainter and fainter until only two remained where the thorns had actually drawn blood. As she turned the tops of her socks down she noticed one was torn, but there wasn't anything she could do about it now. She stuffed her handkerchief into her bag and sat back.

They were entering Beldon proper and the streets were alive with people on their way home from work. They belonged here, they didn't have to run away, they were looking forward to their tea. What was waiting for them? Baked beans? Bread and dripping? Macaroni and cheese? Joanna, who liked all those things, considered jumping off the bus, knocking on a row-house door, and asking, May I come in and stay with you? No one would think of looking for her there.

But on second thought, a fourpenny bus ride from More-haven was too risky. She needed to get much farther away!

The conductor came up to her. "You want the station, right? Then here's your stop." She slipped past him and onto the back platform.

"Thanks," she called to him as she jumped off. When the bus started up again, they waved to each other.

A taxi piled high with suitcases whipped past. It must be going to the station too, she decided, and set off in pursuit. The street ran between red brick houses and over a canal, where two boys were fishing. "Is this the way to the station?" she called down to them.

They looked up, grinning. " 'Is this the way to the station?' " one mimicked. Joanna flushed with annoyance and hurried on.

A few moments later she rounded a corner into the station yard.

She approached the ticket window as nonchalantly as she could. The man behind the grill was reading the evening paper and drinking tea out of a thick white china cup with BRITISH RAILWAYS in black letters on it. His blue peaked cap was pushed back on his head, revealing a shiny scalp and a smattering of ginger freckles.

"Excuse me, please," Joanna said. "What time's the next train to London?"

The man ran his thumb and forefinger along the bridge of his nose and sighed. His hands were grimy and his fingernails were broken. There were ginger freckles on the back of his hand as well. "The six o'clock'll be in 'ere in ten minutes." He yawned and he didn't bother to cover his mouth.

"I'll have a half-single."

"That'll be four and seven." Joanna counted out the money carefully and pushed it under the grill.

Ten minutes to six. She was doing well. At this rate she'd be at Paddington by seven. By the time the supper bell rang at Morehaven and people started noticing she wasn't there, she might even have reached the Arlington!

The evening sun blazed across the platform after a drizzly day. The station was on the edge of town and beyond the railway embankment meadows sloped away to a meandering river. Friesians, like the ones at home, were grazing by the willows, their backs turned to the station. Trains and travelers didn't interest them in the least.

A workman eating a rock bun strolled past Joanna. After the hazards of her escape a rock bun was most appealing. She had already spent four shillings and elevenpence. If she bought a bun for threepence, say, she would have almost five shillings left. Yes, she could afford it.

The workman was strolling back towards her. He wore army

clothes, the clothes he'd been demobbed in at the end of the last war. Pickering still wore his in the garden at Widleigh. The man squinted down the railway line for signs of the train, and as he finished the last morsel of his bun and licked his fingers, he caught Joanna's eye and grinned. "A bit of all right, that was," he said.

Joanna went up to the refreshment stand, a threepenny bit in her hand. The refreshment lady was closing for the night; she wanted to finish and go on home, and she pointedly ignored her customer. Her head was wrapped in a grubby pink cloth and she wiped her eyes with the back of her hand as she took leftovers out of the display case and carried them into the back to put them away until the next day.

"I'd like a bun, please," said Joanna loudly.

As the woman reached for a plate of cheese sandwiches, Joanna wondered, Do you pay the same, regardless of whether a sandwich is newly cut or two days old?

"Buns are finished," the woman said.

"But I saw three on a plate," Joanna protested. "You just put them away."

"You're too late, sorry."

"Give 'er one, Mave, there's a girl!" The workman had come up behind Joanna. "Let the kid 'ave one. Keep 'em another day and you could pave a road with 'em!"

"Mind your own business," said Mavis wearily, "and I'll mind mine."

"You should be glad you've got a taker," the man said with a grin. A whistle blew down the line. "'Urry up, girl, our train's coming."

The woman relented. "Anything to keep you quiet, Terry, you and your lip!" She retrieved a bun from the back and held it for ransom above the counter. "That'll be fourpence, miss."

"Bloody robbery!" exclaimed Terry as the train drew into the platform. "Almost missed it, 'cause of you, Mave. Getting too slow for the job," he added, winking at Joanna. "Come on, nipper, let's get on!" He helped Joanna into a carriage and they sat down opposite each other. "'Ope you're quicker in the mornin', Mave," Terry shouted through the window. "The way she looks, it's a wonder anyone eats 'er food," he added to Joanna with a laugh. "You'd think she's out to *poison* you, wouldn't you. Good though, those buns, when you get your teeth into 'em." Joanna nodded in agreement. "So what're you going to London for? The waxworks?"

"No, I've seen them twice already," Joanna said. "I'm going to the dentist, actually."

"Bit late, aren't you, less 'e works at night."

"My appointment's for tomorrow morning," Joanna said quickly. "I'm spending the night with my uncle. He lives near Hyde Park."

"'E does, does 'e? And what about your auntie?"

"She's in the hospital, having her appendix out."

Terry scratched his head. His hair was light brown and thick and curly. "So it'll just be you and your uncle? 'Ope 'e's nice to you."

"He usually is," said Joanna. She brushed the crumbs off her skirt, adding, "He's brave, too. He won rows and rows of medals in the war — you should see them! He keeps them in a glass case in his study. Each one's labeled. Were you in the war, too?"

"Me? Course I was!" and he told her about stalking Rommel through the Western Desert on a camel. "Nearly caught 'im, too," he said. When he got out at the last stop before Paddington, Joanna was sorry to see him go. "Don't let 'em take 'em all out," he said as he got down onto the platform.

"Take all what out?"

"Your teeth, of course!"

Joanna laughed. She'd forgotten her dentist's appointment.

At Paddington she waved down the first cab she saw, but a man in a bowler hat pushed past her, jumped in, and rode away. The next cab she got without trouble. "The Arlington Hotel as fast as possible," she told the driver.

A church clock was striking seven as they passed by. Far away down the railway line the bell that signaled the end of prep would be ringing at Morehaven. Joanna put that out of her mind; instead she thought about her grandmother and what *she* must be doing now. Drinking whiskey with a friend, probably — Cousin Humphrey, or that old general her mother had introduced to her in the lobby a yearlong month before, when they'd been up to buy her uniforms. At any rate, the friend would be a man. Granny's friends were rarely ladies.

As the taxi turned into Knightsbridge, Joanna was delighted to see Standish, in his brass-buttoned frock coat, on the Arlington steps. "Good evening! How *are* you?" she cried, jumping out of the taxi and dumping all her money into the driver's hand.

"You gave me quite a turn, miss! I wasn't sure it was you, coming on your own. Is Madam expecting you?"

Joanna looked up at him and laughed. "No, this is a *complete* surprise!" A moment later she was in the lift on her way to the third floor. Mrs. Beresford had just come in, the lift boy said. Then it was only a few steps down the plum carpet to her grandmother's door.

She knocked and waited, and when no one came, she knocked again. "Who is it?" she heard at last, but Joanna didn't answer. She wouldn't until the door was open and she was sure of being let in. "Well, who is it?" her grandmother called again, this time much closer. The door swung open.

Half an hour before Mrs. Beresford had returned from tea at Claridges, locked her door against her public, and removed the artifices that shored up her youthfulness.

This was the first time her granddaughter had seen her without make-up. Her sparse hair straggled to her shoulders, her dressing gown was tied slackly round her hips. She didn't offer her cheek to be kissed. "Why didn't you let me know you were coming?" she said dryly. "Since I'd understood your mother had locked you up in that dreadful school, naturally I'm surprised to see you."

Joanna advanced to the middle of the room, dropped her bag, and whirled round like a top. "She *did* lock me up and it *is* a dreadful school" — she stopped whirling and swayed in front of her grandmother — "so I ran away. What d'you think of *that*, Granny?"

Mrs. Beresford tied her belt a little tighter and a little higher, closer to her waist. "It sounds rather clever," she observed, taking some hairpins from her pocket and securing her hair on top of her head. Now that she looked tidier, she felt more in command, and her spirits began to lighten. She went to the mantelpiece, took a cigarette from the ivory box, lit it, and, having realigned her features into some semblance of public order, turned to Joanna. "You must tell me all about this adventure," she said, "but first you need something to drink. Orange juice? It's in the fridge."

When Joanna came back from the kitchen, she sat on the sofa and stared into her glass. She was afraid of looking at her grandmother, afraid of letting her know that, yes, she'd seen how old she really was. "No one saw me leave," she began. "They'll only just have realized I'm not there. They'll ring Widleigh, first, I suppose — if Mummy telephones, please don't say anything about my being here!" She looked up at her grandmother for an instant and then away. "At least don't tell her till tomorrow. By tomorrow we'll have made a proper plan, and with a proper plan it'll be easier to convince her that I'm not going back. Because I'm *not.*"

"If you're so dead set against it after barely a fortnight, it certainly must be an awful place!" Mrs. Beresford exclaimed. "Of course your mother always claimed to have liked it, but she has a very earnest side. *You* don't seem earnest, though, I'm glad to say."

"The point of going to school," said Joanna, "is to be educated, but the teachers were so ignorant I wasn't learning *anything.* So in the middle of last night I decided to leave."

"I admire your decisiveness, I must say," said Mrs. Beresford lightly. "You're truly your grandmother's granddaughter!" She sat down beside Joanna. "I ran away once myself. Did I ever tell you about that?"

"But you never went to boarding school, Granny."

"I didn't run away from *school,* my darling, and this was after I grew up. I ran away from the house of a friend who'd started to bore me. Very early in the morning I slipped out and got a lift with a farmer to the station, and by breakfast time I was miles and miles away!"

"Wasn't she terribly upset?"

"Naturally. My friend was a man, though. Fun to begin with, but at close quarters he turned out to be deadly dull. I couldn't stand him another minute. I simply had to leave! So you see, darling, I do sympathize." She took Joanna's hand. "You know, as you get older, you become more and more like me. I too have always found being bored *intolerable.*"

"I won't find living with you a bit boring."

Mrs. Beresford abruptly let go of Joanna's hand. "You can't really be thinking of living with *me!*" she exclaimed.

"Yes, I am. I can't go home. Daddy and Mummy don't want me."

"What *do* you mean?"

"They don't, it's true."

"But the Arlington's no place for children! That's why there aren't any. If you lived here, you'd be the only child in the entire hotel."

"I wouldn't mind that a bit," Joanna said. "I don't like people my age, anyway. In general I prefer grown-ups."

Mrs. Beresford was becoming increasingly agitated. "Your father would never allow you to live here!" she said, rising from the sofa.

"But Mummy says you always get your own way, so if you make up your mind that you *want* me here, Daddy's bound to give in in the end."

"You'd be perfectly miserable. We both would! This flat's hardly big enough for one person, let alone two!" Mrs. Beresford gave a mirthless little laugh. "And you'd have an awful time fitting into the routine of an old woman like me."

"No, I wouldn't — I'm used to routines. I've had them my whole life! I'll do all your shopping for you in the winter when it's cold and wet and you don't want to go out yourself. I'll be a great help, you'll see!"

"I'm not decrepit yet, Joanna! I'm still capable of doing my own shopping, even in horrible weather." Mrs. Beresford closed her eyes, breathed deeply, opened her eyes again. "Look, my dear, grandparents are not the best people to bring up children, except as a last resort, and *you've* still got two able-bodied parents, both of whom happen to detest me! Your mother fervently believes that I've ruined her life several times over. Your father sees me as an irresponsible, useless old woman who's never done a hand's turn for anyone." She went on, "And there's another thing — you're wrong about their not wanting you. Indeed they want you! The trouble is that they're so completely incapable of sharing you that they had to have a total outsider about whom they knew virtually nothing take charge of you for years! Then when she left, *of course* you had to go to boarding school. Otherwise they'd have been fighting to the death over you."

Mrs. Beresford stubbed out her cigarette and immediately lit another. "While we're on the subject, I'll tell you something else. Your father has such a passion for his parental rights that when you were six and your mother ran away with you, he brought a charge of kidnapping against her. Yes, he accused his wife of kidnapping her own child! And he sold several Drayton treasures to pay lawyers to prove his case and get you back!"

She drew on her cigarette. "I think you should know the facts, Joanna, unpleasant as they are. After you've thought about them a little, perhaps you'll understand what a romantic notion your living here really is. Cheer up," she added, taking Joanna's hand again. "Now I'm going to ring the restaurant and order something delicious." She had her girlish, throaty voice back now. "What are you *longing* for?"

Joanna jerked away. "You've always talked as if you wanted me," she shouted, "but that was just an *act!*"

"In this particular instance, what *I* want is irrelevant," said Mrs. Beresford sharply. "If you have no particular likes or dislikes so far as supper is concerned, I'll order for both of us. I'm going to tidy myself up now," she concluded, and she went into her bedroom, closing the door firmly behind her.

For a moment Joanna remained immobilized on the sofa but then she wiped her eyes on her skirt and got to her feet. She tiptoed to her grandmother's door and put her ear to the keyhole.

Mrs. Beresford was ordering their supper. "The lamb sounds nice," she said, "and the crème brûlée. Make sure to give us plenty of caramel, won't you. You'll send it up in ten minutes? Perfect! Oh, and will you give me the switchboard . . . Mrs. Beresford speaking, yes, good evening . . . I'm really very well. . . . Could you be awfully kind and get my daughter? . . . You know the number . . . Barbara? It's Mummy! . . . Can you hear me? . . . Yes, I *know*. What a drama! . . . She's here . . . arrived half an hour ago . . . Wants to live in the Arlington with me but of course I told her that's impossible. . . . So you'll be taking her back to Morehaven . . . Just as I thought . . . Then I'll expect you here for lunch tomorrow."

March 1957

Chapter 10

The Arlington Hotel

LADY HARRIET COOPER stood behind a rectangular chrome and glass table and poured tea into small white cups. Iris, the Portuguese maid, handed them out to a dozen girls seated on chrome and leather chairs and, having seen to milk and sugar, passed round the cucumber sandwiches.

Beyond tall windows was a patio in which ivy in raised beds grew abundantly. Lady Harriet regretted the uniform green of ivy; she would have liked to plant spring bulbs — hyacinth, narcissus, scilla — but Nigel insisted that the gardening service would be very put out if she interfered.

Years before, when Nigel had brought her to look over the Hill Street house, she had said doubtfully, "Isn't this part of London rather grand for us? I'd be happier in Chelsea or South Kensington than Mayfair, and do we need five floors and a double drawing room?" Her husband had replied, "I think Mayfair's ideal — I don't regret my decision in the least!" Only then had she understood that he'd merely wanted her to *see* the house; he wasn't asking her opinion because he'd already bought it. It had been he, not she, who had chosen the blue and beige decor and then, late the year before, when he'd decided to have the whole house done up again, the clean lines and bare surfaces of the Bauhaus. In Herefordshire, as country squire, he required bric-a-brac, overstuffed chintz-covered sofas, and eighteenth-century sporting pictures, but Olympic Underwear was plunging into the North American market, and as a rising captain of industry, he wanted his London house to convey an aura of efficiency, competitiveness, and drive.

For the past three weeks — ever since she and Gabriella had established themselves at Hill Street for the preliminary activities of the Debutante Season — Lady Harriet had felt as if she were living in a hotel, and despite an extended spell of dry weather, her back had been giving her a good deal more trouble than usual; some mornings she had scarcely been able to get out of bed.

Gabriella had been waiting impatiently to come out for years. She adored rituals and gave every aspect of their enactment the closest possible attention. She relished making up guest lists and writing invitations, scheduling dressmaker and hairdresser appointments, and working out attendance strategies for three tea parties in a single afternoon. She expected her mother to be as enthusiastic as she was. "Why go to just one luncheon, Mummy, when, if you think through the logistics, you could manage two?" she urged. "That way you meet twice as many mothers and make twice as many connections" (which could prove valuable to her daughter's social career). Since food didn't interest Gabriella particularly, the composition of menus was left to her mother, but in most other matters, Gabriella's ideas were clear, and they prevailed.

Lady Harriet had reservations about lavishing so much time, effort, and money on the entertainment of such a young girl. Nigel, however, had none. He had been looking forward to Gabriella's season as much as Gabriella had. For both of them the high point of the decade would come on the twenty-third of June, 1957, when Lady Harriet Cooper would be At Home at Spurlock Hall, Herefordshire, to receive five hundred of her daughter's friends for supper and dancing to Teddy Lightfoot's band (which Nigel had booked two years before). Nigel would pay for everything; Gabriella would go to everything. All they required of Harriet was that she be on hand to perform a few minimal functions.

Lady Harriet hoped that all this activity, this wearing of hats and scurrying for taxis, was achieving the desired — if not necessarily desirable — effect. Since their arrival in London she had carried with her two leatherbound notebooks, both of which were alarmingly full, one with names and addresses, the other with engagements. The early days of March, devoted to luncheons for mothers and teas for the debutantes, had been relatively easy on the spirit, but one week before, Gabriella and her contemporaries had trooped off to Buckingham Palace to be presented to Her Majesty (who, one imagined, might have had better ways to spend two hours than watching a host of seventeen-year-old girls, in heels too high, teeter down a long red carpet to execute a movement only faintly approximating a curtsy), and now the pace was quickening. Lunches and teas were on the wane; cocktail parties were in the ascendancy. In May the balls and dances would begin and would continue night after night into the autumn. To Harriet, Christmas, which marked the true end of the ordeal, was an eternity away.

She had poured the last cup of tea; it was time for her to venture out beyond the protection of the table and do her duty by the girls who were about to become Gabriella's lifelong friends and enemies. In their uniform of cashmere sweaters, pleated skirts, black court shoes, and charm bracelets, it was difficult to tell them apart. Heads bowed, address books out, and sharpened pencils readied, they waited with a certain tenseness round the jaw for the vital business of extending contacts — in particular, *male* contacts — to begin.

Gabriella sat in the center of the circle. With two older brothers, one at Cambridge, the other in the Rifle Brigade, she was in a position of immense strength when it came to bargaining for names. The likes of Giles and Steven Cooper were pearls without price, for in an emergency they could be counted on to drum up legions of fellow undergraduates and subalterns who would be brought on the double to eat and drink the night away at the expense of a stranger. That many of them, after consuming great quantities of smoked salmon and champagne, didn't bother to talk to the girls — let alone dance with them — was immaterial. What mattered to hostesses was *keeping the numbers right*.

"Who have you got for me, Pamela?" Gabriella asked the girl sitting on her left.

"Tommy Phelps," said Pamela.

Gabriella flipped to the P's in her address book. "Chillhurst Manor, Tewkesbury? Got him already. Try again."

"Michael Sainsworth."

"He sounds familiar, too." But Gabriella had *Hubert* Sainsworth down, not Michael.

"They're second cousins," explained Pamela.

"I see. Who else have you got for me, Pam?"

"What about Nicholas Kazakov?"

"A Russian!"

"I suppose his father was."

"What is he? A prince, a duke, a count, at least?"

"A count, I think."

"What's he like to look at?"

"Smallish, wears glasses." Gabriella grimaced. "But he drives an Alfa Romeo," Pamela added in the nick of time.

Gabriella brightened. "Okay, you get both my brothers," she said graciously, and she turned to the girl on her right. By this simple and straightforward method she was fairly certain of getting twenty-two new males on her list by the end of the afternoon.

This was the third tea party the Coopers had given and, Lady Harriet noted thankfully, the last. The next event for which she had major responsibility was a cocktail party on April seventeenth. But that would take place at Nigel's club. Nigel and Gabriella had said the Hill Street house simply wasn't big enough.

"How many are you proposing to invite, darling?"

"A hundred and sixty."

"Gracious, d'you know that many people already?"

"Of course, and so do you, Mummy," Gabriella had answered crisply.

The truth was, though, that Lady Harriet was poor at names and faces. She had intended to glance over the afternoon's guest list before the party, but in the rush of setting out cups and saucers, picking up *Vogues* and *Queens* from the drawing room floor, and dashing round to Searcy's in a taxi to fetch the éclairs, which, by half past three, still hadn't been delivered, she had forgotten about the guests. When she first looked round the room, she wasn't sure that she had ever seen any of them before; but then she recognized Joanna Drayton, who was sitting by the window, gazing distractedly into the patio, her address book neglected on her knee. She didn't appear to be attending to the bargaining process at all.

The last time Lady Harriet had seen her had been in April almost two years before, when she had run into her and her father at Hereford Station. Henry, pacing the platform, hands clasped behind his back, looked unhappy but resolute. Joanna was whispering to a puppy in a traveling cage on the bench beside her. When Lady Harriet greeted her, she looked up cautiously, unsmiling. Intruders were not welcome.

"Is there room for me, too?" Lady Harriet asked, even so. Joanna pulled the cage closer. "You've been at Widleigh for Easter?"

Joanna nodded. "Mummy went to Greece and I came down here."

"Greece? I don't remember your mother traveling."

"She didn't when she lived with Daddy, but nowadays she

goes abroad as often as she can. She's very keen on the ancients. She says the ruins of Greece and Asia Minor give one a sense of one's mortality — they purify the soul. The Arlington makes the soul pretty sluggish," she added, smiling at last. Ah, a ray of sunshine, Lady Harriet thought.

"I do wish Nigel liked Asia Minor," she murmured. "But it's only Cap d'Antibes and the Bahamas for him . . . Tell me about this puppy. A new acquisition?"

"I bought him yesterday for half a crown from a boy in Ludlow Market."

"Is he any breed specifically?" Lady Harriet asked, imagining it chewing crocodile shoes, piddling on Persian carpets, tripping up chambermaids.

"The boy said spaniel, but I doubt it. His legs are too long." Joanna took the puppy out of his cage and lovingly caressed his ears before handing him to Lady Harriet. "Here!"

"What are you going to call him?"

"I haven't decided."

"He looks like Toby," Lady Harriet said. "My oldest grandchild, Victoria's little boy. He's stringy, too."

The train was pulling in. Henry came up, nodded good evening to Harriet, seized Joanna's suitcase, and marched off. Joanna took her puppy, popped him into his cage, and followed her father. Not wanting to force Henry into conversation, Harriet had seated herself in a different compartment.

Now she unhooked her cane from the back of a chrome and leather chair, took a plate of éclairs, and went up to Joanna. "Take two if you like. They're ridiculously small."

Joanna's curly hair hung loose below her shoulders. She hadn't had it back-combed, puffed out, and sprayed with sticky substances like Gabriella's other girlfriends had. Her green eyes were large and deep set. She wore no make-up. An interesting-looking young person, Lady Harriet decided. "The last time we met," she said to Joanna, who had eagerly bitten into one of the

tiny éclairs, "you'd just acquired a puppy of ambiguous origins.
Did it turn out to be a spaniel?"

"No, a sort of poodle, only by the time you could tell that, he
was living in Streatham with the daughter of the Arlington hall
porter. Mummy didn't have the time to walk him while I was
off at school so he had to be given away. I called him Toby,
though, and the name stuck. In Streatham he's still Toby." She
looked longingly at the éclairs. "May I have another?"

"Help yourself!"

"I've been practicing the piano all afternoon and I'm ravenous. I could eat the entire plateful!"

"Why don't you. The others are too busy to be hungry."
Lady Harriet added, "Practicing all afternoon? That sounds
serious. What are you up to these days?"

"I left school last July and since then I've been studying here
in London for the Royal Academy entrance exam. I passed just
a fortnight ago. I'll enter in September."

"My congratulations!"

"Thanks."

"Miss Cathcart must be *thrilled*. A musical career was what
she always had in mind for you, wasn't it?"

"Miss Cathcart doesn't know. We lost touch a long time
ago."

"That's too bad. She was such a vital person . . . I've often
wondered what became of her."

"I imagine she's been tyrannizing a succession of little girls
— the same way she tyrannized me." They both laughed.

"Was she really a tyrant?"

"A benign one."

"By the way," said Lady Harriet quickly, "you don't mind
talking to me, a mere mother?"

"Mind? Why should I?"

"I'm making you miss the serious business of the afternoon."

"That doesn't matter. I'm not really doing the Season. My

mother says she isn't up to organizing a party. She has her hands full with Granny."

"There are far too many parties as it is, and every Monday morning half a dozen more are announced in the *Times*. By the way," Lady Harriet went on, "how *is* your grandmother? Does she take a great deal of looking after?"

"Yes, she has nurses round the clock. They live in the hotel, on the top floor, and have their meals with us, and one or the other of them is always giving notice or getting ill or needing time off, which means a lot of bother for my mother."

Name swapping had come to an end and guests were putting their address books away. In a few moments there would be a rush to the door and each girl, with precious new data in her handbag, would be on her way back to mama. Lady Harriet sighed. She ought to be doing the rounds and relearning by devious means names that she had certainly been told once, twice, in some cases, three times.

Suddenly Gabriella appeared beside her. "Amanda asked me to go with her to supper at her brother's. He lives on a houseboat near Chelsea Bridge. I can go, can't I?"

"You've been out late every night this week, darling," said her mother doubtfully.

"But I'm not *at all* tired."

"Tomorrow night you simply must stay in. Are we agreed?" Lady Harriet turned to Joanna. "I've so enjoyed talking to you. Do give your mother my love and tell her I'll ring soon and make a date for lunch." Picking up her cane and the depleted plate of éclairs, she moved away.

Gabriella looked Joanna over carefully. She noted a wool — not cashmere — sweater, a straight — not pleated — skirt, no make-up whatsoever, and eyebrows that needed to be plucked. Joanna hadn't had the benefit of the Comtesse de Bernard's finishing school in Paris. She looked as if she'd hardly been started, in fact. Gabriella had invited her because she had a

twenty-five-year-old brother who had been at Eton and Christ
Church and had once been perfectly presentable, although ru-
mor had it that he wasn't anymore.

"Don't you adore London!" she exclaimed. "Isn't it super to
be *out!* Last year Mummy insisted on Victoria shadowing me.
Can you imagine, my sister, mother of two and pregnant, wad-
dling into every party behind me — 'No, you can't go dancing
at the Conroy, Gabriella, you have to go home to bed.' 'No, you
can't have a whiskey and soda, Gabriella, you have to wait till
you're eighteen,' et cetera. Now Victoria stays at home with her
infant and I go to parties with my brothers. They're extremely
casual chaperones, I'm glad to say. They're both just as mad
about London as I am. Steven's on some army course in Wiltshire and Giles is supposed to be swotting day and night for his
Cambridge finals. Even so, they both manage to spend a huge
amount of time up here. Two weeks ago, on his way back to
Cambridge at four in the morning, poor Giles fell asleep at the
wheel and ran slap into a cow and completely wrecked his car.
They towed it off for scrap. He'd only got it in January."

"What became of the cow?"

"Its two front legs were broken, so they shot it. It should've
been in its field, not wandering about on the main road. Giles
got a great gash across his forehead where he went through the
windscreen. He's still wearing a bandage. Didn't you see the
story in the *Evening Standard* — 'Tycoon's Son at War with
Beast'? Daddy was livid. He hates being called a tycoon! They
say such ridiculous things in the gossip columns. Why does one
even bother to read them? But nothing stops Giles. He's up
here as much as ever, only now he has to come by train because
mean Daddy refuses to buy him another car until he's finished
at Cambridge. Incidentally," she went on, "I was waiting for
you to give us James's name just now."

Joanna said nothing.

"Herefordshire has been rife with rumors," Gabriella said

after a moment. "I know he left Oxford under a cloud, shall we say, but what happened after that? Last spring Giles spotted a wild-looking creature in the Fulham Road — no socks, jacket out at the elbows, hair halfway down his back — and when he got up close, the creature turned out to be James! He's the last person one imagined as a beatnik — one thought he'd be a don. Where is he now?"

"He's in Spain," Joanna said. "He'd had it in mind to live there for a long time and finally, eight months ago, he went."

"Spain!" exclaimed Gabriella. "How divine!" Last August she had been to the bullfights in Seville; she'd had the most heavenly time. She had begged and pleaded to be allowed to go again to Seville this August, but, she said, "Daddy's dug his toes in. He's making me go to Perthshire with him — he wants me to shiver on some frigid moor and watch while he slaughters grouse. I can't imagine anything more boring!"

Girls hovered round them, wanting to say good-bye. "I must be off," said Joanna.

"You, too? Well, next time you write to James, remember to tell him we're having the party of the decade on the twenty-third of June, so he'd better come back from Spain for it."

"Looks like you 'ad a long day," the lift boy remarked to Joanna, who had appropriated his stool. She sat back, head against the wall, one leg dangling. "'As that piano teacher been knocking you about again? You should learn to stand up for yourself better!"

"I didn't go to Mr. Ehrenreich this afternoon," Joanna replied. "I went to a tea party with eleven other girls."

"Eleven? Crikey! Sounds like the right sort of do for me."

"But unfortunately not for *me*."

"Well, 'ere you are," the boy said, letting Joanna out at the third floor. "You can put your feet up now."

Soon after Mrs. Drayton had come to the Arlington to "do" for her mother, as she put it, she had taken the flat next door, identical to Mrs. Beresford's, for her and Joanna. Now, dressed to go out, she was waiting impatiently in their sitting room. "I'd almost given up on you," she exclaimed as Joanna walked in. "What took you so long?"

"A man was playing the violin in Curzon Street. I stopped to listen, I forgot the time."

"Well, now you're here . . . Nurse O'Hara left at three and since Nurse Darling has bronchitis you're needed till Nurse Channing comes on at eleven." She beckoned her daughter through the connecting door into the other flat. "Let me show you what there is to do."

"How can you think that I don't know? I've done it so many times!"

"But if I don't remind you about details, you forget them, and when I'm out and I'm not certain things are being taken care of properly, I don't enjoy myself."

Joanna dumped her jacket and handbag on a chair, kicked off her narrow shoes, and in stocking feet followed her mother to her grandmother's room. The curtains were drawn and a small lamp was lit beside the wide bed in which Mrs. Beresford lay. The Little Event, as Mrs. Drayton referred to her first stroke in June 1950, had rendered Mrs. Beresford speechless in a wheelchair; the Great Event, the second stroke in September 1955, had deprived her of her hearing and confined her to bed. Her skin was brownish gray; her flaking scalp showed through cropped white hair. Her right eye, blue and sightless, stared perpetually. Her doctor had been unable to get it to stay shut. Her old friends, who never visited her, said it was her indomitable spirit that kept her alive. Her daughter, who lived with her, knew she remained alive out of spite.

"She's changed and dry," said Mrs. Drayton. "Nurse O'Hara saw to that before she left. Her supper's ready in the hot plate. It's puréed chicken. For pudding, there's coconut blancmange in the fridge. Remember, she'll need three pillows. Prop her up so that she's comfy and feed her very slowly, half a teaspoon at a time. Then afterwards there are the pills. Two pink and one yellow. They're here." She indicated a saucer on the bedside table.

"You don't have to remind me, Mummy."

"Once you forgot, though, and she slipped badly."

"That was months ago," Joanna said, "and I haven't forgotten since. Is she asleep now?"

"Yes, she fell asleep before O'Hara left. You'll have to wake her up for supper. It's no good hanging about hoping she'll wake of her own accord because she never does."

"I promise she will get her ammunition," Joanna said flatly. "Both nutritional and medicinal."

"I wish you could be kinder about your grandmother. Poor little thing — what harm did she ever do you?"

Barbara Drayton might complain about being tied to the Arlington, about the wicked expense of running a hospital in a hotel (although it wasn't yet her money being spent), about being nothing more than a maid, a drudge, an unpaid orderly. Nevertheless, when Mrs. Beresford got a sniffle that might turn into pneumonia — it never had, but there might be a first time — Barbara would stay in the flat; she wouldn't go out for days on end, not until the sniffle had cleared up completely. Even though she hadn't forgone her foreign trips entirely (since the Great Event she'd been once to the toe of Italy, once to Tripoli), both times she had come home several days early in a panic, fearing that her mother had died and no one had managed to reach her. In fact, Mrs. Beresford had shown no sustained signs of dying. She had lost her power to betray but not to obstruct; this she continued to do with great effectiveness.

As she followed Joanna out of the old lady's room, Mrs. Drayton said expansively, "I appreciate your being willing to help."

Joanna flopped into an armchair. "Where are you going, anyway?"

"Humphrey and I are having dinner with Tom Thorndike

and Gerald Bayley, two young friends of his who spent the whole winter in the Peloponnese, in a cave, I gather, hundreds of feet above the Aegean, with a sheer drop to the sea."

"I wonder what they were doing in that cave," Joanna said, smiling faintly, "although with Humphrey's friends it's easy to guess."

"One writes novels, the other's a poet."

Joanna sat up. "Writers? In that case, they might have run into James!"

"How could they, darling? He went to Spain, not Greece."

"He said he was going to Spain, but he might have changed his mind — he might have gone to Greece instead." She went on, "And even if they didn't actually run into him, Tom and Dick, or whatever their names are, might have heard of him through the grapevine. There can't be all that many young English writers traveling round in the winter. At least you could ask."

Mrs. Drayton reached round to the back of her neck. "Damn, I forgot these buttons! I can't do them up myself. Would you mind?" She presented her back to her daughter and, while Joanna struggled with the buttons, said dryly, "We've been over this before. We haven't heard a word from your brother for eight months, have we? Yet if he wanted us to know where he is, we'd know. All it would take is one postcard, two minutes of his time, and a stamp. One can only assume that it's his intention to keep us in the dark."

"We don't even know if he's still alive," Joanna said quietly.

"Oh, of course he's alive! If he were dead someone would have found his body and reported it to the authorities. Your father would have been notified. The Spanish authorities are most particular. For that matter, the Greeks' are too. We're not talking about darkest Africa, you know."

Joanna fastened the last button and gave her mother a little push away. "If he were *my* son," she said fiercely, "I'd have hired someone to look for him. That's what private detectives are for — to track down people who don't want to be found."

"As you well know, Joanna, I couldn't possibly afford one," Mrs. Drayton said peevishly. "You should ask your father when you see him next." She gave a short laugh. "I can just imagine his reaction! He was perfectly delighted when at last James took himself off. He must have hated having him wandering round Herefordshire, looking like a tramp. The last thing Henry would do is spend money to get him back! Humphrey will be here in a minute — I'm going to get my coat," and she hurried off to the other flat.

Joanna went to the window. It was almost dark in Hyde Park; there were no strollers on the paths. But who knows, she thought, perhaps James has come back from Spain or Greece or wherever he went to and now he's hiding out there in that clump of laurels, looking up at me. She raised one hand in acknowledgment. "I miss you," she whispered. "I hope you're safe."

Mrs. Drayton reappeared, coat over one arm. "I want you to understand something," she said loudly. "Your brother never cared for me — even as a little boy he didn't. When he was about three he decided I wasn't his type; on the basis of what, though, I'll never know, as he never gave me an opportunity to show him what type I was. He always chose to be with Nanny Hastings or Agnes or your father — anyone but me! Of course when I took you off to Scotland, I sealed my fate with him. Since then he's taken every chance that's come his way to deprecate and humiliate me. I wouldn't wish a son like him on anyone." She sighed angrily. "If you think that it's my responsibility to track him down when he clearly doesn't want to be tracked down — and especially not by his mother — you're mad. For once, can't you try to see things from my perspective!"

Joanna felt an aching numbness round her heart. "There must be something you can do," she mumbled furiously, turning back toward the park.

There was a knock on the door. "That must be Humphrey," Mrs. Drayton said with relief, and she went to let him in.

"What a charming frock, Barbara!" Humphrey Beresford exclaimed, kissing her on the cheek. He smiled broadly as he came into the sitting room. "First time on, aren't I right?"

Mrs. Drayton, flushing with pleasure, followed him. "The dressmaker finished it this morning and I had to wear it straightaway. Childish, I know, at my age."

"I love the high neck — terribly elegant, reminiscent of Mme. Grès." Humphrey wrote the odd concert review and a column on antiques for a Sunday newspaper. His 1952 book on the baroque was regarded by many as the standard work on the subject. Everyone who was anyone, artistically speaking, came to his house in Smith Street to eat his *gran cucina italiana.* His housekeeper cut up the vegetables; the rest he did himself.

Since boyhood he had been a sort of courtier to his aunt Leonora. When she was in London he would escort her to concerts, theaters, and openings; when she was abroad he visited her much more regularly than he did his mother, Mrs. Ashton-Beresford, who lived a life quite without flair in a stockbroker Tudor house just thirty minutes out of town, in Virginia Water, Surrey. Because their tastes in literature, painting, and architecture were different, they argued constantly, but they enjoyed their arguments and always made peace in order to have more. With Barbara a quiet third, they traveled together to Turkey, Egypt, Morocco, and, one summer, to Oyster Bay, Long Island, which they found tedious beyond belief; they stayed only a week before sailing home.

The morning after poor Aunt Leonora's stroke, Barbara materialized to take care of her. Humphrey had seen little of his cousin since her marriage to an unlikely Herefordshire landowner. (As her closest male relation, he had given her away.) As a girl, she hadn't been a bit like her mother; she hadn't been especially clever or good-looking; she couldn't sing a note or play the piano; such opinions as she had she expressed with trepidation, while taking others' opinions, even if patently absurd, too seriously. After twenty-odd years in the country, she didn't appear to have changed much.

Humphrey discovered, however, that now he *liked* having his opinions taken seriously. Soon he was escorting Barbara to the same theaters, concert halls, and galleries to which for so long he had taken her mama. It was clear she needed guidance in many areas and he was pleased to give it. With his encouragement the odes and sonnets of the Widleigh years were locked in a trunk and stored in the Arlington cellar, and Barbara turned her hand to engaging pieces about her Continental travels, most of which she undertook with her cousin; soon she was publishing them regularly in glossy magazines. Humphrey also attended to her appearance. The warring colors faded, the scarfs were given away to the wife of the hall porter, and a handsome woman emerged in good, subtly detailed wools, linens, and silks. Her headaches came less and less often until finally they stopped.

Meanwhile, Humphrey encouraged her daughter, too.

"What d'you see out there in the dark?" he asked Joanna cheerfully. She was still at the window, her back to the room.

"Nothing."

"Then come and sit next to me and tell me all your news."

"Do close those curtains," Mrs. Drayton said quickly.

"Why? There's no one in the park at this hour, and even if there were, what would they see in here? We aren't exactly having an orgy." Joanna came away from the window, leaving the curtains open, and sat on the gold brocade sofa, beside Humphrey.

"Not tired of cucumber sandwiches yet?" he said.

Joanna shrugged. "Today's tea party wasn't bad. At any rate, I enjoyed talking to the mother of the girl who gave it. By the way, Mummy, Lady Harriet said she's going to ask you to lunch."

"Did she? It's difficult to imagine Harriet Cooper in London. One hardly remembers seeing her except in gardening clothes. Harriet was a neighbor of ours in the country," Mrs. Drayton explained to Humphrey. "Shabbily Irish, absent-minded, shy. She was even less in touch with the pulse of Herefordshire than I was, which I found comforting."

"There were all these girls sitting on uncomfortable chairs, exchanging men's names and addresses," Joanna said to Humphrey. "Gabriella kept looking at me, trying to get me to release information about James. Of course I didn't."

"I hope you weren't rude to her, darling," said Mrs. Drayton hurriedly. "When she was a child I found her charming — such beautiful manners . . ."

"I was invited to lots of parties when I was young," Humphrey said pleasantly. "I was friendly, so the mothers liked me, and I didn't get tight at dinner, a common failure among my contemporaries. The food was always delicious and it seemed a pity not to appreciate it, which one wouldn't if one drank too much. In those far-off distant days one could consume incredibly elaborate dinners every night of the week and still keep one's figure." He sighed and sipped his sherry. "How I envy you young people! You never take any exercise to speak of, do you, Joanna, and look at you, a slip of a thing, while I do ferocious daily battle on the squash courts and deprive myself of all kinds of treats and *still* the flesh accumulates!"

"Come on, Humphrey, you're the slimmest sixty-one-year-old in London!" said Joanna.

"What dreadful flattery!" Humphrey laughed. "And how I love to hear it!"

Although these days Joanna was fond of her cousin, it had taken her a long while to warm up to him.

"Why are you so standoffish," her mother would chide her, "when he's kindness itself to you?"

"Did I ask him to be kind to me?"

"No, but he was devoted to your grandmother, and he's

perfectly sweet to me — he's changed my life entirely for the better — it's only natural that he's sweet to you as well."

But the point was, Humphrey *wasn't* natural!

Mrs. Burridge, the practical nurse who used to help with Mrs. Beresford, had told Joanna she had it on good authority: Mr. Humphrey was only interested in boys.

"Then why's he interested in *me?*" Joanna had demanded.

"I don't think he *is,* dear, really," replied Mrs. Burridge. "He likes you, but that's different. All he's after is a family. Why shouldn't he have one, poor man, even if he is as he is? Put yourself in his shoes for a moment."

But Joanna had found that too great an imaginative feat.

Four years before, when she was fourteen, Humphrey had suggested a week at the Salzburg Festival at the end of July. The previous summer he and Barbara had gone together; this time he proposed taking Joanna, too. When her mother telephoned her at Morehaven to tell her about the wonderful invitation, her immediate response had been, "Please tell him no, thanks. I couldn't bear it."

"I don't understand. What couldn't you bear?"

"A week of purple passages, for one thing. It's sickening how he goes on about Bourbon Naples and Moorish Granada."

"We're going to Austria, not Italy or Spain."

"I don't want to go anywhere with Humphrey, not even to the corner of the street!"

But there had been no getting out of the Salzburg. Humphrey had booked and paid for everything. Joanna and her mother would fly to Munich the day after the school term ended and meet Humphrey there. Then they'd travel down to Salzburg together. They had reservations at the Kasererhof, on the river.

It rained all day the first day but the second was lovely and Humphrey suggested they take a bus to the Wallersee for a swim. Mrs. Drayton said she'd rather stay in the hotel with her opera book; she wanted to prepare for the *Abduction from the Seraglio*, which they were attending that night. "But you should go, darling," she urged Joanna.

"I want to take a nap. If I don't, I'll fall asleep in the first act."

"The Wallersee's said to be icy — a swim will perk you up," her mother said firmly.

Humphrey rented two changing cabins on the shore. Joanna changed as slowly as possible, and then with a towel wrapped tightly round her, she burst out, raced past Humphrey in his Italian bathing suit, which was two tiny blue triangles, cast aside her towel, and plunged into the lake. After her swim she dashed out of the water and threw herself facedown on the sand. "I want to sunbathe," she told Humphrey, but it was useless; he wouldn't let her. He pulled her to her feet, insisting that she walk with him along the beach, arms linked in the Continental fashion.

"You're turning into a very original young woman," he said softly. "It's a great pleasure to have you here — I'm so glad you agreed to come!" He went on to tell her stories about Nannerl and little Wolfgang, the phenomena of Europe, and about Leopold and Constanze, on and on about the Mozart family, with whom he was on a truly intimate footing, with whom he wanted to put *her* on an intimate footing. And in return for all this entertainment she knew that he was asking her to admire his body, toned assiduously on squash courts and in gymnasiums, so that he looked fifteen years younger than the fifty-seven he actually was. But she kept her eyes resolutely on the beach ahead, and when finally she summoned the will to extricate herself, she saw he was crestfallen that she hadn't acknowledged his hard muscle and smooth, tanned skin.

For months after Salzburg, whenever there was no avoiding him, in her mind's eye she stripped him of his smart London suits down to those two blue triangles. If he looked into her eyes, surely he would see his almost naked self reflected there.

But little by little she lost her horror of Cousin Humphrey. Instead of fleeing to her room in the other flat when he came to see her mother, she began to stay and talk. He was easily the most interesting person she'd met and now that the sight of him no longer gave her goose flesh, she quite liked going out for an occasional lunch alone with him; she was even willing to sit next to him on the sofa if he wanted her to.

Now he was patting her hand and saying, "It's sad you can't come with us this evening as we're going to the Havana for the first time. There was an adulatory piece in the *Telegraph* a week ago, a mixed blessing, probably, as once a place is recommended in the papers it soon begins to go downhill. I hope we catch it before that happens. If not, you'll forgive me, won't you, Barbara, and do remember, I chose it with your pleasure in mind. By the way," he added, turning back to Joanna, "peasants bore your mother, so how about seeing the Ballet Folklorico with me next Monday? If the Havana turns out to be decent, we could go there for supper afterwards."

"Next Monday Joanna will be in Herefordshire with her father," said Mrs. Drayton quickly.

When Joanna had left Morehaven and come home to the Arlington to prepare for her exam, her few London friends had all seemed to be off in Paris or Florence being finished, and if it hadn't been for Humphrey's invitations to restaurants and theaters, her life would have been very dull indeed. Humphrey also liked to buy her things. One autumn afternoon he swept her off to Harvey Nichols and bought her a chic dark-red coat with a half belt at the back to replace the dingy Morehaven coat, the only one she had. He enjoyed the selection process enormously and hadn't batted an eye at the price. "You'll only be seventeen once," he told her. "You've got to have one or two good things." Then he rushed her on to Harrods to buy what he called a dinner dress. For Christmas he gave her a gold chain bracelet. "Something to clank through life with," he had said when she opened the Cartier box.

Barbara Drayton was grateful for Humphrey's interest in her daughter; but when she realized that he was including Joanna in their outings as a matter of course, her enthusiasm wavered. She found herself "forgetting" to arrange coverage for Mrs. Beresford so that Joanna would have to stay behind to take care of her. If only Joanna would make some friends of her own! Then Barbara and Humphrey could resume the pleasant routine they had established before Joanna had intruded.

"It's seven-thirty," said Mrs. Drayton sharply. "Aren't we meeting your friends at quarter to eight?"

"Dammit, so we are!" Humphrey's face fell. "I was hoping to hear how Opus 109 is coming along, Joanna, but we'll have to wait till after Easter." He finished his sherry and stood up. "Well, enjoy your time with your father and do give him my love."

Joanna nodded. She had no intention of passing on his greeting, though. Her father's comments about Humphrey were always most unkind.

As soon as her mother and Humphrey had left and she was alone, she switched off the lights in the sitting room. She stood at the window, looking out at the darkened park, until a clock struck eight and it was time to chivvy her grandmother awake.

She was deeply sorry for her grandmother. The second stroke ought to have killed her instead of leaving her like this; she was deeply sorry, also, for her mother, so long a captive. But even on bad days she refused to feel sorry for herself because the Arlington wasn't *her* prison. Soon she'd be off — she had to believe that. Soon she'd be leading her own life.

Chapter 11

Widleigh

ON FRIDAY Joanna went to Herefordshire to spend Easter with her father.

When the Little Event occurred in the summer of 1950 and Barbara Drayton, seizing the day, had rushed to her mother's side, James had been almost nineteen. At the end of term, one month later, he'd left Eton, gone immediately into basic training with the regiment, and thence eight thousand miles to fight Communist insurgents in the Malayan jungle. By the time he had completed his national service, returned to England, and gone up to Oxford, he was of age. Where he spent his vacations was up to him; and having switched from Classics to Modern Languages, he chose to spend them on the Continent, catching up with the living, as he told each of his parents, after wasting so much time with the dead.

But when Henry and Barbara Drayton parted, Joanna had been just eleven years old. A great deal of time would have to elapse before *she* came of age. There had been no divorce and no court ruling, but her parents had an immutable understanding that *she must be shared*. Every year she was her father's for Christmas, Easter, the month of August, and one half-term holiday.

"For my sake you've got to go," Mrs. Drayton would tell her. "He doesn't want me — I doubt he ever wanted me. He wants *you* though, as much as ever, and if you don't put in your time on the cross, he'll make *me* go back so he can have you. You know as well as I how wretched my existence was at Widleigh. I'll stick my head in the gas oven rather than live that way again. I mean it, I really do, Joanna. You can't let the side down!"

Ramrod straight, Henry Drayton was waiting on the platform when Joanna got off the train at Hereford Station. He called a porter — he didn't carry suitcases himself anymore — and led her out to the yard where the shooting brake that had replaced the Bentley was parked. Henry was feeling in his pocket for change with which to tip the porter when Nigel Cooper appeared beside them. "I heard you came to Hill Street just the other day!" he exclaimed, flashing Joanna a smile. He looked as healthy, handsome, and expensive as ever, and much younger than Lady Harriet. "How amusing to run into you here! How long will you be down?"

"Till Easter Monday."

"Splendid! Gabriella, the boys, and assorted young will be arriving the day after tomorrow and then you'll have to come over to Spurlock to see us." It was said in the neighborhood that Nigel Cooper had recently given fifty thousand pounds to Conservative party funds, in return for which he confidently looked forward to receiving a knighthood in the next birthday honors. In expectation of his title, he stood a little taller and forced himself a little more insistently on the attention of others. "I suppose you're here often to see your papa," he remarked to Joanna.

Henry Drayton sniffed the hair oil that Nigel used on his handsome head. "Not often enough," he said.

Nigel laughed a deep, rich laugh that made Joanna think of plum pudding with too much brandy butter on it. "I know, one's meant to feel grateful that they come at all. My boys would never darken my door if they didn't want money. They think I should supply it in unlimited amounts on the theory that *they* know how to enjoy it whereas, in my senescence, *I* don't! Naturally they couldn't be more mistaken. Well, I shan't keep you. I hope we see you both very soon," and he strode away to the ice-blue Mercedes waiting for him at the curb. While his master had held court with the Draytons, the chauffeur had been wiping the spotless windscreen. Now he scampered round to open the door and Joanna recognized Stillwell, the butler, dressed in chauffeur's uniform. Having ushered Colonel Cooper into the car, he jumped into the front and drove off. Joanna watched as the Mercedes paused at the entrance to the station yard, then slid to the left and out of sight.

"Get in!" Henry said gruffly. "The door's unlocked."

They drove slowly through the town and as they reached the countryside and picked up speed, Joanna closed her eyes. She was absorbing the confusion that always engulfed her when she first saw her father after three months away. She knew, though, that by the time they reached Widleigh she would have reorganized herself. She'd had plenty of practice, after all.

For the first few years after the separation, the specter of her mother on her knees in the narrow Arlington kitchen with her head in the oven was all that prevented Joanna from letting the side down, because, despite what Mrs. Drayton said about Henry wanting her, he certainly didn't behave as if he did.

The week his wife left him he told Mrs. Burgess to close up all the rooms in the house except the two or three he used himself. Blinds were drawn, furniture was covered with dust-sheets, doors were locked and the keys hung on labeled hooks in the pantry. Before Joanna's visits her father would order her red wallpapered bedroom — formerly Miss Cathcart's — opened and aired, but he made no other concession. The blind piano tuner no longer made his twice-yearly visits; the television, bought a month before Mrs. Drayton's departure, was consigned to the attic; when the gramophone broke it stayed in disrepair. Henry was out on the farm most of the day and his evenings he spent as before, reading Scott and Thackeray, Eliot and Dickens, in the smoking room with the door shut. The smoking room was where he ate his meals, too, from a tray, while Joanna ate hers in the kitchen.

Only once a day did he attempt to include his daughter in his solitary existence — her presence at tea in the dining room was mandatory. But even then he paid her little attention. There were times when he did not talk to her at all and they would sit across the table from each other, rattling cups and buttering crumpets, without even the morning paper as a screen between them. He rarely asked about her life at school and never about her mother. (Having had his wife's clothes, books, and papers packed and sent Railway Express to the Arlington, with a note, "Any matters pertaining to the children will be handled by my solicitor, William Chadwick, whose address you know," he did not communicate directly with her again.)

On some afternoons, though, he would burst out of silence in midsentence, as if he had been talking to her for a long while; and having fulminated about the postal service or the inequitable nature of the British tax system, he would stop as abruptly as he'd started. For the rest of the meal he would stare down the long table, seeing nothing but the images in his own head. But on other occasions, after an interval of silent, mounting bitterness, he would lean across cinnamon toast, digestive biscuits, and odds and ends of cake to denounce classmates who had snubbed him at Eton, masters who had favored tardy, disorganized boys over himself, a woman called Beryl Parker who had broken their engagement to marry a younger, richer man, commanding officers who had humiliated him and passed him over for promotion. (Although he had come out of the Great War deserving to be made a lieutenant-colonel, when he retired from the army, in 1930, he was a major still.) Most often his targets were his own parents, who had never praised him, never missed him during the long years he was away in India, in no way recognized him for being the best son he knew how to be. As he roared and shouted he would search his daughter's face for signs that she accepted what he told her about those two whom she knew only in sepia photographs: her grandfather (the spitting image of her father) in plus fours, her grandmother, in cloche, muffler, and long alpaca jacket, their stern features softened somewhat by the thirty-odd years that their photographs had stood on the drawing room piano. If Joanna shut her eyes in self-protection, her father would shout, "Look at me, damn you! Listen to what I have to tell you and never forget it!"

Once, in a voice that was suddenly most desolate, he cried, "The only truly happy time I've known was with Sybilla. *She was so kind,* then she went behind my back, betrayed me!"

During these early visits Joanna would telephone her mother surreptitiously — asking to reverse the charges so that her father wouldn't discover her disloyalty later, from the telephone bill — and beg to be allowed to leave. Once only was permission granted: one teatime, in rage and despair, Henry seized a corner of the cloth that demarcated the quarter of the table they used and pulled it clear so that plates and cups and saucers, teapot and hot water jug, went crashing to the floor. Joanna fled, weeping, from the room down the pantry passage and through the empty kitchen to Agnes's cottage in the stable yard. That night, when she knew her father would be in bed, she crept into the house and telephoned her mother, who agreed, in the face of choking tears, to the August visit being shortened by six days. But never was Joanna excused from going to Widleigh. "If you miss," her mother told her, "your father will make my life a misery . . ."

Within months of his wife's leaving Henry Drayton sold his horses and let his fishing to a stockbroker from Birmingham. He stopped going to race meetings and county cricket matches.

When invitations to social gatherings arrived he dropped them in the wastepaper basket. Since he didn't take the trouble to respond to them one way or the other, they petered out, and lifelong acquaintances, driving along the river road, would look up at the great pink stone house on the hillside and say to themselves, He must still be alive or one would have read an obituary.

Joanna would rather have died in solitary torment than invite a Morehaven classmate to share with her the silences and rages of her father. His abruptness on the telephone soon put off Lady Harriet in her attempts to arrange tennis dates for their daughters. Thus, her cousins Sep and Cynthia were her only visitors. They would simply appear, as before, for a week each summer, and because they were relations, even Henry Drayton didn't have it in him to send them away. However, he wouldn't allow Joanna to go back to Warwickshire with them as she had in the past. "You're here to visit me, not them," he told her.

That the Knightleys were at least as unconventional as the Draytons was a source of some comfort to Joanna. Following their grandmother's death, Sep and Cynthia spent their school holidays with the servants; their father had removed himself from their lives and their mother, the demented Caroline, came and went as her furies moved her. One August, while the twins were at Widleigh, the furies moved her to walk out of a London theater, take a taxi to the airport, and board a plane to Sydney, whence she was returned under armed guard. But there was something to be said, Joanna decided, for having a mother who was unequivocally, *publicly* mad, instead of privately mad, like her father. Besides, at times, so her children reported, Caroline was sane and cheerful, which Henry never was.

By and large, the twins seemed less upset by their anomalous situation than Joanna was by hers. Then, they had each other, whereas she very rarely had James, who was so often away, off in Aix or Andalusia or, one endless summer, in Canada being a lumberjack. Their evenings in front of the fire in his bedroom at Widleigh receded further and further into the past. But Joanna promised herself that one day whatever had gone wrong between James and herself would be set right.

She spent long hours of her visits in the dusty library, where she read *Travels in West Africa, The Oregon Trail, The Voyage of the Beagle, Life in Mexico.* With Mary Kingsley, Parkman, Darwin, Frances Calderón de la Barca, and a dozen other brave, foolhardy nineteenth-century men and women, she journeyed as far as she could from Widleigh, while bracing herself for the daily encounter with her father in the dining room at tea. Her dread, of course, was that his rage would turn on *her.* She wasn't dead or off in India. She was sitting four feet from him trying not to blink or flinch or weep.

But her time on the cross eventually came to an end.

The first afternoon of her Easter visit just before she was fifteen, as she listened to her father curse *his* father — in 1895 he had had Henry's first labrador put to sleep for no good reason while Henry was away at Winterfields — it dawned on her that she wasn't frightened of him anymore. He'd lost the power to compel her to listen or even to look at him; her mind was wandering and her eyes as well.

Next day at suppertime, just as she was sitting down to eat at the kitchen table, Henry appeared from the smoking room, tray in hand. "Is it all right if I join you?" he said. Later he asked if there was anything in particular that she wanted to do while she was at Widleigh. In almost four years he had never asked her that. "I'd like to be able to play the drawing room piano, and to see a film," she told him. In the morning the piano tuner was telephoned and an appointment made, and after an early lunch, off they went to the cinema in Hereford, where, at two o'clock, the only other person in the audience was an old woman in a black coat with a moth-eaten Persian lamb collar. Head to one side, the woman snored softly.

That evening, as they ate their supper in the dining room —

"Why not," her father said, "we'll be out of Agnes's way" — he told her that he was about to sell his stock — his Friesians and his Cheviots — and let the farms he had in hand to a man called Roger Gillingham, who was new to these parts. "I'll be seventy next January," he told Joanna. "It's wise to slow down."

"But what will you do without the farm to keep you busy?" she said. You've taken leave of your senses, she thought; and then, Or could it be that you've *come* to them?

"I'll have more than enough to do with the Drayton papers. There are boxes that have sat for centuries — no one's looked in them since they were filled up and shut. I shall need plenty of help, though, from some young person with good eyes. How do you fancy the job, my love?"

"I'm going back to Morehaven, Daddy."

"That won't go on forever. One day soon you'll leave that place," he said happily, "and then there'll be enough to keep us busy here for many, many years."

Only I'm going to be a concert pianist, she opened her mouth to tell him, but not having the heart, she said instead, "Miss Hilary could help you in the meantime. She's used to helping her brother with the bishops of Hereford and Gloucester."

Her father ignored the suggestion. "When exactly will you leave Morehaven?"

"When I'm seventeen and I've taken my A-level exams."

"Why must you?"

"So I can earn a living."

"Did I ever say you'd have to?"

"No, but you admire energetic, independent women, and I do, too. A woman who can't make her own way in the world isn't up to much."

Her father shrugged. "There's no harm in having qualifications, I grant you, just in case. But so long as you're living here with me you won't need them."

Soon they were eating all their meals together and Joanna

was accompanying her father and the dogs on the long walks that he still took every afternoon at three (if not at three and a half miles an hour). But when Grizelda died he decided against replacing her. "A puppy would take so much effort," he said. "Dolly's enough for me." He still raged occasionally but his rages rumbled and rambled and rolled away, and as the end of a visit drew near he would plead, "Stay a little longer, just a day or two!" Now that he loved her he took great care of her, thereby letting her know that he needed *her* to care for *him*.

As the car bumped over the cattle grid at the bottom of the drive, Joanna awakened with a start. "I must have dozed off — I'm sorry."

"It's a long journey down from London, lovey. I'm not surprised you fell asleep."

Henry drove round the side of the house and into the stable yard. He stopped at the back door. So he doesn't use the front anymore, Joanna thought. Another retreat.

In the kitchen he said, "We'll have our tea now. I told Agnes not to come in — she's left everything ready for us. I'll just boil the kettle. How do you like my new gadget, by the way?" he added, showing Joanna a blue electric kettle. "Boils water in thirty seconds flat. It was Agnes's suggestion and at first I said I didn't care for anything so quick." He smiled shyly at his daughter. "You know your old father doesn't take easily to new ideas."

"It's a pretty color."

He was pleased. "The others I saw were silver and brown. The silver was too flashy for us and there's too much brown in here as it is." He removed his cap and laid it on the kitchen table as the kettle started to whistle. "See what I mean!"

He led the way to the smoking room, where a fire burned. "Mrs. Crompton lit it in your honor," he remarked. "Put the tray over there." He indicated a low table beside the fireplace.

"You're cold, aren't you, lovey. I'll give you your tea right away."

"A fire makes all the difference in this room," Joanna said gently. "I wish you'd light it every day, not just in my honor."

"But I never feel the cold! Here's your tea." His hands shook a little and the cup rattled in the saucer. "Let's see what we have in the way of cake today," he added, taking the lid off a large tin. Inside was a chocolate layer cake, Agnes's specialty. "Super!" he exclaimed, and cut a big slice for Joanna. "Got everything you need now?"

"Everything, thank you."

Henry lowered himself carefully into his leather armchair, stretched his legs out, and waited for his daughter to breathe new life into him. Joanna took a bite of cake and savored it. "Even better than I remembered," she said, and added, "It's lovely to be home."

"It's lovely to have you here," Henry said softly. Joanna glanced at his glowing face and then away. At the beginning of her visits she always felt in danger of melting, losing herself, if she held her father's loving gaze. Tomorrow she would be able to meet his eyes without fear of being absorbed, but today she needed to ration him, in order to be sure of keeping herself separate, her own person.

He started to tell her about his tenants' most recent attempts to improve or ruin his property, and as he talked his eyes seemed less hollow than before. He got up and went to the window, where she joined him so that he could point out what so-and-so had done here and what so-and-so intended to do over there. "Ready for more cake?" he asked when he had finished.

"No, thanks, I'm full."

"Then perhaps you'd like to get settled upstairs." He was prepared to let her out of his sight for a few moments. "Mrs. Burgess did a tremendous cleaning — she took the carpet down to the lawn to beat it. You should have seen the dust!"

At the door Joanna said, "Have another cup of tea while you're waiting. I shan't be long." She climbed the back stairs and went along the landing. At James's door she stopped and tried the dull brass handle, but of course the door was locked. At Christmas two years before her father had locked it himself and thrown away the key.

That Christmas, the sixth of the separation, Joanna had taken the train to Hereford as usual. "Is James at home already?" she asked her father when she saw him at the station.

"Been home a good while, in fact."

"I haven't heard a word from him since September. I suppose he's working too hard to write letters." James was in his last year at Oxford; he had Schools in June.

"Working hard? I doubt that," replied her father.

As soon as they reached Widleigh Joanna went to the kitchen to greet Agnes. Her cat, Charlie, elderly and fat now, still lay on the shelf above the Aga, but the mongrel, Chip, had been run over by a speeding delivery van. As she put on the kettle for tea she remarked, "I suppose the Major told you."

"Told me what?"

"About your brother."

"Yes, that he's here."

"That's all he said?"

Joanna stiffened. "What else is there?"

Agnes filled the teapot and, when Joanna had a mug of tea and she had one as well, said, "It was two months ago today, at dinnertime, that he walked in. He'd come eleven miles on foot from the station. Left his car in Oxford and all his things as well. Mr. Pickering went down and fetched them later."

"Two months ago!" Joanna pushed her mug away. "I don't understand . . ."

"And he hasn't gone a step past this kitchen since. The first night he was with me, then he moved out to that cottage up against the park wall. No one had lived there since I came on the place, though at one time they used it for sheep. Anyway, *he's* there now. Only comes in here when he knows the Major's out. He was here an hour ago, in fact, while the Major was off meeting your train. If I was you, Joanna, I wouldn't go looking for him," she added gently. "He likes his privacy, does James."

"I'm going to speak to Daddy," said Joanna, jumping up.

"I warn you, the Major doesn't like to talk about your brother," Agnes said, shaking her head.

Joanna found her father listening to the racing news in the smoking room. As she walked in he snapped off the radio, remarking, "Dreadful going at York. They've got a blizzard up there."

"Agnes told me James came home from Oxford in October. Why?"

Henry Drayton shrugged. "Haven't had the chance to ask him. He's been giving me a very wide berth."

"What did Christ Church tell you? He couldn't have walked off without their noticing!"

"Certainly they noticed. They wrote me a rather civil letter, saying that things had got a bit out of hand and he'd had to spend a few days in the hospital. They recommended that he take further rest at home."

"James was in the hospital! What hospital?"

"The Warnford. It's where they lock up Oxford undergraduates who go nuts. Dons as well, I imagine."

"What else did they say in the letter?"

"I've forgotten."

"Can I see it?"

"Afraid not. I threw it in the fire," Henry said matter-of-factly, but his nose had begun to twitch.

"What did they tell you at the hospital?"

"From them I heard nothing. James is of age, you know. Legally I'm not responsible for him."

"Even so, you didn't get in touch with the doctors?" Joanna

sat down abruptly in front of the hearth, across from her father.

After a moment Henry said dryly, "This isn't the first time your brother has made an ass of himself. He did it in Malaya, too. Let's see, when was that? About five years ago, I'd say. But because of Drayton regimental connections his commanding officer sent him down to Singapore — and took him back after he'd had a bit of an airing — instead of sending him home, which, in retrospect, might have been the better move."

"What do you mean exactly by James making an ass of himself?"

"Made out he was Mahatma Gandhi — not even Jesus Christ" — Henry's voice hardened — "so that he could get out of fighting in the jungle. This time I imagine he pulled the same trick to get out of his examinations." He crossed his legs and went on. "D'you know who I really hold responsible? I never approved of your grandmother giving you children money. Of course she didn't ask me for my opinion on the matter, just went ahead, and last August your brother got his. Then he was free to do anything he damn well pleased."

"Five thousand pounds isn't much money."

"It's enough to live in a shepherd's cottage on macaroni and cheese."

After a moment Joanna said, "Have you talked to him once since he came back here?"

"Not even once." Henry leaned forward. "How about you?"

"Of course not — I've only been here fifteen minutes!"

"When you've had the unpleasant experience of trying to talk to him, perhaps you'll be a little less forceful in your tone."

The next morning Henry was off to sell a saddle to a man in Leominster and he asked Joanna if she wanted to go, too. She excused herself — she had Christmas cards to write — and as soon as she heard him drive away she went to the kitchen to wait for James. "Seeing as you're here," Agnes said, "how about peeling these carrots."

When she heard him in the stable yard she stayed where she was, at the sink. He was on the steps, he was rattling the back door handle, and then she turned and saw him on the threshold in his old gray overcoat. He'd just cut himself shaving, and as he walked in he dabbed his cheek with a rag. He seemed taller and thinner than she remembered, as if he'd grown out there on the hillside, even though he was twenty-four and had long since reached his full height. His wrists showed white and bony at the ends of his overcoat sleeves. His hair lay lank on his collar.

When his eyes met his sister's, he flushed a slow, deep red. She washed her hands and dried them on the roller towel above the draining board and then she went to him. "How are you?" she said. But as she touched his arm he shrank away.

"There's lamb stew," Agnes said quickly. "Do you fancy some?" He nodded, but although he unbuttoned his overcoat he didn't take it off. He sat at the table and waited to be served.

Joanna stood across from him, hands shaking. "I'm terribly sorry," she said softly.

"Sorry about what?"

"About the troubles you've had."

He frowned. "I don't know what you're referring to. It's wonderful to have time to write at last."

"What are you writing?"

"Do you honestly think I'd tell you? You might steal my ideas!"

Agnes handed him a plate heaped with stew and vegetables, and he hunched over it and wolfed it down. "More?" she asked when he had finished, but he got up without replying. "Off so soon and your sister just arrived to see you!"

"Well, she's seen me, hasn't she! What else does she want?"

"Stay and talk to me!" Joanna pleaded. "Tell me what's happening!"

"No time for chitchat," James said, buttoning his coat. "I've got too much to do."

The next morning, Christmas Eve, Pickering brought in a pine from the plantation and set it up in the hall. Every Christmas Eve that Joanna could remember she and James had decorated the tree together. This year she draped tinsel and hung up the glass ornaments alone; afterwards she put on her coat and boots and went outside. She walked quickly through the park and climbed the stile into the frosty field behind James's cottage. He wasn't there; from fifty yards she saw the padlock on the door. Feeling like a spy, a thief, she examined the place furtively. James had boarded up one window and replaced broken panes in the other. The putty round the new glass was still fresh. He had attempted to fix the roof by nailing a tarpaulin over it, and there were two new, pale planks in the door. Against one wall, logs were stacked neatly; two buckets, for fetching water from the cattle trough inside the park, as Agnes told her he did, stood side by side in the grass near the door. When she peered inside she made out a cot, a chair, several piles of books on the floor, a packing case strewn with sheets of paper. No desk, no typewriter. Ashes glowed in the fireplace and a blackened kettle stood on the hearth.

Perhaps he had gone to renew his supply of those water biscuits he used to eat in the old days, while he wrote his tales of mystery and imagination in the style of Edgar Allan Poe, Joanna thought sadly.

She turned one of the buckets on its rim and sat down to wait for him, but after an hour and still no sign, it occurred to her that he might have spotted her from a distance; he might be staying away until she'd gone.

When she got back to the house she found Agnes in the kitchen, stuffing the turkey. "D'you think he'll come tomorrow?" Joanna asked.

"If you mean your brother, I wish I could tell you yes, but I can't."

"Out of *habit* he might. At any rate, we'll lay a place for him?"

Agnes sighed and said nothing.

"I knitted them identical V-neck pullovers. Daddy's is maroon and James's is blue. I was hoping they'd wear them tomorrow . . . I do hope they fit! Daddy's ought to, I measured him last summer, but with James's, I had to guess because I hadn't seen him since Easter and I hadn't thought of knitting him a pullover then." Joanna rushed on, "There's a waiter at the Arlington who's about James's size, so one day before the restaurant opened for lunch, I went down with a tape measure and asked if he wouldn't mind. He whipped off his coat and was perfectly sweet about it. Afterwards, though, I wondered whether his arms mightn't have been shorter than James's . . ."

Joanna gave her father the pullover at breakfast on Christmas morning. He put it on immediately and it fitted. "This is a big step up from the scarf you gave me for my birthday, lovey. What an accomplished knitter you've become!" he said. Then he gave her a long, red leather box with gold tooling, inside which was a double string of pearls. Barbara Drayton had worn them for the twenty years of her marriage until she'd chosen — as she sometimes put it to her daughter — "a sort of life with your grandmother over no life at all with *him*." She'd left them in their box on Henry's desk in the smoking room. Henry had put them in the vault in the Hereford branch of the Westminster Bank that same afternoon.

"What's this!" Joanna exclaimed.

"Your great-grandfather gave them to your great-grandmother."

"And *you* gave them to my mother."

"That's right, and now I'm giving them to you."

"But they're meant for James's wife when he gets married."

"I can give them to anyone I want and I want to give them to you. Let's see how they look on you."

She shook her head violently. "I don't want them! I'd feel awful wearing them!" She snapped the box shut and handed it back. "It's not right for me to have them!"

"You're being sentimental," Henry said, hurt and angry. He slipped the box into his jacket pocket, got up, and left the room.

James's present lay unopened next to his place at the table.

Joanna and her father walked in silence through the shrubbery to church, where Henry Drayton read the Gospel: "'I bring you good tidings of great joy. . . . Peace, good will toward men.'" In the graveyard afterwards they exchanged pleasantries of the season with Philip Ogden-Smith, Thomas Edgerton's successor. (Having fallen and broken his hip the previous summer, Mr. Edgerton had retired with Miss Hilary to a south-coast town, where his manuscript was receiving his undivided attention.)

"Got the whole family with you, Major Drayton?" boomed Ogden-Smith, who, until his spiritual awakening at the age of thirty-six, had been a Household Cavalry officer.

"Yes, the whole family."

"Wonderful! I had so hoped to meet your son, James, this morning, but I see he sleeps late."

At lunch Henry carved the turkey and then he filled two plates with a combination of light and dark meat, stuffing, vegetables, and onion sauce. He set one heaped plate in front of Joanna; the other he took himself.

"But there are three of us!" exclaimed Joanna.

"Two," her father said. "Your brother won't show his face in here."

"He loves turkey," said Joanna, despairing.

"No doubt he'll get some later. Agnes spoils him rotten, don't think I don't know!"

After the meal Joanna removed James's present to her room; she'd take it to the cottage later. As she was on her way downstairs she heard her father shout from the smoking room, "I want to talk to you. Come here, I'm waiting, I've been waiting for two months, in fact!"

She hurried across the hall into the pantry passage. At the far end she saw James, unshaven, grimy, framed in the kitchen doorway, with Agnes hovering behind him.

"I want to talk to you!" Henry shouted a second time. He shifted from foot to foot and flexed his fingers, spoiling for a fight.

Agnes gave James a little push and he started off along the passage. Reaching his father, he said flatly, "What d'you want to talk to me about?"

"I'll say what I have to say in here."

Hands in his trouser pockets, James went into the smoking room. Henry followed and from opposite ends of the passage Joanna and Agnes converged on the closed door. Henry's voice came through to them loud and then cracked, the words swallowed and spat out by turn. Joanna imagined him standing at his desk, gripping the back of the chair, as the old rage — the rage she had so often witnessed in the dining room — boiled anew. In an occasional lull she heard James's slow voice, muffled by the door. Nothing father or son said was intelligible to her, but then suddenly Henry's voice came clearly. "You're a deserter, a runaway, James Drayton! You're running away from your life!"

The door sprang open and James plunged out with Henry a step or two behind him. Joanna expected to see him grab his son, shake him, punch him, knock him down, but he stopped short and grasped the doorpost to steady himself as he watched James stumble off down the passage and out through the kitchen to the stable yard. Henry cocked his head, listening, and when he no longer heard footsteps on the gravel, he turned into the room and groped his way past chairs and tables to the window to see James crossing the park. But James was nowhere to be seen — he had gone back to the cottage another way — and after a few minutes, when her father turned from the window, Joanna saw that his face was awash with tears.

Agnes led her to the kitchen. "A cup of tea won't hurt," she said, and put the kettle on to boil.

"What do *you* think is the matter with James?"

"That he's a poor lonely soul is what I think. I wish there was someone to take him as he is, not wanting something different, like your father does."

"Why does Daddy hate him so?"

"He's led the Major quite a dance, has Mr. James. And this didn't begin in October, either, if you ask me. He's been carrying on for years. Even as a child he wasn't easy. Always one to rub you the wrong way."

"He didn't rub *me* the wrong way!"

"No? Maybe not, but you had more patience with him than was reasonable, Joanna, is what I've often thought."

They heard Henry Drayton on the landing above. He stopped for a moment at James's door and came down the back stairs and through the kitchen. In his right hand he held a long, black key. "Where are you going with that?" Joanna cried. Unheeding, he went outside to the well in the middle of the yard. He leaned across the stone parapet, and they heard a faint splash as the key hit the water twenty feet below.

During the remainder of Joanna's visit James didn't come into the house.

When Joanna took his present to the cottage the day before her visit was over, she found it locked, and so she left the parcel on an upturned bucket by the door. She also left a note over which she had agonized for hours. After writing many drafts and tearing them all up, she'd ended with, "I hope this fits and soon I see you wear it."

But she never heard if it fitted, let alone saw him wear it. By the time she went back to Widleigh for her Easter visit, he was gone. "Went off one March morning," Agnes told her. "Without warning, like he showed up in the first place." At least he hadn't gone back to the station on foot — Mrs. Crompton had seen him on the bus, with one small bag. "She didn't try to get him into conversation, he didn't look like he'd encourage that." So no one knew where he had gone to, or why.

One evening the following July, when Joanna was watching her grandmother while her mother went to Glyndebourne with Humphrey, James telephoned. "Hello," he said. "What are you up to?"

"*Where have you been?*" she cried. "I've been so worried!"

"Worried about *me*? I don't believe it!"

"Where are you now?"

"In London, of course."

"Where are you living and who with?" He didn't answer. "When can I see you? Can you come here now? I'm alone, except for Granny. Mummy won't be back till very late."

"I detest the Arlington — I always have," James said. "I shan't go there."

"Just tell me when and where then!"

"The Café Europa in Baker Street, the Euston Station end, tomorrow at four."

"I'll go there straight from Mr. Ehrenreich."

"Still slogging away with him, are you? Faithful, earnest, *resolute* Joanna!" James mocked.

She was silent. "Are you all right now?" she asked eventually.

"Why shouldn't I be? My plans for Spain are set."

"Spain! You're going?"

"Yes, indeed. I'm off there with a friend."

"Which friend? How long do you plan to be away?"

"Possibly forever."

"You're not going back to Oxford?"

"You can bet your life I'm not!" After a moment he went on. "So tell me, what's the boyfriend situation? Scaring them off as much as ever, I bet. Not surprising." He laughed mirthlessly. "Men can't stand pushy girls who keep asking questions about things that aren't their business."

A whimper came from the bedroom. "Granny's awake," Joanna said, tears stinging. "I'd better see what she wants."

The next day Joanna arrived at the Café Europa at quarter to four, sat at a table in the corner, and waited, Elvis Presley blaring, but her brother didn't come. At seven, having paid for five cups of tea, she left and walked home through Kensington Gardens, where dogs and children raced beside the Serpentine and in and out of shadows lying long across summer grass. She let herself into the flat just as her mother and Nurse Channing were sitting down to supper.

"*Where* have you been?" Mrs. Drayton exclaimed, exasperated. "We were about to ring the police."

"Whatever for?"

"Because you're three hours late! We were afraid the worst had happened!"

"What would that be, I wonder," Joanna murmured, and then in a normal voice, "I was enjoying the good weather. Who knows how long it'll last." As she took her place at the table, she added in as casual a tone as she could manage, "Last night James rang."

Mrs. Drayton started. "He did? Good Lord! He's not wanting to come here, is he? We're full up now that Nurse O'Hara's in the spare room."

"He's going to Spain."

"Thank goodness. Can you imagine how awful it would be, having him here!" She added, "If he's going to Spain, he must be out of the state he was in when you last saw him."

"State?"

"Well, what would you call it? Poor way — you *know* what I mean, Joanna!"

If he were out of it he wouldn't have mocked her; he'd have laughed *with* her, not *at* her; he'd have shown up at the Café Europa. "I wouldn't say he was out of it at all."

Each afternoon of her Easter visit Joanna accompanied her father on a tour of his property, and they passed quite close to James's cottage several times. One afternoon, instead of bearing off to the right as he always had before, Henry marched straight up to it. Joanna spotted a rusting bucket in front of the open door. The tarpaulin that James had nailed across the roof had come loose and hung down over the eaves. What remained of his wood supply was scattered through the grass.

"Do you fancy yourself a farmer, my love?" Henry asked, stopping suddenly.

"Me, Daddy?" Joanna was startled out of her thoughts. "I know nothing about farming."

"After I'm dead, would you live here?" Henry looked past her at the door, creaking in the light wind. His fingers tightened on the handle of his walking stick and he held his breath as he waited for her answer.

Softly, reluctantly, she told him, "I don't think so. I'll have my musical career by then. Anyway," she went on, "James will live here. Widleigh's for him, not for me."

"James doesn't give a damn about Widleigh," her father shouted, turning on her. "He wouldn't care if the whole place slid into the Wye. If he ever sets foot here, I'll throw him out! Only I won't have to take the trouble — he's gone for good. He'll never come back again." As he thrust his face up close to hers Joanna smelled his sour breath. "Tell me that James cares about Widleigh, and I'll tell you that you lie!"

There was a childish part of her that still feared his rage and grief, and she had to step back and close her eyes for an instant while she told herself that he was tired and old and bitter, whereas she, at least, was young. She said steadily, "Last time we saw James, there was something terribly the matter with him. That's why he ran away from here, from England altogether."

Henry sighed and she was encouraged, believing he was listening to her.

"We've got to try to find him, Daddy. We can't let him vanish off the face of the earth!"

But he hadn't heard her after all. "I've only got you now," he said flatly. "You're the only one left," and he turned away from the cottage and walked off.

~~~~~~~~~~~~~~~~~~~~~~~~~~~~~~~~~~~~~~~

Chapter 12

Spurlock

THE TELEPHONE RANG when they were in the smoking room
after supper that evening. "It's for you. Some young person,"
Henry Drayton said, handing Joanna the receiver.

"Isn't the country a living death!" a girl said. "After three
days of staring at the rain we're all going out of our minds."

"Excuse me, who's this?"

"You mean you don't recognize my voice and we've been
friends since we were two! You *are* an odd bird, Joanna. It's me,
Gabriella! Anyway, to break the cycle of boredom we're having
a party on Saturday night. There'll be just ourselves and a few
house guests for dinner, but lots of other people will be coming
afterwards to dance. You wouldn't be up to playing the piano,
by any chance? But popular music isn't really your kind of
thing, is it, so I suppose we'll have to make do with the gramophone. You will come, won't you? We'd love to see your papa
as well. Mummy says she's been very out of touch with him."

"Just a second." Joanna put her hand over the mouthpiece.
"The Coopers are inviting both of us to dinner. Would you like
to go?"

"I'd *hate* to go!"

"He says, thank you," Joanna told Gabriella, "but he's not
much of a party goer. He's always in bed by half past nine. I'd
like to come, though."

"Terrific! It was fun seeing you last week. You've been hidden away for so long, we've got so much catching up to do. Of course you drive?"

"I don't, as a matter of fact, but my father will bring me over."

"And we'll get you a lift back. We wouldn't want to keep your papa up past his bedtime. Mummy's just the same — she barely stays awake till the end of dinner. Well, lovely talking to you. See you on Saturday at eight!"

Joanna replaced the receiver and sat down on the stool in front of the fire. "It'll be interesting to go to Spurlock again," she said. "I wonder what Giles and Steven are like now. Do you remember how bumptious they used to be . . ." Her voice trailed off. She had been about to say, when they were at Eton with James.

"Why should they be any different?" said Henry. "As a boy Nigel was impossible and he still is. With the single exception of Harriet, who married in, all the Coopers are identical in character. Shallow, vain, and self-congratulatory. Beats me why you'd want to have anything to do with them."

After a moment's silence Joanna said gently, "We'll have a good dinner and we'll be home by midnight. Won't you change your mind and come, too?"

"What's wrong with Agnes's dinners? And since when have we gone gallivanting about the countryside? I don't see why we should start now."

Joanna counted the brass studs along one end of the firestool; there were fourteen. "There's no harm in going. Besides, when they see what a dull sort I am, they won't invite me again."

Henry went back to reading *Cobbett's Rural Rides*. "Richard Drayton," so the populist reformer had written in 1830, "was most generous of his time and hospitality. Together we fished, shot partridge, and spoke of many agricultural matters. He appears to treat his tenants equitably, and the houses he recently constructed for his laborers are of exemplary design. Each has two bedrooms, an outhouse, a stone sink, and a quarter acre of vegetable garden." In William Cobbett's day the Welsh Marches had teemed with Draytons, but as the nineteenth century wore on they had died or departed for broader futures in Ontario, the Eastern Cape, or on the Queensland littoral; one hundred and twenty-seven years later, only three remained: Henry, his son, and his daughter.

Joanna reached up and took her father's hand. "I'm sorry."

"I see so little of you, lovey," Henry said. "I don't like it a bit when you go off."

After her father had gone to bed Joanna considered the clothes she had brought with her from London. Two skirts, a pair of trousers, a very ordinary wool dress, and a black taffeta skirt that on impulse she had thrown into her suitcase. But she hadn't brought a blouse to wear with it and she didn't want to ask her father to drive her into Hereford to buy one. Besides, she had already spent that quarter's allowance.

A vague memory came to her of a Guatemalan blouse, a memento of Miss Cathcart's exotic past, that had been kept in the dressing-up box. If she could find it, it might just do.

She left her room and tiptoed down the front stairs to the schoolroom. She was lucky; the door was unlocked. She flicked on the switch but the bulb had blown out, so she raised the blinds and moonlight flooded in. She scanned the shelves where once she and Miss Cathcart had arranged their specimens in labeled jam jars. All that remained from those busy days was a set of encyclopedias and an opus on wildflowers. Once there had been a companion volume on birds. Both had belonged to Miss Cathcart, who, at her departure, had forgotten her flower volume.

The dressing-up box had been stored in a cupboard that took up the whole length of one wall. By moonlight Joanna searched through it section by section until finally she spotted an old trunk behind a pile of squash rackets, cricket bats, hunting boots, and assorted accouterments of the sporting life. From the trunk she extracted Henry VIII's hat with an ostrich feather, Charles II's wig, Red Riding Hood's red riding hood, her father's full-dress military uniform, a ball gown of her mother's, the silver lace now nearly black. Near the bottom she found what she'd been looking for and held it up against herself. It would fit where it touched, it would do, and she smiled at the prospect of appearing at Spurlock in a Guatemalan peasant blouse last worn by Miss Cathcart — junoesque Miss Cathcart, that whaling ship figurehead of a woman — in a Midsummer pageant a decade before.

Reports of Miss Cathcart having been sighted in Newcastle upon Tyne, Holland Park (exercising a Staffordshire terrier), the Cathedral Close at Salisbury, and on the beach at Trouville had come in over the years, but the only concrete proof of her continued existence after she swept out of the house on that frigid April morning was the card she had sent Joanna for her eleventh birthday. Joanna hadn't been given it until later, however; on her actual birthday she had been confined to the school infirmary in a state of shock, as Mrs. Kirkland had explained at Prayers to the assembled student body.

Her mother and grandmother had brought her back to Morehaven the afternoon following her escape. "Since I never saw the place, I think I'll come with you," Mrs. Beresford had said, offering to foot the bill for a hired car. (Under the circumstances, a train journey didn't seem like a good idea.) Down they drove, with Joanna mute between them. When they arrived at Morehaven, they didn't stop at the school; they had their instructions to drive on to the infirmary.

"She had plenty to say for herself on arrival at her grandmother's yesterday evening," Mrs. Drayton told Mrs. Kirkland, who came out to greet them on the gravel. "Then all of a sudden she shut up like a clam — isn't that right, Mummy?" — she appealed to Mrs. Beresford — "and when I appeared this morning she wouldn't speak to me either, her own mother!"

Mrs. Kirkland shook her head in sympathy. "It's *horrid* when they won't talk. Makes one feel so ineffective! I can see you've had an awful time. I dare say what you need now is to go straight to the Morehaven Arms for a gin and tonic. Joanna's going to be all right, though it may take a little while to bring her round."

"You can't imagine what the last twenty-four hours have been like for us, for me, especially."

"I know, Mrs. Drayton, believe me, I do know. But she's in good hands here, I promise, so off you go. I'll ring you in a day or two."

"You're being so kind," Mrs. Drayton exclaimed, tears of relief and gratitude in her eyes. "Well, perhaps we *should* be going. It's been a very long day . . . I came all the way from Hereford this morning, London first and then down here." She turned to Joanna. "Good-bye, darling. You heard what Mrs. Kirkland said, you're in good hands." When she bent to kiss her daughter, Joanna jerked away. "See what I mean, Mrs. Kirkland?" Mrs. Drayton stepped back with an exasperated sigh. "It's hopeless — she's like a brick wall! Anyway, unpleasant as the circumstances may be, since we're here, would it be all right for my mother and me to look round a bit before we leave? I haven't seen the school since I was a student here myself."

"By all means! Just give me a minute while I send over for a senior girl to show you about."

"We don't want to put you to any trouble . . ."

"*No* trouble. Be sure not to miss the swimming pool. Lord Tillingden was frightfully generous while his granddaughters were here. Only the best would do — diving boards, showers in the changing room, heating, too, although, alas, we can't afford to use it. The clay courts wouldn't have been here in your day, either."

"No, we played on grass."

"And the gym was enlarged in 1935. You'll find there's lots to see. By the way," Mrs. Kirkland went on, "after our telephone conversation last night I felt I had a much clearer understanding of what this poor child has been through recently. Whatever else she may have been, Miss Cathcart — I've got the name right, haven't I? — must have been terribly engaging. Such people are, of course, and inevitably children become attached to them. Her leaving had to come as quite a blow. But in time the dust will settle, the gap will be filled, Joanna will get over her sadness and resentment. I think it best that she stay apart from her classmates for the moment. It's quiet here — she'll get plenty of adult attention . . ."

"Whatever you say. We trust your judgment absolutely."

"This means no visitors until she's in a better frame of mind."

"No one will come anywhere near her until you give the word!" said Mrs. Beresford. She turned to Joanna. "Look at me, darling. I've told you before, life has its disappointments and it's silly to let them get one down. Come on," she urged, "look at me!" When Joanna refused to, Mrs. Beresford gave a little shrug and, slipping her arm through Barbara's, said, "Actually, a gin and tonic sounds to me like a better idea than taking a tour of the grounds. We'll see the improvements in July when we're down again for Parents Day."

But Mrs. Beresford never saw Lord Tillingden's pool or the enlarged gymnasium; by July she had been rendered speechless in a wheelchair and Barbara came to Parents Day alone.

Joanna lay in a high narrow bed in a room in the Morehaven infirmary. Blue-and-white-striped curtains hung at windows with bars. She watched reflections on the ceiling and rejected tray after tray of food selected and arranged to tempt her. "I wish you'd snap out of this," said Miss Norton, the assistant matron, who came to sit with her each afternoon. "Perk up — today's your birthday, too."

I shan't perk up till James comes, Joanna replied silently. He was on his way, though. He was on the train from Windsor, he'd reached Beldon Station, he was on the bus, he was hurrying up the drive past the copper beech tree. She heard him on the infirmary steps, begging Nurse Bullock to let him in. "I have to see her — I'm the only person who can bring her out of this!" He was racing up the stairs, coattails flying, he was throwing the door open, he was here beside her, hugging her, stroking her hair. I'm so sorry, Joanna, so sorry, so sorry. You have to get better because I love you and I can't bear to see you sad.

She wanted him to come so much, she imagined him coming so often, that she almost convinced herself he had.

At the end of a week she began to communicate in words, not just grunts; she had a little appetite, she was willing to play canasta with Miss Norton, and Mrs. Kirkland telephoned Mrs. Drayton. "As I predicted, the dust seems to be settling. She seems to be coming round."

At the end of a fortnight she returned to school. She was put in a different room with different roommates, and in a different form with a different teacher, and Mrs. Kirkland told her she should forget the first weeks at Morehaven before she ran away; she should make a fresh start.

Staff and students now treated her as if she were a member of some strange species of which they were in awe, and on the whole this suited Joanna. Time passed and a new generation of girls came to the school; nevertheless, the episode wasn't forgotten altogether. Newcomers soon learned, as part of Morehaven lore, that although one mightn't have thought there was anything odd about her, in fact Joanna Drayton had gone round the bend once and run away. Or perhaps she'd run away first and *then* gone round the bend; the sequence hadn't been clear.

No one asked Joanna to explain what had happened. Not Mrs. Kirkland, not her mother, not Jocelyn or Eliza. Her grandmother may have wanted to ask, only, given her circumstances, she couldn't. James didn't ask, either; he went off to the army without laying eyes on his sister, who never knew if he'd been told about her escapade (as Mrs. Kirkland referred to her flight and subsequent confinement). Perhaps it was just as well that nobody asked her, since she wouldn't have been able to explain. Only much later, when the despair that had engulfed her ebbed, became manageable, contained, did she realize she'd suffered a broken heart.

On the card that she found when she returned to school from the infirmary, Miss Cathcart had written in beautiful black italic handwriting, "I want you to understand how much I enjoyed knowing you, Joanna. Whatever else, good and bad, that I remember about my years at Widleigh, I shall always treasure my experience with you. Watching you learn was a great and wonderful pleasure. I hope that you find school challenging and that you continue to be fascinated by the world around you throughout a long, purposeful, and productive life. Meanwhile I shall count myself fortunate indeed if I ever again teach a child as innately talented, as rewarding, as you. Look after yourself during this, your twelfth, year. Sybilla Cathcart, your friend."

The card bore a photograph of the ceiling of King's College Chapel, Cambridge, perpendicular Gothic, soaring to the greater glory of God, but no return address. Joanna tucked it away in the bottom of her writing case, and when occasionally she pulled it out to reread it, she would ask herself, If we ran into each other now, would she be pleased with me?

For a long time Miss Cathcart would undoubtedly have been

disappointed, for even though Joanna appeared to have got over her "shock," this wasn't entirely the case. "I can't play anymore," she insisted to her watery-eyed piano teacher and, when Mrs. Kirkland herself was summoned, to her as well. Her ferocity and joy had vanished; that part of her seemed to be dead.

She learned other ways to keep her fingers busy: crocheting, embroidery, patchwork. Mrs. Kirkland entered a quilt of Joanna's in a national schoolgirl competition and it won first prize.

It was Humphrey, inveterately encouraging Humphrey, who put a stop to all that busy work. For decades he had played chamber music every other Thursday at home at Thirty-eight Smith Street, with Aunt Leonora, if available, as his pianist. Once she was *hors de combat* he tried a succession of replacements, but none "did."

"I'm absolutely desperate," he told Joanna the winter after Salzburg. "So it's going to have to be you. I remember your aunt Leonora sight-reading Schubert duets. You were *both* terrific!"

"But I've forgotten everything I ever knew about music. It's nearly four years since I played."

"We can train you up again — I know it!"

"My fingers crack, my hands are stiff, I can't tell one key from another."

"Instead of being histrionic, sit down and see what you can do. You've wasted enough time languishing; I've got a gun to your head. Come on, try! For your own sake, for your own delight and pleasure."

After she had played for an hour each day for a week, Humphrey observed with a smile, "It sounds to me as if you remember a lot about music. It sounds to me as if you like it a good deal, too. Do you?"

"I suppose," Joanna conceded, and then, quickly, "Yes, I do!"

"Then you must have a teacher." Not a Morehaven teacher, he told her mother.

"But the music there is supposed to be so good! It's Mrs. Kirkland's *thing.*"

"Good isn't good enough. Joanna needs someone *excellent.*"

"Excellent teachers are expensive and Henry *hates* spending money. He's been known to initiate legal proceedings over a seven-guinea dentist bill."

"Did I say a word about Henry? *I'll* pay for the teacher. In fact I've already been making inquiries. She's lost a lot of ground, but with determination and proper instruction why shouldn't she catch up again?" He turned to Joanna. "Well, are you ready to stop being bloody-minded and set to work? If you are, we should go and have a chat with Jacob Ehrenreich."

"Who's he?"

"Your teacher, if he agrees to take you on."

"He doesn't live in Beldon, I don't suppose," said Mrs. Drayton quickly.

"No, he's just round the corner in Albert Hall Mansions. Couldn't be more convenient."

"But Joanna happens to attend a boarding school in Berkshire. She's there eight months of the year."

"There's a perfectly adequate train service."

"Mrs. Kirkland won't like the idea at all."

"Dear Barbara, I shall persuade the tyrannical Mrs. Kirkland of the necessity *myself,* if need be."

Every termtime Saturday morning for her final two and a half years at Morehaven, Joanna had taken the train to Paddington and a taxi from there to Mr. Ehrenreich's large, dark flat. An hour later she would stumble, exhausted, into the street and go back to school. Now that she was in London to study the piano full time, she had her lesson on Tuesday afternoon. True, she toiled along a road that was interminable, but at least she was on it — and it wasn't all toil; there was much joy, too. Should she run into her tomorrow, Miss Cathcart would surely be pleased about that.

"So glad to see you at Spurlock after such a long time!" exclaimed Stillwell, standing back to let Joanna pass. In his black coat and pin-striped trousers he was his old obsequious self, capable, so Joanna imagined, of perpetrating any kind of nastiness on his master's behalf. (She saw him creeping from stable to stable at dead of night, injecting other people's horses with dope.) "How are you and Mr. James?"

"We're both very well, thanks," Joanna replied, noting with satisfaction that she was taller than he was. She could have sworn that he winked at her as he took her coat. Had he, too, heard the gossip about James, or was he merely mocking her Guatemalan costume? At the drawing room door he announced in a ringing voice, "Miss Joanna Drayton!"

Half a dozen people were grouped round a blazing fire. Women in evening dresses sat on sofas, dinner-jacketed men stood about talking to each other; no one paid the slightest attention to Stillwell's announcement. Joanna was considering a retreat to the cloakroom when she heard a familiar tap-tapping in the hall behind her. "Good to see you, my dear," Lady Harriet said warmly. "I'm sorry. I was out talking to the cook and I didn't know you'd arrived. Nigel took Gabriella and the boys racing at Stratford — they only got home fifteen minutes ago and they're still in their baths. That's why there were no Coopers in evidence to greet you. Come in and meet the others."

On one chintz-covered sofa sat a rapier of a woman wearing a long-sleeved blood-red dress. Her hair, dyed jet-black, was pulled back in a chignon. Her mouth was blood-red also, her eyelids heavily blue. "This is my sister-in-law, Mrs. Whittington-Burke, Joanna," Lady Harriet said. "You remember the Widleigh Draytons, don't you, Muriel. Joanna is Henry's daughter. You probably danced with him when you were young."

"I don't remember *ever* dancing with Henry Drayton. He was a quite different generation. He must be pushing ninety now!"

"He's seventy-two," said Joanna.

"Is that all? Well . . . and your mother, who was she?"

"Barbara Beresford."

Mrs. Whittington-Burke nodded slowly. "I don't believe I was at the wedding — something must have clashed. No longer together?" Joanna shook her head. "Pity." She gave what passed with her for a smile, revealing poor teeth, and turned to the man sitting beside her on the sofa arm.

Lady Harriet continued the introductions. There was a mottle-faced man, George Hillbridge — great friend of Nigel's, they went to Winterfields together — and his wife, in cream with fur collar and cuffs, on the other sofa. She examined her nails while her husband discussed investment strategies with a banker called Junkie Carlton, whose wife was off visiting a sister in Australia. Two young men from Giles's Cambridge college swayed in front of the mantelpiece. They had started drinking at five-fifteen; it was now ten past eight. Lady Harriet introduced Joanna to Melissa Montgomery and Jennifer Paxton-Brown, two girls who were sitting on the sofa next to Mrs. Hillbridge. Joanna recognized Jennifer Paxton-Brown from the cover of the previous week's *Country Life.* She gave Joanna the short blank stare that she reserved for contemporaries whom she had no wish to know.

"What will you have to drink?" said Lady Harriet, leading the way to a bottle-laden table at the far end of the room.

Joanna asked for tomato juice, which came in a tin; Lady Harriet managed to cut herself on the lid. "I do wish Nigel would come down!" she sighed. "He's supposed to be barman, not me. I never remember what to mix with what. My sister-in-law returned the first martini I made her this evening. She said it was undrinkable." Joanna poured the tomato juice into a cut-glass tumbler while Lady Harriet bound up her finger in her handkerchief. "I'm sorry we couldn't persuade your father to come," she added, "but I can see that this sort of party mightn't be quite his form. How is he these days?"

"He still walks many miles each day without tiring. I get utterly exhausted trying to keep up." In a low voice she went on, "James is the one I'm worried about — not my father. Last summer he disappeared."

"I heard that he'd not been well," Lady Harriet murmured.

"For all we know, he *still* isn't. We haven't had any news of him at all. You don't mind my talking about this, do you?" Joanna continued urgently. "My parents refuse to discuss the matter. They say there's no point looking for him — he'll come back in his own good time — but I'm afraid something dreadful's happened. Sometimes I have nightmares about him." She looked steadily at Lady Harriet. "He's in some dank cellar somewhere, he's starving, he's in jail . . . he's dead. If you were me, what would you do?"

Lady Harriet looked away. "Is there anything else I can get you?" She offered a bowl of nuts. "Do you like cashews? Someone brought them to us from East Africa." As her husband appeared in the doorway she said quickly, "Young people seem to have to make their own muddles, and if one tries to interfere, one often makes things worse instead of better. If I were you, Joanna, I'd let well enough alone."

Nigel Cooper and his children, bathed and gleaming in their evening clothes, surged into the room. "Forgive us for neglecting you!" Nigel cried. "All the way home the children were shouting at me for not driving faster. I told them, 'Better home late and alive than on the dot and in coffins!' " He made the rounds, kissing cheeks and shaking hands, until he reached his sister. "Wonderful to see you, Muriel! Where's Lucas? Assuming he came with you, of course."

"Oh, he came," said Mrs. Whittington-Burke. "I left him in his bath. He said he'd be down sooner or later, but so far as punctuality's concerned, my son's like you, Nigel — full of promises, but fuzzy."

Mrs. Whittington-Burke was several years older than her brother. She had once been her father's favorite, but when she was about eleven years old the elder Cooper observed that instead of the delightful gazelle-like creature he had hoped for, Muriel was turning into a nervous giraffe; in contrast, baby Nigel was showing every sign of becoming the self-confident, engaging fellow that any newly minted millionaire manufacturer of socks and underpants would want for a son. And so with dismay Muriel had watched her little brother supersede her in their papa's affections. But his habitual way of making amends to people had always been to pay them off, and so he saw to it that his first love was heavily compensated. Short of continuing affection, he provided her with every advantage and, when Frederick Whittington-Burke appeared on the horizon, enough money for the length of her neck to be overlooked. Baby Nigel had spent a lifetime trying to woo his sister, a task he knew to be hopeless but which, nevertheless, permanently engaged him. He had willingly allowed Muriel, who was the only person on earth for whom he was truly sorry, to snub him for fifty years.

Gabriella, in midnight-blue velvet that set off her blond hair, waved to Joanna as she followed her father to the fireplace. "So glad you made it!" she called and then, turning to her friends, the two tight undergraduates swaying at the mantelpiece and the stiff girls on the sofa, exclaimed, "Such a pity you didn't come to Stratford with us! The minute we got to the race-course Steven and I ran into the mad FitzGerald clan. We made a beeline for the members' bar and had a terrific binge. We saw hardly any racing!"

Lady Harriet beckoned to her son Giles. "Come and say hello to Joanna. How long is it since you two saw each other? You've got a lot of catching up to do." She excused herself, explaining that she had to talk to Stillwell, whereupon Giles, who was a youthful version of his father, launched into an account of his betting activities. After he had provided an avalanche of figures Joanna thought it safe to remark, "So in the end you came out even."

"*Even!* What d'you mean? I was down twenty-six quid!" He held his whiskey glass up to the chandelier and stared at it, eyes narrowed. "So as you might imagine, I'm in need of this!" and he swallowed two thirds of the contents. "Things are beginning to look better already," he said with one of his father's opulent smiles. The new scar on his forehead added distinction to his handsome, fleshy face. He was perfectly convinced that any female over fifteen and under forty-five would be delighted to listen to him go on forever about the odds at Towcester or Chepstow. "Trouble is" — he stifled a yawn — "the horses take a lot out of one."

"Dinner is served!" Stillwell announced from the doorway.

Lady Harriet seated Joanna between Junkie Carlton and an empty chair. "That's Lucas's place, but we shan't wait for him," she said.

Stillwell was collecting the soup plates when Lucas Whittington-Burke finally appeared. He waved Stillwell away — "No soup for me," he said — unfolded his napkin, and spread it carefully across his knees. Soon he was moving his head from side to side to stretch his neck muscles while making circular movements with first one shoulder, then the other. After some minutes he slouched down and sipped his wine. He spoke neither to Mrs. Hillbridge, on his left, nor to Joanna, on his right. Since Junkie Carlton was busy with Gabriella, Joanna sat in silence. She fingered the array of forks beside her plate and longed to be at home with her father.

At the far end of the table Muriel Whittington-Burke had everyone enthralled. Her acerbic wit was legendary. At all costs one should avoid drawing her scorn, but it was great fun to hear her be amusing at someone else's expense. Up-and-coming wits paid her close attention, for she commanded a certain turn of phrase and a talent for alliteration that spelled death to the self-respect of all who fell foul of her. As a child she had been assumed by everyone, and especially by her father, to be extremely clever. As a grown-up, however, her intelligence was focused on a predilection for dealing death through scorn. In most other respects she was a rather stupid woman.

Joanna tried to listen to the monologue but she gave up when Junkie Carlton leaned his elbow on the table and effectively blocked her view.

She stole a glance at her other neighbor. Lucas didn't resemble his mother at all. He was of medium height and build; his neck was perfectly in proportion, no giraffe ancestry there; his teeth were white and even. He had abundant wavy chestnut hair and heavy eyebrows which met in the middle. His mouth was wide and soft, his eyes a little slanted. He kept screwing them up as if he were thinking something very profound that demanded a great deal of concentration. After taking a few mouthfuls of creamed spinach he put down his fork, leaving the rest of his food untouched. That no one had addressed a word to him didn't seem to bother him at all. Joanna, who was feeling very unhappy, hoped that she looked as unconcerned as Lucas did. She considered leaving before the dancing began, but after all the regret she had caused him, she couldn't telephone her father to ask him to come fetch her. Perhaps if she claimed a headache Giles Cooper would run her home in his car, but then she remembered he'd crashed it. And of course the supercilious Stillwell couldn't be spared. He had to open doors and announce arrivals and enjoy his moments of glory.

She would just have to wait out the evening, which served her right for having foolish hopes, for imagining that by coming here she might squeeze into some world other than the smoking room at Widleigh or the third floor of the Arlington Hotel.

"If you like, you can have this." Lucas was pointing one

stubby index finger at his chicken *à la Kiev.* "I'm a vegetarian, so it doesn't interest me."

Why not accept? What else is there to do but eat? "Are you sure you don't want it?" Joanna said after a moment.

"I told you, I don't eat meat." Lucas transferred the chicken from his plate to Joanna's. "In my opinion, meat eating should be confined to beasts of the jungle and the zoo. Of course, that's merely *my* opinion. I shan't try to force it on *you.*"

Intending to humor him, Joanna said, "You seem to have a poor view of carnivores."

"I live in hope of man's conversion," Lucas replied evenly.

Was he trying to be humorous? But no, his expression was entirely serious.

"How can one ever find the way if one is consumed with a longing for flesh?" he added.

As someone as yet unconverted, presumably she was free to eat what she was given, and so Joanna cut into the chicken. Unfortunately the butter that filled the space between the meat and the outer shell of bread crumbs spurted in a magnificent dark-yellow arc onto the right sleeve of Lucas's dinner jacket.

"I'm terribly sorry!" Joanna cried. She wet a corner of her napkin in her water glass and dabbed at the oily patch.

"Never mind," said Lucas. "The heating in this house is always excessive and never more than now. This gives me a valid excuse for removing my jacket," which he proceeded to do, revealing a pair of dirty blue suspenders, one end of which was attached to the waistband of his trousers with a paper clip. His collar was grubby, too, and there were brown spots on the frills down the front of his evening shirt.

Seeing his nephew disrobe, Uncle Nigel called down the table, "Getting ready for bed, Lucas?" The assembled company swiveled to look.

"This is entirely my fault," Joanna told them. "I squirted butter on his sleeve."

"Then Stillwell will find him another jacket!" exclaimed Nigel Cooper, and he rang the bell.

"I'm perfectly happy as is," Lucas said.

But Stillwell was already at his master's side. "Fetch Mr. Lucas another jacket, will you? Harriet, where do you keep the boys' outgrown clothes?"

"He's quite all right in his shirtsleeves, Nigel," Lady Harriet remarked. "After all, we're only family and friends."

Mrs. Whittington-Burke, who had been leaning forward to watch the proceedings, observed, "We only have to put up with him till the end of dinner — he'll disappear before the dancing begins. He detests intense social activity."

But Uncle Nigel pressed on. "We've got to do *something* for him, Muriel. Didn't he bring a sweater?"

"He did. Only I warn you, it's pretty unappetizing."

"Fetch Mr. Lucas's sweater, will you, Stillwell?" Nigel Cooper said.

The guests turned back to their conversations and Lucas was left scowling at his plate. Joanna said quietly, "Sorry, I certainly didn't intend to cause you trouble."

"Being a widow," Lucas said, "without other children, my mother depends on me to provide her life with meaning. Therefore I'm perfectly used to being the center of attention. Assuming that you have a mother, who provides *her* life with meaning?"

Joanna smiled. "You wouldn't really want to know!"

"Oh, but I do! That's why I ask. What my mother needs to sustain her is of crucial importance to me, a burning issue, so naturally I'm keen to make comparisons."

"In that case . . . " Joanna considered the small compass of her mother's life. "I suppose that for *her* the most important factor is my grandmother — whether she lives or dies. She's paralyzed, you see, and getting on for eighty."

"For Mrs. Whittington-Burke the most important factor is

whether *I* live or die, but in contrast to your grandmother, I'm ambulatory and I retain, regardless of what Mrs. Whittington-Burke might think, most of my critical faculties. Thus I find such an abundance of concern more than I can easily appreciate." For the first time Lucas opened his eyes properly and Joanna saw that they were large and very black. He smiled for the first time, too. But clearly this strange, long-winded young man wasn't at all amused, so why in the world was he smiling? He made her feel most odd, but since she would have felt even odder had she kept a straight face, she smiled back, and they sat there smiling at each other while laughter and snatches of stories about other people's mothers, horses, houses, wafted around them.

When Stillwell returned with a shabby brown cardigan, Lucas put it on obediently, switched off his smile, and sat, head bowed, through salad, fruit and cheese, and peach melba. By the time Lady Harriet led the women away to coffee in the drawing room, he hadn't said another word.

Chapter 13

The Arlington Hotel

MRS. DRAYTON AND NURSE CHANNING were seated at a baize-covered table playing gin rummy when Joanna let herself into the flat on Monday evening. "I don't have to ask you if you enjoyed yourself," said Mrs. Drayton with a knowing smile.

Joanna pulled her suitcase in after her and shut the door. "Agnes slipped on the back steps on Good Friday and sprained her ankle. She'll have to keep her weight off it for a fortnight. She sent her regards."

"Is that all you've got to report?"

"Surely there's more than that to tell us," said Nurse Channing, whom Joanna thoroughly disliked. In the absence of an ability to knit or sew, or a taste for murder mysteries, Nurse Channing devoted herself entirely to gossip and speculation. "We gather you're spreading your wings at last."

"I've got Mr. Ehrenreich tomorrow," Joanna said, annoyed. "I'm going to bed. I want to get up early to practice. The Widleigh piano was out of tune."

"Wait a minute," Mrs. Drayton cried. "There was a telephone call for you." She produced a scrap of paper from her skirt pocket. "Here — it was some young man who said he'd met you in the country. He wouldn't leave his name, only this number. *Very* mysterious! As I was saying to Nurse Channing, Herefordshire must have changed. In my day no one was *at all* mysterious. That was half the trouble."

Perhaps one of Giles Cooper's Cambridge friends had telephoned. Joanna was surprised that either would want to see her again, and she wasn't flattered. By the end of dinner they had both been so drunk they could barely stagger round Colonel Cooper's study, transformed with the help of a single pinkish light bulb into a nightclub. Joanna had danced with the one called Martin until he'd fallen fast asleep against her, his chin digging into her neck. When she gripped him firmly by both shoulders he woke up long enough for her to get him over to a sofa, on which he instantly collapsed. Then the other one, whose name was Hector, grabbed her, propelled her out through a side door into a pitch-dark corridor, pinned her up against the oak paneling, and thrust his hand between her thighs; whereupon in rage and humiliation she slapped his face and ran away.

But now Nurse Channing and her mother were giving her their full attention.

Long before, Joanna had learned that if she couldn't conceal her private affairs completely, it was best to conduct them in public, so instead of going off to use the telephone in the other flat she went to the writing desk and dialed Belgravia 2604. She counted twelve rings and was about to replace the receiver when someone picked up at the other end. "Is this Belgravia 2604?" she asked, but no one answered. As she repeated the question she felt two pairs of eyes boring into her back. "Joanna Drayton speaking," she added.

"Excellent!" a male voice exclaimed at last. "I was standing on my head, but now I'm down. Hold on a minute." She heard the receiver clatter to the floor. "It was the cat," said the voice a moment later. "He wanted to be let out. Since he was neutered he's developed irregular habits. Can you have lunch with me tomorrow?"

"I don't know who you are!"

"I'm the lucky fellow who sat next to you at dinner last

Saturday. You squirted molten butter over me. Don't tell me
you've forgotten that drama!"

"Lucas?"

"The very same! And now that I'm identified, will you or
won't you lunch with me?"

Joanna wasn't at all sure she wanted to see that strange young
man again, but in order to avoid explanations and excuses in
front of her mother and Channing, she said, "I'd like that."

"In that case, meet me at ten past one at the Times Bookshop. I presume you know where it is? I'll wear the cardigan
that replaced the spattered jacket. It's brown and has a quite
large hole in the right elbow."

Joanna replaced the receiver and, to give herself some respite
before facing her audience, glanced through a pile of letters on
the desk. Nothing for her. She turned to the two ladies and
looked from one to the other. A cardinal rule: Always meet the
eyes of the enemy. If one did not, they moved in even faster.

"That was Gabriella's cousin, Lucas Whittington-Burke. I'm
having lunch with him tomorrow," she told them. "His mother
is Colonel Cooper's sister. I met them both last weekend when
I went over to dinner at Spurlock."

"Nigel's sister? Long teeth and red hair?"

"The hair's black now, but yes, the teeth are longish."

"The Whittington-Burkes used to have a place in Leicestershire. Do they still?"

"I haven't the faintest idea."

"You're lunching with a young man and you don't even
know where he's from!"

"He didn't happen to say, and frankly, I didn't think to ask."

Nurse Channing's chair creaked as she shifted her weight
from one large buttock to the other. "Does seem odd," she
observed.

"Must one always start getting to know someone by asking
for his home address?"

"It's natural to wonder where a person's from," said Channing.

"After all," said Mrs. Drayton, "you don't lunch with young men very often. If I'm not mistaken, this is the first young man to invite you."

"No, you're not mistaken," Joanna said dryly.

"Really, it's your own fault that you haven't been invited out, darling. You're too critical; no one meets your standards. According to you, everyone you meet under twenty-five is irredeemable. You look down your nose at them so, it's not surprising they don't ask you to go out with them!"

"Girls her age do tend to be choosy," added Nurse Channing. "It's only when you get closer to our age that you realize you have to accept people the way they are."

Mrs. Drayton sighed. "Well, anyway, shouldn't we be thinking about what you're going to wear tomorrow, Joanna?"

. "I own four skirts, three shirts, and seven jerseys, some combination of which will have to do. If Lucas doesn't care for my appearance, he needn't ask me out again." Joanna shoved her suitcase a few feet across the floor in the direction of the other flat.

"Is it so heavy that you can't carry it?" said her mother, frowning. "It's making deep lines in the carpet that the Hoover won't get out."

Every Tuesday, as she trailed through Knightsbridge on her way to Mr. Ehrenreich's at half past two, Joanna watched and envied girls her age — and some looked younger — being escorted in and out of restaurants and soup-and-spaghetti places. Some were with their fathers, some were with their Humphreys, but most were with their boyfriends. Glancing surreptitiously through restaurant windows, she would see them tossing bright heads, their eyes dancing; the men ate steadily while the girls only played with their food. All that mattered was the man across the table. How terrible to be so beholden, how terrible to try so hard to please! Joanna would murmur to herself; and then, a little later, How I wish I were in their shoes!

The Times Bookshop was crammed with people browsing during the lunch hour; they jabbed one another with their elbows as they reached for new novels, reference books, biographies. Joanna thought, If I change my mind, if I don't want to be found, it would be easy enough to hide here. But when she saw Lucas edging his way through the crowd, bumping into people, treading on toes, apologizing, she didn't step into a corner; she stayed where she was. He wore the brown cardigan of Saturday night, without a coat, for her benefit, even though the day, April first, was cold and windy. The knot of his green knitted tie was loose and his chestnut hair curled down over one eye. As he looked about the bookshop he would push it off his forehead but it always fell back. When finally he spotted her he waved a folded newspaper. "Why didn't you wait for me in front?" he called. "Come on!" and he turned on his heels and headed for the door. Once outside he began to walk so rapidly along Wigmore Street that Joanna could barely keep up. She was aware that passers-by were looking at her curiously as she rushed after him, her dark hair tangling in the wind.

"Why the hurry?" she gasped when they stopped at a set of red traffic lights. Lucas had to wait, or risk his life and hers as well.

"The table's reserved for one-fifteen and we're late already." He grabbed her arm as the lights turned green and they plunged across the street. On the other side he let her go and dashed off again. Joanna fell behind, cursing her high-heeled shoes.

All of a sudden Lucas plunged into a doorway, but when Joanna followed him inside a few seconds later he was nowhere to be seen. Beyond a darkened foyer were people sitting at tables and waiters scurrying, but the foyer itself was deserted. There was no one about to ask, Did you see a strange young man run through? Standing there alone, she felt conspicuous and silly and her feet hurt. Just as she decided to accost a waiter a door slammed behind her.

"I desperately needed the gents, sorry," and there was Lucas, with freshly plastered-down hair. "Are you hungry? I know I am!" and he made for the table at a point farthest from the door and sat down. As Joanna slid onto the wall bench beside him, he remarked, "They do have chicken *à la Kiev*. I hope you won't order it, though."

"I wouldn't dream of endangering your life again."

"Why the sarcasm?" he said lightly, picking up a menu.

"Could I see a menu, too? Why is this table only set for one?"

"Because they weren't expecting you. Generally I lunch alone and read the paper." He beckoned to a waiter. "Lay another place, please." Turning back to Joanna he said, "Why are you lugging that around?" He indicated the music on the bench beside her.

"I've got a piano lesson at two-thirty."

"In that case we'd better order straight away. I always have the cheese soufflé with broccoli, strawberries, and herb tea."

"Always?"

"Once one knows what one likes, one should stick to it." After a moment's thought he went on, "Are you very serious about music?"

"It's my only talent, so I'd better develop it."

"That sounds like one's mother talking. Do you also suffer from an overzealous mama?"

"If you mean overzealous on *my* behalf, I wouldn't say so, no. My mother has too many preoccupations to be all that concerned about me."

"I'm disappointed," Lucas said, and he really did look disappointed, too. He began to draw with a fork on the tablecloth.

Joanna stared at a picture of a lake on the opposite wall. She recognized Lake Lugano. Once, with Humphrey, she had seen that very view.

If Lucas liked lunching alone, then why had he invited her? She could have been getting in a final hour of preparation before confronting Mr. Ehrenreich. April was a cruel month for Mr. Ehrenreich. In April 1938 he had got out of Berlin and made his way to London, expecting that his wife and sons would follow. But they hadn't, he'd never seen them again, they'd died in Theresienstadt. He constantly punished himself for escaping: his insomnia was bad, his angina was worse, his stomach was terrible. But in April, when sleep deserted him entirely, he punished his students as well. Despairing, he thundered, threatened, whacked their hands. No matter if, like Joanna, they hadn't been born at the time of his desertion; that didn't absolve them from blame for surviving — just as he had — while others had perished.

The combination of the present with this rude boy and the prospect of the afternoon's session, for which she was inadequately prepared, depressed Joanna's appetite, but she ordered sole with parsley butter. "Why did you ask me to have lunch with you, Lucas?" she said when the waiter had gone off again.

"Because your hair's beautiful, for one thing. For another, you're the only young woman I've ever met in my uncle Nigel's house who didn't say something was 'frightfully amusing' in the first three minutes."

"I might have, though, if we'd talked longer."

With a flourish Lucas finished his drawing. "Masterful, wouldn't you agree?" He had drawn a keyboard on the tablecloth. "Eighty-eight keys. Count them if you like." In places he had scratched so hard that he'd made holes in the linen. "Don't worry, the odd act of vandalism's nothing. They make a fortune out of me. I come here every day."

"Why do you?"

"My mother's always out at lunchtime undergoing routine maintenance of one sort or another — hair, skin, legs, feet, stomach, you name it, she has someone working on it. Lunch isn't provided at home in Chester Square, so I'm obliged to fend for myself. What about *your* domestic arrangements?"

"I live with my mother and grandmother in the Arlington Hotel. They send lunch up from the restaurant."

"How does that suit you?"

"Which? Having lunch sent up, or living as and where I do? . . . I wouldn't say either is ideal."

"Move out then!"

"I can't yet. I'm a dependent minor."

"No means of support, other than parents?"

"No, but as soon as I possibly can I shall find some."

"And where do you propose to look?"

"If I'm good enough, maybe the Royal Academy will give me a scholarship, and I'll get a bedsitter."

"I've never actually seen a bedsitter," said Lucas. "They don't sound very appealing."

"Eventually, when I start to earn a proper living, I'll get a flat."

"But remunerative employment is so time consuming," said Lucas with a frown. "When would you have the chance to do what you really want to do?"

"What I really want to do is play the piano, and that's how I'll support myself. I'll teach and give recitals and perform with symphony orchestras on six continents."

"In that case, where will you have your flat?"

"I haven't quite decided. Rio, San Francisco, Tokyo."

"Why not London?"

"I'd rather live abroad."

"Ah yes, as far as possible from the family . . ."

The waiter appeared with their food: Joanna's fish, pristine with lemon wedges, Lucas's soufflé, brownish, puffing high above the dish. "I hope it's soft inside," said Lucas to the waiter. "Yesterday it was all dried out and I had to send it back."

"Will you try it, sir?" the waiter said, hovering.

Lucas spent an extraordinarily long time unfolding his napkin; then he took several sips of water while the waiter watched the soufflé shrink, but at last he plunged his fork into its heart. He took one mouthful and then a second. "A huge improvement!" The waiter smiled, showing bright white teeth. He was a Cypriot, about the same age as Lucas, with dark skin and straight black hair oiled close to his head. Now he hurried off to tell the cook that the young gentleman, the one who leaves ten-shilling tips if he's satisfied and nothing at all if he's not, was happy.

"What do *you* do, Lucas?" Joanna asked.

"I reflect. That takes up a great deal of my time."

"What do you reflect on?"

"The Way."

Joanna paused, a forkful of fish to her mouth. "The way where?"

"From spiritual confusion to inner peace. Isn't that what we all need desperately?"

"Most people just want to be happy," Joanna said mildly.

Lucas gave a snort. "How old are you?"

"Almost eighteen."

"And you haven't yet learned that happiness is a chimera! Reach for it and it vanishes. Spend your life looking for it and you'll die miserable."

Inner peace? Joanna frowned. She was far more familiar with confusion. It nagged and tugged and sometimes frightened her. The Anglican church certainly hadn't quelled it. (Having taken Holy Communion on so many frigid mornings without any increment in spiritual ease, she knew she wasn't one of the elect whose faith was founded on rock.) Music helped, so long as she was actually playing. Sleep helped, too, until the alarm clock rang. She buttered a roll and ate half of it before asking, "Have you been reflecting long?"

"Would that I had! No, alas, I'm only in the early stages. I began not quite two years ago, after I was sent down from Oxford. Mind you" — he grinned — "it wasn't my idea to go up but Mrs. Whittington-Burke said that since all my relations had gone, I should too. I resisted. In the entrance examination I drew Chinese dragons and so failed successfully. But my mother gave a great deal of money to the college of her choice and there I was, accepted after all! I stayed a year, which is the least amount of time it takes to demonstrate total academic inadequacy. Again my mother tried to interfere, but this time they told her they absolutely would not, could not make an exception for her son. Oxford wasn't the *place* for him, they explained to her impatiently, which is exactly what *I'd* been explaining to *them* from the beginning. So there I was, back home, heels kicking, when I saw an advertisement in a newspaper announcing that Swami Krishna had moved to Twenty-one Beech Street, Highgate, and was ready to receive, nurture, and guide seekers of inner peace on Tuesday and Thursday evenings between eight and half past ten."

When he had scraped the last morsel from the sides of his dish and sat back, replete, Joanna asked him, "Will you tell me about the swami?"

"Mightn't you think it 'frightfully amusing' that anyone should seek to emulate a caderous little wog, shivering in his loincloth in the London cold?"

"You said yourself that I'm not the kind of person who finds things 'frightfully amusing.'"

Lucas stared at her in quizzical silence. "What do you want to know?" he said at last.

"*Are* you more peaceful than you were before you met him?"

Lucas said softly, "Absolutely!"

"That's not enough of an answer! What has the swami done for you?"

"That's a long story."

"Tell it to me! What happened the first time you saw him?"

Lucas smiled a crooked smile. "Nothing. When I knocked, no one answered."

"So what did you do?"

"Went for a walk, came back half an hour later, and tried again. This time the door was opened by an old man in a long shirt. He beckoned me inside and led me upstairs. Cats had been peeing on the staircase, the whole place reeked. Later it was explained to me that the house was condemned and scheduled for demolition and the swami was merely squatting in it after being thrown out of a house round the corner. He was constantly being thrown out of houses because landlords don't look favorably on gurus. Anyway, we went into a room completely bare of furniture, just two mats on the floor. The old man whipped off his shirt and sat on one of them and told me to sit on the other. I saw then that he wasn't old at all, really. Although his hair, which was long, past his shoulders, was gray, he was taut and fit. There I was, wondering how we were going to communicate, when he suddenly said in almost unaccented English, 'Tell me what disquiets you.'

"Usually when people ask what's on my mind, they aren't interested in doing anything to help me — they're just hoping to satisfy their curiosity." In a low voice Lucas went on, "But when the swami asked, I felt he had all the time in the world to hear me out, and no reason to use what I told him against me later. If I stopped talking he didn't prompt — he merely sat, with an alert expression on his face, waiting for me to start up again. After a couple of hours he suggested I come back another evening when other people, all searchers like me, would be there, too. Some, like me, were beginning their quest, but others were further along and I might learn from them.

"When I left I wasn't at all sure I *would* go back because I've always loathed organized activities. I stayed away for several weeks, but then I thought, Why not take a chance? The Indian who opened the door said, 'We have been waiting for you — why did you take so long?' The swami was sitting on the floor upstairs with a dozen people. They were having a dialogue. One person would ask a question and the swami would answer with another question. That way he got us to think about a different aspect of the original question. Everything was wonderfully calm.

"Of course, my mother has a quite different view of the proceedings," Lucas said with a wry smile. " 'The flotsam and jetsam of the earth sitting on their haunches while an emaciated fakir fills their heads with mumbo jumbo' is how she describes what goes on."

"She's been there?"

"Not at all, but that hasn't stopped her from forming strong opinions. At one time she aired them in letters, threatening the swami with criminal action. Later, after he had a telephone installed, she rang him constantly, but he always said that although he would be very glad to talk with her about herself, he wasn't at liberty to discuss his relationship with me, as that was private. Meanwhile, she complained vociferously about my standing on my head in the drawing room. At first I did crash down a few times and I broke a few priceless objects, but from the way she carried on, you'd have thought I was doing it on purpose! She also objected to my diet. I had to point out repeatedly that in my own house, which I had inherited from my father, I was entitled to ask my housekeeper, whom I paid with my own money, to prepare whatever I wanted, and if that happened to be brown rice and lentils twice a day, so be it. The truth is," said Lucas with a grin, "if it hadn't been for the swami and what he's taught me about patience and forgiveness, I'd have put Mrs. Whittington-Burke out in the street long ago.

And now," he concluded, "you'd better be off or you'll miss that lesson."

Startled, Joanna looked at her watch. "You're right!"

Lucas beckoned to the waiter, who brought the bill. "I haven't any cash today," Lucas told him. "Put it on my account, will you?"

Joanna picked up her music and, not knowing quite what else to do, offered to shake hands. But Lucas ignored her outstretched hand.

"Do you want to come again tomorrow?" He leaned back against the wall and watched her neutrally. "I'll be here at one-fifteen."

"Do you mean that?"

"Why would I have asked you if I didn't?"

"I'll say yes, and if for some reason I can't, then I'll ring you. I can't remember what I did with your number. It's listed in the telephone directory, I suppose."

"'Fraid not. Mrs. Whittington-Burke is a deeply distrustful woman."

Joanna waited for him to give her his number again, but he didn't. "The sole was delicious," she said quickly. "Thanks," and she picked up her music and walked out.

Joanna threw her music on the sofa. "I'm back late because Mr. Ehrenreich kept me twenty minutes extra. 'When Beethoven wrote *pianissimo*, he meant *pianissimo*, so why do you play like a herd of elephants on a jungle path! I shan't let you go until you get it right!' But I never got it right — my hands wouldn't stop shaking with terror."

"He's hard on you because you need it," said Mrs. Drayton quickly. "He's not being capricious. One day I hope you'll appreciate how lucky you've been to have such a dedicated and distinguished teacher."

Joanna poured herself a cup of strong tea and took a biscuit from the tin that Nurse Channing offered and went to the window overlooking the park. The sharp wind had dropped and a pale spring sun had broken through low clouds. White and purple crocuses ringed the elm trees and scillas splashed blue across the grass.

"What restaurant did you go to?" her mother said.

"I didn't notice."

"Well, at least you know where it was."

"In Wigmore Street."

"What did you eat?"

"Dover sole."

"Did you like the young man?"

"It's too soon to tell. I was only with him for an hour, then I had to go to Ehrenreich."

"What does he do?"

"If you mean, how does he earn his living, his father's dead, so it appears that he doesn't have to." Joanna turned her back on her mother.

"I've got it!" exclaimed Mrs. Drayton suddenly.

"Got what, madam?" said Nurse Channing.

"The father of the Whittington-Burke boy . . . I knew there was a tragedy. For the last twenty-four hours I've been racking my memory and now I remember! Frederick, his name was, he hanged himself right here in London, after the war. And the awful thing was, it was a child who found him in the hall. He'd jumped, you see, from the landing. It was in all the papers. At the time Herefordshire people who'd known her as a girl said, 'No wonder, Muriel Cooper would drive anyone to suicide!' Does Lucas have brothers or sisters?"

"No, he doesn't."

"So of course he was the child . . . Imagine the effect it must have had on him!"

In Hyde Park seven dogs were running together. They raced through the crocuses, barking joyously, while their owners held

their leashes and relished the sunshine; better late than never.
"I'm going out," announced Joanna, putting her cup back on
the tea tray.

"But darling, you just came in!" said her mother. "I've hardly seen you since you got back from the country. Couldn't you
be a little more sociable? Sit down with us and have another
cup of tea."

Joanna got off the Oxford Street bus at ten past one the next
day and walked quickly through the alley into Wigmore Street.
A restaurant called Le Potage seemed familiar, but inside the
foyer was ablaze with light. No, that wasn't right. A hundred
yards farther on she came to Frederick's, and sure enough,
there was Lucas waiting for her in the dimly lit entrance. "So
you did come! I was afraid you wouldn't." He added, taking
her hand, "You don't have a lesson today, do you?"

"No."

"Good!"

At the same table where they had had lunch the day before
he ordered a cheese soufflé, as always, and Joanna, lamb chops.

"What have you been up to today?" said Lucas.

"Practicing."

"You never stop!"

"I'd better *not* stop! In the summer I'll be taking a master
class with Alfredo Correa de Leon at Salzburg and I'm trying to
get ready for that. What have *you* been up to?"

"Lying on my back, as I do between twelve and one every
weekday."

"What ever for?"

"In order to give my free associations to the O.B."

"The O.B.?"

"The Old Boy — Oliver Chesterton, Doctor of the Soul.
He's just round the corner at Twenty-seven Wimpole Street,
which is what makes Frederick's so terribly convenient. It's a

brisk eight-minute walk from the O.B.'s couch to this very table."

"What's a free association?"

"Whatever comes to mind. Unexpurgated trivia."

What's a doctor of the soul, she wanted to ask, as well as, What's a swami? But she had to be careful with questions. She didn't want to appear as completely ignorant of his world as in fact she was. "Is the O.B. helpful?" She thought that was safe. Doctors were supposed to help their patients, after all.

"Mrs. Whittington-Burke claims he's her *sine qua non*. If true, then I'm glad for her. Certainly she's known him a very long time. I doubt that in the last twenty-five years she's made too many decisions, however mundane, without first seeking his advice. As to whether he's helpful to *me*, that's highly debatable. The Old Boy himself maintains that he's *essential* to my health and happiness — how else could he justify the huge fees he demands and gets? As the object of his ministrations, however, I'd say he's a pain in the arse."

"How long have you been doing this?"

"Depends on what you mean by 'this.' Given the O.B.'s special relationship with my family, I can't remember a time when he wasn't in the offing. To me he used to be somewhat in the order of a dentist whom one is obliged to visit intermittently for checkups, cleanings, fillings, and the odd extraction. Our *intimate* association only dates back a couple years. Having received strong hints that I was likely to be sent down from Oxford, Mrs. Whittington-Burke was most distressed — all her greasing of palms might come to nothing! So she had me sweat up to London on Mondays, Wednesdays, and Fridays so that Oliver and I could jointly reflect on my behavior in the hope of rectifying it. But in due course, since I had absolutely no intention of changing my ways, the university had no choice but to carry out its threat.

"Once I was out on my ear," Lucas continued, "it was up to

Oli to make something of the last surviving male Whittington-Burke. Thrice-weekly visits were increased to five and the next few months were truly horrible. Not content with daily so-called therapeutic contact, the O.B. would accompany me to Leicestershire of a Friday, where he would be overbearingly present until Sunday night. One of his favorite activities was to parade through the house — *my* house — telling Mrs. Whittington-Burke which pictures to send to auction. Another was making up menus with the cook, and he was fond of rearranging the furniture, too.

"Finally I couldn't stand him one more second, so I got the gardener to drive me to the station, and I took the first train back to London. Unfortunately it was one of those trains that stops everywhere and by the time I'd reached Euston and taken a cab to Chester Square, there were my mother and the dear doctor positioned in the drawing room, having raced up by car. But I'm happy to say, I'd given them such a nasty shock — they thought I'd left for foreign parts with the swami — that in choking voices they begged me for my terms. 'All right,' I told them, 'I'll come every day to Wimpole Street and I'll come on time, but in the first place, Dr. Chesterton, you will never show your face in Leicestershire again. In the second place, and this holds true for both of you, the swami's none of your bloody business!' "

"Does your agreement still stand?"

"They've been awfully good about their side of it, I must say. As for me," Lucas said with a shrug, "Well, I never miss a session and I'm more or less on time. I don't say much, though. In fact last year between April and November I didn't say a word. Since I have the hour before lunch, it was often quite alarming, lying there on the sofa with the Old Boy's stomach rumbling desperately only inches from my ear. He's excessively fond of his grub and lamentably self-indulgent . . . Ultimately — after seven months of silence — I said, 'It seems to me that you've got a lot fatter.' 'What makes you say that?' he replied, cool as a cucumber. 'I'm worried about you, Dr. Chesterton. If you aren't more moderate you'll suffer a monumental heart attack and die, and what will become of my poor mother then? I'm not up to keeping her *compos mentis* without you.'" Lucas laughed gaily. Clearly he was enjoying himself. "How well up are you on your Freud, Joanna?"

"I know practically nothing about him."

"I envy your ignorance! *My* grounding has been only too thorough. The Old Boy, or the Young Boy, as I suppose he was then, was psychoanalyzed in Vienna by the Great Man, a process that put him in touch with his baser instincts while equipping him, so he claims, with the ability to relieve the afflictions of such poor devils as fall supine on his brown velveteen sofa. Given that I'm what you might characterize as a close-mouthed type of patient, he sometimes finds the urge to fill my silences with lectures on the Great Man's work impossible to resist. But Oli, you should know, is no mere sycophantic disciple — he has a mind of his own! Not content to leave things as Freud left them, he's forever pushing on, adding twiglets to the tree of knowledge, groping for new theoretical insights, searching for scientific breakthroughs. Mind you, his approach has always struck me as quite haphazard. The swami's seems far more scientific. Yoga has made me more fit than I've ever been before and I haven't had bronchitis once since I gave up meat. And that's quite apart from what his philosophy has done for my peace of mind. Without a doubt he is the most extraordinary man I've ever known. I think you'd find him extraordinary, too, Joanna. Chesterton, on the other hand, far from making me feel peaceful, fills me with fury and disgust. I wouldn't recommend him to my worst enemy's dog!"

Joanna had still not entirely rejected her mother's dictum that in order to keep well informed one need only give the *Telegraph* a close reading every morning; total knowledge still seemed comfortably within her grasp, even if she didn't make a consistent effort to attain it. But clearly Lucas's preoccupations lay well outside the scope of the *Daily Telegraph.* "I'd very much like to meet the swami," she said eagerly, "but does he welcome outsiders?"

"Weren't we all outsiders to begin with?" said Lucas cheerfully. "What are you doing tomorrow evening?"

"I'm going to Eliza Lancaster's cocktail party."

"*Cocktail* party, Oh, God," Lucas groaned. "So you're having a perfectly marvelous time, just like my cousin Gabriella."

"I wish I could say I was having a marvelous time," Joanna said, smiling faintly. "Only I don't drink and I don't smoke — if I did, at least I'd have something to do with my hands — and so far I haven't mastered the gasp-and-giggle conversational style, so I spend most of my time at parties watching the clock, and as soon as I think I can leave without appearing rude, I do so."

"Why do you keep going if you don't enjoy yourself?"

"Because I'm almost always alone and I'm tired of it, and, who knows, maybe I'll meet someone I'll like and who'll like me."

Lucas grinned. "Well, you met *me* at the Coopers' party and *I* like you."

"Thank you." Joanna grinned back.

Having finished his soufflé and broccoli, Lucas produced a packet of Gauloises, took one out, and lit it. "By the way," he said after a few puffs, "I used to know a James Drayton. Any relation of yours?"

"He's my brother!" Joanna's heart skipped a beat. "You knew him at Eton?"

"Wrong, I was spared those rigors. Chesterton chose a laissez-faire Swiss school, where I learned to swear in many languages and not a great deal else."

"Then you met him in the army?"

"Wrong again. Oli got me out of that, too. To give him his due credit, he's got me out of a lot of unpleasantness. I met

James Drayton at Oxford, actually. We lived for one short, sweet academic year on the same landing. A solitary fellow. Rarely opened his curtains. Probably didn't care for what he would have seen if he'd looked out — stampeding hordes of Christ Church bloodies shouting their way through Peckwater Quad in the middle of the day. What's he up to now? Swotting for his D.Phil.?"

"He never even took his finals," Joanna said quietly. "He had a nervous breakdown and went down."

"I'm sorry to hear that!" Lucas said, frowning. "He was said to be extremely able — sure thing for a First. Does he reside in the hotel with you and the other two ladies?"

"He said he was going to Spain, but that was getting on for a year ago. I don't know if he went because he never wrote or anything. He simply disappeared." And having started talking about James, she found she couldn't stop.

She talked about him and her father, about him and her mother, and a bit about him and herself. Meanwhile, eyes narrowed, Lucas smoked four Gauloises. Was he listening? Perhaps he was sitting through the saga merely because he was trapped between her and the wall. "In my family," she concluded finally, "there are three armed outposts — my father, my mother, and my brother. I'm in the middle, equidistant from the others. From time to time a message arrives for me from one of the outposts, then I decode it and decide what to do."

She glanced round the restaurant. People were drinking, talking, eating, wielding knives and forks; waiters hurried with trays and plates and glasses. They all seemed very far away. Lucas, one foot from her on the same bench, did too. Never mind, she was used to facing her family alone.

After a little while Lucas smiled his funny crooked smile and said matter-of-factly, "You're a strange and wonderful girl, Joanna. How extraordinary it must be to have you for a sister! Shall we leave now and go to Chester Square? My mother won't be there. She was up and out as usual and on the Old Boy's couch by ten."

"She's Dr. Chesterton's patient, also?"

"His *original* patient! Of course she was Miss Muriel Cooper in those days. When he returned from Vienna he opened his practice with her. She's had the ten o'clock slot for decades. Between eleven and twelve the couch cools off while the O.B. writes a page or two of his magnum opus on differentiation, and then I roll in."

"What's differentiation?"

"In a nutshell, it's Mrs. Whittington-Burke's ability to tell herself apart from her son."

"Can she?"

"It's about that, basically, that she goes to see the good doctor. Anyway, today's Wednesday, so at eleven she nipped round to a quack in Harley Street to have her liver cleansed, quite a long procedure. She won't be home till five. Do come and play the piano for me!"

As their taxi swung past the Arlington, Joanna caught sight of a familiar couple on the steps. "Look!" She clutched Lucas's arm. "That woman in the purple hat is my mother."

Lucas peered out the window. "Purple's a fine color for a woman of a certain age. Who's the splendid fellow with her?"

"That's Humphrey."

"Is he Mrs. Drayton's special friend?"

"They're first cousins."

"First cousins aren't necessarily friends . . . Take me and Gabriella, for instance — it would be hard to say who finds the other more despicable. What's the nature of their association?"

Joanna smiled. "Humphrey doesn't like women, if that's what you mean."

They stopped in front of a massive stucco house. Lucas paid the driver and rang the bell. "I forgot my key again, Mrs. Staines," he said to the woman who opened the shiny green door.

"You should wear it on a string round your neck, sir. What if I'd gone out shopping?"

"Ah, but you hadn't," he said.

"Don't worry, Mrs. Staines won't say a word," Lucas remarked to Joanna as he led her across the black-and-white marble hall.

"Won't say a word about what?"

"*You*, to Mrs. Whittington-Burke. Mrs. Staines is very well trained. She never says anything about who comes to the house while Mrs. Whittington-Burke is out."

"Doesn't your mother like you to bring people home?"

Lucas gave a short laugh. "Nothing makes her more upset! She couldn't possibly believe that anyone would come here just because I invited them. She thinks everyone's out to take advantage of me financially." He pointed at a grand piano that stood in an alcove at the other end of the very large drawing room. "Would you play for me, Joanna? I'd so love it! Or would you like a glass of brandy first?"

"No, thanks." Claude Lorraine satyrs and Delacroix horses hung on all four walls; Sheraton tables were littered with objets d'art. No wonder Mrs. Whittington-Burke objected to Lucas doing his yoga here! "Have you lived in this house long?"

"I was born here. Mrs. Whittington-Burke didn't trust hospitals so she had everyone come to her. Then a few years later a bomb dropped across the road and I very nearly died here. The night-nursery ceiling fell on my bed while I was in it. It's not a house I'm especially fond of but it has one great thing going for it — it's big enough for my mother and me to live almost separate lives." Lucas lay down on a powder-blue silk sofa, placed two pillows under his head, and crossed his legs. "You're really quite lovely to look at," he remarked as Joanna sat down at the piano. "I imagine that any record with you on the cover would sell very well."

*

Throughout the month of April, Joanna and Lucas saw each other almost every weekday. (The Whittington-Burkes, *mère et fils*, were in Leicestershire at the weekend.) Lucas's table at Frederick's was always laid for two. After lunch they went to foreign films if it was raining and they sat in St. James's Park if the weather was good. Or else they went to the zoo. Lucas was very attached to Sinbad, the gorilla, who glowered in black desperation in a corner of his cage. "I know how he feels," said Lucas. "Before I met the swami, that's how I felt almost all the time."

Occasionally they went to Chester Square and Joanna played the piano. They were always out by ten to five, except once when somehow time slipped by, and there was Mrs. Whittington-Burke at the door; but while Mrs. Staines engaged her in the front hall, Lucas and Joanna escaped through the service entrance. When they got back to Knightsbridge they always said good-bye round the corner from the hotel.

"My mother mustn't know we're friends," Lucas insisted. "She has a highly developed talent for mucking things up."

"Why is that?"

Lucas shrugged. "She's your proverbial jealous woman and since word has a habit of getting about, I'd rather your mother didn't know that we're seeing each other, either. Were you to say to her, 'I went to the cinema with Lucas,' and were she to run into Aunt Harriet in the Tube, the cat would be out of the bag and back to Mrs. Whittington-Burke in no time."

"What would happen then?"

"She'd insist on meeting you."

"She already has."

"But that was *before* we knew each other. Unless you enjoy being the object of extraordinary curiosity, be as discreet as I suggest."

"What about Dr. Chesterton? Aren't you meant to tell him everything that passes through your mind?"

"My side of the bargain is only that I put in an appearance and be more or less on time. I didn't promise to tell the Old Boy anything of importance."

It wasn't difficult for Joanna to keep Lucas a secret from her mother. She timed her entrances to coincide with periods of intense activity, such as when Mrs. Beresford was being bathed or changed or coaxed into eating puréed liver and peas. Mrs. Drayton attended to her with full attention, believing that if she were distracted for an instant the old lady would die, as it were, by her daughter's hand. By the time the bedroom had been straightened and medicines dispensed, Mrs. Drayton had usually forgotten to ask Joanna how she'd spent her afternoon. If she did ask, the answer "window shopping" seemed to satisfy.

Was all this secrecy really necessary? Joanna had to wonder. The only time she had seen her, Mrs. Whittington-Burke had seemed strong-willed, a character, one might say, but evidence of actual malevolence was lacking. She supposed she would have to take Lucas's word for it, and so, if he didn't want her in his house when his mother was there, that was his business. But why keep Lucas a secret from her own mother? What, really, did they have to hide?

Lucas had told her that he liked her, that he thought she was beautiful, that he wanted to see her every day. In their time together he talked a lot — about Freud and Chesterton, the swami and his devotees, and about his travels, especially those with his father, whose two great passions had been volcanoes and eclipses. Father and son had observed two Etna eruptions, an island rising from the ocean off the Icelandic coast and a volcano from a field in Mexico, solar eclipses in Kenya and the American Rockies, and more eclipses of the moon than Lucas could possibly count.

"We were always together," he explained to Joanna one blowy day on Hampstead Heath. "He tutored me. I went to school only after his death — by then I was thirteen."

"What did your father die of?"

"A combination of factors."

"I'm sorry," Joanna told him.

"I'm terribly sorry, too. Sometimes in dreams," he said with his funny smile, "I search for him in the places where we went together. Ultimately I find him on that beach in Sicily, watching Etna through the field glasses. An extraordinary redemption."

While she was at Morehaven, Joanna had daydreamed about finding a boy, a soul mate, someone who loved her. Next to getting into the Royal Academy, that's what she had wanted most. This had come to pass — she'd found her boy. Lucas wandered through the streets of London with her; he went with her to Mr. Ehrenreich's and waited outside while she had her lesson. When it was over, they'd go wandering on again.

And yet things weren't turning out quite right. Romance was missing. Lucas hadn't even kissed her yet! Furthermore, supposing he *did* declare his love for her, would she love him back? Although she had certainly got to know a great deal *about* him, she had an unhappy sense that she wasn't getting to know *him*. Sometimes being with him felt far lonelier than being by herself.

One afternoon towards the end of April, while they were feeding the ducks in St. James's Park, Lucas said, "We meet with the swami this evening at eight. Would you like to come?"

"Would I like to! I've been dying to be asked!"

"Then I'll see you in the Knightsbridge Tube station at seven-fifteen."

What should I wear for sitting on a mat in a house that's scheduled for demolition? she wanted to ask him, but didn't.

She told her mother she was going to have supper with Divina Jenkyns, Mr. Ehrenreich's other Royal Academy entrant, who would be going to Salzburg, too. "Like that, in shabby country trousers!" Mrs. Drayton exclaimed to Joanna, on her way out at seven-ten.

"The Jenkynses are very informal," she replied. "They have all their meals in the kitchen because Divina's brother keeps his boat in the dining room."

Lucas was pacing up and down in front of the newsstand. "Thank goodness you're on time!" he said. "The swami's a stickler for punctuality." Buttons were missing from his tweed jacket; his baggy gray flannels were held up with a knotted tie. He's even shabbier than I am, Joanna thought.

They took the Underground to Highgate, where they got out and walked quickly for fifteen minutes. "This is it," Lucas said, turning into the driveway of an elegant white house set back from the street.

"You told me the swami lived in a slum!" exclaimed Joanna.

"Used to. I bought this place for him last December. It suits him better."

"*You* bought this for him!" No wonder Mrs. Whittington-Burke worried about people taking advantage of her son!

They had reached the front door and Lucas was searching through his pockets for something, a key, perhaps. Curtains were drawn across the windows and behind them Joanna imagined the faithful waiting in silent meditation for the Thursday dialogue to begin. Tonight, she told herself, my life will change irrevocably. The Way will be opened to me, too. She shivered with excitement.

But suddenly Lucas was pushing past her and running down the drive to the street. Absorbed by her fantasy of rebirth, Joanna didn't at first believe what she was seeing. "Wait, Lucas!" she shouted when she came to. She raced after him. At the curb she turned her ankle and fell flat on her face, then scrambled up again and ran on. Lucas stopped at the corner a hundred yards ahead, glanced back, and saw her muddy trousers, her wild hair. He watched impassively as she limped up to him.

"What's the matter? Why didn't you go in?" she said furiously. "Why did you run off like that? Have you gone mad?"

For an answer Lucas waved down a taxi, jerked the door open, pushed Joanna in, and jumped in after her. "The Arlington Hotel," he told the driver, and he hunched down in the corner, as far as possible from her. "The swami wasn't there," he mumbled.

"Then why were the lights on and why was the house full of people? I saw their shadows on the curtains. You must have, too."

"*He* wasn't there, though."

"I don't believe you! You got cold feet, admit it, you decided I wasn't *spiritual* enough!" But she couldn't get another word out of Lucas. When they reached the Arlington he didn't even look up as she ducked past him and out of the cab.

"Evening, miss." Standish stood tall on the front steps. "Did you enjoy your party?"

"I didn't enjoy it at all, as a matter of fact!"

"Then the next one 'as got to be better, 'asn't it."

Mrs. Drayton was out; Nurse O'Hara was watching television in Mrs. Beresford's sitting room. "Good night!" Joanna called through the connecting door. "I'm tired — I'm going to bed."

It wasn't quite nine o'clock when she turned off her light to weep with rage. Once again she'd been made a fool of. She should have slapped Lucas's face, right there in front of Standish, just as she'd slapped that fellow Hector at the Coopers' dreadful party, where she'd met the creep Lucas in the first place. Standish would have stood up for her! He was a real supporter. *He* never vanished — he was always there, regardless of the weather or the tempo of the times.

When she left the hotel the next morning she saw Lucas in the entrance of the department store opposite. He waved. She ignored him and set off towards Harrods to buy stockings.

Lucas crossed the street and fell into step beside her. "It's early for lunch but what about a second breakfast? Don't be grim, Joanna," he said to the side of her face, "it's too nice a day." He kept up a steady patter until, half a block from Harrods, Joanna came to an abrupt halt.

"To stop your *pestering*, I'll have a cup of coffee."

They went to a Viennese café in Lancelot Place. It was just opening, the cream cakes and linzer torte weren't out yet, the coffee was still perking. "We could go somewhere else," Lucas offered.

"I can wait five minutes," Joanna said sharply. "Can't you?" She sat down at a very small table on a very narrow chair.

Lucas sat down opposite her and immediately started talking about his mother's latest plan for his future. "She wants me to study forestry with a view to keeping me busy in the country growing Christmas trees, transplanting seedlings, pruning, weeding. Actually, if it means no more visits to Wimpole Street —"

"What happened last night?" Joanna interrupted.

"I told you what happened. I made a mistake in the schedule, that's all. I *do* make mistakes occasionally," Lucas said mildly. "I tell you what, if you haven't got another of those dreary cocktail parties, let's go to the theater this evening. It's perfectly safe. Mrs. Whittington-Burke never sees a play. No plot is simple enough for her to follow all the way through."

Lucas invited her to the theater twice within a week and once to the cinema, but he didn't ask her up to Highgate again.

One May morning Joanna was at the piano working on a composition for Mr. Ehrenreich when Mrs. Drayton appeared from the other flat. She was wearing a brown-and-white checked suit and new suede shoes. "How are things going, darling? I've missed you — we've both been so busy." She had begun to feel more warmly towards her daughter now that she was seeing less of her. "I haven't even had a chance to ask you about supper in the kitchen with Divina. Did you have fun?" She came up to the piano. "Have you got a few minutes?" Joanna put down her pencil. "You'll be eighteen a fortnight from today," her mother went on, "and Humphrey and I are going to give a birthday party for you."

"For *me!*"

"Why not?"

"I can't remember the last time I had one."

"Your birthday comes in termtime and you were away at Morehaven for so many years," said Mrs. Drayton quickly. "We've been talking about a party for some time, and yesterday over drinks we said, 'Let's do it!' Humphrey even offered to have it at Smith Street. He proposed putting on one of his Italian productions, but I told him absolutely not — I couldn't allow him to slave for days beforehand. So we agreed on a compromise — fifty for cocktails at Number Thirty-eight and on to dinner and dancing at the Conroy. Remember that party you went to there when Lucy Wheelock's father got his peerage? You said you liked the band."

"Are you really sure you want to do this?" Joanna said, astounded.

"Of course we're sure, darling!"

"It'll cost a lot of money . . ."

"You'll only have one eighteenth birthday . . . You do understand that although this is a joint effort, Humphrey is actually *paying.* Of course I would if I could, but you know the situation — the housekeeping money can't be made to stretch that far." Mrs. Drayton went on brightly, "There's no big social event on that night that I know of, but people do get terribly booked up so we must get the invitations out as soon as possible. Who do you want to invite, apart from the Coopers and your Knightley cousins? I really don't know who your friends are. If I can't put a face to them I never remember names. (Joanna, terrified that a door might swing open to reveal her stricken grandmother having her nappy changed, rarely shared the truth of the decay she lived in with her contemporaries.)

"There's no point in asking the Knightleys," Joanna said. "Cynthia's down with hepatitis — she caught it on a dig in India — and Sep would be bored to death."

"Didn't you have dinner a week ago with someone called Archie? And you mentioned a Jeremy Tyler, too . . ."

"I don't know anyone called Archie."

"There's the Whittington-Burke boy — wasn't he smitten with you at Easter?"

"I never said that!"

Mrs. Drayton sighed. "Joanna, this is an exceptionally generous offer on Humphrey's part. Must you turn what is intended as a treat into a chore?"

"I'm sorry," Joanna murmured. After a moment she asked, "Do you know if Humphrey's at home today? I'd like to go over and thank him."

"Would you?" Her mother smiled. "I know he'd like it very much if you did. He's been such a great friend to all three of us! We've all got so *many* reasons to thank him. Well" — she buttoned her suit jacket — "I'm off to buy some Vicks Rub for Granny. She's wheezing, poor love. So it's agreed, we'll make up the guest list this evening."

After her mother had gone out Joanna dialed Humphrey's number. "Mr. Beresford's in his study," the housekeeper told her. "He said on no account to disturb him, but you're not no account, are you?"

"Do please come!" Humphrey cried when Joanna was put through. "I'll have had enough of the doges of Venice by four, and I've found a Weber sonata I want to try. It's for piano and flute *or* violin."

When she arrived at Smith Street, Humphrey was in the music room on the second floor, tuning his violin. He had on a green cardigan that Joanna had knitted him and corduroy trousers — his working clothes in which he wrote his reviews and his Sunday column. "I've had a beastly day," he told her. "Bursitis in the elbow, the typewriter stuck, et cetera, et cetera." He chuckled. "But once I knew you were coming the bursitis vanished. Shall we have Weber first, or tea?"

"Tea, if you don't mind. Mr. Ehrenreich was truly punishing today."

"Worth it, though. I can't tell you how proud I am of you! I always think, Terribly sad that Leonora isn't aware. She was the one who started you off in the first place."

"That's not quite true."

"She always claimed the distinction . . ."

"My playing the piano was Miss Cathcart's doing, actually. You never met her, did you?"

"I never did. Not your mother's favorite, I've gathered."

"She was mine, though. She used to whisper in my ear, 'One day you'll be a great musician,' and since I believed everything she told me, I believed that, as well. For her sake, I'd become one."

"All that work, just for her!"

Joanna nodded. "Pleasing her was the most important thing in the world. I suppose that's why when she went away I stopped in my tracks. It had never crossed my mind to play for my own sake . . . I remember how cross I was at first when you pushed and prodded me back to the piano. I thought, Why won't he leave me alone!" She smiled. "It may have been the best thing you ever did for anyone, Humphrey.

"Mummy told me about the birthday party," she went on. "It's very sweet of you to do this."

"It isn't *just* a birthday party. It's to celebrate your successes, too." He added simply, "They give me a great deal of pleasure."

The housekeeper came in with the tea things and laid them out on a table by the window. "Sugar or lemon? Do have a scone," said Humphrey. "Just out of the oven."

Joanna took one. "It's sweet of you to give a party for me."

"You've already said that. Don't keep on about it, you embarrass me!"

"No one's ever given a party for me before."

"It's not just *me* who's giving it, Joanna. The invitations say Mr. Humphrey Beresford *and* Mrs. Henry Drayton. I ordered them last night and they promised to do a rush job. We'll have them tomorrow."

"I've been asked to so many parties, and I've never had a chance to pay anyone back." She added, "There's something else I want to talk to you about."

"I can guess — you want a car. Sorry, I won't help you there, Joanna. I want you in one piece."

"It's not a car, Humphrey. I want to talk about James . . . My father says James is legally of age — he can do what he pleases. My mother says James doesn't tell us where he is because he doesn't want us to know. When I say, 'But he's *ill*, he's not responsible for his actions,' she says, 'If he were ill they wouldn't have let him out of the hospital.'

"But I tell you, he wasn't himself when I talked to him last summer! He was impenetrable, *cruel.*"

"What are you asking?" said Humphrey quietly.

Joanna drew in a deep breath and let it out again. "Mummy always listens to you — you can convince her of practically anything. Will you try to convince her that James must be looked for?"

"Your mother's had a difficult time with your brother," Humphrey said slowly. "It seems they've always got on each other's nerves . . . Supposing she's right, though, and James is staying away on purpose, how do you think he'll like being found? I don't imagine he'd appreciate our efforts."

"What James does is *his* business, regardless of his state of mind. Is that what you're trying to tell me?"

Humphrey sighed. "I suppose so. Mind you, I haven't got anything against him personally — I've never known him terribly well. I met him a few times with Leonora but by the time your mother moved to London, he'd grown up and gone. Anyway, I'd gladly go look for him myself if I thought that finding him and hauling him back here would help. But the fact is, when a person has deep troubles he usually doesn't want anything to do with his family. Remember the old adage, 'You can only help those who help themselves.' There's a great deal of truth to it, Joanna."

The next day at lunchtime Joanna went to Frederick's to meet Lucas. She had decided that he was her last hope. When she entered the restaurant he was drawing with a fork on the table-cloth. Slipping into the bench beside him she said, "I've a very big favor to ask you."

"I can guess. You want money."

"I'm afraid I do, yes."

He stopped drawing and turned to her. "It's okay," he said pleasantly. "This happens to me about twice a week. What d'you want money for?"

"To hire a private detective to look for my brother." She hurried on, "My parents won't lift a finger, neither will Humphrey. When I asked I admit he was nicer than my mother or father, but still he refused. I haven't any idea how much a detective would cost — I haven't checked into it yet — but I've got three hundred pounds in my savings account and if I could double that, it would be a good start. I'm asking for a loan, Lucas. I'll pay you back as soon as I possibly can."

"I shan't lend you a penny," Lucas said, and went back to his drawing.

"In that case I'll have to steal a Drayton treasure, hock it, and use the proceeds."

"Why hire a detective?" Lucas said.

"I just told you."

"Why not look for him ourselves?"

"You and I?" Am I dreaming? she thought.

Lucas put down his fork. "What use would some burly British detective be compared with you and me? As his sister, you know James better than anyone else does — his character, habits, preferences, and so on — and although I know him only slightly, I feel a certain sympathy . . . Didn't you say that when you last heard from him he was headed for Spain?" Joanna nodded. "How well do you know that part of the world?"

"I've never been there."

"I have. I spent several summers in Torremolinos, two, alas, with Dr. Chesterton. And how horrible they were! Mrs. Whittington-Burke was very poorly and the dear doctor was assiduously on hand. You should have seen him sweating in the summer heat. A pretty sight he was not. Anyway, I speak the language passably." Smiling, he said, "The idea of looking for your brother quite intrigues me. In fact I've been playing with it for weeks, ever since we talked about him. If you hadn't raised the subject I'd intended to do so myself shortly. If we're going, we've got to be off pretty soon."

Dizzy with astonishment, Joanna gasped, "Why are you offering to do this?" Was Lucas her soul mate after all?

"I'm insisting, not offering. You ask why? Well, after a long, dull winter, I'm ready for an adventure, and this is a cause after my own heart." He went on, "As I said, we have to be off soon — a week from Friday, that's the eleventh, to be exact. Mrs. Whittington-Burke will be away that weekend and Oliver is taking that Friday off to squire her, so I'm absolved from my Wimpole Street session. I shan't be missed until the Monday morning, and by that time we'll be half a continent away. We'll go by train. It's slow, of course, but one is less easily detected in trains, traveling with the multitudes, than on airplanes."

"The eleventh!" Joanna exclaimed in alarm. "But I can't miss my party."

"What party?"

"My mother and Humphrey are giving a birthday party for me on the fifteenth. I can't miss it, Lucas! Think how they'll feel if I don't show up for it."

"I wouldn't waste my time thinking about how they'll feel if I were you. You're only doing what they should have done many months ago. Now," Lucas said matter-of-factly, "let's get down to strategy. Spain's a big country. The question is, Where is James most likely to have gone? What clues have we got? First, he's not well, or wasn't when last you heard from him. Second, he's trying to be a writer. Third, he isn't rich. One asks oneself, if one were in his situation, where would one go? Somewhere cheap and peaceful! So we shan't find your brother in Madrid, shall we? It's noisy, quite expensive, and full of soldiers with submachine guns." Lucas frowned at the picture of Lake Lugano on the opposite wall. "If I were James," he said after some moments of reflection, "I'd go to the Balearic Islands. They do marvels for the soul, psyche, spirit, or whatever one's designation for the part that's out of whack might be. So we'll try Ibiza first, and if we don't find him there, we'll go on to Minorca, Majorca, and every island in the Mediterranean if need be!"

They would cross to Paris on Friday, reach Toulouse on Saturday night, make their way over the Pyrenees to Barcelona the following day, go down to Valencia, and catch the boat to Ibiza from there. "Just as we reach the open sea on Monday morning, here in London the penny will drop — Mrs. Whittington-Burke will realize that she's breakfasting alone!" said Lucas gleefully.

"What will she do then?"

"She'll telephone Oliver."

"What will *he* do?"

"Take a cab up to Highgate for an audience with the swami."

"Will the swami know where you are?"

Lucas shrugged. "Maybe yes, maybe no. In any event, he's the most discreet man in Britain — he won't divulge a thing."

Lucas sat back. "There's nothing I enjoy more than a clandestine adventure. Do you like them, too?"

"I haven't had much experience ... although once I ran away from boarding school."

"Undetected?"

"If you mean was I caught en route, the answer is I wasn't."

"Was it an enjoyable adventure?"

"So long as it lasted."

Lucas smiled a slow smile. "This one's going to be tremendously enjoyable — ferryboats, dilapidated taxis, snowy mountains, sun-scorched plains, crashing waves on rocky headlands, cloaks, and — who knows? — even daggers, and always the great thrill of evading the authorities." He laughed joyfully. "In the course of tracking down your brother, we'll have the time of our lives!"

Chapter 14

France

As THE TRAIN RAN through gray working-class Paris suburbs
relieved here and there by pink geraniums in window boxes,
Joanna watched Lucas, on the seat across from her, decorate a
lunch menu that he'd taken from the restaurant car with red
Chinese dragons. He hummed to himself as he drew. He had
covered the front of the menu and the inside; now he was
working on the back.

He had been smiling ever since they left London.

On the Channel steamer, as the White Cliffs of Dover had
receded, Joanna had asked, "What's making you so happy?"

"Happy? I'm *intoxicated*," he'd told her, "*drunk* with possibilities!" and he'd got up from his canvas chair and walked off.

She had glimpsed him striding up and down the crowded
deck, smiling towards France. His curly hair bobbed wildly in
the wind, his tie streamed over one shoulder, his tweed jacket
flapped. Occasionally he glanced in her direction but he didn't
wave or beckon. Was she just another passenger traveling from
Dover to Calais, simply part of the landscape that his smile
happened to embrace?

Looking for James on her own would have been a daunting
proposition. She might have let the spring slip by as she practiced for Salzburg, and if ever the moment arrived when she
thought that she had practiced enough, summer would have

come and with it, the moment to go to Austria, not Spain. But Lucas had taken charge; he had insisted on their setting off as soon as possible, and she was grateful to him for that.

He has a right not to talk to me if he doesn't want to, she told herself. Unfortunately, though, she wasn't enjoying the company of her own thoughts much.

She had told her mother that her father had expressed a wish to see her for her birthday, and so she was going to Widleigh for an extra weekend. (In fact, Henry Drayton had long ago forgotten the month, let alone the day, of her birthday.) Her alibi covered her until seven o'clock on Monday evening, after which her mother would grow restless; and if she still hadn't arrived at the Arlington by five on Tuesday, her birthday, there would be a hunt, led zealously by Nurse Channing, through her room for clues. In the drawer of her bedside table she had left a note: "Since no one else would, I've gone to look for James. Mr. Ehrenreich wasn't expecting me today; I'd arranged for a time on Thursday afternoon instead. I'm sorry about missing the party. Give my apologies to Humphrey. I hope he'll understand. I'll be away as long as necessary. Please tell Mr. E. I won't be coming on Thursday, either." When Barbara Drayton read the note, remorse would finally strike her, a development that Joanna had been anticipating with relish. What she hadn't anticipated, however, was that remorse would strike *her*, too.

Ever since the boat train had pulled out of Victoria Station at nine o'clock that morning, an initial twinge of spiritual discomfort had been sharpening implacably; now, at seven in the evening, it had developed into undeniable full-blown guilt: she had completely sabotaged her mother's sole sustained attempt to be generous to her. The taffeta dress, green to match Joanna's eyes, would stay on its hanger; the shoes, green also, would stay in their box. Barbara Drayton (in mauve Thai silk from Fortnum's) wouldn't be saying how d'you do in the drawing room at Smith Street with Humphrey beside her. Instead, she would be at the front door telling guests, "The party's off, Joanna's vanished, you can't imagine the anxiety she's putting us through!"

At least I should have persuaded Lucas to wait till *after* the party, Joanna told herself for the hundredth time, and for the hundredth time, she reminded herself why they hadn't waited: This was their golden opportunity. Instead of driving to Leicestershire with Lucas, Mrs. Whittington-Burke was taking a long weekend in the country with Oliver Chesterton.

Lucas completed the elaborate scaly tail of his final dragon just as the train drew into the Gare du Nord. He jumped up, grabbed their suitcases, and dashed out of the compartment without a word.

"Where are you going?" Joanna shouted, but he raced on. She battled her way up the platform and found him outside the station as he was climbing into a cab. It was evident that he'd already given the driver directions.

"We have to be at the Gare St.-Lazare by eight tomorrow to catch the Toulouse train," she said, gasping. "Where are we going to spend the night?"

"Get in," Lucas ordered. "You'll see."

They set off through Friday evening traffic jams towards the center of the city. Joanna had been to Paris once before, in late summer, when litter lay under the bushes in the Tuileries Gardens and tired streets waited for the chilly autumn rains to drive back the tide of tourists. "Next time you'll see it in the spring," Humphrey had promised. "When the sun dances on the river and the tulips blaze, it's so lovely one could weep." Now, on a May evening, the sun was too low to dance on the river and the tulips were wilted and dead, but the air was soft, horse-chestnut candles shone in the fading light, and Parisian boys and girls wandered, arms entwined, through the Place de l'Opera and the Rue de la Paix and kissed on wrought-iron benches. Lucas, turning from the window to Joanna, grinned gleefully. "Paris is incredible," he exclaimed, "a place of infinite delight. I'm simply thrilled to be here!"

"Please remember," Joanna told him as they turned into the Place de la Concorde, "I can't afford anything expensive. I may have to make my money last for months."

Their taxi stopped before the eighteenth-century façade of the Hôtel Crillon. "Here we are!" said Lucas happily. "Despite the traffic we made excellent time."

"But I can't afford a *croissant* in a place like this!"

Lucas hauled out their suitcases, paid the driver, and beckoned to a bellboy.

"*Comment allez-vous, Monsieur Lucas? Quel grand plaisir!*"

"*Guardez-les, s'il vous plaît.*"

"*Très bien!*"

"That boy knows you!" exclaimed Joanna.

"I come here rather often. I was here just before Easter, in fact." As Lucas entered the lobby he glanced at his reflection in a huge gilt mirror, smoothed down his hair, pushed up the knot of his tie. He crossed a great expanse of purple carpet to the reception desk and said to the liveried gentleman behind it, "Could you tell me if Mrs. Whittington-Burke is already in Suite Seventeen?"

"Certainly, sir. She arrived this afternoon."

"Has she come down to dinner yet?"

"I don't believe so, sir."

"Thank you so much." Lucas nodded graciously and turned to Joanna, who was trembling with astonishment and horror at his side. "Shall we have a drink while we're waiting?"

"Why did you tell me your mother was going to the country?" Joanna demanded in a low and furious voice.

"I didn't say that," said Lucas mildly. "I don't believe I said where she was going."

"*You knew from the start that she was coming here!*"

Lucas shrugged. "She shops twice a year in Paris — early

May and late September — and Chesterton comes with her to
proffer his opinions and to carry the boxes and bags." He
glanced at the clock over the desk. "It's only five past eight.
They won't be down for a bit. Mrs. Whittington-Burke takes
infinite pains with her toilette when she's in Paris. Bubble bath,
face mask, pedicure, the whole bang shoot."

Guests, most of whom seemed to be Italian or Brazilian,
milled about. "We're in the way," Lucas said. "Do let's sit
down somewhere. I hate being bumped into, especially by
dagos."

"What do you intend to do when your mother and Chesterton appear?" said Joanna grimly.

"Let's have a drink," Lucas suggested, ignoring her question.

"I don't want a drink, I want to get out of here!"

"We can't leave yet. We haven't seen them."

"*Exactly!* I don't understand why you do most of the things
you do, and as long as I'm not directly affected, I don't *care*.
But in this case, we're on our way to look for my brother.
That's the agreed purpose of this expedition. Furthermore,
your mother and your psychiatrist were *specifically* not to be
informed. We agreed on that too, remember?"

"If you really don't want a drink, I shan't have one either,
but at least let's sit down." Lucas made his way to a Louis
Quinze sofa upholstered in striped silk, and for lack of a better
plan, Joanna followed. "From here we've got a direct view of
the lift and the main staircase," Lucas said cheerfully. "Which-
ever way they come down, we'll spot them right away."

"And they'll spot us," Joanna said, "and *that* will be the end
of this little adventure."

"Mind if I smoke?"

"It's unlike you to care about my preferences," Joanna said
bitterly.

Lucas lit a Gauloise, crossed his legs, and sat back. "This
hotel is sadly in need of renovation," he observed. "D'you see

that crack in the ceiling. It could collapse on one's head at any moment! That happened to me and Mrs. Whittington-Burke once before. Not an experience either of us would care to repeat. Why, there *is* the dear lady!" he exclaimed. "She and the doctor have chosen to make a grand entrance. And she's got on such a smart new frock! . . . She must have bought it on her way in from the airport. Not to my taste, though. Too melodramatic."

Mrs. Whittington-Burke, striped in black and white from neck to toe, was coming down the broad staircase on the arm of a dinner-jacketed, barrel-stomached man, with whom she was deeply absorbed in conversation. "You have to admit they make a striking pair," Lucas murmured, eyes riveted. As they reached the bottom step Chesterton threw back his head and gave a great bark of laughter. "Amusing though she can be on occasion," Lucas remarked, "Mrs. Whittington-Burke is a debilitating companion. The Old Boy certainly deserves his dins." But instead of proceeding directly to the dining room (past the sofa on which Joanna and Lucas sat), Chesterton and his patient-patroness turned in the opposite direction. "Heading for the bar," said Lucas. "A quick martini before oysters, turtle soup, and duck *à l'orange.*"

He sat for some moments staring at the door through which the two had disappeared. "That was very satisfactory," he said at last with a contented sigh. "We *could* lurk behind pillars, shadow them down a corridor or two, and dine a few tables away with our backs steadfastly turned, but I suppose we should be getting on — we have our own agenda. Just wanted to make sure they were enjoying themselves. They are, too, wouldn't you agree, Joanna? They seem quite wrapped up in one another . . . I'll just retrieve our cases from that boy and we'll be off."

"Where are we going now?" said Joanna, faint with relief.

"First we'll have some dinner at a bistro I adore — I've got a penchant for a mushroom omelet and a slice of *tarte aux pommes* — and then I know just the hotel, near the Gare St.-Lazare, to fit your budget."

An orange neon sign, Hôtel d'Orléans, crowned a drab gray building in a drab little square. "This is it," announced Lucas. "You'll note a contrast. I hope it's sharp enough." As their taxi came to a halt, Joanna glanced at her ringless hands, pulled a grubby pair of gloves from her handbag, and put them on.

The Hôtel d'Orléans had no bellboy, no hall porter, nobody to carry in suitcases at ten o'clock at night — or even at ten o'clock in the morning — so Lucas carried them in himself. He went up to the mountainous bleached blond woman behind the desk, who, hair notwithstanding, would never see seventy again. While Lucas wrote "M. et Mme. Richardson" and a fictitious address in the register, she scrutinized Joanna. What wife would wear such an unbecoming skirt, such an ugly sweater, or have smudges on her chin? Those dirty gloves deceived no one — this wife wore no wedding ring! But she didn't bother to test her suspicions by asking to see their passports; the Hôtel d'Orléans wasn't of an order to require proof of identity from anyone.

She took a key from a hook, eased her way out from behind the desk into the lobby, and indicated to Lucas and Joanna that they should follow her. She swayed up three dim flights of stairs and along a landing and, at the far end, with much bending and squinting at the keyhole, unlocked a door. *"Voilà!"* she said as she switched on a weak overhead light and glanced round the room. There was a brass bed with a bluish counterpane, a single chair, a marble-topped washstand, a table, and an armoire. The floor was bare, and no towels were provided. The old woman sighed heavily, handed Joanna the door key, and left. They heard her making her ponderous way back to the stairs.

Joanna shut the door and Lucas put the suitcases side by side on the table, went to the window, threw the shutters open, and leaned out across the sill. After a shower an hour before water lay in puddles in the gutters and between the cobblestones. Every so often a car swished by.

Joanna removed her gloves, kicked off her shoes, and sank to the edge of the bed. She was utterly exhausted, dirty, and cold.

Lucas turned back to the room. He waved at the rickety furniture and the peeling ocher walls. "This is an excellent jumping-off place, don't you agree?"

"I find it sinister," Joanna replied flatly, without looking up.

Unheeding, Lucas said, "I like the *atmosphere* of this hotel. One comes, one goes, there's no record, no memory. No one will ever know that we were here."

Joanna shivered. No memory? Until the end of her days she would remember that old woman and her dark-rooted straw-colored hair. "I'm worn out," she said. "I'm going to sleep."

Lucas produced a pack of cigarettes, lit one, turned back to the window, and leaned out.

Joanna found her key in her bag and unlocked her suitcase. Once smart, shiny black, it was dull, scratched, and battered now. A label hanging from the handle announced in childish capitals, MISS JOANNA DRAYTON, WIDLEIGH PARK, HEREFORDSHIRE. She tore the label off and stuffed it in her pocket. Then she pulled out her nightdress, hairbrush, sponge bag, dressing gown. The room afforded no privacy at all and so, for fear that Lucas would whip round and see her pink bra, blue slip, and grayish suspender belt held together with safety pins, she undressed in haste. She drew her long-sleeved Viyella nightdress, intended for damp spring nights alone in her own bed at Widleigh, over her head. Having been to the lavatory in the restaurant, where Lucas had had his omelet and she'd had *escalope de veau,* she could last until the morning, so she brushed her hair fiercely and climbed into bed. It was icy and she very nearly jumped out again and put on her dressing gown, but vanity prevented her. Convinced though she was that nothing romantic could ever occur between her and Lucas, her gray Morehaven dressing gown with coffee stains down the front simply would not do; at least her nightdress was clean, even charming, in a sprigged, Victorian sort of way.

She lay, hands between her thighs for warmth, and waited for sleep to creep up on her; then the morning would come quickly and they'd be on their way to the sunlit south. She hoped that sleep would help allay her many misgivings about her companion, too. But it refused to come and she found herself thinking about who had occupied this bed before her, what they had done together and alone.

Shutters clanged together, a bolt was pulled to. There were plopping sounds as garments dropped to the floor and the bed creaked and swayed as Lucas lay down. He struck a match and lit another Gauloise. Joanna, meanwhile, kept her eyes determinedly shut.

"You're awake," Lucas said. "If you were asleep, you'd breathe more deeply." He leaned across, took hold of her shoulder, and shook her. "You're not deceiving me!" She opened her eyes and reluctantly pushed herself up to a sitting position. The dim light was still on. Lucas sat back against the brass bedstead in his underclothes, puffing on his cigarette and regarding her through the smoke. He held his left arm across his chest as if to conceal from her his youth and hairlessness. He no longer smiled. Thoughts that had entertained and exhilarated during the day had deserted him. Joanna stretched her legs out and arranged her nightdress carefully over her knees. She noted that her toenails needed cutting and that Lucas's did too. He coughed and spluttered. He was an expert smoker; he smoked with style. It was the first time she'd heard him cough while smoking.

As he turned to extinguish his cigarette in the ashtray on the bedside table, Joanna saw how slim and slight he was, how narrow and bony his back. He pulled up the bedclothes, clutched them to his chin. "I'm cold," he said, shivering.

"Didn't you bring any pajamas?" Joanna said, and when he shook his head, she added, "If you like, you can wear my dressing gown." She had heard that line about being cold before. An arrogant boy she had met at a house party that past summer had rolled onto a playroom sofa, patted the cushion beside him, and told her, "I'm so cold! Come and warm me up." "But we're having a heat wave!" she had replied, standing her ground. The boy had jumped up and stalked out and at breakfast the next morning had cut her dead. But Lucas wasn't arrogant; he wasn't angry. He was scared and it *was* cold. She regretted her practical approach. "No," she said, "you wouldn't want my dressing gown. It wouldn't fit, it's much too small."

Lucas ran his tongue over his lips and his hand through his hair and said, "I want to have intercourse with you."

He didn't say, "I want to make love to you," which was how the idea had been proposed to Joanna in the past. Furthermore, *intercourse* was the word used by the female gynecologist who came to Morehaven each July to address students about to venture forth into a sexually hazardous world. Such an act, she declared, ought to occur only between individuals who were married to each other.

"I should explain," Lucas went on, his eyes fixed on a point to the side of her left ear, "that Dr. Chesterton and I have gone into this a fair amount."

"Gone into what?"

"The issue of my having intercourse with girls." His voice was barely audible.

"You mean, you generally do it with men?" She couldn't quite bring herself to use that antiseptic word, even at a passionless time like this.

"Not at all!" He paused. "I use streetwalkers exclusively."

Joanna had heard boys tell stories about tarts — Lucas's vocabulary was more technical — but she'd guessed from their nervousness and laughter that they hadn't been any closer to a tart than she had herself, going home along Piccadilly in the evening. "But in a sense," Lucas was saying, "streetwalkers are unnatural. They impose certain emotional constraints on the proceedings. Chesterton has suggested that it might be helpful for me to have intercourse with an ordinary girl. Would you object very much to my having intercourse with you?"

Neither Eliza Lancaster nor Lucy Wheelock — not even Divina Jenkyns, whose family was so informal — would ever find herself in a seedy Paris hotel with a man who proposed to take her virginity for psychiatric reasons, his own psychiatric reasons, no less — not even hers! Joanna laughed until suddenly tears came and she was weeping.

Lucas, watching her wipe her eyes on a corner of the sheet, said quietly, "Now I've put my foot in it."

"You haven't got the faintest *clue* how another person feels," she exploded. "All you know or care about is *yourself!* You're the most totally self-centered person I've ever met in my life, and I've met some horrors, let me tell you!"

"It wasn't my intention to make you cross," Lucas said sadly. "I'd been hoping that you'd help me out, but you don't have to. I'm sorry I brought the matter up. If we want seats on that Toulouse train, we'll have to be up and out very early, so now we'd better get some sleep. Goodnight," and he turned off the light.

Joanna lay on her back and stared at the ceiling. Whenever a car turned into the street below, headlights flashed through the slats of the shutters, streaking the room. She reviewed the weeks she had known Lucas — so many afternoons and evenings of being careful, stepping on eggshells, letting him have his own odd way. She should have taken stands! What a fool he'd made of her! But after a while her indignation subsided and she found herself feeling sorry for him. The cramped world of Widleigh and the Arlington Hotel seemed to have prepared her better for the real world than all those special effects, that exotica, had prepared Lucas. He was much more likely to get lost in life than she was, she decided, and she turned to him, lying two feet from her, so confused.

"Lucas?" She spoke his name softly. "If you're still interested, I'd like to try."

He started at her voice, stirred, propped himself up on one elbow, and pushed his hair out of his eyes. In the light that filtered through the shutters he looked at her hopefully. "Why do you say that now?"

She shrugged. "I was thinking things over and I changed my mind."

"Thanks," he said softly. "I'm so glad you did." After a moment's silence he asked, "Have you ever had intercourse before?"

"Not quite."

"Pity. It would be simpler for both of us if you had."

She had heard that young men were in awe of virginity and that the prospect of being the first in, so to speak, pleased them, but Lucas wasn't pleased. "Sorry to put you to the inconvenience," she said sarcastically.

"It isn't as important as all that." He smiled, moved over to her, kissed her, eased himself on top of her. Rather to her surprise she liked that; she liked the way he kissed her, too. He was more accomplished than she had imagined. Those street-walkers must have taught him a thing or two. He stopped kissing her long enough to order, "Take this thing off!" He pulled at her nightdress. "It's appalling!"

"Aren't you going to take off your underclothes?" she said as she tossed her nightdress onto the floor. He pulled her to him again without answering. "Do this." He took her hand to instruct her.

Joanna was beginning to enjoy herself. She regretted their

afternoons in the zoo with Sinbad and feeding the ducks in St. James's Park when they could have been upstairs in Chester Square, doing this! They tumbled about on the grubby blue counterpane and nerve endings that she hadn't known she had came to life and thrilled all over her. She waited for him to come into her — that had to happen now — but suddenly he flung himself away from her, turned on his side, and drew the bedclothes up to his ears. "Did I do something wrong? If I did, please tell me!" she begged, kneeling naked at his side, but when she touched his blanketed back he told her, "Enough of that. Leave me alone!"

She picked her nightdress up off the floor, put it on, back to front, and slipped under the covers. This time sleep did come, although her dreams were real enough to make her think a dozen times that she was wide awake.

They got up in the cold dawn, dressed quickly, and took a taxi to the station. Joanna said she was hungry, she was going to get something to eat. Lucas accompanied her to the buffet and shifted from foot to foot while she ate her breakfast; he drank half a cup of coffee.

He had smiled all day from London to Paris, but today, as they went on again, he didn't smile at all. He didn't speak to her; he didn't let his eyes meet hers. Whenever the train stopped at a station Joanna would leave their crowded third-class compartment to stretch her legs and to air her pounding brain; each time Lucas followed her and then, on the platform, left her and walked briskly away. She would tell herself, He's off, that's that, he's gone; but when the whistle blew he would come racing from some distant corner to his seat.

Wedged between a fat lady who smelled of garlic and an ancient one-eyed man, Joanna asked herself, If I've set off with one lunatic to look for another, does that mean *I'm* a lunatic as well?

Lucas had insisted on the slow route to avoid detection, to

get into the spirit of things. Orléans, Châteauroux, Argenton, Limoges, where they changed, then on over the Dordogne River, the Lot, and the Tarn. The train chugged across green plains, through forests and river gorges, past medieval towns and villages with ruined castles perched above them, round the foothills of the Massif Central. For short periods Lucas would watch the passing countryside with seeming interest, but mostly he leaned back against worn brown plush, eyes shut. He didn't go with Joanna to the restaurant car for lunch, and worried about his not having eaten since the night before, she brought back two rolls from supper, wrapped in her handkerchief. When she touched his knee to rouse him, he shook his head; he didn't want her rolls, he didn't want anything. Then she spotted Fruit Gum wrappers at his feet. He had secret supplies!

After sunset when Joanna could no longer see the country, she took out *Heart of Darkness,* but she couldn't concentrate. She dozed in the corner seat across from Lucas; she awakened, dozed again, and dreamed of a tumble-down cottage, a Balearic version of the one in which James had spent his Widleigh winter. In her dream she found him staring out to sea. I've had such an awful time, Joanna, so confusing, he said as he turned to her. I hoped you'd get here somehow — I hoped you wouldn't let me down. I couldn't be sure, though, could I? But after all, you made it — now I'm going to be okay. She awoke just before midnight as the train drew into Toulouse.

Lucas didn't push aside the other passengers in order to get the suitcases down from the overhead rack, as he had when they'd reached Paris. In the scramble to get out, plenty of people bumped him with their packages and parcels, and yet after everyone had departed, there he sat, eyes closed, oblivious.

"Lucas, Lucas," Joanna shouted in his ear, "wake up, get up! We've arrived — we have to get out here and find somewhere to spend the night."

His eyes flicked open and he jumped up so suddenly and

with such force that he knocked her sprawling across the seat. He seized his suitcase, leaving hers.

"Wait for me!" Joanna shouted, but of course he didn't wait. He was running to the door, leaping from the train, racing the length of the platform, out of the station, across the Place de la Gare, as Joanna lugged her battered case in pursuit. She paused to look at a schedule posted on a wall, and by the time she had discovered that the Barcelona train left at nine in the morning, Lucas was clear across the square and up the steps into the Hôtel de la France. As she darted into the street Joanna was almost run over by a *deux-chevaux* that shot from shadow into light. The driver swerved and swore at her, and she took one look at his scarlet face before struggling on. She entered the Hôtel de la France just in time to see Lucas enter the lift with the diminutive night porter.

"Wait, *attendez-moi, s'il vous plaît!*" she yelled across the lobby, but the gate clanged shut; the lift rose and disappeared. There was nothing to do but wait for the porter to return; then she would explain that she had been delayed at the station and wanted to be directed to the room where her husband, *le jeune anglais,* was expecting her. As she stood in the lobby, half a dozen men walked by. Despite her physical and mental condition, they scrutinized her hips, legs, breasts. But she wasn't a pretty girl welcoming attention; she was an escapee who had just come seventeen hours on the train from Paris only to be left high and dry by her lunatic companion!

When the porter returned she almost threw herself on him. She had forgotten to put on her gloves; she'd left them in the Hôtel d'Orléans. The porter watched impassively over gold-rimmed spectacles as she gesticulated with ringless hands and chattered her request for succor. He turned wordlessly to the reception desk, opened the register, and ran his finger down the page headed *samedi, 12 mai.* M. Richardson had signed only for himself; he had made no mention of Madame. "But

I'm English," Joanna cried. "Why would an English girl come alone to a place like this? Of course I came with my husband — he's waiting for me upstairs." Tears splashed down her cheeks. "Please take me there!" A fat man in a belted corduroy jacket had stopped to observe her hysteria. Now he pursed his lips in sympathy, consternation, disapproval, who knew what, and went out into the night. With the sadism of the very small, the porter watched her for some moments longer until finally, when she had wiped her eyes and blown her nose, he closed the register and pointed first to the lift and then overhead. "*Allons!*"

At first there was no response when the porter knocked at Number Twenty-three, a front room on the third floor. His eyes flashed scornfully over his glasses, but he knocked again and this time the door opened a crack. "*Qu'est-ce qu'il y a?*" said Lucas.

"It's me, Joanna. Let me in!" and to her amazement the door opened wider. She gave the porter a small smile of triumph before slipping through. The door slammed behind her and there stood Lucas beside a brass bed just like the one in Paris, only its counterpane was grubby yellow instead of grubby blue. "That was a vicious thing to do!" she shouted. "Can you imagine how I felt? Why did you rush up here, why didn't you wait?"

Lucas regarded her in silence. By the light of one low-wattage bulb that hung, shadeless, from the middle of the ceiling, his heavy eyebrows ran clear across his face.

"That's what I always seem to be asking — 'Why didn't you wait?' I sound like a cracked record, even to myself," she said. He hates me, she thought wearily. He's forgotten who I am, but all the same, he hates me . . . who knows why.

Lucas turned from her and flung himself face down on the bed, and there he lay, a fistful of counterpane in each hand. "Speak to me, Lucas," she begged, leaning over him. "You spoke to the night porter — you must have. You *can* speak if you have to, if you want to enough." She clutched the brass bedstead and, in her agitation, shook it, as if she were shaking him. "Unless you tell me what's the matter, I can't help you." But Lucas lay there, rigid, muscles, nerves, and sinews steeled against her, an invisible armor plate covering every square inch of his body.

He's afraid of me, she realized suddenly. It's because of *fear* that he hates me. Nevertheless she continued to beg, cajole, plead, promise, until finally she was so utterly exhausted that her voice trailed off in midsentence. She dragged herself to an armchair by the window, turned her jacket collar up against the night air — cool still, despite its being May and so close to Spain — and fell asleep immediately.

When she awoke it was nine o'clock and Lucas had disappeared, although his suitcase still stood near the door, next to her own. She got up from the chair, stretched, felt the ache in her legs and shoulders, and threw open green shutters. In the square below a flock of pigeons whirled. She lifted her face to the sun, closed her eyes, and imagined, when she got back to London, people asking, Where did you get your color so early in the year?

There was a wash basin in the room, and judging from the brown stain on the porcelain, the tap produced water. She removed all her clothes and washed herself from head to toe. Then she got dressed in clean clothes. When she looked at herself in the mirror she half expected to see the worn face of a stranger, but she saw her own face, no older than two mornings before when she'd set out on this adventure. Encouraged, she smiled at her reflection, gave her hair a hundred strokes, put on her shoes. I'm ready now, she told herself, although she didn't know for what.

It was possible that Lucas had gone for good, but then again, perhaps after a day of Fruit Gums he was ravenously hungry and had taken himself off to get something to eat. She was pretty ravenous, too. She decided to go into town to find a pleasant café; she wouldn't give a thought about what to do next until after breakfast. So she went downstairs and gave the room key to an affable young man at the reception desk. He wished her good morning without a trace of curiosity as to why she was without Monsieur.

She walked through the Place de la Gare and into a tree-lined boulevard. She felt suspended, as if she had left one world and not yet arrived in the next; the people she passed in their Sunday best, sober suits, pretty summer dresses, seemed very far away, very small, like dolls placed in a plaster model of a city yet to be built. She smiled at one young woman on the off chance of getting a response that would tell her, Yes, Toulouse is real and the people here are real too, but the woman looked back, startled. I meant to smile, Joanna thought to herself, but perhaps I didn't; perhaps I stuck out my tongue. Has Lucas affected me so drastically already?

After crossing the River Garonne, high with Pyrenean snow waters, she bought a newspaper and continued on along the boulevard until she found the sort of café she'd had in mind. Red umbrellas with Pernod written across them in large white letters shaded blue-clothed tables. The café was already quite full of families refreshing themselves after the diligence of Mass. She chose a sunny table from which she could watch the comings and goings in the street. She ordered and, while she waited for her breakfast to come, opened her paper, looked at photographs, and read the captions. She hadn't the will or energy just then to tackle full-length columns. She thought she could feel freckles forming on her cheeks. Every spring they appeared with the first strong sun, and in the autumn they faded away.

The waiter, bringing croissants and coffee, roused her. She ate one croissant and a second with large dollops of plum jam. Then, as she sat back to sip her coffee and watch the people strolling by, a smartly dressed middle-aged woman and her son stopped in front of the café. The woman was tall and fair, large-bosomed, statuesque; her son was several inches taller, narrow-shouldered, fair, too. They didn't look French; Swedish, per-haps, or German. Joanna watched them make their way round knots of playing children to a deeply shadowed corner and the only table that was still free. The young man stooped ever so slightly. Perhaps he had suffered from ailments all winter and with spring his mother had decided to take him south. He sat down, back to Joanna, shoulders hunched. The mother leaned towards him and in a low voice assured him that if he felt too cold they would find a sunny table in another café, but he shook his head and they stayed.

Joanna started on a third croissant. She ate slowly in order to delay the moment when she would have to begin thinking in an organized fashion again, but finally that last croissant, too, was finished. She paid the bill, folded her newspaper, brushed the crumbs from her skirt, and rose to leave. She was about to walk out of the café when the large blond woman, wanting more butter, turned to summon a waiter.

There under the red umbrella, her shining face unaltered by the years, sat Miss Cathcart.

The moment their eyes met she surged up and over to Jo-anna. "Has it been seven years?" she cried. "Is that really possi-ble?" Her delight at seeing Joanna seemed unalloyed. "You were a mere child and now you're a young woman!" She seized Joanna's hand and shook it with all the old, enthusiastic vigor. "A charming one you've turned out as well, if I may say so. I do like your hair long! I can see that you were leaving, but it's Sunday and such a lovely day. Please don't rush off! My dear, how *good* it is to see you. Won't you join us for a little while?"

Café patrons watched the blond woman sweep the slight, dark girl off to her table in the shaded corner, and as the two approached him, the fair young man pushed back his chair and rose to his feet. "What a strange coincidence!" he murmured. In neatly pressed gray flannels, white shirt open at the neck, and beige sweater that bore creases of newness down the sleeves stood James Drayton. He kissed his sister on the forehead mechanically. "We scarcely expected to see Joanna here, did we, Sybilla," he said in a voice that conveyed no surprise, no warmth.

Joanna took the chair that he pulled out for her. "I didn't expect to see you, either," she replied, awestruck. Knowing that her gaze would waver and slide, she couldn't bring herself to look at either of their faces; but on Miss Cathcart's lapel she recognized the brooch of lapis lazuli, the Talbot children's farewell present, and she fastened her eyes on that. "What brings you to Toulouse?" she said as evenly as she could manage.

"We were in the Balearics all winter," Miss Cathcart replied. "I've grown rather fond of islands and Jamie likes them, too. But after the middle of May they start to get crowded, so we're beating a retreat — we're on our way north. We hope to find something that suits us on the coast of Normandy." She went on cheerfully, "We were sad to leave the islands, mind you. We had a nice little place on Ibiza with a spectacular view. It was two miles out of the village of Santa Eulalia del Rio, high above a lovely *cala*. *Cala* is the Catalan word for inlet, by the way. Late last summer when we first arrived there we had great fun with the underwater fishing, but alas, we had to leave before the sea got warm enough to do it again this spring. Being so far away from the village was rather a trial for shopping — we had no car — but all in all it suited us. We preferred to be off on our own."

"Some people find village life intriguing," James said. "Church bells, vegetable markets, drunks shouting in the plaza, that sort of thing, but I can't stand the racket."

"Peace and quiet, that's what was most important for Jamie, after the troubles he'd had," Miss Cathcart went on. "As for me, I was busy being domestic. We had someone in to clean but I did all the rest."

"Sybilla's paella was out of this world," James said. "I don't know what her secret is."

"Lemon. I marinate the chicken in it. Six hours, not a moment less, and then I braise it."

At last Joanna was able to look at her brother, who sat with elbows on the arms of his chair, hands folded in his lap. His hair was short and lighter than she remembered. He had washed it that morning with a shampoo that smelled faintly of pine. His fingernails were short also. For an instant Joanna saw him on Christmas Day as he ran from the smoking room, unshaven, grimy, anguished. But now beside her, close enough to touch if she wanted to make certain he was real, sat this placid boy whose eyes were a deep, dark blue, the color of the English Channel on a summer day.

Periodically Miss Cathcart would appeal to him for his view of some incident or other that had occurred during their island sojourn; then he would reply, "I agree absolutely" or "I had my reservations to begin with, but later on I saw how right you were." The voice that for so long had been tinged with skepticism, disgust, fury, now — as he echoed his companion — conveyed admiration, subjugation, and content.

Since the other two were behaving as if there were nothing especially remarkable about her being with them at a table in a café in Toulouse, even though she hadn't heard from James for nine months or from Miss Cathcart for seven years, Joanna did her utmost to appear as unsurprised as they. When Miss Cathcart had finished her account of what she and James had seen and eaten and read together, she laughed her deep, rich laugh. "Now that you know what *we've* been up to, Joanna, *we* want to hear about *you!*"

Perhaps she only said this in order to fill awkward concluding moments. Nevertheless, Joanna took the opening she was offered and talked about Mr. Ehrenreich, the Royal Academy of Music, the Salzburg master classes in July. She said, "One student will be chosen to play the Mozart two-piano concerto with Correa de Leon himself and the Salzburg Mozarteum. I've been studying the score for weeks in the hope that I'm the one who's chosen. You used to say, 'One day we'll play the E-flat Major with the Hallé Orchestra — we'll toss to see who'll play first piano and who'll play second.' Do you remember?"

Miss Cathcart shook her head. "I confess I don't. What I do remember, though, and most vividly, is your promise, your potential, and to hear that you're fulfilling it in this marvelous way is quite thrilling!" She added, "Since Widleigh Park wasn't the optimal artistic environment, I have to say I was concerned about how you'd keep your music up, but you moved right along!"

"That's not true," Joanna said quietly.

"How can you say that, my dear, when you've accomplished so much!"

"I mean, I didn't move right along. For three and a half years after you went away I didn't touch a piano — I never played at all. James didn't tell you?"

"I don't believe so, dear. We rarely talk about Widleigh and its associations. We made a conscious decision to put all that behind us."

"James isn't the only one who's had troubles," Joanna said.

Miss Cathcart sneezed loudly. "Allergies," she said, digging in her handbag for a handkerchief. "It's the lime trees. France, unfortunately, is full of them."

It was she who gave life at Widleigh meaning, James had told his sister long ago.

"You held everything together," Joanna said after a moment. "It was only because of you that we had a family at all. When you left us" — she held out empty hands — "that was that. I took it pretty hard." She looked into Miss Cathcart's eyes, lapis blue. "Why *did* you go away?"

"You needed companions your own age, Joanna. School was the right place for you."

"So you told me at the time. But you also said, 'When you're older, perhaps you'll understand.' Well, I'll be eighteen the day after tomorrow and I still don't understand. Was it because of jealousy?" she asked at last. "Was my mother jealous of you and my father?"

Miss Cathcart shook her head. "Not especially, no."

"Was my father jealous of you and Mr. Edgerton?"

Miss Cathcart shook her head again.

"Sybilla and I were lovers," James said dryly. "When the secret got out, as in time it had to, Sybilla was given a lift to the station. By the way," he added, turning to Miss Cathcart, "did you have to pay for your own ticket? I didn't ask you at the time."

"Your father paid."

"Uncharacteristically generous of him, I must say!" James's voice had the old ring of sarcasm. So he hadn't been totally remade, not yet.

Joanna gazed at him while umbrellas swayed above them, cups rattled in saucers, café au lait spilled on tablecloths, napkins blew away. Eventually, when everything had come to rest, she said, "Were you always, from the beginning?"

"Of course not!" Miss Cathcart exclaimed indignantly. She leaned towards Joanna. "When I arrived at Widleigh Jamie was a mere *child*. Why, he hadn't even started to shave!"

"We held off for years," James said. "Until my eighteenth birthday. That was the first time we made love, after cake and presents. Remember the shepherd's cottage beyond the park wall? We made love there, and after that we made love everywhere we could think of, didn't we, Sybilla!" He sat back with the glimmer of a smile. "So now Joanna knows. Strange, I must say, that such a bright girl hadn't worked that one out before."

"Have you been" — Joanna sighed enormously — "lovers ever since?"

"There have been gaps," James said. "I went to Malaya for two years, remember."

"And I married," Miss Cathcart said.

"You did!" exclaimed Joanna.

"It wasn't a success, though. My name's Sybilla Henderson now."

"Did you divorce?"

"That didn't turn out to be necessary because my husband died. He was quite a lot older than I was — a widower, a former colonial judge, retired from the Kenya high court. He'd been chief justice, actually."

"And a K.B.E.," James said. "That makes Sybilla Lady Henderson."

"He seemed suitable, but turned out not to be so . . . Jamie knew how to get in touch, should he want to, and eventually he did. I was living in the Channel Islands and his letter was forwarded to me there. I received it just about a year ago."

Joanna had been brought up to date now; there was nothing more to talk about, and all three tried to find a way of bringing this chance encounter to an end as gracefully as possible. James said, "We're catching the midday express up to Paris where we'll spend a couple of days. Sybilla wants to see the Goyas in the Louvre."

Miss Cathcart said, "If only we weren't dashing off, we'd walk round the city again with you. Romanesque Toulouse has a lot of charm."

"I don't have time for sightseeing," Joanna began, intending to continue, I've got schedules to work out. But instead she found herself saying, "Neither of you asked me how I happen to be in Languedoc in the springtime. Maybe you haven't because you don't want to know, but I'll tell you anyway.

"When you hadn't come back by Easter, James, I became obsessed — I was convinced something terrible had happened to you. Everyone I talked to said you'd dropped out of sight on purpose and I shouldn't worry, but I couldn't stop. Mostly what I thought about was you."

She went on, "We've never talked about my first term at

Morehaven, have we? Were you told about my going round the bend?"

"I was," James said quietly.

"I was desperately sad then, and desperately angry ... I hated everyone but you. They said I had to be quiet, that I couldn't have any visitors. As I lay there in the infirmary, I imagined you knocking down the nurse when she tried to stop you. I imagined you forcing your way in." She paused for a moment. "Of course you didn't come, though, and somehow I picked up anyway, got out of bed, went on about my business, and my memory of that dangerous deadening time grew hazy. But I never forgot what it felt like to long to see your face ... And so two days ago, afraid that you had despaired as I had despaired once, hoping that my coming would make all the difference in the world, I set out to find you. A man I met suggested looking first on islands — the Balearics were a good point to begin, he said — so I was on my way to Valencia to get the ferry over. Lucky I ran into you or I'd have wandered all over the Mediterranean for nothing."

Finally she said, "Last summer on the telephone you told me you were off to Spain with a friend. Had I known who your friend was, of course I would never have come to look for you ... As soon as I've taken care of a few odds and ends here, I'll be on my way back to London." She waited but neither James nor Miss Cathcart spoke. Had she really said what she thought she'd said? Had she imagined everything? Oh, well ... She stood up and shook hands with both of them. Miss Cathcart did her best to cover her discomfort with a smile. James blushed. The crimson of his face made a striking contrast with his pale, clean hair. He murmured, "I was in a bad way at one time, much better now."

"He still has spells occasionally," Miss Cathcart said, "but we're hoping a quiet summer will do the trick."

"And after that?"

"I shall stay as long as he needs me." Miss Cathcart brightened. "It's been splendid talking to you. I'm glad we had a chance to iron out a few things. The very best of luck in Salzburg!"

"Do you still play?"

"Alas, very little. But that's all right. You're playing for both of us, Joanna!"

When she got back to the Hôtel de la France the key to Room Twenty-three was not at the desk. "Monsieur has returned already," the affable young man informed her. She found the door ajar and Lucas in the armchair by the window, looking out into the square. When she came over to him he looked up but not at her. "Careful," he cautioned, "it could break."

"What could?"

"My crown," he said. "It's very delicately made."

On the floor behind the armchair she spotted a scrap of paper and retrieved it. It was the receipt for a telegram sent to Whittington-Burke, Hôtel Crillon, Place de la Concorde, Paris.

"So they'll be coming soon," she said softly. "That's good. I'll wait with you." But Lucas didn't say another word.

In the early afternoon she went out to buy bread and cheese. She gave Lucas half; he accepted it and ate it without looking at her. He also ate an orange and a slim chocolate bar and drank half a bottle of Vichy water.

Joanna took out *Heart of Darkness* but made little headway. It was hard to read about mystery and horror when one was sitting close to a madman, even if he was pacific; and so until the light faded she watched people passing, children playing, pigeons hopping, pecking, whirring in the square below.

From the window at about eight the next morning Joanna saw a dusty limousine pull up in front of the hotel. She watched as Mrs. Whittington-Burke emerged, dress creased. She looked very tired. Behind her came Chesterton in a rumpled London suit. Joanna jumped back from the window and grabbed her suitcase. To Lucas, who was sitting on the edge of the bed, she said, "They're here — they'll be up in a minute. Good luck, safe journey," and she patted his shoulder before fleeing from the room and along the corridor. As she reached the stairs she heard the lift clank open behind her and Mrs. Whittington-Burke's voice: "What could have brought Lucas to Toulouse, of all places?"

Downstairs Joanna positioned herself in an alcove near the front door.

Soon the lift descended and out came the proprietor, the uncle of the affable young man, followed by Mrs. Whittington-Burke and Dr. Chesterton. Between them, in lock step, marched Lucas, blank-faced, wooden. They stopped at the desk and while Chesterton paid M. Richardson's bill, Lucas looked round the lobby. For an instant his eyes met Joanna's, but he betrayed no sign of recognition. Chesterton replaced his wallet in the inner pocket of his coat, took hold of Lucas's arm, and led him out to the waiting limousine. The two got into the back while the chauffeur settled Mrs. Whittington-Burke in the passenger seat. Then he scampered round, jumped in himself, and drove off.

Joanna walked slowly across the Place de la Gare, relishing the early sunlight and the fresh, cool smell of newly washed cobblestones. At the station entrance she put down her suitcase and waved her arms, sending the pigeons whirring skyward. "Don't touch, be careful," she called out to them. "My crown is very delicately made!"

From the Dover–London train she watched urgent green countryside fly by. How could it be that after such a journey, such turbulence and tumult, it was still spring in England? She had half expected to see stubble fields and blackening branches against a late autumn sky; but there were hardly more leaves out on the hopvines, hardly more dandelions shining in the grass than she'd seen four days before.

She had found what she had lost. That James hadn't needed to be found because, other than to her, he hadn't been lost, didn't matter. What she had set out to do she had done.

Her quest had been a secret and so it would remain. At the start she had thought, Lucas and I are sharing this adventure, this clandestine rescue operation. She hadn't understood that it wasn't possible to share with Lucas because he experienced life alone — so much alone that she wouldn't have to worry about his giving their secret away. He had erased her and their adventure, completely.

Tidings that James was safe, better (if not quite well), and in Miss Cathcart's care might reach Barbara Drayton eventually. If so, she would seize upon them, harp upon them interminably to the Channings of this world. If they reached Henry Drayton, he would tell no one; he mightn't acknowledge, even to himself, this further evidence of betrayal. In any event, neither would hear the news from their daughter, who would protect as long as possible those two whom she had so long loved.

As the train reached the outskirts of London, fields gave way to yellowish brick houses. Each had a narrow strip of garden running down to the railway line, in which, defying soot and grime, cherry blossom wafted, magnolia burst into huge white stars, phlox crept pink and purple, ajuga and grape hyacinth painted sunny corners blue. Then gardens were crowded out by blackened station yards; the train came to a halt; passengers seized their belongings and scrambled out of the compartment, leaving Joanna alone. Her watch said four twenty-four. After ups and downs and shocks and surprises she was back in one piece, in time for her party. A passing porter glanced in and, seeing her smile, called, "Want any help, miss?"

She shook her head. "No, thanks. I'll manage on my own," and she pulled her case from under the seat and climbed down to the platform.

May 1964

Chapter 15

Widleigh

ON THE NINTH OF MAY, 1964, Joanna Drayton played the Beethoven C Major with the Vancouver Symphony Orchestra and as she came backstage for the last time, a sheaf of white and yellow lilies in her arms and applause still ringing in her ears, she found Lawrence Farmer, the musical director, and Hester Furgusson, the wife of the chairman of the board, waiting in the corridor. "We need to have a word with you, Miss Drayton," Farmer said. "I'm so sorry . . . Hester, perhaps it would be better if you . . ."

"But not out here." A patrician-looking woman in a gray silk dress, Mrs. Furgusson drew Joanna away from the autograph hunters, the young pianists hoping for an argument about tempo and interpretation, and the tall man with the sad face who had followed her from city to city, from Tulsa by way of San Diego, all the way up to British Columbia, without once attempting to speak to her.

Mrs. Furgusson led Joanna into a room lined with tables piled with coats and hats and shut the door. "It's your father, my dear. I'm afraid he's passed away. Your agent, Mr. Rothman, called from New York, and our housekeeper reached us with the message during the interval. We decided to wait until after the performance to let you know . . . I hope we did the right thing."

"I've got to sit down," Joanna said, but there were no chairs, so she pushed hats and coats to one side and hitched herself up on a table. The small room was hot and airless and her black velvet evening dress had long sleeves, yet she shivered.

"This wasn't expected, was it?" Mrs. Furgusson said.

"He's seventy-nine — he's never been ill a day in his life. *Was* seventy-nine, I mean." After a moment Joanna added, "Although you might say that he'd been old for a very long time." She bent to her sheaf of lilies, but they didn't really smell of anything.

"Your mother, is she still living?"

"Yes, but my parents separated years ago. My brother and my father didn't get along either, and so" — she glanced up at Mrs. Furgusson, who stood before her, hands clasped, an expression of deep concern on her handsome face — "it's not much of a family. The sooner I get home the better."

"I perfectly understand, and we'll do everything we can to help you get away."

Joanna looked down at narrow floorboards; the varnish was wearing off. She saw through them and beyond them to a black and silver river threading south between green hills and she heard Henry Drayton's voice: You can't beat this view anywhere on earth, Joanna!

"I'm going to have to miss your supper party, I'm afraid," she said. "You'll go ahead without me? After so much preparation it would be a shame to cancel it. None of your guests knew my father and only a handful know me."

Mrs. Furgusson's elegant hand rested on Joanna's shoulder. "*I'll* take care of the party, Miss Drayton. At this point all you should worry about is *you*. First thing, you'll want to make calls and travel arrangements. There's an Air Canada flight to London that leaves at ten in the morning, and tomorrow being a Saturday, you should have no trouble getting on. Lawrence went to get his car — by now he must be outside waiting for you."

As soon as she got back to the Georgia Hotel, Joanna telephoned her mother. "So he found you!" Mrs. Drayton exclaimed. "When Agnes rang last night with the news I told her you'd been dashing about so much lately, I hadn't any idea where you were. Luckily you'd given me Rothman's number the last time you were over, so I rang him. All I got was an answering service — he was out for the evening, they said — but eventually he rang me back at four A.M. our time. Can you hear me? I *hate* these transatlantic calls! I was just saying to Humphrey, 'I hope when Joanna rings I'll be able to hear her.' That time you telephoned for my sixtieth birthday from — where was it? — San something in Texas, the static was awful."

"Mummy," Joanna shouted, "how did Daddy die?"

"Heart attack. Agnes found him yesterday, after tea. He'd been listening to a cricket match on the smoking room radio. She went in to take the tray away and he'd collapsed on top of it — there were biscuits and sugar lumps all over the carpet. She got the ambulance and they rushed him into Hereford but they couldn't revive him. Merciful, really. He'd have hated being in hospital, attached to tubes. Anyway, Agnes telephoned here about nine and then it was a question of getting hold of Rothman. When finally I did, he was very pleasant, I must say, though he does speak English with a most extraordinary accent. Sounds Russian. Is he?"

"He was born in the Bronx," Joanna said.

"By the way, where *are* you?"

"Vancouver. I just came back to the hotel from the concert hall."

"How many more have you got?"

"How many more what?"

"Concerts."

"Only Toronto and Montreal, and I'll get Rothman to cancel them. I'll be home sometime early on Sunday morning. Don't meet me — I'll take a taxi in."

"*Ought* you to cancel, darling? I mean, this is your first proper tour. Is it wise or necessary to break it off? You might get a reputation for being temperamental. The funeral could wait till you've finished. After all, your father's safely in the morgue . . ."

Joanna took a deep breath. "Does James know?"

"Not yet."

"He's in Brighton, isn't he?"

"Of course, where else would he be? Only remember, he won't answer the telephone between eight at night and eight in the morning and it's only half past seven here. At eight sharp Humphrey's going to ring him. He does rather better with your brother than I. We'd planned to motor down to Wiltshire to lunch with friends but since we got virtually no sleep last night, we don't really feel up to it. Besides, if you arrive early enough tomorrow morning, we can go to Widleigh straight away, and two long car journeys two days running aren't my idea of fun."

"You and Humphrey are going up to Herefordshire with me?" said Joanna incredulously.

"I think I should." Mrs. Drayton gave a short laugh. "I'm still your father's lawful wedded wife, and Humphrey's offered to drive us up and stay till after the funeral. As you know, he's marvelous at arranging events, and we can't expect much from James. When Granny died, he only came to the cemetery — never set foot in the church."

Having left messages with numerous East Coast answering services, Joanna made a reservation on the Air Canada flight to London.

She flew through a short spring night and a long Atlantic sunrise. Her plane circled above hawthorns frothing pink and white in parks and playgrounds and landed at Heathrow just before six.

Since finishing at the Royal Academy she had spent little time in England. After nine months in Paris with Alfredo Correa de

Leon she had gone to study with Vera Lermantov in New York, at Juilliard. When her fellowship had ended she returned to Europe to compete at Avignon, where she was runner-up, and, at the end of the summer, at Sheffield, where she won. But instead of remaining in Europe she had gone back to New York. All her teachers had been displaced persons, refugees from tyranny: Ehrenreich from Hitler, Correa de Leon from Franco, Lermantov from Stalin. She too felt like a displaced person, longing for home, unable to live there, and since her lover was in New York, she decided New York would do for the time being. She spent her grandmother's money, when she received it, on an American Steinway which she had hauled into her fourth-floor apartment in a decaying building on East Fourteenth Street.

Her lover was a cellist called Leo. He was fifteen years her senior, celebrated, married, and the father of three sons. Lately he had started to talk about leaving his wife, Cecilia, in order to marry Joanna, a prospect she didn't relish nearly as much as she had imagined she would. For one thing, she suspected that Leo as lover and Leo as husband might be two different species. Despite his ardent declarations to the contrary, she was afraid he might demand of her the same degree of self-effacing domesticity that he exacted from Cecilia, whose promising career as a violinist had been shelved in favor of caring for him and bearing and raising his sons. For another, Joanna wasn't as enamored of New York as Leo was. (He was from Battle Creek, Michigan, and believed New York was the center of the universe. Joanna did not — she hadn't decided where she wanted to settle. Once she got to know them, she might very well prefer Rio, San Francisco, or even Tokyo to the searing egotism of New York City.)

Or was it that she was habituated to the clandestine, that she was free to love only in secret? Once it was open, legitimated (routinized), mightn't love wither and die?

She would be twenty-five next Thursday. Wherever her music took her she would go — to Kansas City, Missouri, as it had that past March, or to Bucharest, Rumania, as it would in August, to play the Mozart B-flat Major. So far, she had no more carefully articulated plan than that.

She told Humphrey, who was at Heathrow to meet her, "You oughtn't have got up so early for my sake!"

"Don't worry, I have senile insomnia — I'm always awake by four. So why not pop in the car and come down and get her, I said to myself. Although I'm sorry about the reason for your visit, I'm awfully glad you're here. I do wish you weren't so Anglophobic, Joanna."

"I'm not Anglophobic! Never a day goes by that I'm not homesick. It's just that I had to leave England in order to recover."

"Recover from what?"

"Growing up."

"And how long is that going to take you?"

Joanna smiled. "It might take my whole life!"

"I do so hope it doesn't," said Humphrey gravely. "Even when you do come over, you're usually too busy to play chamber music with your old friends. Now your mother tells me you're about to make a recording of the Schubert Impromptus, and once that's out, you'll be even more sought after — you won't have any time for us at all! By the way," he added, "I thought we'd go to my house first and have a cup of tea. We shouldn't disturb your mother quite this early, and I want to hear all about your concertizing — that's the correct American expression, isn't it?"

When, at age eighty, Mrs. Beresford had expired of heart failure while being fed puréed peas by Nurse O'Hara, Barbara Drayton gave her mother's portrait by Augustus John to the

Tate and most of her furniture to the Edgewater Home for Unmarried Mothers. The portrait of her father she sent to the Worshipful Company of Goldsmiths, of which he had been master from 1897 to 1898. Then she moved out of the Arlington and into Number Thirty-two Smith Street, three doors down from her cousin. This was the first house, indeed the first habitation of any sort, that she had called her own. "If I want I can put a fountain in the drawing room and potted palms and parrots in cages on the stairs," she told Humphrey joyfully.

She'd done nothing of the sort. With Humphrey's help her first house became a model of conventional comfort — articles about it appeared in several of the same magazines to which she continued to contribute. Now she wrote on exhibitions, entertaining, and London gardens, as well as travel, which tended to be to places farther afield than hitherto — Alaska, Sikkim, Fiji, were spots she'd touted highly. All her pieces were lavishly illustrated with photographs taken by Carl Butterfield, who was one of Humphrey's younger friends. She was still a captive, but third time lucky; her cousin was infinitely more benevolent than either her mother or husband had been.

Mrs. Drayton hoped for grandchildren. As she told her hairdresser, who until the Great Event had done Mrs. Beresford's hair also, "One starts out all right when the children are little, and then, I don't know, suddenly one finds oneself being dreadful. Mummy was perfectly dreadful to me, too, and yet she couldn't have been sweeter to the grandchildren. I'm sure I'll be just as sweet to mine as she was — I'll delight in every new accomplishment." But so far Joanna had shown no interest in obliging — she was too busy being a rising star — and neither had James. Indeed, apart from the Brighton bookshop in which, with the money Mrs. Beresford had given him, he had bought a share, James appeared to have no interests.

Since his mother's move to Smith Street, he had come to see her only once, to look for a story that he said he'd left in the spare room bureau when Barbara was still living at the Arlington. But the bureau was in his mother's bedroom now, full of underclothes — no trace of his story. He had snorted with disgust, turned on his heels, and marched out. Henceforth mother and son met from time to time for lunch at Number Thirty-eight where, over scampi, Humphrey would draw him out about fads and fluctuations in the book business while Barbara sat silently by.

After returning from his Continental sojourn, almost seven years before, James had not been to Widleigh — or seen his father — once.

Barbara was up and dressed in a tweedy coat and skirt (right for Herefordshire) when Humphrey and Joanna arrived at nine. "Darling, you look awful," she exclaimed. "And surely you're thinner than when you were over last summer. You didn't sleep a wink on the plane, I don't suppose. I never do, either. I *hate* crossing the Atlantic — I'm always terrified of falling in. I'm sorry your triumphant progress round North America had to be interrupted. You must be so cross!"

"Daddy didn't die on purpose."

"Still, he might have waited a week until all your concerts were finished . . . Have you two had breakfast?"

"A cup of tea and half a grapefruit," said Humphrey. "She wouldn't even let me make her toast."

"On the plane they were constantly trying to feed me," Joanna said. "You know how it is. By the time you reach Ireland you never want to see another pepper steak with salad in your life."

"Well, come into the kitchen while I have *my* breakfast and we'll go over what we've decided so far."

Barbara Drayton's kitchen was a splendid aggregation of butcher block and Italian tile. Ferns cascaded in the sunny bay window; French cooking utensils for every conceivable purpose hung above the eight-burner stove. Barbara didn't cook, but Humphrey did, and she had designed her kitchen to his specifications. Their dinner parties were more often at Number Thirty-two than Number Thirty-eight because Humphrey preferred the proportions of Barbara's dining room to those of his own. He preferred most of the furniture he'd helped her buy for it, too. He especially coveted her Hepplewhite table. Letting her have it instead of keeping it himself had been a stupendous altruistic act.

Barbara poured three cups of coffee and put a slice of whole wheat bread into the toaster. "It was too late to get your father's death into Saturday's paper," she said, "but it'll be in the *Times* and the *Telegraph* tomorrow: 'Funeral private Tuesday, memorial service to be arranged.' We didn't think it would quite do to have the funeral open to everyone. I mean, would we be up to dealing with all those Herefordshire people we haven't seen for years when we've hardly seen *each other* for years, either? So we decided, better to have a memorial service later, when things have settled down a bit. Humphrey said you'd probably want to choose the hymns, Joanna. You were the one closest to your father, insofar as he was ever close to anyone . . . I suppose he was attached to Agnes, in his way, but otherwise he only cared for dogs. No doubt there'll be some to dispose of. How about taking one back with you to America, Joanna?" Barbara laughed. "To protect you from those Central Park muggers one's always reading about."

"Daddy had his last dog put to sleep at Christmas," Joanna said. "He wrote and told me."

"That's a blessing. More coffee? . . . Humphrey spoke to James, of course."

"How did he take the news?"

Humphrey smiled. "Said he was dropping everything, leaving the shop in his partner's hands, and going up to live at Widleigh for the rest of his life!"

"You told me he sounded euphoric, didn't you, Humphrey," said Barbara. "Knowing he had Widleigh coming to him, I suppose it's no wonder that, at thirty-three, he's done so little with his life. Now that the plum's fallen off the tree, I certainly hope he's happy. The death duties will be tremendous, as Henry made no effort to avoid them, so far as I know. To pay them, James will probably have to sell off half the estate and turn the other half into a safari park, with hot dog stands and elephant rides for trippers from Birmingham and Cardiff. If he thinks of it as a challenge to his creativity, he might enjoy it. According to his school reports he used to be very creative. In the holidays he would write like mad in his room, instead of riding his pony. He drove his father to distraction! Not that I ever read any of his masterpieces. You were the only one he allowed to see them, weren't you, Joanna, and poor darling, you found some of them awfully muddled, I remember. But James has never done anything straightforward."

"He was perfectly straightforward this morning," said Humphrey.

"In at the kill," said Barbara, "or as soon afterwards as he can get there." She smiled. "One thing that's given me great satisfaction is the knowledge that despite Henry's efforts to turn him against me, ultimately James disliked his father at least as much as he disliked me . . ."

She went on after a moment, "Anyway, I asked myself, is there anyone who should know before tomorrow morning's papers, but honestly, I couldn't think of a soul except Harriet Cooper — she was always nice to your father in the old days — so I did ring her yesterday. We had a lovely chat about Gabriella, once we'd got over the I'm-so-sorry-to-hear-it part at the beginning. Harriet says Gabriella's deliriously happy with her new husband — well, not so new, the baby's already a year old. There she is, at twenty-four, running a huge property in Scotland as if she'd been at it all her life. Can you imagine *yourself* organizing Christmas parties for a thousand tenants,

Joanna? Of course Gabriella's always had a knack for organization ... Oh, I did get in touch with the vicar, Mr. Ogden-Smith. A very different sort from Mr. Edgerton, I must say. Don't you remember him salivating over Miss Cathcart? His successor sounds much more in control of himself. So the funeral's at two o'clock on Tuesday and he'll see to the grave-digger. They'll bury Henry next to his mother, the admirable Catharine Hannington, to whom I was unfavorably compared for twenty years.

"We'll have time to sort through things and go to the solicitor before the funeral. It isn't Mr. William Chadwick anymore." Barbara turned to Humphrey. "He was the martinet I dealt with over school fees — he's retired now. We'll be dealing with his son, Mr. Harold. Or rather, James and Joanna will be dealing with him, possibly with your assistance. You were wonderful with Herriott when Mummy died. I don't know what I'd have done without you! *I* don't intend to lay eyes on Mr. Harold myself. Henry's will, thank God, will have nothing whatsoever to do with me." She glanced at the kitchen clock. "Do you want to take a nap, Joanna, darling? Heaven knows what time it is in Vancouver."

"If I need to, I'll sleep in the car. I'd like to get to Widleigh as quickly as possible."

They drove through a showery morning to the White Hart at Evesham, where they had lunch, and then on up to Hereford, where they stopped off at Jackson's Funeral Home in the Market Square. On a Sunday, with no funeral scheduled, Mr. Jackson wore a tweed coat and gray flannel trousers, instead of his everyday shiny black suit. "Birch should do for the coffin," said Barbara. "After all, once Henry's in the ground, who will see?" But Joanna chose mahogany with brass handles. "Your brother mightn't want to spend the money," Barbara said.

"I do, though, and now I'd like to see my father."

"Darling, don't feel you have to! I didn't see Granny. I simply couldn't bring myself to, poor little shriveled up thing!"

"I want to see him. That's why I asked."

"I buried both your grandparents," Mr. Jackson told Joanna as he led her down the passage to the morgue. "They died within six months of each other, as I remember. Big funeral they had for your grandmother. Must've been close to seven hundred there." In the morgue were three tables, all occupied. "We had an accident yesterday on the Shrewsbury road. A boy and a girl on a motorbike. Ran into a lorry in the rain. Too bad, really," he added, forehead furrowed. He led Joanna to the table farthest from the door and pulled the shroud back with care. "If the light's not good enough for you . . ."

"It's quite all right." Her father lay there in the yellowish-brown suit that Agnes, with Pickering's help, had chosen, looking faintly encouraged. Had he been pleased with the way the cricket match he'd been listening to was going? Worcestershire had beaten Sussex in the last over, but by that time he'd had his heart attack.

"Would you like a few minutes alone with him, Miss Drayton?"

When Mr. Jackson had withdrawn, Joanna reached for her father's icy hands, folded on his chest. If my leaving made you sad, she told him silently, I'm truly sorry, but if I'd stayed I'd have made us both sadder still. Widleigh is for James — it always has been. He'll thrive there, just you see!

"Now that I don't have to face Henry, I'm quite excited about being back," Barbara remarked as they drove up the hill to the house. "It *is* pretty," she added. "When I lived here I hardly noticed, I hated being here so much!"

"Isn't that James's Mini-minor at the door?" said Humphrey.

"Fully installed already," Barbara said, laughing. "Next he'll have his portrait painted, in his father's plus fours, to hang with all the other Draytons in the dining room. On second thought, they wouldn't fit him, would they? He's far too tall."

"I could recommend an excellent portrait painter," said Humphrey as he pulled up behind James's car. "Although I imagine there'll be a number of things to see to before that. For instance, those." He indicated the downspouts on either side of the front door. "They're rusted out."

Agnes came slowly from the stable yard. She was seventy-five and her bunions were killing her. In other respects she was well, she assured Mrs. Drayton. "You're looking very well yourself, madam. London suits you — Joanna's always told me that. Sad about the Major," she added, but he'd had a long life and he'd gone quickly, without pain, and for that you had to be thankful.

"Do you remember Mr. Beresford, Agnes?" said Barbara. "He was last here thirty years ago."

Joanna hugged Agnes. "The burden fell on you, and I'm sorry, but we're all here now," she said.

"Wasn't no burden. I was used to your father and he was used to me. I'm ever so glad to see you, Joanna! Your brother's in the library — he can't have heard the car." She added, "Would you want tea in there, seeing the dining room's shut up?"

Joanna went into the house ahead of the others and through the hall. James was at the library window looking out across the park when she walked in. "Hello," she said. "We just arrived. How are you?"

"There used to be a grove of walnut trees down near the cattle trough," James remarked. He didn't turn round. "When were they cut down?"

"I don't remember. Five years ago, perhaps."

"The Roman emperors in the conservatory . . . they're gone, too."

"They weren't marble, they were plaster. In the end they crumbled away."

"In the end . . . when was that?"

"Dates are hard to pinpoint. Every visit something or other

was different from the visit before, but I couldn't put the changes in order now, not for the life of me."

"Well, I shall replace the emperors. I shall also plant walnut saplings by the trough," said James briskly, turning to his sister at last. His hair, receding at the temples, was white. (Like his mother he'd gone white before he was thirty.) His face was pale and bony, his eyes were a chilly grayish blue. "The place is shockingly dilapidated! The parapet will fall into the flower bed if something isn't done immediately, and the gutters are shot. The garage ceiling's collapsing, the drains are all clogged up. It's most disturbing to see how seriously the old man neglected things. One wonders, How did he spend his time? Reading George Eliot, I suppose, while Widleigh went to pot!"

How have you spent *your* time? Joanna wanted to ask him, but James had long ago stopped giving proper answers to her questions.

In recent years she had seen little of him, since he had steered clear of the Arlington and, when their mother moved there, of Smith Street too. Their few meetings had been in Brighton, where Joanna would spend an awkward hour in the back of the bookshop, or at the Café Europa in Baker Street. It served the best coffee in London, James claimed.

"I'm back from the Continent. Meet me at the Europa at four," he had told Joanna on the telephone one October evening in 1957. She had gone the next day, knowing he wouldn't be there, but he was, at a table in the corner, in clothes like the ones he'd worn in his Oxford days — corduroy jacket, heathery sweater, dark-blue shirt.

"Where's Miss Cathcart?" she said as she sat down opposite him. "Isn't she with you?"

"She went back to Jersey," James replied evenly. "She's hoping to go into the property business — building bungalows for retirees, that sort of thing. I think she'll be good at it. She has a talent for deducing what a person needs and then providing it."

"You mean, *you* don't need her anymore?"

"I absorbed a good deal of her time and energy," James said. "We both had to move on."

"Is that what she told you?" — and when he nodded — "she told me that once, too. When did she leave you?"

"About a week ago. We'd been at Granville in Normandy since May and on the twenty-ninth of September she went to St. Malo and took the boat over to the Channel Isles. I stayed on a few days longer, then I came back here . . . What about you, are you well? Any boyfriends?"

"No one special. I've had fun, though, and in Austria particularly. Abroad suits me, too. I hope to go to Salzburg again next year."

"I'm back in England permanently," James said quickly. "No plans to go abroad again." The waitress stood over them and they ordered cappuccinos.

Joanna gave news of James's Etonian classmates whom she'd run into at parties, adding that once she had begun to meet musicians, whom she liked much more than she did debs and debs' delights, she'd stopped going to coming-out parties. Instead of going to Gabriella's, she'd drunk rot-gut Spanish claret in someone's basement flat in the Earl's Court Road. James seemed to be listening, but since he said nothing, she couldn't really tell. Eventually she said, "Daddy and Mummy don't know about Miss Cathcart. I didn't tell either of them about seeing you two together in France."

"I should hope you didn't!" James exclaimed. He was drumming his fingers on the table. "It was no concern of theirs — for that matter, no concern of yours, either — my being with her on the Continent, or even" — his nose twitched — "in bed with her at home."

"Is it completely over?"

"It was time to move on."

"And you're not devastated!" Joanna cried. "I was, when she left *me*. But then," she went on softly, to herself almost, "I lost both of you at once."

James was looking over her shoulder to the street. "I should be off," he said, feeling in his pocket for change to pay the bill.

"Should I tell them you're back?"

"Why don't you. It'll save me the unpleasantness of contacting them myself. Nice to see you, anyway, Joanna."

He had come through his ordeal, she could see that, his two feet were on the ground. But he no longer laughed or even smiled — he no longer loved her, or anyone. He won't let me know him and he has no interest in knowing me, she told herself as he walked out, and her heart ached, but less than it used to.

Now, as heir to Widleigh, he had his hands full. "It boggles the mind," he told his sister. "It's outrageous how the old man let things go!" And Joanna detected glee in his voice as he added, "I'm certainly going to be busy, getting this place straight."

The next morning all four of them went to see the vicar. "It's *pro forma*, really," Barbara Drayton said. "There only *is* one funeral service, but he'd like to see our faces. He told me he doesn't have a lot on this week. Next week, on the other hand, he'll be very busy — he's taking the Widleigh hale and hearty on a pilgrimage to the shrine of Our Lady of Walsingham. They'll go by bus to Norwich and walk from there. I can't imagine Henry approving of such exhibitionistic piety, but I suppose, with clergy hard to come by, he had to grab whatever he could get. Ogden-Smith told me he holds prayer breakfasts in the vestry, too. Scrambled eggs and instant coffee over a paraffin stove . . ."

As they trooped into his study, which had a view across purplish moors into Wales, Mr. Ogden-Smith boomed at James and Joanna, "I understand you two haven't spent much time at home lately."

"True," James agreed, "but now I, at least, am back for good, and I'll be looking to you to help me get my bearings. In fact, I've written down a list of questions which I'd like to go over with you. Tomorrow's out, of course, but perhaps you'd have time later in the week? Would Wednesday suit you? How about eight-thirty, nine o'clock?"

In the afternoon Humphrey went round the garden with Pickering and two barrows. They filled them with lilac, rhododendron, azalea, white spirea, Japanese iris, and wheeled them over to the church. There Barbara and Joanna arranged the flowers in vases that Humphrey positioned on the altar, the pulpit, and all through the chancel and the nave. "I'm not sure why we're doing this," said Barbara with a laugh. "No one's going to see St. Mary's in her finery except the servants and ourselves."

It looks as if we're going to have a wedding, Joanna thought, as if Daddy were getting married joyously at last.

James hadn't come to the church; he had stayed in to sort through his father's file cabinet before the meeting the next morning, the morning of the funeral, with Mr. Harold Chadwick, who would read the will. "The accounts are chaotic," he told the others when they came back to tea. "It will take me months to put them in order. There's no indication that he ever consulted an accountant."

"Miss Cathcart used to help him," said Joanna lightly. "They always did the quarterly accounts together. Sometimes I even got off lessons because Miss Cathcart was so busy." She added, "She could be very systematic when she chose."

"In this instance," James said, "her system, whatever it was, didn't stick."

On Tuesday morning Joanna drove into Hereford with James in James's Mini. Soon he would trade it in, together with Henry's shooting brake, for a Volvo. "Volvos are hardy," he told Joanna. "Just what one needs for these country roads." He had decided to take a diploma course in agriculture at the University of Wales. "Quite a trek down to Cardiff," he said, "but I hope to fit my lectures into a couple of days a week, which will leave most of my time free for running Widleigh."

"The land's all let," Joanna pointed out. "When you get your diploma, what will you farm?"

"Leases fall in eventually."

Mr. Chadwick was bespectacled, fortyish. He wore a gray suit and an Old Salopian tie. On his desk in his offices at Twenty-one Haymarket, which Chadwick and Chadwick, Solicitors, had occupied since 1854, was a vase of bluebells. When Joanna admired them, Mr. Chadwick said they had been picked on Sunday, between showers, by his seven-year-old daughter. "We're having a damp spring," he murmured. "What was the weather like in British Columbia?"

"I wasn't there long enough to notice — I had to leave in a great hurry."

James and Joanna declined the coffee they were offered. "Then I imagine we should go to the business at hand." Mr. Chadwick's left eye blinked involuntarily. (His father, Mr. William, had had a tic as well.) He cleared his throat before proceeding. "Major Drayton wrote four wills altogether," he said. "The first, as a bachelor, before the Great War, the second when he married, the third in 1950, which, I understand, was the year he and your mother separated, and ultimately a fourth, which of course supersedes all those previous to it. This is the will that I shall read to you now."

After bequests to servants, St. Mary's, Widleigh, Eton College, the Herefordshire Hunt, and the Thirteenth Hussars Memorial Fund, Henry Drayton left his daughter, Joanna, twenty-five thousand pounds, the Drayton pearls, and the Stubbs painting of Robert Drayton, eighteenth-century explorer, and his blackamoor, that hung in the dining room. To his son, James, he left twenty-five thousand pounds also, and a first edition of *Cobbett's Rural Rides*.

"Is that all!" James jumped up, his face a burst of scarlet. "There has to be a mistake!"

"We have a letter from your father," Chadwick said quickly. "Please be seated, Mr. Drayton. It's dated April third of this year. That's just five weeks ago. It's addressed to both of you." When James had stumbled back into his chair Chadwick began to read.

" 'Your lack of constructive concern for your home was a source of great sadness and distress to me for many years. Early on, James indicated that his interests lay elsewhere and so I looked to Joanna to step into his shoes; but soon she began talking of a musical career that would take her far from Widleigh. Although I lived in the hope that one of you would reconsider your decision, as time passed and neither showed any indication of doing so, I realized it would be necessary to make other provisions. I considered my options with great care and ultimately came to the conclusion that one person only was capable of giving Widleigh the attention it merits and requires. That person, my dear friend whose departure to this day I deeply regret, is Sybilla Cathcart.

" 'To her I bequeath all my property, investments, and other possessions, in the belief that in the future she will cherish Widleigh as much as I have in the past.' "

"This is incredible, absurd, *illegal!*" James exploded. He leapt to his feet, swayed momentarily, and sat abruptly, grasping the arms of his chair. "My father had no right to do this!"

"I'm afraid," said Chadwick dryly, "your father had the right to do whatever he wanted."

"Does Miss Cathcart know?" Joanna managed to ask at last. She felt dangerously lightheaded, close to tears, close to laughter. "Did my father tell her about this will?"

"I have no evidence that he did, Miss Drayton. Apart from myself and my secretary, who typed it, no one knew of its existence. The next step, of course, is to inform the beneficiary." He went on, "Would either of you have any idea as to her whereabouts?" James stared in silence at a spot on the wall an inch above Chadwick's head. The color had drained away; his face was pale as alabaster.

"I have no idea," said Joanna.

"Then we'll start with an advertisement in the *Times.*"

"That's how Daddy got her in the first place," Joanna said softly.

"What was that?"

"My father put in an advertisement: 'Governess/companion wanted; imagination and initiative essential.'" She added, "He was looking for someone who'd suit him as well as me."

"Is that so?" Behind thick lenses Chadwick's hazel eyes were wide. "Since Major Drayton did not elaborate on the identity of the beneficiary, I assumed Miss Sybilla Cathcart was a relation on the maternal side."

"In some respects, she did remind him of his mother . . ."

Hearing the news, Barbara Drayton became hysterical with laughter, and when, tears of mirth still on her cheeks, she had collapsed on the library sofa and accepted the glass of sherry Humphrey offered, she gasped, "Henry's last perversity! True to character to the bitter end! My darling" — she looked up at Joanna — "I'm deeply sorry for having perpetrated this father upon you. Believe me, had I known, I would have spared you, but as we met and married in a month flat, really, I had no idea." She wiped her cheeks with Humphrey's handkerchief. "So Miss Cathcart got away with James's patrimony as well as his virginity! Yes, Joanna, that was why she was bundled off so quickly. While you were in the drawing room playing Mozart, she was debauching your brother! Naturally I couldn't tell you, darling, you were just too young — you still believed in storks and water babies. I assumed you'd hear about it from James sooner or later. Better from him in the fullness of time, I decided, than from me."

"He told me," Joanna said.

"Believe me" — her mother blew her nose loudly — "the love affair between your governess and your brother was much the most exciting thing that happened in all my years here. A pity it had to be interrupted, I've sometimes thought, but really, as a responsible parent, one couldn't allow her to stay. I'm sorry you never had the thrill of knowing Miss Cathcart, Humphrey. Although personally I couldn't *stand* her, I admit she was a vital force." She went on, "At least you got the pearls, Joanna. They'll look so pretty on those velvet dresses you wear when you perform. You will insure them, won't you, darling? The Stubbs may turn out to be more trouble than it's worth, though. How will you ever get it up the stairs to your apartment? Unlike a piano, you can't take it apart and bring it in through the window. Better loan it to a museum. Or leave it here. If you take it away, it'll leave a huge patch on the wall and Miss Cathcart will have to have the dining room done up. Incidentally," she added, "where's James?"

"The meeting with Chadwick very much upset him," replied Joanna. "He asked me to drive home, and when we got here, he didn't come in. He said he had to be alone and rushed off."

"I do hope he comes in soon. I told Agnes we'd have lunch at twelve-thirty, to give the servants time to do the washing up." Barbara sipped her sherry. "So Miss Cathcart will be running the wildlife park, not James. Well, she was very adept at dealing with the public and she had a flair for the theatrical as well. I remember her Midsummer pageants. Those crowd scenes were wonderfully done, I must say. One year we had the Battle of Hastings fought out on the lawn."

After lunch, when family and servants assembled on the front steps, there was still no sign of James. "I'm going to look for him," Joanna said.

"But where?" said Barbara.

"On the moor. I saw him heading up there."

"Don't go, Joanna," Humphrey said gently. "If he doesn't show up for his father's funeral, it's his choice."

"He's a great one for disappearing acts, is James," said Barbara. "He'll come back, of course he will — he always does in his own good time — but we can't keep poor Mr. Jackson waiting."

The sky soared for the occasion above a shining river and sun-drenched hills studded with white lambs growing rapidly into sheep. To this the Himalayas don't hold a candle, whispered Henry Drayton in his daughter's ear.

They set off two by two, down the rhododendron walk, through the shrubbery: Humphrey and Barbara, Mrs. Burgess and Pickering, Rhys and Mrs. Crompton, with Agnes and Joanna taking up the rear.

Tenants waited in the flower-decked church; the coffin, heaped with wreaths of yellow roses, lay in the chancel; Felicity Ogden-Smith played Bach. Poor black-suited Mr. Jackson and his henchmen waited, arms folded, at the door. Philip Ogden-Smith, in pristine vestments, advanced to greet the family as they came through the graveyard gate. "How lucky we are with the weather!" he exclaimed. "But where's James?"

"Taking things hard, I'm afraid," said Humphrey. "He couldn't make it over, so Joanna will read the lesson in his stead."

"For All the Saints," they sang, and "Onward, Christian Soldiers" ("Not terribly funeral," Barbara Drayton whispered; "They were his favorites," Joanna whispered back) and finally "Jerusalem," after which they followed Philip Ogden-Smith and the coffin out into the sun.

A Hereford taxi was pulling up at the churchyard gate. "An

architectural enthusiast come to admire and photograph the Norman tower," Barbara remarked. "Well, they won't get the vicar's attention just yet, not until we've finished," and she walked off arm in arm with Humphrey, between lichened gravestones, over new grass strewn with celandines. The other mourners straggled after them, but Joanna waited behind to help Agnes, who was having trouble walking because of her bunions, and because of burying the Major, whom she'd served for sixty years.

A tall woman in a smart black suit and hat, snakeskin shoes, and bag to match got out of the taxi and came through the gate into the churchyard. She hurried across the flagstones.

"I saw the death notice in the paper yesterday morning. Funeral private, it said, but I was so fond of your father!" She held a gloved hand out to Joanna. "Sybilla Henderson, used to be Cathcart. You haven't forgotten me, have you? It's been so many years!"

"Could I ever forget you?" Joanna replied, smiling. "It's wonderful to see you."

"How kind you are . . . I wasn't sure I was doing the right thing by coming. The train was late and then I had to wait for a taxi. I was frightened I'd missed everything."

"The service, yes, that's over, but not the burial. The others are waiting at the graveside — Agnes and I are on our way over there now. Please join us, Miss Cathcart. Isn't it a lovely day," she added. "Did you ever see Widleigh look more beautiful? Welcome back!"